M.. Desire
line and can't imagine a better job. A seven-time finalist
.......he prestigious Romance Writers of America RITA®
.......rd. Maureen is the author of more than one hundred
ro......nce novels. Her books regularly appear on bestseller
.......and have won several awards, including a Prism
......ard, a National Readers' Choice Award, a Colorado
Romance Writers Award of Excellence and a Golden
......ll Award. She is a native Californian but has recently
.......ed to the mountains of Utah.

USA TODAY bestselling author **Anna DePalo** is a
Harvard graduate and former intellectual property
lawyer who lives with her husband, son and daughter in
her native New York. She writes sexy, humorous books
that have been published in more than twenty countries.
Her novels have won the *RT Book Reviews* Reviewers'
......ice Award, the Golden Leaf, the Book Buyers Best
......he New England Readers' Choice. You can sign up
......her newsletter at annadepalo.com

SIX NIGHTS OF SEDUCTION

MAUREEN CHILD

SO RIGHT…WITH MR WRONG

ANNA DEPALO

MILLS & BOON

First Published in Great Britain 2021
by Mills & Boon, an imprint of HarperCollins*Publishers* Ltd
1 London Bridge Street, London, SE1 9GF

www.harpercollins.co.uk

HarperCollins*Publishers*
1st Floor, Watermarque Building,
Ringsend Road, Dublin 4, Ireland

Six Nights of Seduction © 2021 Maureen Child
So Right...with Mr Wrong © 2021 Anna DePalo

ISBN: 978-0-263-28288-7

SIX NIGHTS OF
SEDUCTION

MAUREEN CHILD

To the heroic nurses, aides, doctors and staff of the
George E. Wahlen Ogden Veterans Home
in Ogden, Utah.

I can't thank you all enough for the love, kindness and
care you gave my mother and, at the end, the rest of us.
I've always believed in angels, and now I can say that
I know a lot of them.

A special thank-you goes to Alex, Andrea, Marcia, Jan,
Rose, Linda, Evelyn and Nate.

If I didn't name you personally, know that I love you.

What you do matters.

One

"Get Matthew on the phone." Noah Graystone flashed a brief glance at his assistant, Tessa Parker. "I want to know how he's doing on getting us that distributor in Michigan."

Tessa made a note on her iPad, then said, "Uh-huh. He's supposed to be calling in at four today to update you."

Noah's gaze lifted to her again and this time, he met her blue eyes steadily. "And we both know he won't. He's a great salesman and good with clients, but checking in on time is not one of my little brother's strengths."

The whole Graystone family was involved in the business—Graystone Fine Spirits—and together, the three of them had built their grandfather's dream into a billion-dollar company. But Noah had long ago accepted that neither his brother nor his sister would ever be quite as committed to the business as he was.

His office, on the top floor of a towering building in Newport Beach, California, boasted views of the harbor and the ocean beyond. Not that he spent much time admiring that view. Usually, he was too focused on his computer screen. Still the office itself was huge and plush, with hardwood floors, rugs in muted colors that picked up the soft gray on the walls. The walls themselves were dotted with framed photos of their distillery, and crowded shelves held awards that their different liquors had won over the years.

But there was one trophy missing. One award that Noah was determined to win. World's Best Vodka in the international competition. Graystone Vodka had been his grandfather's baby. He'd built his company on single malt whiskeys, but vodka was his heart. Now Noah was focused on winning that award in his late grandfather's name. Once he'd done that, he'd move on and win every damn vodka award there was. And nothing was going to stop him.

"Yes, Matthew's a bit loose with his schedules, but you're so rooted in punctuality, you pick up the slack."

His eyebrows rose. "Is that a dig?"

"Possibly," Tessa admitted. She checked her tablet, tapped the screen then said, "Your sister sent an email saying she needs to talk to you about a few promotions she's pushing through."

He waved one hand. His sister, Stephanie, was the COO so he didn't have to be. "Tell her to do what works best for her. I trust her to make the right decisions, besides, I don't have time for another meeting today."

"Okay, and speaking of meetings, the one you can't get out of—with the print company making the new labels—has been moved to three o'clock."

"What?" He dropped back in his chair. Noah's schedule wasn't open to discussion. He expected the people he worked with to have the same focus. "Why?"

"Apparently, Ms. Shipman's babysitter canceled on her. She'll meet with you as soon as her mother arrives to watch the kids."

Kids. Why did people with families insist on also trying to run businesses? *One or the other, people. You can't do both well.* Hell, that was the main reason Noah avoided any kind of commitment to a woman. He'd decided long ago that his focus would be honoring his grandfather. Trying to make right what Noah's own father had practically destroyed.

When he wanted a woman, he had one. But he never considered keeping her around. If that made him a bastard, he thought, well at least he was an honest one.

Shaking his head, Noah muttered, "This is what I get for taking a chance on a small company."

Tessa blew out a breath. "We held a competition to find someone new because our old labeler had gotten stale, remember?"

"I do." That had been his sister Stephanie's idea. They'd received thousands of entries from companies large and small and the publicity had spiked sales for months.

"Well, then, relax and give Ms. Shipman the opportunity to prove you wrong. She has a great reputation and the new logo she came up with is fantastic and you know it."

Scowling, Noah stared at her. Five years she'd worked for him. Had she ever once seen him "relax"? "None of that matters if her kids are keeping her from doing the work."

"They're not. They're simply slowing her down a little today and you're doing it again."

"Doing what?"

She tipped her head and her blond hair swept to one side. "The whole, if-this-doesn't-work-when-I-want-it-to-there's-a-crisis thing."

Noah glared at her and wasn't surprised in the slightest that the look had no effect on Tessa. She'd stopped reacting to his temper after a month on the job, and sometime during the last five years, she'd started actively arguing with him when she thought he was wrong. Not that he was wrong now. Or practically ever.

But Noah had discovered that having Tessa's honest opinion, even when he disagreed with it, was helpful. Except when it wasn't. Like now.

"Fine. Ms. Shipman at three."

She made a note on her tablet. He pretended he didn't notice the small smile of satisfaction curve her mouth. Noah did that a lot, he realized—avoid looking at Tessa because as her employer he shouldn't be aware of the floral scent of her hair, or the curves he couldn't touch. So, rather than fire her and hire a less distracting and less efficient assistant, pretense was his only option.

Scowling to himself, he said, "Don't forget we're leaving for London in a few days."

"Not likely to forget that," she said.

Neither was he. The international awards for the best spirits of the year included best vodka awards and that was something he would never miss. As far as the powers that be were concerned, Graystone Vodka was the new kid on the block, so the chances of a win were slim. But the contest itself was important, because people would notice them. Talk about them. In next year's contest, he'd have both the varietal and the pure neutral vodka entered and by damn, he promised himself, he'd have that award and he'd lift a glass to his grandfather's memory.

Meanwhile, "Well, there are things I need wrapped up before we leave and the new label is one of them. Ms. Shipman had better show up."

"She will. And it will be done. At three instead of two," Tessa said. Then she added, "I would think you'd be a little more understanding. Callie Shipman's running her late husband's company on her own. She wants to grow it and build something for her family. Sound familiar?"

Noah bit back what he might have said. Of course it sounded familiar. It's what he was doing with the spirits company founded by his grandfather. "The difference is, I keep my appointments."

"And so will she. At three."

Since there was nothing he could do about it anyway, Noah graciously accepted. "Fine. Three."

"And the Barrington hotel in London emailed to confirm our reservations. Your special requests will be taken care of."

"Good." One thing he could always depend on. Tessa Parker would get things done. She might be a distraction at times—like now, for instance. Why did she have to smell so good?—but she was the most organized human he'd ever met. She kept the office running and never missed a step. Hell, he didn't know what he would have done without her the last five years.

"Do you really need the eighteen-hundred-thread-count sheets?" she asked.

He laughed shortly. "If you'd ever tried them, you wouldn't ask."

"Hmm. Is that an invitation?"

He shot her a quick look. "No."

That wasn't flirtation; it was just her sense of humor. Although if she weren't his assistant… Long blond hair, sharp eyes the color of summer skies. Her skin was smooth and pale and she was tall, with more curves than were fashionable at the moment.

And, he told himself firmly, *you're noticing. Stop it.*

"Fine," she said. "The hotel manager also arranged for the car you wanted—though why you had to have an Aston Martin is beyond me."

"James Bond," he quipped and lowered his gaze to the stack of papers on his desk. There was still too much to do before they left for London.

"Right. Of course." He looked up. She tapped her finger against her chin. "Maybe I can get you a meeting with M and Q."

Surprised, Noah stared at her. "You like James Bond?"

"I have two words for you," she said wryly. "Daniel Craig."

"Really. He's your type?"

"Um, let's think. Gorgeous. Built. Strong. And then there's the accent."

He scowled at her, though why it bothered him that she was attracted to some actor, he couldn't have said. "Ah. Well, it's his car I want."

"Of course you do."

"I hear disapproval, but I'm disregarding it."

"Naturally." Tessa took a breath and said, "The Arizona bottler is having an issue, keeping up with the new orders we're sending them."

"That's good news," Noah said. "Means we're going to need to contract with another bottler soon. Tell Stephanie to start putting out some feelers. I want a few different operations to choose from."

He'd been working for years toward this step up. Family money was all well and good, because damned if it didn't make getting a company up and running easier. But rebuilding Graystone Spirits was the driving force in his life and Noah wouldn't stop until he'd put the company at the top.

"Graystone is going to be bigger than ever." It was a vow, not a statement. "And we'll need companies who can keep up with us."

"I'll tell her," Tessa said.

He looked up at his assistant and asked, "Anything else on the England trip?"

It was important. Not just to Noah personally, but the future of the company.

Graystone had been left to founder the last twenty years, well, until Noah took over ten years before. Since then, he'd been fighting to turn it around. He was on the path now and he wouldn't let anything detour him. One day, he would lift a toast at his grandfather's gravesite and let the old man know that Noah had saved his dream.

While the family fortune had been built on whiskey, Graystone Vodka had been Noah's grandfather's "baby." The old man had dreamed of creating a world-class vodka as a tribute of sorts to his own father. But then his competitive nature had taken over and he'd built their whiskey line into a brand known worldwide and the vodka had taken a back seat. He worked on it when he could and vowed that one day, the vodka would be as popular as their whiskey blends. And it might have happened, but then Noah's father had taken over the reins, and he'd personally ended that.

Jared Graystone had wanted the family money, but hadn't been interested in building it, or in safeguarding the companies that provided him with the lifestyle he loved. Jared hadn't affected most of the businesses because they'd been too protected under the umbrella of a board of directors. But Graystone Vodka had stood alone, a company of the heart for Noah's grandfather. And so it had been easy for Jared to run it into the ground.

He'd drained it of money, allowed employees to drift away, losing distillery masters to greener pastures. Jared had indulged himself in women, hard living and finally had died the way he'd lived. In a car with his latest girlfriend, both of them drunk, sailing off a cliff in Northern California to land in the ocean.

Noah's fingers curled around a pen he snatched off the desk. Even after all these years, he could still feel the surge of anger and shame at the man his father had been.

"Noah?"

He blinked and came out of his thoughts to find Tessa staring down at him, a question in her eyes. "Are you okay?"

"Yeah. I'm fine." He brushed her concern aside and forced himself to stay in the present, and to avoid the past. Ghosts couldn't help him now anyway.

"Ooookaaaayy…" She drew the word out and practically made it a paragraph all on its own. He heard the curiosity in her voice but Noah didn't feel a need to satisfy it. Instead, he kept quiet and waited. Finally, Tessa shrugged and continued, "The jet's being checked over, to get it ready for the flight."

"And?"

"And, your mother called again."

Noah tossed his pen onto the desk and leaned back. His mother was happily remarried and now living in Bermuda and Noah was glad for it. God knew she'd put up with a hell of a lot from Noah's father. She deserved to be happy. But he didn't have the time or inclination to listen to his mom tell him that he was wasting his life, devoting himself to work. To remind him that his beloved grandfather had spent more hours with his company than he ever had with his family. That time was passing and if he didn't do something soon, he'd end up the world's loneliest billionaire.

He wasn't lonely. Hell, he was never alone unless he wanted to be. He had friends. He had women when he wanted them. And as for working too much, hell, he'd never found anything else that could completely captivate him like the company did. There was always another merger or another deal. And mostly, there was the driving desire to build Graystone Vodka into the top brand in the world. And if he had to work twenty-four/seven to do it, then that's what would happen.

"Did she leave a message?"

Tessa checked her notes on the tablet again. "She said and I quote, 'Tell him he can't avoid me forever.'"

He scowled. He wasn't avoiding her per se. He was just busy. Which was, he allowed silently, his mother's point.

"Fine. I'll call her later."

Tessa snorted.

"What was that?"

"We both know you're not going to call her."

"Do we?" he countered.

Tessa held her tablet to her chest and crossed her arms over it. "You don't want to give her the opportunity to tell you to get a life."

"I have a life, thanks," he said.

"Sure you do."

Irritated now, Noah looked up at her. Her features were tightly drawn and she seemed, now that he thought about it, wired pretty tightly. In the five years she'd worked for him, he'd never seen her less than professional. Why the difference today?

"What's going on with you?"

Tessa took a breath and huffed it out. The only way to do this, she told herself, was like taking off a Band-Aid. Do it fast. "I'm trying to figure out how to tell you that I quit."

Frowning, he asked, "Quit what?"

Her eyes rolled. "*My job*, Noah. I'm resigning."

"Don't be ridiculous." He waved that off with a low chuckle.

"I'm not." Tessa watched him, waiting for the reality of what she was saying to hit him. When it finally did, he stared at her as if she had two heads.

"You're serious?"

"Absolutely." This had been building inside her for several months. And she'd finally come to the realization that the only way she would ever find a life for herself was to leave the job—and the man—she loved. The sooner the better.

He shot to his feet. "Why would you do that?"

Well, she couldn't exactly give him the driving reason behind her resignation. She wasn't about to tell him that she'd been in love with him almost the entire time she'd worked for him. How pitiful was that? No, thank you.

So she gave him the secondary reason, which in its way was just as important as the first.

"Because I want time to focus on my own business," she said honestly. "I've got enough money saved now to make it possible for me to work for myself—"

"You have a business?"

Tessa wanted to sigh again, but why bother. She'd mentioned it to him before. Several times over the last couple of years, but if you didn't have *Vodka* stamped on your forehead, he pretty much didn't hear or see you. "Yes, I do. I make lotions and soaps and things and sell them on Etsy and it's recently started taking off. I want to build on that."

He pushed one hand through his dark blond hair and shook his head. "Well, if you've built your business while working for me, why do you have to stop?"

Because she just couldn't face coming into this office every day for the next twenty years and being silently, pitifully in love and having to pretend she wasn't. Because she didn't like making dinner dates for him with some model or actress. She didn't like shopping for gifts for the women who spent the night in his bed so he could send them on with a friendly *thanks but goodbye* note. Honestly, there was only just so much a woman could take.

"Because unlike you, Noah," she said firmly, "I'd like to have a life outside this office."

He stared at her. "You just admitted you *do* have one."

"No." She shook her head. "What I have are bits and pieces of time that I can devote to my work because I'm on call for you twenty-four/seven."

"You're exaggerating."

"Am I? Last Sunday night, where was I?" She didn't wait for him to answer. "I was at your penthouse because you called at eleven thirty to tell me you'd had a brainstorm about the varietal vodkas you want to produce next spring. You needed me to research it to make sure we were coming up with something new and exciting."

He frowned at her. "That was an anomaly."

"Really?" She hitched one hip higher than the other and tapped the toe of her taupe heels against the burgundy carpet. "The day before I was out with a friend and got a text from you saying you needed me to come to the office, pick up the Finnegan file and take it to your place."

She'd been to his home on the cliffs in Dana Point countless times over the last five years. But, Tessa thought, she'd never been upstairs. Never been in his bedroom. To her, it was like the promised land—and she'd likely never see it. Because she'd *never* had him look at her and feel that he was actually seeing *her*.

"It was important. Old man Finnegan was trying to hold up the merger and—"

She didn't let him finish. Because the longer she talked to him about this, the more it struck her that she should have quit two or three years ago. Nothing would ever change between them and hanging around wishing things were different wasn't helping her in the slightest.

"Don't you get it? It's *always* important, Noah. I left my friend at the movies, went to the office to get the file and then spent the next ten hours at your home, *working.*" Frowning at the memory, she added, "I ended up napping on the couch in your living room because as much as *you* might be driven, I need sleep once in a while. And I got a crick in my neck for my troubles."

"Is this about your salary?" he countered. "Because I'll give you a raise."

Another sigh. She just couldn't help it. He wasn't getting it and she was pretty sure he was remaining oblivious on purpose. "It's not about the money."

He came around the edge of the desk and stopped when he was only about a foot away from her. For one brief, shining moment, Tessa fantasized that he would come closer, sweep her into his arms and declare undying adoration for her. She almost laughed at herself.

"How about a company car, then?"

"You're not listening to me, Noah. I don't want a car, either."

"What the hell do you want, Tessa?"

"Again, I point out that you're not listening. I already told you. I want a life, Noah. And if I keep working for you, I'll never get one." She looked around the luxurious office and briefly paused to take in the ocean view through the wide windows, before turning back to him. "I'll end up just like you. Only alive within these four walls. No time for friends. For love."

"Seriously?" he asked. "My mother couldn't get to me, but she got to *you*?"

"Believe it or not, I didn't actually need your mother to tell me that finding someone to love is important."

"I'm not stopping you from that," he argued.

Oh, he really was, because *he* was the one she loved, and he was so blind to everything that wasn't Graystone

Vodka, he'd never notice her. To him she was an efficient piece of office furniture. A dependable printer. A top-of-the-line computer.

"I don't want to argue with you, Noah. I just want you to know that this is my two-week notice." No point in dragging this out any longer. "If you want me to interview people for my position, I'm happy to do it."

"No." He shoved both hands into his pants pockets. "I'm not going to discuss this further right now. Just… get Finnegan on the line, will you? I need to iron out a few more details."

"Sure." She turned for the door and when she reached it, he said her name and she stopped, then looked over her shoulder at him.

"This isn't over, Tessa."

"Yes it is, Noah."

She left the office and felt like a shipwreck survivor finally reaching shore. Her knees were weak, her heartbeat was racing, but she had to give herself an imaginary pat on the back. She'd done it. She'd actually quit. Now all she had to do was get through the next two weeks.

Because Tessa knew Noah Graystone very well and he wasn't finished trying to get her to stay.

Two

Tessa stopped, took a deep breath and blew it out. That wasn't easy, but she'd done it. And she survived. And now all she had to do was make it through the next two weeks.

Then she'd be free. She'd be running her own business from her home. And she wouldn't have to come here every morning and face a day of being with a man who looked at her and never really saw her. Not that she could blame him entirely, Tessa told herself.

Even if he was attracted to her, he was her boss so couldn't say anything. But she'd been telling herself that for five years and even she didn't believe it anymore. There'd never been the slightest flicker of interest from Noah. So rather than long for a man who would never see her—time to leave.

The phone on her desk was ringing, thank God, so Tessa pushed her own thoughts aside to walk over and answer it. "Noah Graystone's office."

"Hi, Tess!"

Matthew Graystone, calling in, she checked the clock—seven hours early. One thing you could count on with Noah's brother—he was always unpredictable. "Matthew. How's the trip going?"

"Excellent. That's why I need to talk to the boss."

"I'll put you through."

"Thanks."

She rang Noah's office and said, "Matthew's on the phone."

"Hmm. Early for a change."

When she hung up, she dove into work because that was the one thing she could always do to keep her mind busy. But an hour later, she had to admit it wasn't working. Now that she'd finally set her plan into motion, Tessa couldn't stop wondering if she'd done the right thing.

Of course she had. It was just the tiny voice in the back of her mind, taunting her with the knowledge that she'd probably never see Noah again that had her questioning herself. Which was beyond irritating because the reason she was quitting was so she could put some distance between herself and Noah.

Noah had been starring in her dreams for years and it was time to admit those dreams were never going to be reality. *But*, that treacherous voice whispered, *how can you give up what you've never had?*

Frowning, Tessa brought up Noah's schedule for the international vodka awards. While she made corrections and notes for herself, that little voice kept talking, damn it.

Sex, Tessa. I'm talking about sex.

Well, she'd had sex plenty of times. She'd even had

a fiancé once upon a time. Until he'd cheated on her with her former best friend. Still, she'd told herself that it was better to find out *before* the wedding that her fiancé was a no-good-lying-cheating dog. And her ex-friend was even worse.

That was one of the reasons she'd left Wyoming for California and a fresh start. Her parents had been happily married forever. Her older brother was married with kids and even her cousins were in relationships or marriages that made her heart hurt at every big family gathering. So she'd packed up and left. Now she only had to hear about what everyone was up to on the phone. She wasn't faced with it all the time.

So sure. She'd had sex.

But not with Noah.

Of course not. He was her boss.

Not anymore.

Her fingers stilled on the keyboard. Did that voice have a point?

Yes.

Her frown deepened, but she couldn't quite dismiss the notion that annoying voice had suggested.

Two weeks and she was gone. Two weeks with Noah and then he would be out of her life. But had he ever really been *in* it? Yes, she'd spent nearly every day for the last five years with him, even the occasional night. But those nights had not been spent the way she would have wanted them.

Maybe sex is what you need.

That voice was really irritating now, because it had a valid point. If she was going to say goodbye to Noah forever, then why not indulge in one night of memorable sex—and she knew it would be memorable, because, well, just look at the man.

Technically, he's not your boss anymore.

True. She *had* quit her job. This two-week thing was just…considerate. There was nothing ethically or legally icky standing between them now.

So, if there's nothing stopping you…what's stopping you?

She sighed and started typing again, but she wasn't paying attention to what was popping up on the screen. Instead, she thought of Noah.

Of seducing Noah.

And damned if she could come up with a reason not to.

Although she had to silently admit, she wasn't trying very hard to talk herself out of it. Why shouldn't she get the one thing she'd dreamed of for five long years before leaving?

"Are you listening to me?" Matthew's voice carried the sting of irritation.

"What?" Noah shook his head and tuned back into the conversation at hand. "Of course I'm listening. You got the distributor in Nashville."

"Try to contain your enthusiasm. It's embarrassing."

"Sorry. Good job." Noah paused, then asked, "Weren't you supposed to be nailing down the Michigan distributor?"

"Yes and I did that. Consider Nashville a bonus," Matthew said. "I got their agreement this morning. Thought I'd tell you right away since we've been after this deal for six months."

"Right." Noah swiveled in his chair and faced the

wide window with its view of the ocean. On that expanse of blue, boats with colorful sails skimmed the surface while charter fishing boats chugged far out of the harbor, headed for open sea.

The view should have been soothing. It wasn't.

"Okay, I can only assume you're dying or something. You're never this disinterested in business."

"What?" Scowling fiercely, Noah turned his back on the window and forced himself to focus. "I'm interested. And happy you got both of those distributors nailed down."

"Uh-huh," Matthew said. "What's going on?"

Still frowning, Noah shot a glance at the closed office door. On the other side, he knew Tessa sat at her desk as she had for the last five years. She was the warrior at the gate. No one got past her to see him unless she approved it. She knew the names of every one of the employees here at Graystone Spirits and probably their kids' names, too. She was the one who reminded him about birthday bonuses for the office workers and the one who shopped for his mother at Christmas.

Tessa kept his schedule, ran his life and pretty much managed the whole company; he had to admit that, even if only to himself.

They'd been a damn good team for years and suddenly she decides, *that's enough*? No. he wasn't buying it. There was something else going on here and he would find out what it was.

But his brother was still waiting for an explanation, so Noah blurted out, "Tessa just quit."

"Seriously?" Matthew sounded as stunned as Noah felt and for some reason that made him feel better. "Why?"

"She says she wants a life. What the hell does she have now?"

"A job."

"A damn good job," Noah countered, feeling as if he suddenly had to defend himself as an employer. "She's never complained."

"Right. So you have to ask yourself...what did you do?"

He hadn't considered that. If he'd pissed her off at some point, he had no doubt at all that she would have let him know about it. But as he thought about the question now, all he could come up with was, "Nothing."

"Well, something prompted this, so talk to her. Try to figure out what went wrong. Hell, Noah. You're the *fixer*. If you can't solve this no one can."

True again, he told himself. Since he was a kid, Noah had been the one to look at a situation and find the best route through it. He never missed a loophole. Never let opportunity slip past him. He could find the lone diamond in a pile of rocks dismissed by everyone else.

"You're right."

"Hell," Matthew said on a snort of laughter, "this phone call was worth it just to hear *that*."

"Yeah, don't get used to it." With thoughts of Tessa worming through the back of his mind, Noah set his subconscious to work on the problem. Meanwhile, though, "Any news on the distributor in Kansas City?"

"And, it's back to business," Matthew mused. "Yeah, I've got a call in to him. Just waiting to hear back. I'm flying out there tomorrow to do an in-person meet and greet."

"Good. Tell me about the Nashville deal." He only

half listened as his brother talked, while his mind looked for the solution to the problem of Tessa.

"I did it."

After work, Tessa took a seat at her neighbor's kitchen table and reached for the glass of wine Lynn had already poured. Tessa took a long drink and let the cold, dry wine ease away the sharp edges that had been tearing at her for hours.

Noah had spent most of the day trying to talk her out of resigning. Reminding her about how well they worked together—which she knew. How much they'd accomplished. And the fact that if she left, she would be breaking up the team.

The man was relentless. But in spending all that time with her, he'd only managed to underscore her need to quit. Being with him all the time was just too much. She couldn't take it anymore. Tessa was tired of fighting her attraction to him.

"Well, hey," Lynn said with a grin, "congratulations. Really didn't think you would."

Lynn was five feet two inches tall, with curly black hair, a wide smile and a warm heart. She was the neighborhood "mom" even though she was only thirty-five. Everyone in this part of Laguna knew that if they needed help, go see Lynn.

"Thanks for the support," Tessa said and twirled the stem of her wineglass.

"Oh, come on." Lynn gave her a nudge. "You know I'm on your side. How'd he take it?"

"He offered me a raise."

Lynn laughed. "So typical of men. Toss money at a problem."

Tessa nodded. "He honestly looked stunned when I told him I quit."

"Why wouldn't he be?" Lynn shook her head. "You've been there five years, honey. You do everything for him but trim his hair."

Tessa took a sip of her wine and otherwise kept her mouth shut. How could she admit that once she actually *had* trimmed his hair? Oh, not a whole haircut, but Noah hadn't liked the wave in his hair and since they were on his jet on the way to a meeting, he'd asked Tessa to trim it. She'd had her fingers in his thick, wavy hair and if she admitted that to Lynn, she'd never hear the end of it.

Every Friday night for the last two years, she and her neighbors had a standing wine-and-snacks date. They traded off locations every week and tonight, thank Heaven, was Lynn's turn. Because her "snacks" were always so much better than the ones Tessa came up with.

She reached out for the plate in front of her, picked up a bacon-wrapped stalk of asparagus and took a bite, just managing to squelch a sigh of approval. There was cheese and crackers—warmed Brie, of course, not the supermarket cheddar Tessa used. Baked chicken tenders on toothpicks and homemade salsa and corn chips.

"What are you thinking?" Lynn asked.

"Just that it's a wonder you and Carol don't weigh five hundred pounds each. You're way too good in a kitchen."

Lynn grinned. "I've even managed to get the kids to eat vegetables. Watch." She turned in her seat and called out, "Jade. Evan."

The girl and boy, ten and eight years old respectively, came running.

Their mom asked, "Want some asparagus?"

"Sure!" Jade grabbed one of the bacon-wrapped stalks and took a big bite. Evan took one, too, unwrapped the bacon and handed the vegetable to his mother. When they left again in a mad rush back to their Disney movie, Tessa laughed.

Wryly, Lynn said, "One out of two isn't bad."

Carol walked in the back door just then, dropped her purse on the kitchen counter and walked straight to the table. Even before she grabbed an empty wineglass, she bent down to kiss her wife hello. "Oh, boy, I'm glad to be home."

She dropped into a chair, poured some wine and snatched a cracker off the plate.

"Busy day?"

"You have no idea," Carol said. "I had a mom's group come in today, with all eleven of their combined children because one of them has the chicken pox. They all wanted the kids looked at—just in case. And I had to tell them that keeping them all together in a herd will pretty much guarantee that they'll all get it."

As a pediatrician, Carol was perfect. She loved kids. It was the parents who frustrated her at times. Her long blond hair was pulled back into a ponytail that hung down her back and her big blue eyes looked tired.

"Don't they have vaccinations for that now?"

"Bingo." Carol pointed her finger at Tessa. "But do people get them? No. You wouldn't believe..."

Lynn held up both hands. "This is officially a work-free zone," she announced, giving her wife a hard look. "No complaining, either."

"Not even about Colton Briggs biting me again?" Carol shook her head. "Three years old and the kid's got a bite like a Great White."

Lynn laughed, but shook her head. "Not another word until we've all had enough wine that we won't care."

Carol opened her mouth to argue, then shut it again. "You're right, sweetie. Just feed me and keep the wine coming."

Envy whispered through Tessa as it always did when she was with her friends. The two women had the best relationship she'd ever seen. Oh, they argued like anyone else, but they were always there for each other. The love between them was practically palpable. They'd been together nearly fifteen years and they were still so happy.

The kids were in the living room watching a movie, and their laughter drifted to them through the house. Lynn slid the plate of cheese and crackers closer to Carol and said, "She did it."

"Who did what?" Carol took a swig of wine.

"Who do you think?" Lynn said, laughing. "Tessa did it. She actually quit her job."

Carol's eyes went wide. "Seriously?"

Tessa smothered a groan. Was she really so pitiful that her friends were actually proud of her for quitting a job that she had loved for five years? "God, you guys, it's not miraculous or anything. I just handed in my two weeks' notice. No big deal."

Carol picked up her wine and toasted Tessa with it. "Sure. No big deal. Except you've been talking about doing this for two years."

"I think this is a sign of the apocalypse," Lynn whispered.

"Funny." Tessa grimaced and grabbed another asparagus stalk.

"Oh, come on honey, we're just teasing," Lynn said.

"Yeah," Carol added, "we're just glad you finally did it. Now the trick will be to stick with it."

"I know you're kidding, but come on." Tessa sipped at her own wine. "Of course I'm sticking with it. What would be the point of quitting in the first place otherwise?"

Lynn shrugged. "Noah's not going to give up easily."

True. He would miss having her at his beck and call. Who else could he hire who would put up with working weekends and nights?

"I know, but I've made up my mind."

When both women just stared at her blankly, Tessa argued. "I *have*."

"Prove it," Lynn said.

"How?"

"When he calls this weekend—"

"And he *will* call," Carol tossed in.

"Don't answer," Lynn said. "Or better yet, turn your phone off completely. Let him get used to not having you to run interference for him all the time."

Tessa thought about that for a moment. It would be weird having her phone turned off, which was probably a bad sign—she was too addicted to the darn thing. But if she didn't and Noah did call—and Carol was right, he would—she would probably cave and answer the phone. What did that say about her? Was she really a glutton for punishment, as her grandmother used to say? "Okay, you have a point, though I am still working for him for the next two weeks…"

"During the week. During the day." Carol's eyes narrowed on her. "Nights and weekends are yours. Supposedly. Even I get every other weekend off."

Tessa took a deep breath. "You're right. I know you're right and that's why I quit and that's also why I'll turn my phone off this weekend."

And to show both of her friends that she was serious, Tessa pulled her phone out of her pocket and shut the power off. Watching it shut down gave her a little pang. Of course, the voice in her head whispered, *But what about emergencies?* No, the only likely "emergency" was Noah wanting her to work on some plan or other. So, better she do this than get sucked into Noah's world again. She had to start distancing herself from him. For her own sanity.

Lynn chuckled. "Are you okay?"

"Not sure yet." Tessa gave her a wry smile. "I'll survive. Probably."

"Here's to you breaking out. Building your own business. And maybe," Carol added as she lifted her glass, "finding a *man*."

The problem, Tessa thought, was that she'd already found the man she wanted. Sadly she couldn't have him.

"Although," Lynn offered, "if you want to spread your wings, I have a friend…"

Tessa laughed and shook her head. "No, I'll stick to men, but thanks anyway."

She wanted of course, to stick to Noah. But that wasn't going to happen.

Then that little voice whispered, *He's not your boss anymore, Tessa. Seduce him before you leave. What do you have to lose?*

Noah had never been to Tessa's house. Hell, he'd had to pull up her information from Human Resources just to find out *where* she lived. Which annoyed him. He should have known, shouldn't he? Tessa had been to his home in Dana Point several times, but he hadn't even been aware that she lived in Laguna. Practically around the corner from him. And he'd had no idea.

He parked by the curb in front of the tiny house and stepped out of the car. Pausing for a moment, he looked up and down the narrow street, taking it all in.

It was a well-settled neighborhood. The trees were old and spread shade across the street from both sides, making a leafy green tunnel. Homes were small and well-tended and seemed to be an amalgam of every type of architectural style. There were mini-Tudors, Craftsman bungalows and even a couple that were starkly modern. Lights shone through windows, basketball hoops stood in driveways and a lone kid whizzed past him on a skateboard.

"It's like being in a Norman Rockwell painting," he muttered, finally turning his gaze on Tessa's house.

Naturally, her home stood out from the rest. It looked like a miniature castle, complete with a turret room and crawling ivy on the gray stones. Of course Tessa wouldn't be living in some ordinary place. He could have seen her in a Spanish style or a Craftsman style with bright colors and uneven lines. What he'd seen of her the last five years, he knew her to be anything but ordinary. Flowers lined the walkway of cobbled stones leading to the front porch, but he barely noticed them as he approached.

This place, he thought, was as far removed from his own home as Mars was from Earth. He glanced around quickly and shook his head.

He preferred his home, of course. Four thousand square feet, rooftop private pool and a wide view of the Pacific. He only saw people when he chose to. On this street, you could be ambushed by neighbors determined to suck up your time and draw you into unimportant conversations.

But he wasn't here to talk to Tessa's neighbors. He was here to convince Tessa to stay at Graystone. And he didn't care what he had to do to make that happen.

The yard was small but tidy and he idly wondered if she actually mowed the grass herself. Out by his pool, there were potted flowers and trees and even a trellis with some kind of flower crawling all over it. He couldn't remember even *seeing* the gardeners who cared for the gardens at his home. It was just done. Like elves coming in the night. That was just how Noah liked it.

A light shone down on the narrow front porch and highlighted the tumble of flowers and some kind of ivy spilling from a huge terra-cotta pot. The front door was an arch of dark, heavy wood that looked as if it would be at home on a real castle.

The house was more…whimsical than Noah would have expected from someone like Tessa. She was always so pragmatic. So realistic. Seeing this side of her was eye-opening in a way and made him think that maybe he didn't know her as well as he thought he did.

"Ridiculous," he muttered. Of course he knew Tessa. They had spent so much time together over the last five years, he knew her better, apparently, than she did herself. Because he knew she didn't really want to quit. She liked her job. She was good at it.

He knocked firmly on the thick door and waited impatiently for her to answer. When she did, though, Noah was speechless.

Tessa's blond hair was long and loose around her

shoulders. She wore a pale blue T-shirt that clung to her figure in a way that her business attire never did. The hem of the shirt was short enough to display an inch of bare skin above the waistband of her black shorts and when she inhaled sharply, that waistband dipped lower over her belly, sending a hot blast of lust blasting through Noah. Her long legs were bare and her toenails were painted bright scarlet. She looked, he thought… edible.

"Noah?" She stared up at him and confusion shone in her blue eyes. "What're you doing here?"

Was her voice normally that husky or was he just imagining things?

"We need to talk." He pushed past her into the house.

"Please," she said from behind him. "Come in."

Three

Noah stopped just over the threshold and shot her a wry look. Then he took a moment to glance around the interior. Stone walls in the entryway, too, continuing the whole magical cottage feel. There were colorful rugs on the hardwood floors and paintings and framed photographs on the walls.

He kept walking and stepped into a tiny living room filled with an overstuffed couch and twin matching chairs. Tables gleamed from polish and the lamps lit in the room threw a soft, golden glow across the scene that made it all seem…homey, not claustrophobic. Which was impressive since the whole room was about the size of his walk-in closet.

He turned to face her and briefly let his gaze sweep over this unexpected Tessa. He had to admit, he liked the look. A lot. She swiveled to close the door and he had a half second to admire the curve of her butt and knew he'd never forget it. Reaching up, he briefly rubbed the bridge of his nose hard enough, he hoped, to wake up his brain.

"Why are you here?"

"I already told you," he said. "We have to talk."

"Yes," she said, folding her arms beneath her breasts, lifting them to dazzling heights. "But usually when we 'have to talk,' I get a phone call telling me to drive to your place. Heck I didn't even think you knew where I live."

"Of course I knew." The lie came easily. He wasn't about to admit that he'd had to look up her address. Five years she'd worked for him and her personal life was a blank page. He'd had no idea she was running a business in her "free" time. No idea she lived in a cottage that looked as if it had popped out of a fairy tale.

And zero idea she looked *that* good in shorts.

Not the point.

"Huh." She was surprised, but she accepted what he said. "So again. Why are you here?"

"Like I said, we need to talk."

"About what, Noah?"

"You know what," he snapped and wasn't sure who he was more bothered by. Her? Or himself? Catching her like this, relaxed, casual—tempting—was feeding all sorts of intriguing possibilities in his mind. "You quit, Tessa and I don't accept it. It's ridiculous."

"No it's not. Actually, it's long past time I did," she said and walked past him, heading down a short, narrow hallway as if he wasn't there at all.

Noah followed because what choice did he have? Tie

her to a chair? Or a bed? No… "Where are we going?"
he asked.

"I'm going to the kitchen and then the garage. I don't
know what you're doing."

"Following you." He walked into the kitchen and
wasn't surprised to find it a small—he supposed *cozy*
was the right word—room. Dark green walls, pale oak
cabinets and the same hardwood flooring in here. There
was a two-person table sitting under the window and
a kitchen island where dozens of small, empty jars sat
waiting. For what?

Tessa moved directly to a stove that looked older than
she was and picked up a wooden spoon. She stirred the
contents of a stainless steel pot and lifted the scent of
jasmine into the air.

It was warm in the closed-up room, so Noah slipped
out of his suit jacket and walked over to hang it on the
back of one of her chairs. "What are you doing?"

She threw a quick glance at him. "I'm making candles."

"Seriously? You make your own candles?" He'd
never known anyone who did something like that.
"They sell them, you know. Is that what this is about
really? A big raise? Do you make your own soap, too?"

"Yes, no, no and yes," she answered all four questions. "I could buy candles but I can make my own. Plus,
I'm making these to sell on my Etsy site and third, no,
it's not about a raise. I already told you that. And, I already told you I make soaps and lotions."

Had she? He didn't remember.

Once she'd finished stirring the pot, she took the
spoon to the island, dripped a bit of melted wax into the
bottom of the jars and then affixed a wick to each splotch.

Noah frowned as he watched, but kept quiet. He didn't understand what she was doing, but damned if he wasn't enjoying watching her do it. She moved gracefully, soundlessly, in her bare feet and for some reason, he was really enjoying those bright red toes of hers. When she swung back to the stove, he had another good view of her behind and noticed with interest that there was the hint of a tattoo at the small of her back, just peeking over the waistband of her shorts.

And he instantly wanted to find out what that tattoo looked like.

He undid the button of his collar and loosened his tie.

A few minutes later, she swung her hair back over her shoulder before she picked up a hot pad, then lifted the pot off the stove. He bit back a warning about how dangerous hot wax was, because no doubt she was already aware. Yet still, he kept quiet as she poured the wax into the waiting jars, adjusting the wicks so that they remained straight as she poured. She filled six jars before she was finished, propped up the wicks with what looked like chopsticks, then turned and set the pot back on the stove.

Finally, he asked, "How do you get the rest of the wax out of the pot?"

"I don't," she said. "I'll reheat this for the second pour once this pour sets up."

"Second pour?" Why was he interested? Because she was talking and he was watching her mouth move and wondering why he'd never noticed how full her bottom lip was.

She sighed. "The first pour will settle and a sort of concave will open up along the wicks. The second pour will correct it."

"Okay." He didn't really care. He just wanted to keep watching her.

"Whatever residual wax is left over will become part of the remelt in a couple of days. This is my jasmine pot and I'll use it again for more candles then."

"Remelt." Noah shook his head and watched her set the pan down on one of the front burners.

"That's right. I've got to go to the garage. I'll be back in a minute."

He wasn't going to stay behind and look like an idiot alone in her kitchen, so he followed and enjoyed the view of her butt as he walked behind her. The edges of that tattoo kept drawing his gaze and he wondered what it was. Dolphin? Rainbow? Mermaid? Hmm.

Noah shook his head. Tattoo aside, he approved of the view of her behind. Somehow, Tessa had managed to camouflage her really amazing butt beneath business suits and skirts, and he never would have guessed she would have a tattoo. This was a nice surprise…and a little unsettling. He didn't like what looking at her was doing to him, but there didn't seem to be much he could do about it.

A breeze shot up out of nowhere and still did nothing to ease the heat building inside him. Noah scowled, stuffed his hands into his pockets and glanced around at the darkened yard as they walked to the garage.

Small again. Surprising, really that she could have so many flowers and trees in such a tiny space. Everything was neatly tended and he imagined that in summer, the explosion of flowers would be spectacular. Even now, there were flowers with dusky colors dotting the garden line.

Tessa opened the side door to the garage, flipped a

switch and a sword of light pierced the gathering darkness. He followed it like a path and stepped inside behind her.

Again, surprise had him stopping in place to look around. Now he understood why her car was parked in the driveway.

This wasn't really a garage, he told himself, it was more of a workshop. There were two sturdy tables set up in the middle of the room with boxes stacked neatly at the ends of both of them. Along the walls were shelves, neatly arranged with boxes of glass jars, and gallon-sized jugs filled with pastel-colored liquids and other shelves holding huge boxes of who knew what? Stacked neatly on the floor were several more jugs filled with a milky fluid. And what looked like a tension rod between cabinets held roll upon roll of ribbons.

"What is all this?" he asked, a little dumbfounded.

"My business," she said from the corner where she was dipping into one of the mystery boxes. She came up with a single white block about ten by eight and two inches thick, broken up into small squares. "I store my candle wax, scents and lotion bases out here. And I use the tables to fill big orders."

"When do you have time for all this?" he wondered aloud before he could stop himself.

A wry smile curved her mouth and he found the motion…tantalizing.

"Good question," she said. "I work whenever I can, stealing a few minutes here and there. I don't have enough time to devote to my business. Which is the reason I resigned. Remember?"

He frowned. "You'd rather work in a garage than work for me."

"I'd rather work for myself, yes." She nodded firmly and headed for the door.

When she got close enough, he reached out and grabbed her arm, dragging her to a stop. The instant he touched her, Noah felt a blast of something desperate and undeniable shake him. What the hell was happening?

He'd worked with Tessa for years and but for the occasional moment, he'd paid no attention at all to the fact that she was gorgeous and seriously built. Now it seemed that was *all* he could see. Or think about.

He let her go quickly, but the burn sizzling his fingertips remained.

"We could work something out," he blurted out, staring into her eyes. Were they always such a deep, rich color?

"Noah, it wouldn't work." She took a breath and he absolutely did *not* notice her full breasts rise and fall with the action.

"You can't know that," he argued.

"Please. Who would know better?" She took a tighter grip on the block of wax. "I can't be on call for you twenty-four/seven and still find the time for my own stuff. I've been trying for five years and it doesn't work."

He took the wax from her and was slightly surprised at how heavy it was. "Now that I know you've got this business—" he broke off and gave her a hard look "—which you could have told me about long before now—we can make the time."

She smiled slightly and shook her head. "That's sweet. You might even mean it…"

"I don't say things I don't mean," he said, interrupting her.

"...but it wouldn't last," she went on as if he hadn't spoken. "Noah, you're so focused on your own work, that's all you see."

Not at the moment, he thought, letting his gaze briefly drop to the impressive cleavage she was displaying in that V-neck shirt. Right now, work was the furthest thing from his mind.

"In spite of the fact that I give it so little time, my business is growing. And now I'm also selling jewelry that my neighbor makes, so I'm expanding. I need the time, Noah. So thanks, but I made the right call." She turned for the door and Noah walked right behind her.

Quietly fuming, frustration bubbling inside him, he switched off the light, closed the door behind him and followed her back to the house. The heat of the kitchen was a distinct difference to the chill outside and yet it was *nothing* compared to the heat flaring inside him.

Noah set the block of wax on the tiny island then watched as Tessa reheated the wax she'd been working with before. "What are you doing now?"

"I'm getting the second pour ready," she murmured without bothering to turn and look at him.

Ridiculous as it sounded, he wasn't used to her ignoring him. He didn't much care for it, either.

"How many pours are there?" he asked.

"Usually two, but you can do more. All depends on how the wax settles and what you're looking for."

He glanced at the candles and saw she had been right. The wax was settling, sinking. He'd never thought about candles. Why would he? But now he could see how much work went into such a simple product. Give him the liquor business any day.

Distilleries that worked seamlessly, employees who

handled any problems instantly. He knew his way around the business world. He was damn good at it. And he hated to admit it, but Tessa was one of the reasons for his success. His spine stiffened. He couldn't lose her.

He *wouldn't* lose her.

And he would start by tempting her with what mattered most to her—her business.

"You know, if you stayed," he said and paused until she turned to glance at him.

Those eyes of hers captured him again and Noah almost lost his train of thought. Unheard of. He prided himself on his ability to focus on the situation at hand and suddenly, being around Tessa was scattering his thoughts.

"Yes?" she asked, waiting.

Scowling, he muttered, "We could do something about your work setup."

She laughed shortly. "Could we now?"

Noah frowned again, but she didn't see it as she'd already dismissed him and turned her attention back to the pot she was stirring gently.

"I'll remodel your garage," he said abruptly.

"What? Why?" Now she turned to stare at him wide-eyed.

"Seriously?" He walked closer to her but stopped soon enough to keep a safe distance between them. "You want to grow your business, but you're working in this claustrophobic kitchen and a garage that's already stuffed to the gills. How can you expand if your space is limited?"

She sighed loud enough for him to hear it. "Expanding my business will be as easy as having more time for it, Noah. I'm not trying to be the biggest candle/lotion/soap supplier on the West Coast."

Well, that statement went against everything he'd been taught about business. If you were going to do something, then you should damn well shoot for the top. Be the best. Be the *only*, if you could.

"Why not?" he demanded. "Why wouldn't you want to be the best and the biggest?"

She turned her head to look at him. "We're not *all* as driven as you are, Noah. What I want is for my business to support me and maybe a little extra. Not everyone wants to be a tycoon. Some of us even want to have a life, too."

"I have a life."

She snorted derisively and his scowl turned fierce.

"Not that I've seen," she said and picked up the pot. Carrying it to the island, she carefully poured a stream of hot, scented wax into each candle, one at a time. The air in the kitchen was suddenly alive with the scent of jasmine. It was thick and warm and, damn it, seductive.

When she set the pot down on the stove again, she faced him and put her hands at her hips. The action tugged the material of her shirt tighter, highlighting those breasts he couldn't seem to stop noticing.

"Noah, I appreciate your self-interested offer of generosity, but I don't need it. I'm happy working out of my kitchen."

"Even if the offer includes a commercial-grade stove and all the equipment you might need to run your business more efficiently?"

She paused, considering, and he knew he'd caught her interest at least. But then she spoke and he knew he'd lost her just as quickly.

"I don't have room here for a commercial-grade stove."

"We'll remodel your kitchen."

Tessa laughed then and shook her head. "I resigned, Noah. It's not the end of the world. You'll get on fine with a new assistant."

No, he wouldn't, damn it. Tessa knew his company as well as he did. Where was he supposed to find that? "No. It'll take years to break her in."

"Or down," she muttered.

"What was that?" he asked, though he'd heard the guttural comment.

"Nothing." She lifted one hand and waved her own comment away. "I only meant that I've done my job and now it's time to do something else."

"Sure." Broke her down? Had he done that? He didn't see how that was possible, since the woman rarely treated him with any kind of deference. She ran his office. Hell, she ran his *life*. No. He wasn't going to accept her words without countering them.

"How in the hell can you say I broke you down?" The question hung in the scented air between them and simmered there for a long minute or two before she answered.

"I'm not getting into this, Noah. Not now."

"Well, you quit your job," he argued hotly, "so if not now, *when*?"

"Does *never* work?" she quipped and his eyes narrowed on her.

Her own fault, Tessa told herself.

She never should have let him in the house. But he hadn't given her a choice on that. And she certainly shouldn't have let him stay. Or muttered that comment just loud enough for him to hear it.

Tessa's kitchen felt incredibly small right now. Normally, the room was perfect. It held memories of her grandmother, whose house it had been. When her grandma died, she'd left the house to Tessa, because she was the grandchild who'd loved it most. Her family had come to visit Grandma nearly every summer and this house brought every one of those memories to life.

It was big enough for Tessa and her business and she liked that the kitchen was cozy. It made her feel... safe. But tonight, Noah's presence had shrunk the space until she couldn't draw a breath without the essence of him filling her. She hardly detected the jasmine—only his aftershave, a woodsy blend that had always smelled like heaven to her.

And that was totally beside the point—and yet one more reason why she'd quit her job.

Her heart was pounding and her mouth was dry. Completely normal. She was so accustomed to her body, her emotions and her thoughts jittering whenever he was near, it didn't even surprise her anymore. But having him level his laser-like focus on her was brand new and a little unsettling. His blue eyes seemed darker, bigger, somehow, and the way he was clenching his jaw made her wonder what exactly he was thinking.

She had to say something, though, so she started talking. "Maybe that was a little harsh," she said. "It wasn't so much breaking me down as *wearing* me down. I don't want a job where I'm always on duty, Noah."

"You're not."

"Really?" She spread her hands out as she looked

up at him. "Because it's Friday night and here you are. In my kitchen."

His frown deepened and Tessa wondered why it was that that expression always seemed more endearing than forbidding.

"I'm not asking you to do any work," he argued.

He was asking her to stay, though, and she couldn't do that. Heck, she'd be mortified to tell Lynn and Carol that her resignation hadn't even lasted twenty-four hours. But it wasn't just that. This was for Tessa's own sake. She needed to find a future that didn't include Noah. If nothing else, his visit here tonight had proven that.

Just being this close to him was driving her crazy. Normally, at the office, she could push aside what she was feeling because it was inappropriate. Boss-assistant attraction was so clichéd even she couldn't stand it. But he was here now. In her space. And he was so close that the temptations she'd fought for so long were rising to the surface, refusing to be ignored.

But ignore them she would.

Why ignore me? that voice whispered almost instantly. *Indulge me instead.*

"Sure you are," she argued, resisting the lure of that voice. "You're trying to bribe me to stay in a job I already quit."

"*Bribe* is a strong word."

"Really?" She had to laugh because Noah could go over the top easily and never realize it. "You just offered to remodel my garage and my kitchen and stock it with top-of-the-line equipment."

"Well," he snapped, "have me shot at dawn for offering to make your life easier."

She sighed. "That's not what I'm saying, Noah, and you know it."

"I thought I knew *you*," he said. "I'm just realizing that I was wrong about that."

Well, good. She was happy to have surprised him at last. Even though it meant having him here, breathing her air, smelling wonderful, radiating enough heat that her skin felt as if it were sizzling.

No, he didn't know her at all. If he did, he wouldn't have come here when she was feeling the rush of leaving her job. When she knew that she didn't have to be circumspect in how she treated him anymore. Because he wasn't, technically, her boss anymore.

So isn't it nice that he's here?

No, it wasn't.

Honestly, that inner voice was getting extremely annoying. Mostly because its whispers were becoming more and more tempting.

"Hello? Earth to Tessa," he said and Tessa realized she'd been thinking too much and talking too little.

"I'm just busy, Noah. I don't have time to go over all the same territory again and again." *Good. Get him to leave.*

Ask him to stay.

"Maybe I can help."

"What?" She goggled at him. The master of his universe wanted to step down into the real world, however briefly, and work in a tiny kitchen? "You want to help me make candles?"

"Doesn't look that difficult," he said with a shrug. "And while we work, we can talk some more."

"Fantastic."

Or, you could forget about the candles and do something else.

"Okay fine," she said abruptly, in an effort to silence that tiny voice inside, "candles it is. There's a walk-in pantry right over there." She pointed to a door in the corner of the kitchen. "Just grab one of the melt pans off the bottom shelf."

"Any one at all?"

"Yeah. We'll make whichever one you choose."

She watched him go and admired the view as she had been doing for five long years. Honestly, no man should have a butt that good. And his long legs, narrow hips, flat stomach and broad chest? Deadly. Really.

What are you waiting for, Tessa?

A sign maybe? A meteor? Asteroid crashing into earth?

He bent down to get one of the pans and Tessa sighed. This was going to be a very long evening.

An hour later, the kitchen was a mess, four new jars of cranberry candles had been filled and Noah was peeling hardened red wax from his five-hundred-dollar shirt. Perfect.

"I'll pay for the shirt," she said.

"Why should you pay for it?" he muttered darkly. "I'm the one who splashed the damn wax."

"You said it didn't look difficult."

"It isn't. It's just…" he frowned. "Dangerous."

Tessa moved in closer, batted his hands away and took over for him. With her fingernails, she could get at the wax still clinging to the fabric. And this close to him, she couldn't avoid dragging his scent into her lungs, or the heat pumping from his body. She heard his every breath and swore she could also count the beats of his heart. When they sped up suddenly, she was sure of it.

Slowly, she straightened, lifted her chin until she could look him in the eye. What she saw there startled that inner voice into shrieking, *This is it, Tessa. Time to make a move.*

Noah's eyes darkened and somehow, at the same time, lit with a heat that she felt burning inside her, too. He lifted one hand and smoothed a strand of her hair back from her face and the tips of his fingers slid across her skin like a wish. Her blood simmered in response and it felt as if she were on fire. She didn't mind the flames at all. She'd been quenching them for five years.

Maybe it was time to fan them instead.

"You're not my boss, Noah. Not anymore."

"Until I get you to change your mind," he said with a satisfied smile that told Tessa he wasn't through trying.

Do something, Tessa. Even if it's wrong, do something.

So she did. She released a breath she hadn't realized she'd been holding and said, "For right now, you're not my boss."

"No," he agreed. "I'm not."

"Just so we're both sure of that." She went up on her toes to kiss him and that voice inside was blessedly silent.

Four

Tessa stunned him.

She felt his shock when she hooked her arms behind his neck and laid her mouth over his. But it was astonishing how quickly he recovered from his surprise. In an instant, his arms came around her middle and pinned her to him as he kissed her back.

It was everything she'd thought it would be. Everything —and more than her dreams had conjured. His mouth was firm and soft and oh, so expert. Her nipples tingled, pressed against his chest so tightly. Her breath caught in her lungs and she didn't mind. Who needed to breathe?

Tessa gave herself up to the moment, letting it fill her and tempt her with the promise of more. The surge of emotions was tangled and confusing, so she ignored them and concentrated on sensation alone. His hands swept up and down her back, cupped her butt and squeezed until she groaned into his mouth.

The sound must have tripped a switch inside him, because Noah tightened his grip on her, swung her around and pressed her up against the refrigerator. Through the heat pulsing inside her, she didn't even feel the sting of cold metal. Seconds ticked past and the only sound was the hard thumping of their hearts. His tongue swept into her mouth and she gasped at the electrifying feeling that jolted through her.

She'd opened Pandora's box here and she wasn't sure what to do next. When he slid one hand up to cup one of her breasts, she at first sighed, enjoying the moment she'd spent so much time dreaming about. But then reality reared its ugly head, her brain woke up and she knew she needed to stop. Think.

No thinking!

The opportunity is right here in front of you. Grab it.

But she couldn't. Not when she had to face him at work for the next two weeks.

Deliberately, Tessa pulled her mouth from his, then pushed out of the circle of his arms. Her knees were weak and her sense of balance was completely gone. If she hadn't slapped one hand down on the kitchen island she might have tipped over.

"What?" Frowning, Noah took a step closer to her. "What the hell, Tessa? Why'd you stop?"

She held up her free hand and took a couple of deep breaths. It wasn't going to help. Nothing would help. *An orgasm might.* But that wasn't going to happen, she insisted silently.

"Because," she finally managed to say, "I promised myself I couldn't leave my job without doing that at least once. And now I have. So, I'm done."

"Uh-huh." He scrubbed one hand across his mouth.

"You're done." His breath came as fast and sharp as hers. "You know, there are lots of other things we could do—at least once…"

Oh, boy. There was literally nothing she wanted more. The very idea of being with Noah, naked bodies tangled together on cool, smooth sheets, was enough to make her breath hitch. But resolutely, she shook her head and said, "We still have to work together for the next two weeks, Noah."

"We're not working now," he pointed out.

"No, we're not," she said. "So maybe you should go."

He looked surprised again—not in a good way, this time.

"Seriously?" One eyebrow lifted. "You kiss me like that and then tell me to go?"

"Yeah. Sorry." Boy, she was sorry. Sorry she'd stopped. Sorry they weren't going to go to her bedroom. Sorry she now had to spend the next two weeks thinking about that kiss.

Nodding grimly, he said, "All right. I'll leave."

No. Don't let him leave. What are you thinking?

That inner voice had a point.

He walked over to the chair where he'd hung his jacket a couple of hours ago, shrugged it on, then came back to her. For a moment, Tessa thought he might even lean in to kiss her again, but then she realized he would never do that, now that she'd called an end to it.

"I'm going," he said. "But I'll see you on Monday."

"Right. Monday." Which meant she still had Saturday and Sunday to get past this. Sure. She could do that.

Noah moved in, cupped her cheek in the palm of his

hand and tipped her face up so that their eyes met and held. "You will be there, right?"

She blinked at him. "Of course I will."

Nodding, Noah smiled briefly. "Good. Wouldn't want you to chicken out."

Chicken out of what? Facing him? Leaving him? Either way, Tessa was a little insulted even though she knew he was playing his own game. In challenging her, he was making sure that she'd show up. That she wouldn't phone in her last two weeks.

"I don't chicken out."

"Really?" His mouth quirked. "Seems like that's exactly what you just did."

She didn't like the sound of that, but maybe he had a point. "I just came to my senses, is all."

"Yeah, I don't think that's it."

Frowning, Tessa whispered, "You don't scare me, Noah."

"Glad to hear it." He nodded. "Scaring you is the last thing on my mind right now." He left then and from halfway down the hallway, he called back, "See you Monday, Tessa."

Sighing, she sort of slumped against the kitchen island and felt the cold of the granite bite into that inch or so of bare skin at the small of her back. It was a good wake-up call, she told herself. Didn't do anything for the heat still crawling through her body, but the touch of cold was enough to draw her out of the semitrance state that kiss had left her in.

You missed your chance.

"Come on, Tessa," she muttered out loud. "Finish up these candles, then clean up and drink some wine. A lot of wine. And maybe a cold shower."

Cold shower. That's pitiful.

"Be quiet," she snapped to that voice and wondered if it was a bad sign that she was now apparently arguing with herself.

It was a long weekend.

Noah had spent far too much time thinking about that kiss in Tessa's kitchen. He'd tried to brush it off as just a kiss. Nothing special. But even he wasn't believing his lies. Tessa had starred in his dreams and haunted his thoughts for the last two days and he hoped to hell she'd had a bad weekend, too. Only fair, since she was the one who'd started—and ended it.

On Monday, he got to the office early as per usual.

What was *unusual*? He wasn't on the phone or going over paperwork or even plotting his next move in his quest for worldwide vodka domination. Instead, he was still thinking about Tessa. Waiting for her to arrive. Wanting to see if she'd brushed off that kiss or if it had tormented her as it had him all weekend.

It took a lot to surprise Noah. He prided himself on always being one step ahead of his competitors and even his friends. His long-range thinking had stood him in good stead for years.

Until Tessa kissed him.

He pushed away from his desk and paced to the bank of windows overlooking the Pacific. Staring out at the water and the heavy gray clouds gathering on the horizon, Noah instead saw Tessa's big blue eyes staring up at him. The passion shimmering there had spiked something inside him that he hadn't expected.

Desire, hot and thick, had pumped through his veins and when she'd called a halt, Noah's entire body went from need to frustration in a blink of time. And there he'd stayed all weekend. He hadn't been able to stop thinking about her and when he tried to sleep, she was there, too. In his dreams, smiling at him, opening her arms to him as she tumbled onto his bed.

"At least once," he muttered and pushed back the edges of his suit jacket to shove both hands into his slacks pockets. "So that's good enough for her? Just one kiss?"

Muttering under his breath now, Noah admitted that he didn't like this at all. The kiss, of course he'd liked. He would have had to have been a dead man not to enjoy that kiss—and probably even death wouldn't have been enough to dull the fire Tessa had caused.

What he *didn't* like was the fact that he'd thought about her all weekend and was still thinking about her now. Tessa was a distraction—a hell of one, if he were being honest. And he couldn't risk being distracted now. He couldn't afford to take his eyes off the prize.

Noah was closer now than ever to achieving what he'd been working toward for years. He had a duty to his late grandfather. To the rest of his family and he wouldn't step away from that. Not for anything. Not even for another taste of Tessa.

His hands curled into fists at his sides and Noah fixed his gaze on the ocean and the cloud-swept sky. But as he stared, his mind raced with images from his past.

His father, Jared, had taken over the family company and nearly driven the vodka division into the ground. His father, Thomas, Noah's grandfather, had watched as his son threw away family duty—to the company, to his wife and children—in favor of fast women and even faster cars. Noah was ten when his father left them. And fourteen when a drunk Jared finally drove one of his cars off a cliff, killing himself and his latest woman. It was almost a relief.

Noah's grandfather, an old man, had taken over the reins of the company again, but his heart wasn't in it. He'd taken Noah to work with him, showing him the business, teaching him and basically being more of a father than grandfather. Noah had taken it all in. He'd wanted then so much to make up for what his father had done, he'd promised his grandfather that when he grew up, he'd make Graystone the best in the world.

As memories faded and the present rushed in, Noah gritted his teeth in frustrated anger that hadn't abated over the years. His own father had lost everything in his relentless pursuit of women. Noah had no intention of making the same mistakes.

He was focused on the company. The family. His duty was to build on his grandfather's dream and somehow, some way, erase his father's sins.

Not even Tessa could sway him from that goal.

So during the hours he'd spent thinking of and dreaming of Tessa, Noah had decided over the weekend that this morning, he would act as if nothing had changed between them. He put that kiss, that night, down to a momentary brain blip.

"And now I'm back." He took a deep breath, let his gaze focus on the ocean and told himself that he was unchanged. Unaffected.

"I'm also lying," he muttered, but if there was one thing he'd learned when starting out in business…don't let anyone see you doubt yourself.

So he was prepared when Tessa walked into the office and said, "Good morning, Noah."

"Tessa." He glanced at her. She was wearing one of her conservative suits, this one in a subtle blue with a white shirt and sensible black heels. Her long hair was pulled up into a messy bun that only made him want to free the whole mass and watch it tumble over her shoulders. Grimly, he nodded before returning his gaze to the window and the view beyond. "Work up a schedule for London, will you? I want to know exactly where we'll be and what's happening every day."

"Sure. I'll have it for you in a couple of hours."

"That works." Still not looking at her because how could he? Now he knew what kind of body was hiding beneath that unimaginative blue suit. He knew the toes hidden in those black heels were painted a deep red. And he knew she had a tattoo that was completely camouflaged by the persona of "perfect personal assistant."

No, if he looked at her again right now, he'd be thinking about that night at her place. That kiss. And he'd already vowed to wipe it from memory.

"Anything else?" she asked.

So many things, he thought, but didn't say. "Yeah. Ask my sister to come in when she's free. I've got a few things I want to go over."

"Sure. Is that it?"

"Yes," he said and silently, he added, *just leave.*

"Okay." She didn't leave, though. He could sense her there. Waiting.

Finally, Noah turned to face her and just looking at her made him want to rethink his whole plan.

"Is everything all right, Noah?" She tipped her head to one side and in her eyes, he read confusion.

"Everything's fine." His voice was clipped and as neutral as he could keep it.

She studied him for a long minute. "Should we talk about what happened on Friday?"

"No." One word. Deliberate. He headed for his desk, effectively dismissing her. If he looked at her again, he might lose his resolve.

"I think we should," she said. "It's clearly bugging you."

He looked at her, locking his eyes with hers. Bugging him? No. What bugged him was that he could be so easily drawn off the path he'd laid out for himself. And he wouldn't let it happen again.

"You're wrong, Tessa," he said.

"I don't think so, Noah," she answered, shaking her head. "I was there. I remember. And you do, too."

Oh, yeah. He remembered. Not that he wanted to, it was only that the kiss itself, that moment in time, had been burned into his memory so deeply, he'd never be able to shake it.

But that didn't mean he couldn't ignore it.

"It was a simple kiss. Don't make more of it than there was."

"Don't make less of it, either."

"We're not talking about this," Noah said.

"Funny. Sounds like we are."

He gave her a hard scowl and wasn't the slightest bit surprised when it had no effect on her at all. "We both have work to do," he snapped. "Let's get on it."

"Right. We'll do that." She turned for the door and paused on the threshold. Looking back at him, she added, "But we both know you're lying, so don't think you're getting away with something."

She closed the door a moment later, as if to make sure she got the last word. And Noah had to admit, it had been a good one.

Tessa took the extra time to walk down to Stephanie Graystone's corner office at the opposite end of the floor. Yes, she could have called, but she needed the movement. As if she could walk off Noah's reaction—or non-reaction. Who did he think he was kidding, anyway?

Over the weekend, Tessa had imagined all sorts of ways the conversation with him would go this morning. Some of them had ended with him locking his office door, lying her down on the sofa and—

She broke that thought off quickly. One thing she didn't need was to indulge an imagination that had been on overdrive since Friday night. Heck, she'd spent most of the weekend working in her kitchen and every moment of that time reliving the kiss. The feel of his arms around her. The hard slam of his heart against hers. And mostly, the wild, overwhelming taste of his mouth fused to hers.

And her dreams had been off-the-chart erotic. She woke up horny and aching and exhausted.

Then he tried to tell her it was nothing? Did he think she was stupid? Was *he* stupid?

Who cares if he's stupid? that little voice shrieked. *He's a hell of a kisser—let's see how good he is at the main event.*

Well, yes, she would really like to, but she'd need his cooperation, damn it.

Tessa barely saw the people she passed. Everyone was at their desk, working busily, while she was fighting raging hormones and a rising temper. The office was huge, open and filled with sunlight through the wide bank of windows overlooking the Pacific. Of course the windows were tinted, but still the light and the view made this a beautiful office to work in. Tessa stared straight ahead, though, down the hall to Stephanie's closed door.

When she got there, she looked at Steph's assistant, Angie. "Is she free?"

"Sure," the woman said. "She just got off a call and her next meeting isn't for half an hour."

"Great, thanks." Tessa opened the door, peeked in and said, "Stephanie? You have a minute?"

"I'd love a break. Come on in." Stephanie Graystone was tall—nearly five feet ten inches and was, to put it bluntly, gorgeous. Her dark blond hair was pulled back from her face by a simple headband and then fell past her shoulders in thick waves. She wore a white dress shirt, black slacks, and her black jacket was hung over the back of her chair. Her eyes were a darker blue than Noah's—almost violet, really—and her wide mouth was curved in a smile.

"What's up, Tess?"

"Noah needs to see you, he said. I'm guessing it's something about plans for while we're in London…"

Stephanie's eyebrows lifted into perfectly sculpted arches. "And you had to walk down here to tell me?"

"No," Tessa said and dropped into one of Steph's visitor chairs. The two women had long ago developed a friendship that went beyond employer/employee and today, Tessa was grateful. "I just needed to walk."

"Ah." Stephanie sat back in her chair and swiveled it a little. "Noah's aggravating you, too?"

"Too?" Tessa echoed. "What's he doing to you?"

"Oh, treating me like it's my first week on the job." Stephanie waved one hand gracefully in the air, as if dismissing her older brother. "It's okay—I'm used to it. I hear him out and then do things my way. Keeps us both happy. He is a major control freak after all."

"True." Noah thought that only *he* could run the company the way it should be run. He kept his finger on the pulse of every department and personally oversaw every decision. Well, that wasn't entirely fair. His department heads made their own calls, but Noah wanted to know about them.

"What's going on, Tessa?"

"Nothing." She shook her head, wondering why she'd come to Stephanie. Sure, they were friends, but Noah, no matter how aggravating, was still the other woman's brother. And even when Tessa's brother Joe irritated her beyond belief, she would still stand up for him to everyone else.

"So, what's bugging you?" Stephanie asked.

"I quit on Friday—did he tell you?"

"Yes." Frowning a little, Stephanie said, "He told me Friday evening before he left for the night. He was outraged that you would leave the company."

Outraged. That about covered it. "Are you?"

"No." Stephanie grinned and shook her head. "If you've got a business you want to build, you'll never do it if you're dancing attendance on the king."

Tessa snorted and some of the tension lessened in her chest. "Thanks."

"No problem. But, is there an issue with Noah about this? Is he giving you a hard time?"

I wish.

Oh, stop it, she warned that voice in her mind. That was a terrible pun.

"He did come over on Friday to try to talk me out of it, but he eventually dropped it and helped me make some candles. But it's not about my resignation. Well," she corrected, "not entirely."

Steph smiled slowly and leaned forward. "Ooh. There's a story here. Do I get to hear it?"

"Probably," she admitted. "But first, I've got a question for you that is wildly off topic, but it's something I've been trying to understand for years."

"Now I'm curious. Ask."

"Okay," Tessa said. "I want to know why Noah is so driven. Why does this vodka award mean so much to him?"

"A long story that I'm going to try to cut down to size," Stephanie said on a sigh. "It goes back to our father. First you have to know that dear old dad was just no good at all. He took over for our grandfather—who was already raising us along with our mom because father-of-the-year dumped us."

Tessa winced and immediately compared her own amazing parents to what Steph, Noah and Matthew had grown up with.

"Anyway," Stephanie continued, "it broke Papa's heart to see what his son became and it was hard to watch the old man sort of shrink into himself in response. Noah was the oldest, so he just naturally assumed the obligation to make Graystone what it was before our dad wrecked it.

"Like I said, our grandfather took in Mom and all of us. Gave us a home. And a legacy to live up to." She smiled a little, remembering her grandfather. "Matthew's a lot like our dad without the whole 'terrible human' thing and Noah is practically a clone of our grandfather. Family, duty, matter most to him. I don't think he'll ever give up until Papa's dreams become reality."

Tessa was listening, and didn't like it. Oh, at last she understood what was behind Noah's focus, but that didn't make her feel any better.

Yes, he was driven, successful and focused on the prize he could see right in front of him. But what, she wondered, would he do when he finally *won* that prize? When he met his goal? Would he try for a life then, or would he just shift his focus to the next challenge?

"Speaking of tangents," Stephanie said softly, "I'm actually looking forward to Noah being in London for a week."

"Why?"

"Don't sound so judgmental," Stephanie teased. "It's nothing drastic. But while he's gone, I'm giving everyone three or four days off so I can get painters in here to change the boring, snow-blind white walls and I'm having hardwood floors laid to give the place warmth."

"In three or four days?"

Stephanie winked. "It's amazing what the word *bonus* will get you."

Tessa laughed. "On the way to your office I was thinking this is the most beautiful place to work I'd ever seen."

"Well, sure, we have the ocean view, so that really helps. But come on." Stephanie rolled her eyes. "Let's face it. Noah wouldn't notice his surroundings if they were on fire. But why should the rest of us put up with his bland decorating style? Nope. COO here and I'm making an executive decision. Or two."

"You know what?" Tessa said. "You're right. Noah wouldn't notice unless the Graystone label was splashed across the walls. Go for it, Steph. And text me a picture of it once it's done."

"That's right." Stephanie's shoulders slumped. "You won't be here to see it. And now I'm sad. Who will I complain to about Noah?"

"You can always call me," Tessa offered. She probably shouldn't want to get reports on him as much as she did.

"I may take you up on that," Stephanie said. Then she was quiet for a moment or two before blurting, "You know, Tessa, you should just go for it."

"It?"

"Noah. I mean you won't see him again after London. You've been in love with him forever. So seduce him."

"You knew?" Tessa just blinked at the other woman.

"Not hard to notice," Steph said. "Unless of course you're Noah."

"He's ignoring me."

"Don't let him."

"It's not that easy."

"It's not rocket science, Tessa. It's sex."

Exactly what I've been saying.

She frowned as her inner voice and Stephanie seemed to gang up on her.

Then she decided to just tell her friend what had happened last Friday. Maybe she'd planned on telling Stephanie all along. Why else would she have walked down here when a phone call would have handled it? And who better to give her a little insight than the woman who'd grown up with Noah?

"I kissed him on Friday." She said it before she could lose her nerve.

"And about time, too," Stephanie said.

Not the reaction she'd been expecting. "What are you talking about?"

"Please, Tess." Stephanie sat back in her chair and shook her head. "Just because my brother has apparently been wearing blinders for the last five years doesn't mean I have."

"Oh, God…" How embarrassing was this? How many other people in the office had noticed that Tessa was in love with the boss?

Stephanie laughed. "It's not a tragedy. So? What happened?"

"Oh, he kissed me back. I think he curled my hair, actually," Tessa mused. "Then he left and I didn't hear from him all weekend. No business problems to handle. No plans to make."

"Unusual, I grant you," Stephanie said, nodding.

"And this morning when I saw him, he acted as if it had never happened." That still annoyed her. "He brushed it off. Said it was nothing and we wouldn't be talking about it again."

Tessa's temper began to bubble as she described that meeting with Noah. Honestly, she'd been so surprised at his attitude, she hadn't really processed how she was feeling about it.

Now that she was processing it, though, she was beyond annoyed and deeply insulted.

"Typical." Stephanie laid her forearms on her desk and leaned toward Tessa. "Well, he's lying."

"I know that. I was there. Doesn't change the situation, though." Except for making her want to charge back down the hallway, breach his office door and confront him. *Make* him admit that the kiss they'd shared was way more than he was pretending it was.

"I think it does," Stephanie said. "If it didn't mean anything, he wouldn't mind talking about it. He'd say something stupid about inappropriate behavior and be done with it." She pointed her finger at Tessa. "But him saying it doesn't mean anything and refusing to talk about it means that it *did* mean something to him and he doesn't want to think about it."

"Believe it or not, I followed that," Tessa said with a half smile. "But what does knowing it change?"

While it was great having her own thoughts on this validated, Tessa didn't know what else it did for her.

"It changes how you handle it—if you still want to," Stephanie said, then added, "and I totally understand if you just want to write him off."

"No…" The chance for writing off Noah had come and gone years ago. The day she had first realized that she was in love with her boss. With a man who would never see her as more than part of his office.

But hadn't that changed Friday night? Hadn't he, at last, really seen her? For the first time?

I told you, Tessa. Sex is the answer.

Who said anything about sex?

You should.

She shut that voice down again and focused on Stephanie.

"If you want my advice, don't let him bury it. Talk about it. The kiss, I mean. Talk about it a lot. Make him remember."

Making him remember would bring her…what? Was

finally giving in to what she felt for Noah the answer? Or would it be better to just leave her job with the same hungers that had tortured her for five years?

How was she supposed to know?

"I can see you thinking," Stephanie mused aloud. She shrugged. "Up to you, obviously. But I know my big brother. Ever since our grandfather died, Noah's been obsessed with fulfilling Papa's dream. Making Graystone the name you think of when you buy a bottle of vodka.

"It's going to take being hit over the head to sway him from that course—figuratively, of course." She grinned. "Although sometimes I consider a literal hit over the head—though I restrain myself."

Tessa laughed a little because honestly, she'd been pushed to the edge with Noah herself many times. It wasn't easy working with a driven perfectionist. Wasn't easy pretending not to care for him, either.

"Like I said," Stephanie went on, "it's up to you. But if it helps, I'm on your side."

It was good to hear, anyway. Tessa had a lot of thinking to do. Decisions to make. But meanwhile, she also had a job to do.

"It helps," Tessa said and stood up. "I don't know what I'm going to do yet—beyond get back to work, at the moment."

"Okay, well, tell Noah I'll be there in a few minutes. I just need to make a call to Marketing, get them to send me the latest report."

"I'll tell him," Tessa said and headed for the door. Stephanie was already on the phone when Tessa left the office. She took her time walking back to her desk.

Looking around the office space, she had to admit that she would actually *miss* coming in to work every morning. Not just the people she knew and liked, but also the rush of the work itself. Helping to put Graystone on the map was exciting and now she was leaving just as Noah was within reach of the award he'd been working toward for years.

Still, she had to do this. For herself. Noah's dreams weren't hers. Tessa knew her future didn't lie here, at the company. Or with Noah. So difficult or not, she had to move on.

Now she just had to decide if she really wanted to leave and never indulge herself with Noah.

She was pretty sure she knew the answer.

"Tessa said you wanted to see me."

Noah looked up as his sister walked into the office. Stephanie was smart, capable and since taking over the position of COO had done incredible work for the company. Noah trusted her implicitly—and yet still kept up with the decisions she was making for the family business.

"Yes," he said, "since I'll be in London for a week, I thought we should talk, make sure we're on the same page."

"What page is that?" she asked, dropping elegantly into one of the visitor chairs opposite his desk. She crossed her legs, folded her hands in her lap and waited.

Patience. Steph had always had it and it worked to her favor in negotiations with competitors and clients alike. It didn't work with Noah.

"I want to know what you're planning for when I'm out of town."

"Not a thing," she said, lifting her hands now in a show of innocence.

"Right." Shaking his head, Noah continued, "I've taken care of the meetings I need completed before I leave. The new labels designed by Ms. Shipman's company look good. I'm having her send you some mock-ups with several different colors, so you can make the final decision."

"Seriously?" Her eyebrows lifted. "Okay, good. These are labels for the varietal vodka, right?"

Their signature mix of blackberry-and-lime-infused vodka was a winner; Noah was sure of it. Once he had that award, he would focus his efforts on the pure vodka line.

"Yes, she's going to work on a different approach for the pure vodka bottles, though I think we should keep the Graystone font the same, to provide continuity to the customers. Still, I want your opinion."

"You'll have it." She smoothed the crease of her black slacks. "Tessa said you were at her house last Friday."

His head snapped up and he glared at his sister. He knew Steph and Tessa had become friends. He just didn't know if that friendship included gossip.

Hell. Of course it did.

"What else did she have to say?"

"Nothing."

He snorted. "She said nothing."

"That's right," Stephanie said with a shrug. "She said you helped her pour a couple of candles—which by the way, I would have loved to see—and that you left soon after."

"That's it."

"That's it," Stephanie repeated. "Why? Is there more?"

His frown deepened. Had Tessa really not said anything about that kiss? Or was Steph playing him? Hard to tell. Which was irritating.

"Okay then." Stephanie stood up. "If that's all, I've got a meeting with Devon in Marketing in a few minutes. He's got a couple of ideas for our next campaign that I think are brilliant."

"What are they?"

"Oh, I'll save that for when you get back from London." She headed for the door then paused and turned around. "Be sure to call me if we win."

"*When* we win, I will," he said.

"I like the attitude. You and Tessa have fun in England."

"It's business, Stephanie. It's not about fun."

She heaved a dramatic sigh. "It never is with you, is it, Noah?"

"What's that supposed to mean?" Sisters could get away with a lot more than most people, but Noah had a limit and she was cruising very close to it.

She walked back to his desk, planted both hands on the edge and leaned down to look her brother in the eye. "It means, that you don't have to sacrifice your entire life to be the Anti-Dad."

"I'm not sacrificing anything," he countered, wondering how they'd taken this turn in the conversation.

"Sure. Noah, you might as well be a monk."

"That's ridiculous—and where is this coming from?"

"I talked to Matthew today and he's taking a couple of days in New Orleans. And I realized it's been years since you've done the same."

Noah scowled at her. "Matthew takes too many breaks."

"You think he's turning into our father or something, don't you?"

He didn't like to think it, but yeah, his younger brother had a lot of their father's less-than-great attributes. Jared Graystone had left nothing but misery in his wake, which was why Noah had done everything he could to steer his own life in the opposite direction.

Matthew had been young enough that he hadn't really been aware of the pain their father had caused. He hadn't heard their mother crying. Hadn't seen the disappointment and despair in their grandfather's eyes.

Matthew hadn't made a vow to reclaim what his father had ruined, as Noah had.

"Matt likes women, Noah," Steph said. "He likes having a life."

One eyebrow lifted. "So did Dad."

"But Matt isn't a drunk. He isn't cruel or thoughtless or any of the other things our illustrious parent was."

Noah stood up and Steph straightened to face him. "He could be, though," Noah said. "The temptations are right there and if he heads too far in the wrong direction…"

Stephanie pushed her hair behind her shoulders and sighed. "*This* is why Matt's always on the road," she said. "Yes, he's Head of Sales, but he could delegate a hell of a lot more than he does. He takes these trips to get away from your disapproval."

"Bull." Was that true?

"Noah, you're so busy worrying that Matt will become like Dad that you don't see that in the ways that matter he's *nothing* like the man. And you constantly expecting him to suddenly morph into a wastrel is exactly what's keeping him away." She shook her head. "Honestly, Noah, there's a difference between having fun from time to time, and being a complete jerk who tosses away everything that should matter."

Rationally, he knew Stephanie was right. And still he couldn't help worrying about his brother making bad decisions. Scrubbing the back of his neck, he admitted, "I don't want him staying away because of me. He does a great job here, Steph. I just…"

"Worry. Always worry." Stephanie walked around the edge of the desk and gave him a hug. When she pulled back, she said, "Maybe you could try dialing it down a little? Remember, Papa raised us, too. Not just you. And we saw how unhappy Mom was when Dad left. And how much happier she is now. Do you begrudge her that?"

"Of course not."

She smiled at him. "Good answer. Then don't get bent out of shape when Matt and I take a vacation. Or actually have sex once in a while."

Noah winced. "Yeah, I'm not talking about my little sister's sex life."

She laughed. "Fine, let's talk about yours. Or your *lack* of one."

"My sex life is none of your business." His voice was clipped, with the dismissive tone that clearly said the conversation was over. "Don't you have a meeting to get to?"

"Maybe if you *had* sex occasionally, you'd be easier to deal with."

"Butt out."

She shrugged. "Fine. But maybe you should ask

yourself something. Now that Tessa doesn't work for you anymore…maybe your trip to London could be a 'break' as well as a business trip."

His eyes narrowed on her. "You said she didn't say anything to you."

Stephanie patted his cheek. "Clearly, I lied."

Five

Three days later, Noah was on edge.

Yes, he and Tessa had always worked closely together. But these days, that closeness had really become...overwhelming.

It seemed every time he turned around, she was there, leaning over his desk, brushing her hand against his as she handed him a report. Even when she buzzed his office and spoke to him, her voice sounded different. Huskier. Softer. Tempting.

Scowling, he realized that thoughts of Tessa were clouding his mind when he most needed clarity of thought. With the international spirits awards the following week, he needed to be on his game now more than ever.

Some would say that it didn't matter. The votes had been counted, the award decided. There was nothing he could do at this point. But Noah didn't believe that. Sure, the awards were sealed and would be announced in the middle of the conference. But before and after the ceremony, there were people to talk to. New links in the chain to be forged. Commitments to be made. He wanted to get Graystone Vodka around the world and to do that, he needed to make alliances with his counterparts in Europe.

Before the awards, he would be laying down the groundwork for what might come. And once his vodka had won that blasted award, he wanted to be able to move fast on distributors and marketing and every other damn thing required.

The problem was, he couldn't focus on any of it if Tessa kept filling his mind.

Which was why he was here, outside her house again. Not because he missed her, he told himself firmly. Not because he wanted another taste of her. No. This visit was strictly business. To lay down some ground rules. To remind her that this trip to London was too important to blow.

He stopped on her front walk in the darkness and looked at the would-be fairy-tale cottage. Inside was the woman who had been driving him insane for days. Was it a mistake to be alone with her outside the safety of the office? Probably. Had he *ever* been afraid of a challenge? Never.

Scowling to himself, he thought he had also never encountered a challenge quite like Tessa, but that wasn't important right now. What was important was to get a few things straight between them so that the upcoming trip wouldn't be affected.

His long legs made short work of the cobblestone walk and when he got to the porch, he might have knocked on that heavy wooden door a bit harder than was necessary. The door swung open a moment later and there she was. A little breathless, a little harried. Her long blond hair was pulled up into a ponytail at the back of her head and she wore yet another short, clingy T-shirt—this one red. She wore skin-tight yoga pants with a red-and-green floral pattern and her toes were now painted blue. He shook his head at that, but he didn't have long to admire her.

"Oh, thank God you're here." Tessa grabbed his hand, pulled him into the house and swung the door shut with a slam behind him. Tugging him along behind her toward the kitchen, she was saying, "I need help. The overnight service will be here in a half hour and Lynn, my neighbor, had to go home because her son was sick. There's no way I'll get it all done on my own—" she glanced over her shoulder at him "—so you've just been drafted."

This was *not* going as he'd planned it. Noah had assumed that he'd have a calm, cool discussion with Tessa. Tell her that there would be nothing between them so they should both concentrate on business. His gaze dropped to the curve of her butt and he noted that the stretchy pants dipped low enough on her hips that a bit more of her lower back tattoo was visible. Not that it helped him identify what it was, but the view was intriguing.

Internally groaning, he reminded himself that Tessa's tattoo had zero to do with why he was here. "Drafted for what exactly?"

"You'll see." She entered the kitchen, dropped his hand and headed for the table on the far wall.

What he could see was...chaos. The scene in that tiny kitchen went against everything he'd ever known about Tessa. One of the things he'd always admired about her was her innate sense of organization. Hell, as he remembered it, even her stock of supplies in her garage were methodically organized. This... He shook his head, for once in his life, speechless.

The kitchen island, under a hanging pendant lamp, was brilliantly lit, which made it easy to see the candles in a dozen apothecary-style jars, three rolls of jewel-toned ribbon, stacks of empty boxes and packing material strewn across the counters, some of it falling to the hardwood floors.

"What happened in here?" He turned his head to look at Tessa, huddled over the small table.

Her ponytail swung as she looked over her shoulder at him. "I had to work late," she said with a tone of accusation, "so that made me late getting to all of this, but I've made a commitment to get these candles and earrings out tonight and like I said, I've only got a half an hour, so if you don't mind, we can chitchat later and you can help *now*."

"What do you expect me to do?" He knew nothing about her business, and sadly, it looked as though she didn't, either. *This* was what she was resigning for? She was walking away from a great job, good salary...*him*, for this kitchen table nightmare?

"I expect you to measure off sections of ribbon ten inches long, then tie bows around the necks of the labeled jars."

"Tying bows? Seriously?" He looked at her as if she'd asked him to perform surgery.

"Noah," she snarled, "I don't have time for this. Help me or get out if you can't handle it."

His eyebrows shot up.

"Can't handle tying bows? Please." Damned if he'd be sent away before he'd had that talk with her and if that meant dealing with ribbon, then he'd do it. How hard could it be?

"Fine." He took off his jacket, tossed it onto an empty space on the kitchen counter and picked up the wide red ribbon to begin. He used the ruler lying there to measure, then cut it and tied it around the neck of the jar. Looked pretty good, if a little lopsided, to him. So he moved on. While he worked, he asked, "What exactly are *you* doing?"

"Hand addressing the boxes, packing them and sealing."

"Hand addressing?" He cut a green ribbon and repeated the bow action. "Are we cavemen? Don't you have a printer?"

"It's the personal touch, if you must know. How many jars have you done?"

"Two," he said as he finished.

"Hurry up."

His eyebrows lifted. He hadn't taken orders in a long time and he didn't care for it, but there was no time to object. He had to help Tessa finish this so they could talk. White ribbon was next. He watched her as she walked from the table to the counter to grab two more boxes and packing material. Once she had them set up, she came to pick up the two candles he'd finished. She lifted them, stared at them wide eyed for a moment or two, then looked at him and asked, "Did you tie these with your feet?"

"Excuse me?"

"Come on, Noah…" She undid the red bow and quickly redid it, talking the whole time. "Haven't you ever wrapped a present before? No wait a minute, I know you haven't. I wrap your presents for you, don't I? Never mind. I should have known better."

He was only half listening, but he watched every move her nimble fingers made. She made it look very easy, he silently admitted, but he could replicate her moves. "Fine. Do the packing. I can do this."

She frowned and considered it.

"Damn it, Tessa, I'm the president of a multimillion-dollar company. I can handle tying bows onto candle jars."

"Fine." She huffed out a breath. "I don't have the time to be picky. Just…be better."

Well, that was insulting, but he simmered silently as he worked. He could admit, at least to himself, his redone bows looked considerably better once he imitated Tessa's moves and he was finished in a few tense minutes. "Done."

"Great, box them up. Two to a box. Use the packing materials so the jars don't crack in shipping."

"Sure you can trust me?" He thought he'd muttered that low enough, but she heard him anyway.

"No, but I'm out of options." She wielded the strapping tape like a sword in battle. She was fast, efficient and as soon as he had the candles boxed, she was sealing them shut, slapping labels on them and pushing them to one side.

They were a good team, Noah thought. Even at something as incongruous as this. Which was exactly why her resignation made no sense. She was the right hand of the president of a huge company. She was in on every decision. Every marketing meeting, and her suggestions were always considered and usually accepted. Why would she want to toss all of that aside for…this?

When the doorbell rang, her head snapped up as she bit her bottom lip. "Get the door, will you? That'll be Travis, here to pick these up. As soon as I strap the last two boxes, we'll be done."

"Right." Shaking his head, Noah walked down the hall, opened the door and faced a tall, dark haired guy with a wide smile on his face. Slowly, that expectant smile faded.

"Who're you?"

Irritated, Noah said, "That doesn't concern you."

The man gave him a scowl designed to intimidate. It didn't work on Noah, but that didn't stop the man from trying. "Hey, I know Tessa and I've never seen you before. Where is she?"

Exasperation was quickly swallowed by outrage. What? Did he look like a serial killer or something?

"Back here, Travis!"

At Tessa's shout, the man stepped around Noah and headed for the kitchen. Naturally, Noah was right behind him. Travis certainly seemed comfortable in Tessa's home. Just how well did she know him?

Apparently very well. Noah entered the kitchen in time to see Tessa greet Travis with a big hug as she laughed and said, "My hero!"

Travis enjoyed that hug a little too long from Noah's point of view, then he stepped back, jerked a thumb at Noah and asked, "Who's the stiff?"

Stiff?

Tessa laughed, glanced at Noah and immediately tried to swallow her smile. "That's my boss, Noah Graystone."

"No way. As in Graystone Scotch?"

"That's the one," Tessa said.

Travis turned, grabbed Noah's hand and gave it a hard shake. "Good to meet you. You make my favorite drink."

Noah bit back his annoyance long enough to say, "Thank you."

"No problem." Travis turned back to Tessa and reached out to tug at a lock of her hair. "Ready to go, Tess?"

"All set." She picked up a waybill and handed it to him. "All of the addresses are there and my account number."

"Great!" He folded the paper and tucked it into the inside pocket of the dark blue jacket he wore, then picked up five of the boxes. "I'll come back for the rest."

"Don't be silly—I can help."

Noah scowled. He wanted Travis gone as quickly as possible, so he picked up five of the boxes and Tessa grabbed the last two. "We can help," he said.

"Great." Oblivious, Travis just grinned and headed for his truck, talking to Tessa the whole way. "So when are you going to come to dinner with me?"

Was he really asking her for a date while Noah was right there? Who the hell did that?

"I'm super busy right now, Travis," Tessa said, "but maybe soon."

What the hell kind of name was Travis anyway? Was he a cowboy?

"I'm going to hold you to that," the guy said and gave Tessa a wink.

Then he stopped flirting long enough to load the truck. When everything was tucked inside, he shut the loading door and locked it. "Good to meet you," he said to Noah, then looked at Tessa. "I'll see you next week?"

"Oh, no," Tessa told him. "I'm going to be out of town for a week, so I'll call when I'm home and have a delivery going out."

"Okay, and maybe when you get back from wherever, we'll get that dinner."

She ignored Noah as if he wasn't standing *right there* and said, "Maybe we will. Thanks, Travis."

"Not a problem. See you soon, Tess!"

He hopped into the delivery truck, fired up the engine and drove off, leaving Noah and Tessa alone in the suddenly silent darkness.

Then she turned to look up at Noah. "Thanks for the help. I never would have made it in time without you."

Still annoyed, Noah muttered, "Oh, I think Travis would have waited for you."

She tipped her head to one side, frowning at the tone of his voice. "Maybe he would. He's a nice guy."

"Seems to like you a lot."

Tessa laughed. "Is that a crime now?"

"Not a crime no, just…nothing."

"Uh-huh." Nodding, she said, "Well, thanks for stopping by. See you at work tomorrow."

He caught her arm as she started to leave. "I didn't come to tie ribbons, Tessa."

"Why are you here, Noah?"

"I thought I knew," he muttered and looked off down

the street where the brake lights on Travis's truck were fading.

She sighed a little and he turned his attention back to her. "Noah, I'm tired. I want to go sit down with a glass of wine and order some takeout."

"Sounds good."

"That wasn't an invitation."

"That's how I'm taking it. Consider it payment for my expert ribbon tying."

She laughed again. "You expected to be paid for what you mangled?"

"All 'your hero' did was pick up the damn boxes and he got a hug out of it."

A thoughtful expression crossed her face. "Jealous?"

"Of course not," Noah snapped. He wasn't. Obviously. He didn't get jealous because he was never in the kind of relationship where he might feel territorial. So it wasn't that at all. He just didn't like how Travis had looked at Tessa. And he really hadn't liked how long that hug she'd given the man had lasted.

A soft, chill breeze slipped past them and wrapped Tessa's scent around Noah like a ribbon of warmth. He drew it in, holding it deep in his lungs until it felt as if it were branding itself on his soul.

Which was a completely ridiculous thought.

"Jealousy has nothing to do with it," he said and hated that his voice sounded stiff, even to himself. "I didn't like the way he was looking at you."

She waved that off. "Travis is a friend."

Tessa might see it that way, Noah thought, but it wasn't reality. "That's *not* how he was looking at you."

"Why do you care?"

"I don't." It had been aggravating to watch. That was all.

"Good. So, if it doesn't bother me, it shouldn't bother *you*."

She was right. It shouldn't. And yet.

He saw her turn for the house, wrapping her arms around her middle. "I'm going in. I'm freezing out here."

Funny. He felt as if he were on fire. But he followed her into the house anyway. They still had to have that talk, though at the moment, talking was the last thing on his mind. Tessa walked directly back to the kitchen and Noah was right behind her. He liked the view.

While she gathered the detritus left in the wake of the shipping emergency, she asked, "What did you want to talk to me about, Noah?"

Good question. For a second, he blanked on it and couldn't remember why the hell he'd come over here in the first place. His gaze was locked on the curve of her mouth and he was mesmerized. That mouth of hers. How had he never noticed before last week, that her lips were full and tempting? How had he not wanted to know what they tasted like? How had he gone the last several days without taking another taste?

Duty, he reminded himself. Duty was the reason he'd kept his distance. The reason he was here.

He shoved his hands into his pockets. "I wanted to tell you to take tomorrow off."

She blinked, clearly surprised. "Really? Take Friday off when we're leaving for London on Saturday? Are you feeling all right?"

He frowned. Was it really so strange for him to give her a day off? He supposed it was and he'd have to think about that. Later.

"Yes. I'm fine." Tortured, but fine. "I just think it's a good idea for each of us to get ready for the trip and there's no reason to be in the office. We've taken care of everything."

"Uh-huh." She pulled the elastic from her ponytail and released her hair to frame her face and fall across her shoulders.

Was it always that wavy, with a tendency to curl at the ends? Why did he want to touch it? This was not going the way he'd planned. And he realized that was what he'd thought the last time he was in Tessa's house. Apparently, his brain took a vacation the minute he entered the place. And that should tell him he was right about what he'd come to say tonight.

Duty. That one word could keep him on his path and help him avoid the very real temptation that Tessa represented.

"There's something else," he said tightly, silently amazed that he was able to squeeze any words at all past the knot in his throat.

"I thought there might be," she mused, tipping her head to one side so her hair fell like a golden waterfall. "Think I'll pour some wine for the rest of this. Do you want some?"

"Sure. Fine."

He watched as she took two glasses from a cupboard, walked to the fridge and opened it. In a few seconds, she had the cold white wine poured. She walked back to him and handed him one—her fingers brushing lightly against his. Just what she'd been doing to him all week. Tessa took a sip of the wine and sighed in pleasure, and that tiny sound shivered through him.

Then she took a deep breath and her high, full breasts

rose and fell with the action. His gaze dropped briefly to enjoy the show, then he looked into her eyes and saw the gleam there. She'd noticed. Damn it.

He set his wine down untouched. Hell, his brain was already a sieve, no point in adding alcohol to the mix. "Look. Maybe it was a mistake not to talk about that kiss."

"You think so?" She bit her bottom lip, tugging at it until he felt that tug deep inside him.

"Cut it out." His voice was deep and strained.

"What do you mean?"

Her voice was all innocence and he wasn't buying it. "You know exactly what I mean."

"I really don't, Noah." She leaned against the kitchen island, hitching one hip higher than the other. Taking another sip of her wine, she then set the glass down. Shaking her hair back, she said, "Maybe you should explain it to me."

"Yeah," he ground out. "That's what I'm talking about."

She shook her head. "Still don't get it."

"Tessa, this isn't going to happen."

"Sounds dire," she said, smiling. "What isn't going to happen?"

"You. And me. Together."

There. He'd said it.

"Okay. I'll try to heal my broken heart…"

"Funny."

"I'm not trying to be funny, Noah," she said, pushing off the island to face him. "I'm trying to understand why you think, for some reason, that I'm wasting away for you."

"I didn't say that."

"Good. So what are you saying, then?"

"Fine. You want me to spell it out?" He took a step closer and instantly regretted it. She smelled like summer and her scent wound around him like a promise.

"That kiss was…good."

"Agreed," she said with a sharp nod.

"And can't be repeated."

"Okay." So reasonable. But he looked into her eyes and saw not innocence but humor and heat, tangled together.

"Said so easily, though all week you've been…"

She smiled. "I've been what, Noah?"

"Tempting," he admitted, though it cost him.

Grinning, she reached out and laid one hand on his arm. Instantly, heat slammed into him.

"Isn't that a nice thing to say?"

Figured she'd be pleased by that. "It's not a compliment."

"Like you said earlier, I'm taking it as one."

"Fine." Shaking his head, he said, "Hell. Maybe you should. I don't want you in the office tomorrow, because I think it's best if we have some time apart before we board the plane for London."

"Afraid you can't trust yourself around me?"

Yes.

"Of course not. It's just that I can't be distracted by you, Tessa," he said firmly. "I'm closer than I've ever been to putting Graystone Vodka at the top of the list of premium spirits and I'm not letting anything get in my way."

"I'm not in your way, Noah," she said simply. Tucking her hair behind her ears, she added, "I never have been. In fact, I've done everything I can to help you reach your goal. I understand what your business means to you. It's why I quit, remember? Because I feel the same way about *my* business. So I get it. I do."

"Good." His body was still tense, his heartbeat still racing as if he'd just run a marathon.

"And in a little more than a week," she added softly, "you won't have to see me at all. I'll be out of your life completely."

He didn't like the sound of that any more than he had the day she'd turned in her resignation. Yes, he wanted to avoid entanglements that could split his focus on the driving ambition that had been pushing him forward for years. But he also couldn't really imagine his everyday world without Tessa in it.

They'd worked together for so long. He trusted her as he trusted very few people. She was a part of his life and losing her wouldn't be easy. But having her as more than his assistant would be even more difficult.

"Then we understand each other." He looked down into her pale blue eyes and couldn't seem to tear his gaze away.

"I guess we do," she said softly.

"So I'll see you on the plane Saturday morning. We leave at eight."

She nodded, still keeping her gaze locked with his. "I'll be there."

"Good. And then we'll handle business and get through the week like professionals."

"Absolutely."

"And we'll forget about that kiss."

"I don't think so," she said with a tiny shake of her head that made the curls at the ends of her hair dance.

"Yeah," he admitted, "I don't think so, either."

"So," Tessa said, "what you're really saying is stay away *and* come closer."

He scrubbed one hand across his face. Noah couldn't even remember the last time his brain had been so... muddled. "Yeah. That's what it sounds like."

Hell, why was he even here? He didn't want the distraction. Couldn't afford to have his focus split.

"Noah..."

He looked into her eyes and felt himself being drawn in. Focus? Duty? Everything he'd devoted his life to was fading away until all that was left was Tessa. And the hunger clawing at his insides.

She kept her gaze locked on his as seconds ticked past, taking his resolve with them. Hell, maybe he'd known that going to her house was a bad idea. But he'd come anyway.

Tessa took a step back suddenly and he frowned. "What?"

"In the five years I've known you," she said quietly, "I've never known you to be indecisive."

"True."

"Yet now that you're here you're not sure you want to be."

Also true, but he wasn't going to admit it. Turned out he didn't have to speak because she wasn't finished.

"You know," she continued, "I had planned on seducing you."

"Is that right?" His entire body went tight and hard in response to that confession.

"Yes, but I think I've changed my mind."

"A little late for that," he mused, "since you've been doing it all week."

"Excuse me?"

Shaking his head, Noah said, "The touches of your hand. The leaning over the desk to show me a file. Smelling so damn good the scent fills my head and empties it of everything but you."

"Thank you?" It was a question, as if she didn't know whether to be insulted or flattered.

"You're welcome." Noah's gaze swept over her quickly, thoroughly, and the heat sliding through him intensified. "So saying you've changed your mind doesn't carry a lot of weight."

"Okay, say I was doing that, now I'm not." She took another step back as if for physical reassurance. "I admit I wanted you, but I don't need to want a man who doesn't want me—or at least can't make up his mind if he does or doesn't."

Couldn't blame her for that, but she was wrong if she thought he didn't want her. He'd never wanted anything more. Never spent the better part of a week thinking about one particular woman. Never had his dreams been tormenting him with possibilities.

"Well, what if he made up his mind before he came here?"

"Did he?" Her eyes went soft with an almost liquid fire.

"If he hadn't," Noah said, taking a step closer, "he wouldn't be here in the first place."

"Okay…"

Clearly she wanted more, but Noah didn't know what else he could give her. There wouldn't be promises between them. He wasn't talking about diamond rings and white picket fences. All he was thinking about were cool sheets, hot bodies and an end to the wanting.

"You were right, before. I'm not your boss anymore. You already quit."

"I did."

"So whatever happens now is just between us." One more step and he was so close to her now he could see the flare in her eyes and hear the hitch in her breath. "Like you said when you kissed me. You wanted it, at least once. Well, there's something I want. At least once."

She licked her lips and sighed a little and Noah knew that for good or bad, the die had been cast and there was no retreat. But then he never had been much for retreating. It was always about taking the next step. Advancing. Always.

"So," he asked, "seduction over?"

"Looks that way," she said and moved toward him.

That was all the invitation he needed. He swept in, wrapped his arms around her and pulled her in close. She tipped her head back and he took her mouth in a long, deep kiss that had warning bells clanging in his brain. He shut them down because he already knew the dangers and at the moment, didn't give a flying damn about them.

Six

All Noah wanted was the taste of Tessa filling him. The feel of her body pressed to his, the brush of her breath on his cheek. He wanted to slide his hands up and down her body and to finally...*finally*, see that tattoo above her butt, up close and personal.

Her arms linked behind his head and held on as she opened her mouth to him and his tongue tangled with hers. Breaths mingling, heartbeats racing in tandem, he let his hands roam up and down her body and then slid both palms beneath the waistband of those floral yoga pants. She groaned from the back of her throat when his palms cupped her butt and squeezed, pressing her to his aching dick hard enough to ease some of the tension while at the same time creating more.

Suddenly, she broke the kiss, pulled her head back and said, "Take off your jacket."

"What?" Trying to think after that kiss wasn't easy.

Her hands were already pushing at the shoulders of his jacket so he had to pull his hands free of her behind to shrug out of the damn thing. While he was at it, the necktie went next and her fingers pushed the buttons of his shirt free. She slid her hands across his chest and the soft glide of her skin against his fired him even further, and Noah wouldn't have thought that possible. He was a man on the edge. He'd never wanted any woman the way he wanted this one and if he didn't have her in the next few minutes, it was going to kill him.

Tessa slid her hands around to the small of his back, looked up at him and grinned. "Once you make a decision, you're good to go, aren't you?"

"Stop talking, Tessa." He buried his face in the curve of her neck and tasted the pulse beat at the base of her throat. It hammered against his tongue and he smiled to himself, knowing that she was as crazed as he was. Good. She'd been torturing him all week, and Noah was glad to know that seduction was a two-way street.

"I'll stop talking if you'll get busy."

He lifted his head and met her gaze. Breath came hard and fast from his lungs. "I thought I was busy."

"There's busy and then there's *busy*," she said, pushing his shirt off his shoulders to slide off and hit the floor.

"Good point." Kissing wasn't enough. Touching her wasn't enough. He needed to be inside her and it was good to know that she was feeling the same way.

Noah lifted her off her feet and she hooked her legs around his middle, locking her ankles at his back. With both hands cupping her butt, he left the tiny kitchen with long strides and muttered, "Bedroom?"

"Upstairs."

"Of course it is." He took the stairs at practically a run and turned left when she told him to. He should have guessed.

Naturally, her bedroom was in the turret room. The curved walls, the curtains across diamond-paned windows. A four-poster bed covered by a quilt in blues and greens. Paintings of forests and oceans hung on the walls. It was as fairy-tale-like as the rest of the house and it suited her, damn it.

As much as he'd always been impressed with her business abilities, he'd seen, since he'd been to her house and noticed floral pants and painted toes and candles and lotions, that she was also creative. And less…conservative than he'd always believed her to be. So a cottage completely suited her.

It took only a heartbeat of time for Noah to see the whole damn room and then dismiss everything but the bed. That was the only thing they needed. And hell, wait much longer and he wouldn't need the bed, either. He'd just back her into a wall and slam himself home, driving them both out of their minds.

He stalked to the bed and Tessa leaned down to toss the quilt aside. Good enough, he told himself and reluctantly set her on her feet. He felt the loss of her body pressed to his instantly. And he wanted that sensation back. He didn't have to wait long. In a few seconds, they were both naked and rolling across those floral sheets in a tangle of heat and desire.

Noah's mind was empty of everything but the feel of her. The sight of her. Full, beautiful breasts, curvy behind and wide, generous hips. He'd had his fill of skinny women with more bones than flesh and he much preferred Tessa's body. He couldn't seem to stop touching her, having the silk of her skin beneath his hands. She was so responsive that every stroke of his fingers drew a sigh or a groan from her throat that nearly choked Noah.

She twisted and writhed in his arms and let him see exactly what she was feeling. She held nothing back from him and Noah had never been more aroused. Her reactions fed his own until the two of them should have set the bed on fire. And then she turned the tables on him, eagerly.

Tessa's hands smoothed over his body across his chest, down past his abdomen until her long, beautiful fingers curled around his aching dick and stroked him into a frenzy of need that blinded him to everything else. Then she slowly slid her hands across his hips then up, dragging her nails against his back and he groaned tightly, leaning down to kiss her mouth hard and fast. "You're killing me, Tessa."

"Right back at you," she whispered, licking her lips again as if to remind him how much he loved that small action.

He wanted her more than his next breath and yet, there was one thing he had to do first. Smiling to himself, he released her long enough to roll her over onto her stomach so that he could finally see her tattoo.

"What're you doing?" She looked over her shoulder at him.

"Had to see the tattoo," he said, tracing the tips of his fingers along the line of delicate marks on her skin. "I've been wondering about it for days. Your T-shirts kept giving me little peeks at the edges and now I want to see the whole thing."

She went up on her elbows but stayed in place while he continued to define the design with his fingertips.

"So?" she asked. "What do you think?"

Noah thought she had a great butt, but the tattoo? "I like it."

Just above the dimples at the small of her back was a miniature, beautifully detailed line of snowcapped mountains beneath a sea of stars. It was the stardust he'd been getting peeks at and maybe in an hour or two, he'd take the time to explore it more fully.

"Tell me about it. Later." He lowered his head to her behind and traced each shooting star with his tongue until she was writhing beneath him and his own blood was pumping so hard, he felt the solid slam of his heartbeat. When he couldn't take it another moment, Noah went up on his knees, then lifted her hips until she, too, was kneeling.

And it was only *then* that he remembered he didn't have a damn condom with him. "Damn it."

"What?" Breathless, she tossed her hair back and looked over her shoulder at him again. "Why are you stopping? What's wrong?"

"Protection." He looked into her eyes and read the same desire he knew was shining in his own. "I don't have any."

"Seriously?"

He squeezed her butt and swallowed a groan of disappointment. To be this close to claiming her and have to stop was like…finally winning that vodka award then turning it down. "Believe it or not, I haven't carried condoms in my wallet since I was a hopeful sixteen."

She actually laughed. "Good thing one of us was thinking, then. Bedside table."

He reached for it, yanked the drawer open and pulled out one of the foil-wrapped packages inside. Yeah, she was prepared. But for *who*? Travis? Had he been up in this room, rolling on this bed with Tessa? Oh, hell no. Noah pushed that thought and the accompanying images out of his mind. All that mattered right now was this moment. This woman.

Noah sheathed himself, then went up on his knees behind her. Sliding his hands up and down her spine and back to the curve of her hips, he took his time, in spite of the heat pulsing inside him. If this was truly going to be an "at least once" kind of night, then he was going to take his time and make it one to remember. Which meant, he told himself, he wanted to be able to look into her eyes when he took her.

Flipping her over onto her back, he caught the flash of surprise in her eyes and smiled. "I want to watch you. I want to see your eyes."

"I want to watch yours, too," Tessa said and lifted her legs while she opened her arms to him.

Mouth dry, breath catching, he said tightly, "It's not going to be fast." Though silently he wondered how long he could last without losing what was left of his mind.

She swallowed hard, licked her lips and nodded. "Slow is good, too."

He smiled, stretched out alongside her. She ran her fingers through his hair, her nails scraping against his skin, then down to his shoulders and across his chest where her thumbs flicked against his flat nipples and he felt that touch right down to his bones. Noah bent his head to her left breast. He took that hard nipple into his mouth and teased the nub with his tongue and teeth.

She arched her back, groaning, as she lifted herself

into his mouth and Noah smiled against her skin. While he suckled her, he slid one hand down the length of her body and dipped his fingers into her hot, damp center.

Instantly, her hands clutched at his shoulder, her fingers digging into his skin as she cried out his name. Her hips rocked into his touch and he watched her open features as she fought for a release that was just out of reach. Her eyes glazed over and he loved it.

"Noah... Noah...damn it, be in me. Be in me now."

He watched her react to his touch and felt a responding fire erupt inside him. "Screw slow," he muttered and moved to kneel between her thighs.

"Oh, yeah. Slow can come later," she whispered brokenly.

Later. Yes. Because he already knew that once wouldn't be enough.

Noah grabbed her hips, slid her closer and pushed his body into hers. Instantly, her tight, hot muscles closed around him and he groaned in satisfaction. This was what he'd been needing for days. Keeping perfectly still for a long moment, Noah savored the feel of her body clenched on his, until Tessa moved impatiently and shattered that tension.

He moved then, rocking his hips against hers, setting a pace that she raced to match. She lifted her legs, hooked them over his shoulders, to pull him in deeper, tighter and still, he wanted more.

Every sigh that slipped from her lips, every hitched breath pushed him to claim more of her. He'd been thinking about nothing else for nearly a week and he gave himself up to the glory of finally having her beneath him. Of looking into her eyes as she climbed a mountain of sensation, straining for the peak.

Noah took that climb with her, staggering forward, step by step, enjoying the climb, reaching for the top. He felt her release before he read it in her eyes and an instant before she shrieked, eyes flashing as her body shattered.

Tessa's body was still trembling when Noah found his own release a few moments later. It was more than he'd ever known before. More than he'd thought it would be. That staggering climax shuddered through him and all he could do was hold on and shout as the power of it jolted through him, splintering everything that had come before.

Tessa struggled to breathe. And that voice inside her whispered, *Who needs to breathe? Let's do that again.* She was totally on board with that, but first she needed to calm her racing heart and get air into her lungs if only so she could scream out Noah's name again.

Noah. Finally, Noah.

Collapsed on top of her, he was a heavy, warm blanket that she'd longed to feel for five years. He was still inside her, their bodies linked, and she felt something stirring inside her in response. She wasn't finished. One mind-exploding orgasm would not be enough; she knew that now. Her whole theory of do-this-at-least-once with Noah was shot down. Once was beyond great. Dozens of times wouldn't be enough. She'd waited too long for this and now she wanted more.

He pushed himself up onto his elbows and looked down at her. His eyes were a dark blue that still simmered with the heat that had claimed them both only moments ago.

"Well," he said, with a half smile curving his delicious mouth, "that was...a revelation."

"Good word for it," she agreed and lifted one hand to smooth his hair back from his forehead. Then because she had to keep touching him, she let her fingers slide down the line of his face until she could cup his cheek in her palm.

He turned his face into her touch, kissed her hand and Tessa's heart melted even further. Was that just a reaction to what they'd shared? Did he feel more for her than he could admit to? And if he couldn't admit it, what good was it? What was the hold he had on her? What was she going to do when their time together was over? How would she get past loving him, when the memory of this night would be burned into her brain forever?

"Am I crushing you?" He leaned in to plant a quick kiss on her mouth that made her lick her lips in anticipation of another one.

"No," she said, sliding her hands up and down his back, loving the feel of his sculpted muscles beneath her fingers. "I'm fine."

"Okay." He moved slightly and everything inside her lit up.

She inhaled sharply and arched against him.

"Oh," she whispered, "either stay perfectly still, or move faster."

He grinned and did the latter, as she was hoping he would. While his hips moved against her, he dipped his head and suckled at her right breast. That drawing sensation moved through her and she held one hand to the back of his head to keep him right there. His lips and tongue and teeth tormented her in the most amazing way possible while he continued to move inside her, pushing her already sensitive core to reach new heights.

God, she loved a man who could multitask.

In seconds, she was panting for release again. He lifted his head and stared down into her eyes and she was mesmerized.

Her earlier soul-splitting orgasm was forgotten as she raced toward another one. She planted her feet on the mattress and rocked her hips into his as they pistoned against her, pushing his body higher and deeper inside her. She felt every stroke. Heard every one of his racing heartbeats. Felt his breath against her skin and could only cling to him as he drove the rhythm again. As he set their pace. She wanted to do more. To push *him.*

"Roll over onto your back," she said, her voice hitching with every catch of her breath.

He grinned at her and for a second, she was absolutely lost in the power of that wide smile that she saw so rarely. But then the next second came and it was hunger. Mind-numbing hunger that drove her.

When he rolled over, he took her with him and then Tessa was on top. She sat up straight, her body impaled by his. She groaned and let her head fall back, relishing the feel of him filling her. Then she took a breath, braced her hands on his broad, muscled chest and began to move. She ground her hips against him, creating an amazing friction that drove her to move more quickly. Her body's demands couldn't be ignored, so she gave in to them gladly.

His hands were at her hips when she moved, lifting up on her knees and sliding back down his length until the pace she set took them both over. She looked down into his eyes and watched his expression shift from strain to pleasure and back again. She knew what he was feeling because she was caught in its grip, too.

Lifting her hands, she cupped her own breasts as she rode him and saw the flash in his eyes as his fingers at her hips tightened. She kept their gazes locked as she took him on a ride that she controlled this time. Her breasts were sensitive and when she pulled at her own nipples, he groaned aloud.

And then the tingling sensation at her core erupted and Tessa knew her release was coming. "Come with me, Noah."

He shook his head on the pillow. "You first. Always, you first."

"Together," she insisted and dropped her hands to him. Reaching behind her, she cupped him and gently squeezed and she saw his eyes glaze over as his body began to buck. Tessa let herself join him and she screamed when the pleasure rolled up and over her, crashing down on her with a force she'd never known before.

Her entire body trembled along with his and she felt the tiny earthquakes breaking inside her. And this time, when it was over, she collapsed on top of Noah and felt his arms come around her.

What could have been hours later, but was probably no more than a few minutes, Tessa heard him say, "Okay, I'm going to need a little more time before we try that again."

She laughed and even that tiny action set up a chain reaction of anticipation buzzing through her body. "Yeah," she admitted with a sigh, "me, too."

His hands were moving over her, sliding up and

down her spine, cupping her bottom, then back up, as if he were trying to map every inch of her skin. She was good with that. Actually, while he was stroking her, she felt like purring but that might be a little much.

Finally, though, he rolled to one side, taking her with him, Their bodies separated and she sighed at the loss even as she looked up at him and smiled.

There was a lamp burning in one corner of her room, but otherwise it was dark, so there were shadows on his face and in his eyes, but that one soft glow was enough to show her that his expression was both satisfied and confused.

Braced on one elbow, he stared into her eyes and said, "Okay, we've got a few minutes. Tell me about the tattoo."

Her smile still curved her mouth as she smoothed his hair back again, loving the silky feel of it. "You know I'm from Wyoming."

He frowned, thinking about it and then nodded. "I remember."

"Well," she said, "when I moved to California, I got that tattoo to help *me* remember."

"You thought you'd forget?" There was a laugh in his voice.

"I didn't want to risk it," she said with a shrug. "I love Wyoming. The mountains, the trees, the sky when it's so blue your eyes almost hurt to look at it. I guess I wanted a piece of it with me."

"If you loved it so much, why'd you leave?" he asked, voice soft as he smoothed one hand across her breast. "You never said."

Her breath caught and she sighed a little at the caress. Hard to think when he was touching her.

"There's a story," she said, remembering what had prompted her to leave her home. Her family. Everything she'd ever known.

"We have time."

She looked up at him and saw in his eyes that he really was curious—as she was about so much of his background. Thanks to Stephanie, she knew quite a bit about how they'd grown up, but she'd never heard it from Noah. How it had affected *him*. Maybe, she told herself, if she shared something of herself, he would return the favor.

"Okay," she said, trailing her fingers along his arm and the hand that was currently cupping her left breast. "Well, my mom and dad still live on the ranch where I grew up."

A quick smile blossomed and disappeared in a blink. "You grew up a cowgirl?"

"You could say that," she mused though she'd never thought of herself that way. It was just ranch life. Riding out to check the herd, making sure all the animals were fed and working in the blistering heat and freezing cold. "My brother and sister and I worked the ranch from the time we were little. I swear we learned how to ride a horse before we could walk."

"Sounds nice."

His voice sounded almost wistful, but she took his words at face value.

"It was," she admitted, and let herself go back into her memory. "Anyway, I got engaged to a man I'd known since we were children. He was perfect, as far as I was concerned, which just proves how wrong a person can be."

His hand on her breast stilled. "What happened?"

Tessa grabbed the edge of the quilt and dragged it across her like some sort of fabric shield she could hide behind. Which was just ridiculous when she thought about it like that, so deliberately, she tossed it aside again.

"He decided, a few weeks before the wedding, that he'd rather have my best friend," she said and couldn't quite stop the wince that accompanied the words. Not that she was still hurt or even that she regretted not marrying the no-good worthless son of a—

"He cheated on you?"

"Yes." Didn't that sound pitiful? The completely clueless bride, planning a wedding with a man she thought loved her, never suspecting that he was lying to her the whole time. "That's the simple answer. I found out later, that he and my 'friend' had been having sex for six months and I was the only one in our group who didn't know."

"No one told you?"

"No one wanted to be the one to hurt me." She still wasn't sure whether to be grateful or angry. Would they have let her marry him? Probably. And what a disaster that would have been. "Well, except for my fiancé and my best friend. They didn't mind a bit."

"I'm sorry."

"You don't have to be," she insisted, meeting his gaze squarely. "It was a long time ago. They ended up getting married, and divorced a year later, so…karma. As for me, I think it worked out in the end."

"I know it did."

"Really?" She smiled up into his eyes. "Why's that?"

"Because you're here. In a bed with me in a round

room in a tiny castle, of all things. If not for them, you'd be a wife in Wyoming."

"Good point." The truth was, Tessa had gotten over the betrayal and the hurt years ago. But hearing Noah say those words brought it all home how much she would have missed if not for going through that pain.

"So that's why you left?"

"Mostly," she admitted, stroking her hand across his chest and smiling to herself at his quick intake of breath. "But then, there was my brother with his wife and kids and my sister with her husband and kids and my parents looking at me and obviously wondering when I was going to find a new man and have more grandchildren for them." She sighed a little. "After a while, it got old continuously telling them to back off—in a loving way of course."

"Of course." One eyebrow lifted again and his eyes registered his surprise. "You don't want kids?"

"I didn't say that," she countered. "I'd like to have some…eventually. But it was the feeling that everyone was counting off *my* biological clock that was irritating."

He chuckled and she scowled at him. "I don't see you with any kids," she pointed out.

"And you won't," he said fervently.

"There's that decisive tone I know so well," she mused.

"I can't be a good parent *and* make Graystone the best in the world," he said simply.

"Hmm. My father used to tell us there's no such word as *can't*." She shrugged. "You just keep trying until you can."

"Right," he said. "That presumes you want to try."

"And you don't."

"No." One word. Unequivocal.

"Why?" He went quiet and still, but she'd told him her most humiliating story, so it was her turn and she wouldn't let him figuratively back away. "Is it because of your father?"

Scowling now, Noah asked, "What do you know about my father?"

"Stephanie's told me some…"

"Of course she has." He sighed and shook his head.

"But not all. So is your dad the reason you don't want kids?"

"Let's just say I learned early that if your heart's not in it, you'll make a mess of parenthood."

He was pulling back and she didn't want that, so Tessa moved into him and draped one arm across his hip as if she could hold on to him and keep the intimacy from fading. "Steph said that you took it upon yourself to be the 'man' in the family when you were just a boy."

"Steph talks too much." His scowl told her what he thought of that, too.

"So why don't you tell me?"

Noah thought about that for a moment long enough to convince Tessa that he wasn't going to say any more on the subject. Then he proved her wrong.

"You probably already know most of it. My father left. Grandfather took us and my mom in and helped raise us and he's the one I owe. Nothing I do is about my father, Tessa," he told her, and gave her butt a squeeze. "It's always about my grandfather. I owe him. I have a duty to my family and the company and I can't just set that aside. I won't."

"No one asked you to, Noah," she said softly, carefully. "But I'm betting your grandfather wouldn't have expected you to sacrifice everything in your determination to make him proud."

"We'll never know that, will we?" Shaking his head, he pulled away from her and stood up. Then changing the subject he asked, "Where's the bathroom?"

She pointed. "In the hall. We passed it on the way here."

"Be right back." She watched him go and admired the view of his naked butt and long, muscled legs. He might seem as though he was always working, but clearly, Noah found time for working out, too.

She lay down, stared at the ceiling and sighed. Hearing him talk about his father, his grandfather, Tessa began to get a picture of why Noah was so driven. Stephanie had laid it all out so dryly, it had been almost easy to dismiss. But hearing the strain in Noah's voice as he recapped his life in a few short sentences had told Tessa just how important his duty was to him.

And she didn't see a way to change it. His grandfather was dead, so the old man couldn't give Noah permission to live a life. And until Noah finally put Graystone Vodka at the top of the market, he would never give himself the freedom to have more in his life than the company.

This night was becoming everything she'd ever dreamed of. Noah was an amazing lover and beyond sharing his body, he was also sharing something of himself. But at the same time, she felt as if this was nothing more than a very long goodbye.

Noah was perfectly clear about devoting his life to the company. And just because he wanted her didn't mean he loved her. Or needed her. It seemed he felt as if he didn't *need* anyone or anything, but success.

A few minutes later, he was standing in the open doorway, one shoulder braced against the jamb, his arms crossed over his chest. He looked like a sculpture. One created by an especially talented master. And then one corner of his mouth lifted and something inside her stirred in response.

"You look amazing," he said, "laid out across the bed, naked and waiting."

Maybe he didn't need her. But obviously, she thought, as her gaze drifted down that amazing body of his, he *wanted* her.

Tessa let go of the wishful part of her—that stubborn part that hoped for more from him—and became the woman who had agreed to a night with him. *Take what you can get, Tessa*, that voice insisted and maybe she had a point.

Lifting her arms high over her head, she stretched languorously. "I was just thinking something similar about you," she admitted.

"Well, then," he said, "are we done waiting?"

Whatever her thoughts had been moments ago, all she could think of now was Noah. "I think we are."

"We agree again," he said, pushing away from the wall and heading toward her with determined strides. "I've always said we make a good team."

And then he showed her just how good they were.

Seven

A couple of hours later, they were picnicking in Tessa's bed. Naked, with only the quilt pulled across their laps, they dug into Chinese takeout and sipped ice-cold white wine.

Halfway through the Kung Pao chicken, though, Noah thought they should talk about a few things. After all, he'd had a plan when he came over here—in spite of the fact that he hadn't stuck to it. Although, in his defense, he thought, how the hell could he keep from touching her when she looked so damn good?

Glancing at her now, with her tumbled hair and bare breasts, he felt his resolve weaken again as it had pretty much all night. It had probably been a huge mistake to go to bed with her, but he could hardly bemoan that when all he could think of was sex with her again. She got to him as no other woman ever had. He'd come here to reinforce the idea of staying away from her and had instead spent the night having the best sex of his life. Before that all started up again—and damned if he didn't want it to—it was time for reality to be reckoned with.

"What's causing the frown?" Tessa asked. "Already regretting tonight?"

Did she know him that well?

"No," he said, because no matter what, he wouldn't regret what had happened between them. "But—"

She took a sip of wine and swung her hair back behind her shoulders. "I knew there was a *but*."

He gave her a half smile. He'd talked more, laughed more with Tessa than he had with any other woman he'd ever known. Even *during* sex, the laughter and talking hadn't stopped and that was new for him, too. Usually sex was just a physical need that he was looking to satisfy. He didn't form relationships, didn't want to chat or laugh or connect in any way with whatever woman happened to be in his bed.

Tessa was different. And he wasn't sure how to react to that.

"The *but* is, that this—between us—it's not going anywhere, Tessa."

She sipped at her wine again, tipped her head to one side and asked, "Are you trying to let me down easily?"

When she said it like that, it sounded stupid. "I just don't want you making more of this than there is."

"Well, thank you," she said and picked up a piece of chicken. She popped it into her mouth, then sucked at her finger to get the sauce off.

Watching that made Noah's dick go to stone—as it had been for most of the night. Taking a breath, he said,

"I only meant that we were doing the 'just once' thing and now that's done."

"And more than once," she pointed out.

"Yeah, that's true. But we need some ground rules now, before we go to London."

"Okay," she said, the soul of reason, "what did you have in mind?"

Well, that was the question, wasn't it? What he wanted, was Tessa. Again. What he didn't want, were messy complications. So he took the honesty route and told her exactly that.

"Messy," she mused with a sip of her wine. "As in, me clinging to your manly self, begging you to love me?"

His gaze narrowed on her. Hearing her say it out loud sounded extremely stupid. "No. That's not what I meant."

"Okay, then what?"

"Tessa, this isn't going to be anything more than it is."

"Noah, you already said that. And if you think I wasn't aware of it before tonight, you're wrong."

That surprised him. "Is that right?"

"Oh, Noah." She waved one hand, smiled and shook her head. "For five years, I've watched you sidestep any woman who wanted more than a night or two with you. I've bought your 'goodbye' gifts to the women who got too close." She sighed a little. "You avoid relationships like they're garlic and you're a vampire."

He snorted. "Thanks."

"I'm just saying, I'm a big girl and I'm not asking you for anything—" she pointed to a carton near his thigh "—except more fried rice."

He handed it to her and watched as she put some on

her plate. She seemed fine. Not all soft and gooey. But somehow, hearing her dismiss him stung more than he'd thought it would. He was accustomed to giving the "no expectations" speech. He was not accustomed to having that speech brushed aside as if it didn't matter in the slightest.

After a few seconds of silence, she huffed out a breath, glanced at him and said, "You're looking at me weird."

"No, I'm not. I just didn't expect you to be—"

"Realistic? Pragmatic?" She sat up straight, lifted her chin and added, "Eminently reasonable?"

"Yeah," he said. "All of the above."

"Great. I love being surprising."

"Of course you do." Shaking his head, he reached for the beef and broccoli and took a bite.

"Honestly, Noah, don't worry about it." She reached out and laid one hand on his thigh. "Remember, this was just a onetime thing."

He laughed at that and had a sip of wine. "A onetime thing that turned into how many?"

"Okay," she said, still smiling, "then a one-*night* thing."

"Right. And that's okay with you?"

"Sure."

Well, it wasn't all right with him. He didn't want a lifetime with Tessa or anything, but he damn sure wanted more than one night. He wasn't going to get it, but it would have been nice if she'd been a little more… upset about the situation. And even as he thought it, Noah knew he was being ridiculous. Didn't change anything, though.

"So we put tonight behind us, go to London and take

care of business." It wasn't a question, but he still waited to see what she would say about it.

"Well, we could," she said, licking her fork now, forcing Noah to watch her tongue flick at the tines. He just managed to stifle a groan.

Forcing his concentration back to what she was saying—not doing, he said, "We could. Or...?"

"Or," she said, looking at him with a small smile tugging at one corner of her mouth. "We could take the time in London to...enjoy each other before we go our separate ways."

"Enjoy each other." He stared into her eyes and told himself that had to be the best suggestion he'd heard in a very long time. Maybe it wasn't the smartest thing to do, but damned if it didn't *feel* right.

"Why not?" She shrugged and her magnificent breasts moved with the action.

Noah knew that he should probably get up and get dressed and leave now. He was usually a one-night-and-goodbye kind of man. More than one night risked connections, emotions from women who always wanted more from him than he was willing to give.

But leaving right now wasn't even on his radar. A week with Tessa in his bed sounded too good to pass up. Hell, he had nothing to lose here. Besides, Tessa was being extremely reasonable. She knew this wasn't going anywhere. Knew he didn't do relationships. All they were talking about was sharing six amazing nights before they said goodbye.

"If I haven't told you this often enough," Noah said, "let me say, you're a brilliant woman."

"I'm glad you think so," she said, smiling. "And I agree. More wine?"

* * *

Friday night snacks was at her house this week and Tessa went all out. For her. She was never going to put out a spread as nice as Lynn's, but neither would they starve.

Sliced bell peppers and ranch dip, salami and cheddar on crackers, popcorn and plenty of wine. For the kids, she'd pulled up a movie on Netflix and plied them with ice cream.

"This is really good," Carol said, reaching for another salami cracker.

Lynn just looked at her. "Have vegetables, too. What kind of doctor are you anyway?"

"A hungry one." Carol bit into the cracker and salami then grinned.

The kitchen was warm and cozy, the rumble of laughter rolled in from the living room and Tessa was there with her friends. She sighed happily and listened to Carol and Lynn argue the merits of meat versus veggies. Meat was winning.

Tessa grabbed a red pepper and dipped it before taking a big bite. Shrugging, she looked at Carol. "It's actually pretty good."

"Fine." She took one just to please Lynn, took a bite and looked at Tessa. "So, interesting thing…we saw Noah's car in your driveway last night."

"Is that right?" Tessa poured them all some more wine.

"Carol, you said you wouldn't tease her."

"Much," she corrected her wife. "I said I wouldn't tease her *much*."

Lynn rolled her eyes and looked at Tessa. "Sorry about her."

Tessa laughed. "It's okay—yes, Dr. Nosey, he was here last night."

Thoughtfully, Carol tapped one finger to her chin. "Pretty late, too…"

Still laughing, Tessa asked, "Were you clocking him?"

"No," Carol said in an unconvincing protest.

"Yes," Lynn corrected. "Okay yes, we kept tabs on him. We were…worried."

"We were nosey," Carol admitted and snatched another cracker with salami and cheese. "So what happened?"

"You know what happened," Tessa countered with a quick look down the hall to make sure the kids were still in the living room. She didn't want to end up giving a surprise sex-ed course.

"Come on, honey. Control yourself," Lynn said, shaking her head. Carol only looked at her wryly in challenge until Lynn confessed, "Fine. I'm as curious as she is. I admit it."

"Hah. Vindication," Carol muttered and toasted Tessa with a glass held high.

Lynn kept talking. "I was feeling so bad about having to leave you with all of the packages to wrap up and address, but Evan was sick—"

"As the doctor in the family," Carol tossed in, "I'm going to say it was chocolate-chip syndrome. Lynn found the empty bag in the back of the pantry. Apparently, our son decided he needed chocolate and ate them all."

"Yes, well it seemed like the flu at the time." Lynn frowned at Carol, "I was working in my office on the new earrings when he did it and—"

"Not your fault, Lynn. Our son's love of sugar is leg-
endary." Carol sighed. "I should have been a dentist."

Lynn laughed, then looked back at Tessa. "Anyway,
while I was taking care of him, I glanced out the window and saw Noah arrive."

"And never saw him leave…" Carol's eyebrows lifted
high on her forehead. "So how was he?"

Now that she could finally get a word in, Tessa said
on a sigh, "Amazing."

"Oh," Lynn sighed, too. "That's wonderful. Worth
waiting for then?"

"Big time."

"And?" Carol asked.

"And what? There is no more." Tessa shrugged and
kept a blank expression on her face. She didn't want her
friends to worry about her and even more than that, she
didn't want to hear any protect-your-heart speeches. She
knew what she was doing. Probably.

Sex, Tessa. Great sex.

That was true enough, but it was so hard to keep the
words *I love you* from spilling out when Noah touched
her. And if she did that, it would be the end. Well, she
wasn't ready for it to end. Not yet.

Continuing, she added, "We shared amazing sex,
very little sleep and I had today off to get ready for the
London trip."

"Uh-huh." Lynn took a pepper, bit into it, then waved
what was left of it to make her point. "He didn't say anything about—you know, more than one night?"

"He did." In fact, Tessa squirmed a little in her chair
as she remembered the discussion they'd had after de-
ciding to be together while they were in London. "We're

going to enjoy ourselves in England and then we're done."

"And you're okay with that?" Lynn looked worried.

So was Tessa, but she wasn't going to admit it. "It's an extra week with him, so yeah, I am."

It would be devastating later, but she would deal with the pain if it meant she could have him to herself for just a little longer.

"And you're going to be cool with walking away at the end of the week?" Carol didn't look convinced.

"*Cool* isn't the word I'd use, but I will walk away." She lifted her chin. "I have to."

"Oh, sweetie…" Lynn reached out and squeezed Tessa's hand. "That's going to be so hard for you."

It was going to be really ugly and Tessa knew it. She accepted it. But she was willing to pay the price. Love made you stupid, she thought, and wished, not for the first time, that she weren't so nuts about a man who couldn't have been less interested in love.

"She'll make it." Carol nodded sharply. "I think you're doing exactly the right thing, Tess. Use him then lose him."

Tessa laughed sharply.

"Carol!" Lynn just stared at her.

"Well, come on, honey," Carol said. "Tess has been in love with this guy for freaking ever. She can get her fill of him in five or six days and then move the hell on."

"Right. Would it be so easy for you to walk away from me?"

"Come on, you guys…" Tessa looked from one woman to the other.

"Of course not, honey," Carol said. "I love you."

"Just like Tessa loves Noah, though he probably doesn't deserve it, if he can't see how wonderful she is."

"See there?" Carol grinned. "We agree! Tessa, do what you have to do. We'll be here when you get home."

She looked at her friends and smiled. From the living room came Jade's and Evan's laughter. No matter what happened after England, Tessa told herself, she'd be all right. It might take a while, but she'd live through it. She had a life to build, a business to work on and friends she could count on.

For six nights of seduction with Noah, Tessa was willing to risk the pain.

Flying private was really the only way to travel, Noah told himself. The company jet was sleek and comfortable and flew on *his* timetable, not the airlines'.

They'd get into London early evening and go straight to the Barrington. He'd already arranged with the hotel to have dinner and champagne waiting when he and Tessa arrived and then he had other plans. Plans that had been building in his mind since leaving Tessa Thursday night.

He shifted a look at her now and felt his blood buzz. Her hair was pulled up and back from her face, but she wasn't wearing her usual uniform of conservative suit and sensible heels.

Instead, she wore a red, off-the-shoulder blouse tucked into a short black skirt and mile-high red heels. Had she chosen the outfit just to drive him nuts on the hours-long flight? If so, she'd succeeded. She was tapping diligently on her iPad, getting some work done while she relaxed on the brown leather sofa. She wasn't paying attention to him. Wasn't deliberately trying to be seductive. And yet…he was practically salivating as he watched her.

Amazing how a man's view could change so completely. For five years, he'd worked with Tessa and had only occasionally acknowledged that she was an attractive woman.

Now he looked at her and felt his heartbeat thump, his blood quicken and his body go tight and hard. One week with Tessa stretched out in front of him and Noah was determined to relish every moment of it. Yes, there was plenty of work to do during the week and she would help him with that, as she always had. But at this conference, there would be so much more between them.

"You're watching me," she said and never looked up from her tablet.

He grinned. "How do you know?"

"I can feel it."

"Nice to know I'm so powerful," he mused and stood up to walk over to her. Taking a seat on the couch himself, he glanced at the iPad. "You're looking at dogs?" Surprised, he added, "I thought you were working."

She glanced at him. "I was, and when I finished, I went to the website of the animal shelter near my house."

"Okay," Noah said, watching her scroll through the faces of dogs from Great Danes to Yorkies. "Window shopping?"

She gave him a quick smile. "In a way. I'm going to get a dog. I've wanted one since I moved to California. And I don't want to buy some special puppy, either," she said firmly, "I want to get a rescue from the shelter. Find a dog who needs me as much as I need her—or him. I don't care if it's a girl or a boy."

"Why didn't you get one before?"

She turned to look at him and her hair slid across her shoulder in a thick blond rope. "Because I was never home, Noah. It wouldn't have been fair to the dog to be left alone all the time."

He felt a little stab of guilt even though it made no sense. He'd given her a great job with excellent pay and benefits and now he was supposed to feel bad about her not being able to have a pet?

As if she knew what he was thinking, Tessa said, "It's not your fault, Noah. Lots of people keep pets even though they work too much. But I couldn't do it. Anyway, none of that matters now, because now I can have one."

Because she wouldn't be working for him anymore. Because after this week, he wouldn't see her again. Funny. That thought was more depressing than he would have thought it would be. She wanted a dog. She wanted time to work on her own business. Maybe she could have all of that. Maybe, Noah told himself, he could come up with an offer that would keep her with him at work—even if the affair would have to end.

He frowned thoughtfully. But would it have to end? After all, an adult, sexual relationship didn't have to be bogged down by hearts and flowers and expectations of love and forever. They were *great* together, so why should they stop? Hell, it was actually a perfect arrangement. He smiled to himself as he considered things from all angles.

Tessa had already admitted that she knew he didn't want a relationship. She wasn't looking for one, either, so why shouldn't they enjoy the sexual bombshell they created together? With no promises given on either side, they were simply adults enjoying themselves.

So instead he thought about finding a way to keep Tessa at work and make sure she had what she was so convinced she needed.

"What kind of dog are you looking for?"

"Growing up, I had a black Lab, so that would be perfect," she said, scrolling past hopeful, furry faces. "Oh, look at that cutie. But honestly, it doesn't matter to me. I just want a dog to keep me company while I work from home."

He frowned again. A dog to keep her company sounded better to her than working with him. Well, he wasn't going to give up so easily. He was going to come up with the perfect compromise and use their week in England to convince her to stay on with the company. With him. They could find a way around their sexual relationship and still work together. Why the hell should he lose the best assistant he'd ever had just because they were great in bed together?

And Tessa would see that it made more sense to stay at her job than to risk everything on a from-home business that might or might not ever support her. Hell, get the dog, he thought. Noah would make sure she was home enough to ease her conscience.

He smiled to himself and when she caught him, she asked, "What're you thinking?"

"I'm thinking," he lied smoothly, "that it's time to relax before we start the next frantic week."

"I am," she said and pointed to the tablet. "Dogs."

"Yeah, I've got a better idea, Tessa." He took the iPad from her and tossed it to the end of the sofa.

"Hey…"

He pressed a button along the wall and Hannah, his flight attendant, appeared from the cockpit. "Yes, sir?"

"We're ready, Hannah. Can you set it up?"

She smiled. "Of course."

"What are you up to?" Tessa asked warily.

"You'll see." A few moments later, Hannah was back, carrying a tray holding a bowl of popcorn and two iced glasses of soda. "Thanks, Hannah, you can start when you're ready."

"Yes, sir. If you need anything else, I'll be up front with the pilots. Just buzz me."

"Fine."

"What's going on, Noah?" Tessa accepted one of the glasses and took a sip.

"You'll see."

A moment later, the jet's window shades slid smoothly down, the lights dimmed and a wide screen dropped from the ceiling at the front of the plane.

"A movie?" she asked, turning to smile at him.

"Why not?" He dropped one arm around her shoulder as the movie opened. "We'll eat some popcorn and have a good old-fashioned make-out session."

She leaned closer and gave him a quick kiss. "That sounds great."

When she turned her head to watch the screen, Noah watched her. And he ignored the twinge of something unexpected squeezing his heart.

Eight

The Barrington was everything a five-star hotel should be.

Bordering beautiful Hyde Park, the Mayfair district boasted elegant Georgian homes, exclusive hotels and a wide selection of gourmet restaurants. And the Barrington, in Tessa's opinion, was the crown jewel. It was dignified and stylish, with a gray stone facade, and two uniformed doormen patrolling the entrance in bright red topcoats and black caps.

The interior was just as impressive, with gleaming tile floors, ruby-and-emerald rugs and scarlet couches and chairs set up in conversational groups. Of course, Tessa knew that by Sunday, there would be more chairs, more sofas dotting the lobby, to accommodate the two thousand people attending the spirits conference and awards. But for now, the hush of the luxurious hotel only added to the exclusive feel that surrounded them.

When they checked in, Noah and Tessa were whisked to the private elevator that took them to a penthouse suite. And now, while Noah was on the phone, Tessa explored their suite, admiring it all.

Polished hardwood floors with beautiful rugs in muted tones. Wide windows and a set of French doors in the living room and the master bedroom that opened onto a long balcony that provided a view of London that took her breath away.

There was a dining room with elegant Georgian-style furniture, and the main room boasted three overstuffed sofas, several tables and lamps that looked, and probably were, antique. A gas fireplace with red tile accents was cold and quiet now and the wide-screen TV hanging above it was dark.

She looked toward the hall that led to the bedrooms and felt her heartbeat quicken. There were two bedrooms, but they'd only be using one. Tessa's insides sparkled with expectancy and she squashed it momentarily. She had to start getting a grip on her feelings. She was in so deep now that she knew the pain of leaving Noah was going to be tremendous. If only she were able to keep love out of the equation. But then, if that were possible, she wouldn't be in this situation at all, because she'd have stopped loving him years ago.

She threw a quick look at him when she recognized the friendly but cool tone he was using on the phone, and knew he was talking to a potential business partner. Probably someone who had also arrived early for the conference.

"That's very good news, Henry," Noah was saying as he walked toward her and drew his fingertips along the length of her arm. Tessa shivered. He gave her a smile while he listened to Henry, then said, "I'll have my sister call the lawyers. We can leave our legal team and yours to hammer out the details."

Tessa smiled to herself. Henry... Had to be Henry Davenport of Davenport Freight, operating out of Birmingham. She knew that Graystone and Davenport had been doing some negotiations for nearly a month, but it seemed as if they'd reached a compromise. Barely an hour in England and he'd already sealed at least one deal. Noah Graystone was, if nothing else, a formidable businessman.

But then, Tessa had known that for years.

She opened the French doors and stepped out onto the balcony. There were huge terra-cotta pots every five feet, boasting actual trees that were bare now for winter, but at their bases were a few of the last winter flowers bravely blooming in spite of the cold.

The iron railing seemed sturdy, but since they were so high up, she didn't test it by leaning. Still, Tessa let her gaze sweep across the spread of London as lights jumped into life. The sky was clear, the wind was icy and in the room behind her was her lover.

She folded her arms across her middle and hugged that thought to her. Noah Graystone was her lover. It was temporary, yes, but no less real.

"Aren't you freezing?" Noah came up behind her and wrapped his arms around her.

Every trace of cold disappeared instantly as heat swamped her. "I was." She tipped her head back to smile up at him. "Now I'm not."

He held her tighter. "Are you tired? It was a long flight."

"Not at all." Flying in Noah's private jet was a lot less exhausting than flying commercial.

"Glad to hear it," he said, and turned her in his arms so he could kiss her.

And even if she'd been asleep on her feet, that kiss would have woken her up completely. He lifted his hands to cup her face, holding her still for a kiss that opened up every cell in her body and sent that voice inside her to singing an abbreviated "'Hallelujah' Chorus."

She could have stood there with him forever, but there was a knock at the door and he lifted his head, took her hand and said, "Come on. That'll be dinner."

Her knees were a little shaky, but when he tugged her along behind him, she followed. "When did you have time to order?"

"Yesterday," he said with a wink. "Made a few calls. Set a few plans into place."

"Is that right?" Tessa's smile blossomed. "Anything I should know about? I mean, I am your assistant. I should probably be kept up to speed on your plans."

"Oh, you're intimately involved," he assured her and gave her a wide grin. "Be right back."

The full force of that smile was really tremendous. She saw it so rarely—though more in the last week than in the last five years—that it still took her breath away.

He opened the door to room service. A man in a tuxedo jacket pushed in a soundless cart with a crisp, white tablecloth covering it. On the cart were dishes beneath silver domes, heavy flatware, crystal flutes and scarlet napkins. Another man followed the first, carrying an ice bucket and a bottle of champagne.

Noah signed the tab, thanked the men and saw them out.

"What's for dinner?" Tessa walked to the cart and lifted one of the heavy domes. Instantly, the scent of pasta and steak lifted into the air and she was suddenly hungry. "That smells amazing."

"But first, some champagne. Nothing wrong with toasting to a good week, is there?"

She set the dome back in place. "Not at all."

He poured for them both, then handed her one of the crystal flutes. He tapped the lip of his to hers and the chime seemed to ring out in the quiet room. She took a sip to ease the sudden dryness in her throat.

As she did, Tessa tried to figure out what Noah was up to. Yes, they'd agreed to having a week-long affair, but why was he being so over-the-top seductive? First the movie and make-out session on the jet. Now champagne in a penthouse? He didn't have to work this hard at seducing her so why was he?

Was it possible that he'd realized he *cared*?

"No thinking," Noah said as if he could see the wheels in her brain turning.

"Okay. No thinking." It was almost impossible to keep her mind straight around Noah anyway. There would be plenty of time later to try to decipher what was going on with him.

He moved in on her to plant a kiss on her mouth. If he was trying to make her stop thinking, he was doing a great job of it. Tessa dove into that kiss, letting everything but the moment fade away. This was what she'd waited for, dreamed of, for five years. Why would she waste a second of it?

When his phone rang, he lifted his head and she slanted a quick look at it. "No thinking. And no phone?"

"Definitely no phone," he agreed and left her long enough to walk over, pick up his phone and turn it off.

"I've already left a do-not-disturb order at the desk, so the hotel phone won't be ringing, either."

Okay, something was definitely up, Tessa thought, as her heart raced. The man never turned off his phone. The fact that he was doing it tonight had to mean something. The question was…*what?*

He walked back to her and Tessa didn't need another sip of champagne to make her blood bubble. The look in his eyes was enough to do it.

"Dinner now?" he asked, setting his glass down. "Or later?"

Staring up into those dark blue eyes, Tessa set her flute down beside his. "Later," she said, telling herself it didn't matter right now what his motivation was. She'd already decided to revel in the time they had together. The future could take care of itself. She was more interested in the present. "Definitely later."

"Good choice."

He swept her up into his arms and stalked toward the master bedroom. The bed had been turned back already and she barely had a moment to enjoy the huge room with its luxurious appointments.

The bed was gigantic and covered in a burgundy comforter. Bright white sheets stood in stark contrast to the darkness of the duvet. A mountain of pillows was stacked against the headboard and one of the bedside lamps was turned on, its low light spilling across the mattress in invitation.

Noah set her down and hurriedly undressed. She watched him as she did the same, each of them tossing their clothes to land all across the floor and the chairs drawn up near a small, tiled fireplace on one wall.

When they were naked, Tessa took a moment to

enjoy what a picture he made. Then he gave her a slow smile that lit off fireworks inside her.

"I didn't just order dinner. This time, I'm prepared," he said and pulled the bedside drawer open. When he pulled out two boxes of condoms, Tessa grinned.

"I like preparation. It's very sexy."

"Damn straight," he said, taking one of the condoms before dropping the boxes back into the drawer.

She watched him slide the latex on and thought about what he'd done. Two boxes. He was planning a busy week. And Tessa was all for it.

When he was ready, he came to her, gave her a gentle push that had her tipping over onto the bed. Her laughter died though when he reached down and flipped her over onto her stomach. Instantly, her mouth went dry and her body quivered.

Her hard nipples scraped against the duvet, cool against her skin, and sent sensation shooting through her. Taking a breath, she looked back at him and saw his eyes burning with desire as he scraped his hands up and down her back and onto her butt. He squeezed her flesh hard and she gasped with pleasure. Then he stroked her core with his fingertips and in an instant, Tessa's body was coiled and waiting.

He grabbed her hips and hitched her up higher. Tessa went up on her knees, eager now for what was coming.

He bent low to kiss her tattoo and she was never so glad as then that she'd had it done. It seemed to fascinate him and Tessa loved knowing that.

"Higher, Tessa," he whispered.

She lifted her hips higher and rested her head on her forearms, braced on the bed. He pushed himself deep inside her and she sighed as she took him all the way in. Her body trembled with every stroke. Tessa groaned aloud when she couldn't hold it back any longer and clenched her fingers into the silk duvet beneath her.

She moved back into him, helping him claim her. Taking him as deeply as she could while she matched the hard, fast pace that Noah set for them. Electricity seemed to buzz all around the room, where the only sound was strained breaths and the muffled groans that erupted from their throats.

Tessa had never needed so much or felt so much or wanted so much. To have Noah inside her was everything. To hear his breath rushing from his lungs, to feel his hands at her hips, holding her to him, was more than she'd ever imagined. Every time with him was better than the last time. They were linked. Whether he could see it or not, that connection between them was real and strong.

And it deserved more than a week.

"Come on, Tessa. Come. Let yourself go and come." His words were ground out as if it had been a personal victory to be able to speak at all. And maybe it had been.

Tessa didn't think she could have formed words at all.

Then her mind emptied as she raced toward that next release. She fought for breath, felt her heart pounding in her chest, the tingling sensation rising up from deep inside her. She bit her lip and tightened her grip on the cool silk of the duvet. Again and again, he pushed her, silently demanding she give him all she was. Refusing to accept less. And finally, she did. There was no stopping it. No prolonging it.

She screamed into the bed, hoping the mattress

would muffle the sound, and pushed her body back against him in one frantic last jump into oblivion.

Moments later, he held her tighter, ground himself against her and shouted her name like a warrior's triumphant call after a battle.

When he collapsed onto the bed, he wordlessly rolled over and drew her with him, tucking her into the circle of his arms. Tessa laid her head on his chest, draped one leg over his and smiled as she listened to the hard beat of his heart.

She loved him. She always would.

And the heartbreak was, she couldn't tell him.

The Aston Martin Noah had requested was delivered to the hotel and on Sunday, their first full day in England, they went for a ride. A long one, as it turned out, since Tessa had mentioned that she'd always wanted to see Stonehenge. Noah had instantly jumped into action. Salisbury was almost two hours from London and they probably should have simply taken the train. But nothing was going to stop Noah from driving that car.

Early December in England was cold and damp, so they were dressed for it in jeans and jackets, and they'd brought a couple of umbrellas with them. Still, the weather didn't dissuade people from making the trip from London. There were a lot of tourists at the site and Tessa guessed that a good number of them were in London for the conference.

"Does it meet expectations?" he asked, staring at the ancient standing stones ten yards from them.

"Oh, yes," she said. "I wish we could get closer, but this is wonderful."

He held the umbrella over both of them to keep off

the soft, steady rain. "If I'd known you were interested, I'd have arranged a private visit in advance."

Tessa looked up at him. "Oh, thanks, but this is great." Shifting her gaze back to the massive stones, she shook her head and said quietly, "Can you even imagine what it took for people to set these stones in place?"

"Is this another lesson in 'there's-no-such-word-as-can't'?"

She glanced at him and saw him smile. "Let's just say my dad would approve of those people's determination." Turning her gaze back to the stones, she sighed a little. "You can almost feel the magic, can't you?"

He was looking at her when he said, "Yeah. I suppose so."

"You're watching me again."

"I like the view."

She turned to face him and the cold wind racing across the open ground lifted her hair and threw it across her eyes. She plucked it free and said, "Thanks for bringing me here, Noah. I've always wanted to see it."

He frowned a little. "You should have said something last summer when we were in London."

"We were working every minute," she reminded him.

"We could have taken one afternoon," he argued.

"Really?" She gave him a wry smile. Because they both knew that would never have happened. Noah's focus was on the company and everything else in the world simply didn't exist for him. She hated knowing that he was deliberately missing out on so much, but she'd never been able to make him see the truth.

"Okay, I probably wouldn't have," he admitted. Shifting his gaze to the stones where ancient people had once lived and prayed and died, he added, "I should have, though."

"You're here now," she said, and leaned her head against his shoulder. "That's enough."

Rain pattered against the umbrella and the mist lay heavily across the open land surrounding the stones. Magic seemed to pulse in the air and for a moment, when Noah took her hand and folded his fingers around hers, Tessa felt that magic deep in her bones.

Noah's first meeting on Monday went even better than expected.

He left the dining room, satisfied with the progress of his negotiations with Billingsley Bottling. Charles Billingsley was eager to grow his company and taking it international was a huge part of that. Noah wanted a bottling plant in the UK, to help sales grow and to meet the rising demand they were already experiencing. He'd call Stephanie to let her know so she could run backup and nail this down, hopefully this week.

He hadn't seen Tessa in several hours and silently, Noah told himself that was probably a good thing. After their excursion to Stonehenge, it felt as if something had changed between them. Rather than just the heat of desire, he'd been feeling something…deeper. Richer. And he wasn't sure what to do about that.

Sex was one thing.

Relationships were another.

He'd begun to rethink his idea of somehow getting her to stay at the company. Especially if they continued this affair. If what was between them became messy and involved, then that would be too big a distraction. He couldn't afford that. He had a business to grow. He had neither the time nor the inclination to build anything else.

No, the only way to keep Tessa at the company was to end the affair and try to wipe his memory of the times spent with her. Not easy, of course, but necessary.

With that thought in mind, he caught a glimpse of Tessa, across the lobby. She wore a deep blue blouse with a high collar and long sleeves along with that short black skirt she'd worn on the plane and a pair of black stilettos that somehow made her long legs look even longer. She stood out in this crowd of stolid, conventional people and he wasn't surprised to see heads turn as people passed her. Noah frowned, though, as he watched a tall man walk up to Tessa, shake her hand and give her a smile designed to charm.

Of course, he recognized the man as Marcus Campbell of Campbell Bottling, out of Glasgow. The man took Tessa's hand between both of his and held it for longer than necessary, then leaned in and said something to make Tessa laugh. Noah's scowl deepened as he wondered what the two of them were laughing about. And why did Tessa look so pleased to see Marcus Campbell?

Noah had seen her with competitors and allies alike over the last five years and he'd long ago acknowledged that she'd always had the ability to smooth things over, or to make inroads with people who were of interest to Graystone. But he'd never seen her smile like that before. Or maybe he'd never noticed. Hard to believe but it was a possibility, because until the last week and more, Noah had never treated Tessa like a "woman." She was his assistant. Someone he depended on.

No doubt she was talking to Campbell about the

meeting Noah had scheduled with him for breakfast tomorrow. They were supposed to be discussing a shipping agreement between their companies and Tessa was most likely paving his way.

She reached out and laid one hand on Campbell's forearm and the man smiled down at her like she was the last dessert on the table. What the hell could they be talking about for so long? And why did paving the way require touching?

"Noah?" Still frowning, he turned to say hello to Anna Morgan, the daughter of one of his biggest competitors, as she hurried up to him on four-inch heels. Morgan Bourbon was well-known stateside and Anna was no doubt here to start building connections in Europe.

"Hi," he said, shaking her hand and darting another look at Tessa and Marcus at the same time. "How are you, Anna?"

"Good, good." She tipped her head to one side. "Who are we watching?"

"What?" He reluctantly pulled his gaze from Tessa. He was more than a little annoyed to be caught staring. "No one. Just my assistant, setting up a meeting."

She looked, smiled and said, "Oh, Marcus. He's so much fun."

"Is he?" Yeah, Tessa seemed to think so, too. Frowning again, Noah forced himself to concentrate on Anna. "So, I hear your father stepped down last year and you're the CEO now."

"I am," she said, clearly pleased, as she should be. "I'm making a few changes—we'll be adding more spirits to our brand soon. I've found the most wonderful master distiller—" she broke off when it was clear his mind was elsewhere. "Never mind. We can talk business anytime. It was good to see you, Noah." She laid her right palm on his chest and leaned in to kiss his cheek. "I hope we get some time together this week."

He nodded and really looked at Anna for the first time. She was lovely, with short, dark brown hair, and big brown eyes. Her honey-colored skin was toned and muscled and she had a Southern drawl she often used to reel men in like trout. She was smart, ambitious and had a reputation for getting what she wanted. He could admire that in anyone.

But otherwise, he felt nothing. No attraction. No buzz of awareness. No heat from where her hand rested on his chest. And when she stepped back, it was a relief.

"We'll make a point of it," he said and watched her go for a long minute before turning back to Tessa and Marcus Campbell.

The two of them looked to be having a good time and that was more than annoying. Oh, Noah knew Tessa was laying groundwork with Marcus for the meeting that was coming up. But did she have to have such a good time about it? Maybe the better question was, why did it bug him so much? He was being downright territorial and that was something he'd never done. He didn't like it.

What the hell was he going to do without her? Was he crazy for starting this affair? Probably, though he couldn't really regret it.

But losing her from the company was going to be a nightmare. Hell, he hadn't even set up interviews to try to find a replacement, because how could he possibly replace a woman who knew his company as well as he did? A woman who could talk to anyone and make them comfortable? A woman who had the ability to entertain clients and find a way to connect with possible partners?

The truth was, Tessa was far more important to him—his business—than he'd ever realized. And now that he was acknowledging it, he had to let her go? He didn't think so.

She smiled at Marcus and her whole face lit up.

And that smile did something to Noah that he'd never really experienced before, which told him this thing between them had to end.

An affair he could accept—welcome. A relationship was something he wasn't interested in. He had a focus already and wouldn't try to divide it between the company and a woman, only to fail at both because neither had gotten his best.

So, since he was about to lose his lover, he might as well try to keep his assistant if he could.

The Tower of London, Westminster Abbey and Buckingham Palace—it had been a full couple of hours and Tessa was loving it. The crowds in London weren't slowed down by weather so she refused to let it affect her day, either. Streets were jammed with cars and those great double-decker buses and pedestrians taking their lives in their hands darting through the traffic like ballet dancers.

It was wonderful. All of it.

"Is there anything else you want to see?" Noah asked, keeping the umbrella positioned over both of them. The rain had come back, but it hadn't stopped them from exploring. And if Tessa were honest about it, she'd admit that the rain almost made it better. Under their umbrella, they were locked together in their own little world. It felt insulated. Private.

"Actually, I'd love a cup of coffee—or tea, I guess."

Noah winced. "Tea's the safer bet. We passed a tea shop about a block back, if you're interested."

"Sure." She hooked her arm through his and they walked down the sidewalk to the rhythm of the rain beating against the umbrella. Shop windows were brightly lit and customers flowed in and out. And in a few shops, Tessa spotted the first signs of Christmas decorations.

Noah opened the door to the tea shop and ushered her in. The room was warm and dry and smelled like heaven.

They claimed a table by the front window, giving them a view of the rain-drenched street. When a waitress arrived, they ordered tea with sandwiches and scones. Tessa shrugged out of her jacket and hooked it on the back of her chair as Noah did the same.

"This was really nice of you, Noah," she said. "I never would have believed that you'd take the time to do the tourist thing."

"I can be flexible," he argued and when she only smiled, he acknowledged, "Fine. I'm as flexible as a steel pole."

"But you admit it and that's a start."

"Oh, thanks," he said with a choked off laugh.

"Anyway, knowing how you must hate this only makes me appreciate it more. I had a great time."

"Even in the rain?"

"It's atmospheric," she said.

"And freezing," he pointed out. Then he quieted while their waitress brought out a tray with a fine-china pot of tea along with two cups and saucers, a small pitcher of cream and a dish of lemon slices, as well.

She smiled at them both and said, "I'll be right back with your sandwiches and scones."

"Thank you." Tessa poured a cup of the steaming black tea. With a dollop of cream in it, it was perfect and tasted just right. She sighed at her first sip and Noah laughed.

"I get a sigh over coffee. But tea?"

"Don't knock it till you try it," Tessa teased.

Once he had, he was forced to nod. "Not bad. Especially on a day like today."

When lunch arrived, they helped themselves, and while they ate, they talked about the conference and what they'd noticed so far.

"I talked to Steph," Tessa said. "Gave her a couple of names and asked her to get Legal on them."

"That's good. I ran into Anna Morgan this morning."

"Really. How is she? Doing well as the new CEO?" Tessa knew Anna had been trying to convince her father for years to retire and hand over the reins. It seemed she'd finally gotten what she wanted.

"Seems to be," he said and poured them each more tea. "I saw you talking with Marcus Campbell."

His tone sounded weird, but Tessa ignored it. "You should have come over and said hello."

"I'll say hello at our meeting tomorrow morning." He picked up his cup. "You two seemed to have a lot to say to each other."

"Well, yeah," she said. "I haven't seen him since last year's conference. Marcus is fun to talk to."

"Is he?" One of Noah's eyebrows lifted. "His Scottish accent is so thick I can hardly understand him half the time."

Again, weird tone, but who knew what was going through his mind? Tessa chose to skip right over it and smiled. "I love his accent."

"Yeah," he muttered. "I noticed."

"Okay, what's going on with you, Noah?" she said abruptly.

"Nothing. Just wondering how close you and Marcus are."

"Close?" She laughed. "He lives in Glasgow and I live in Laguna, so not very."

"You know what I mean," Noah said.

"Yeah I do. And I'm wondering where this is coming from." She looked at him and saw he wasn't angry. If anything, he looked distant, remote, as if he was pulling back from her even while sitting still. What the heck? They'd had a nice couple of hours and he'd shown none of this. How was he able to go from fun and charming to robotic in a finger snap?

"I just told you I haven't seen Marcus since last year."

"Uh-huh. What about Travis?"

Tessa shook her head. *"Travis?"*

"He's a lot closer than Glasgow, isn't he?" Noah shrugged and leaned in closer so he could lower his voice to avoid being overheard. "You had a stock of condoms that first night we were together. And Travis seemed to know his way around you and your house."

She sat back and shook her head. What had happened? What was he thinking, and why now? In the five years she'd known Noah, she'd seen every aspect of his personality and mean wasn't a part of him.

"Okay, this is going way beyond weird. Do you have a fever?"

"What? No."

"Are you sure, because you seem pretty delusional. A fever would explain it."

He scowled at her. "I don't have a fever. Just a question. How close are you and Travis?"

"That's none of your business," she said, feeling the first stirrings of her temper beginning to boil.

"That close, eh?" He nodded thoughtfully and leaned back in his chair.

"Why *yes*, Noah," she ground out and now it was her turn to lean forward. The lovely shop, the warmth of the place and the heavenly scents all seemed to wither away. Locking her gaze with his, she whispered, "You've cleverly discovered my darkest secrets. Travis is a wild lover. We meet at the full of the moon and dance naked under the elm tree in my backyard. You should see it in summer. We have fireworks."

His mouth worked as if he were biting back words he wanted to say and Tessa thought that was a very good idea. If he said anything else insulting, she might just pour what was left of their tea in his lap.

"Sarcasm? Really?" He finally asked. "That's all you've got?"

"It's all your question deserved," she snapped. "Believe it or not, I'm a grown woman who has had sex many times before I ever met you. I've had dates that went pretty well and I've brought men home—*my* home. My business. I've never questioned you about the bimbos you buy off with a serial gift of a diamond necklace—"

"They're not bimbos."

"—and I'm the one who has to wrap those stupid

gifts and have them delivered. Have I ever once insulted you about your choices?"

Noah swallowed hard. "No, and I didn't mean to—"

"Well, you did." She stood up, gathered her coat and shrugged it on. "Congratulations, Noah. You took a perfectly lovely day and turned it to trash."

"Tessa, don't leave."

"I don't want to be near you right now."

"At least take the umbrella," he said and held it up.

"If I take that from you, I might put it somewhere you would find uncomfortable." Tessa headed for the door, stepped outside into the now pounding rain and welcomed it. She would need a storm of icy rain like this to quench the fire inside.

Nine

"**D**amn it, Tessa, wait!" Noah shouted loud enough for several people to turn and look at him, but Tessa just kept striding away. Everyone she passed gave her a wide berth, so he knew she was still furious. And why the hell wouldn't she be?

She didn't slow down a bit as he tossed money onto the table then chased after her, but his much longer legs made it easy to catch up quickly. Noah grabbed her arm and spun her around. The driving rain hammered down on him and the closed umbrella he was still clutching. "You'll get pneumonia or something— use the umbrella."

"I don't want anything from you." She pulled free and started walking again.

Noah watched her go, gritted his teeth and started to follow, when a woman came out of a shop, holding her purse over her head as a shield from the rain. He held out the umbrella and said, "Here. Take this."

She was startled, but grabbed it. He didn't stand around to watch her open it. Instead, he took off after Tessa, who was making damn good time.

Puddled water splashed up his legs as he ran after her, and with every pounding step, Noah cursed himself. He didn't know what the hell was happening to him lately. He'd never lost control like that before and didn't blame Tessa a bit for walking out. He was lucky she hadn't hit him over the head with that china pot.

"Come on, Tessa! Stop!" Then she did and that surprised him. He'd expected to have to chase her all the way back to the hotel.

Turning to face him, she demanded, "What do you want now? Have a few more insults for me?"

He took a breath and pushed his soaked hair back from his forehead. She looked miserable. Hair a thick wet rope on either side of her head, her face wet, clothes drenched and still, she was the most beautiful thing he'd ever seen. Everything in him wanted to grab her and hold her close, but he had the distinct impression that move wouldn't be appreciated.

"No. No, I don't."

"You sure?" She snapped out the question. "Was that why you were so nice all day? Is that what it was really about? Taking me to all those beautiful places? Being warm and funny and so damn charming? Were you just setting me up? Lulling me into complacency so you could start the interrogation and still feel good about yourself?"

Fury rang in her tone and flashed in her eyes and he

couldn't blame her for that, either. Just like he couldn't blame himself for noting that even furious, she was breathtaking. Then what she said registered.

"Of course not!" Where the hell had that come from? He might be feeling a little crazy at the moment, but apparently he wasn't the only one.

She reached up and shoved her wet hair back from her face and gave a fierce scowl to a man who slowed down as if to enjoy the show. He hurried on. When they were relatively alone again, she asked, "Then what was that all about, Noah? Where do you get off throwing accusations like that at me?"

"I don't know." Shaking his head, Noah looked down the street, trying to gather the threads of thoughts in his mind, but they scattered at the attempt. Looking into her eyes, Noah added, "I don't know where that came from or why I said it. Damn it, Tessa, since this thing started between us, I feel like my brain's been on vacation."

People hurried past them, trying to escape a downpour that most of them had to be used to, he thought. But not he and Tessa. They stood there, facing off like a couple of crazy people in a storm.

He could still see the anger glinting in her eyes, but maybe it wasn't quite as fierce as it had been before.

"I guess I know what you mean," she muttered. "Because I've felt the same way once or twice. But I'm not going to stand still and let you dump your frustrations on me, Noah."

"I know that and you're right." Furious at himself now, Noah tried to figure out what the hell was happening to him. Tessa was still watching him. Waiting. For an explanation he couldn't find. Being jealous was way out of character for him. Being territorial about a woman was just nothing he'd ever felt before.

Hell, he wasn't happy about any of this. For the first time in his life, Noah felt out of control. He didn't like it.

"Tessa," he finally said, scrubbing one hand across his face, "I don't even know where any of that came from."

"I do," she said, tipping her head back, letting the rain splash against her face so she could meet his gaze. "It's been too good between us. For days now, we've been happy. And you couldn't stand that. So you sabotaged it."

"What does that mean?"

"It means you don't want to be happy, Noah." Taking a deep breath, Tessa let it sigh from her lungs as if her anger had drained away in a rush, leaving her exhausted. "You want to be focused on the company. Determined to build your brand. Anything that cuts into that focus has to be excised."

He wanted to argue with her, but wasn't that just what he'd been telling himself? Which told him that maybe he'd had the right idea before. End the affair and save his assistant. That was the only way to get through this. He probably didn't have much chance at keeping her at her job after all of this, but he was going to try. Because losing his lover would be hard. But losing Tessa out of his life completely was unfathomable.

Still, there was no way he was bringing that up *now*. Not exactly like their conversation had put her in a receptive mood.

But he had to say something to try to fix this. To repair what he'd broken. Over and beyond what they'd shared lately, he'd always liked her. Admired her. He didn't want that ruined.

"*Sabotage* is a little strong."

She shook her head and the rain kept falling.

Okay, trying for humor wasn't the best idea. "Look, I don't know what it is. Maybe you're right. Maybe you're not. The only thing I am sure of is that we've got to get out of the rain before we drown standing here."

"Fine." Her eyes weren't flashing now. But they weren't shining as they had been the last week or so.

Noah missed that.

The next morning, Noah and Tessa left their room together, but separate. For the first time since they'd made their bargain, there hadn't been any sex the night before and Noah had to wonder if there would be sex again anytime soon. Had they already been together for the last time? He hoped not.

It was only Tuesday. They should have had until Friday and now he wasn't sure what they had left at all.

"I'll see you later," Tessa said when the elevator hit the main lobby.

The doors swished open with a sigh and they stepped out of the silence into the dull roar of a couple thousand people, all talking at once. Used to be, these conferences energized Noah. Making new business connections, seeing old friends, picking up new and innovative ideas to push his business forward.

Now he silently wished all the people here were on the other side of the world.

"Meet for lunch?" he asked tentatively. "We can compare notes on our meetings."

"I can't," Tessa said. "I'm having lunch with Morris from the glass company."

"Right." Noah nodded. She was taking that meeting

for him to get the basic information needed on his idea for a new style of bottle for their scotch line. "Okay then."

She started to leave, then stopped and looked at him. "Noah, let's just take care of business and we can talk tonight."

By the tone of her voice, he wasn't sure he wanted to have that "talk," but what choice did they have? And maybe he should take a page from her book. Start setting the boundaries in place now. He hated it, because damn it, he'd had a good time this last week or so. Spending so much nonworking time with Tessa had introduced him to more fun than he could remember having in years.

"That's fine," he said. "Good luck with Morris."

She nodded. "Say hello to Marcus for me."

As he watched her walk away, he told himself she'd said that deliberately. To remind him of their argument. Tessa wasn't a woman to sit back and say nothing when she was pissed, and apparently there was plenty of anger still inside her from yesterday. And whose fault was that? he asked himself in disgust.

Breakfast with Marcus didn't improve his mood.

The Campbell family ran a bottling and distribution business out of Glasgow, Scotland, and Noah was interested in having more than one distributor in the UK. Though why he'd chosen Marcus was something he couldn't answer at the moment. Surely there were dozens of others who would be less aggravating.

The other man was about Noah's age and wore a clearly custom-tailored suit. His reddish brown hair was neatly trimmed, his green eyes were sharp and didn't seem to miss much. At least, Noah thought, they hadn't when they'd been locked on to Tessa yesterday.

After talking business over breakfast, they lingered over tea to hammer out a few more details. Noah was still not a fan of tea, but expertly made tea was better than badly made coffee in his opinion.

"You'll have your ever-efficient assistant Tessa contact me, then?" Marcus asked, though his Scots accent was so thick, it was hard to be sure.

Noah frowned thoughtfully. "Yes, I'll have her call you and get the information we need, then it will be up to the legal teams to come up with a contract we can both agree on."

Marcus lifted his cup and took a sip. "Oh, I don't think that'll be a problem." Setting the cup down in its matching saucer with a quiet clink of china, he mused, "I think this deal will be a benefit to both of us."

"I agree," Noah said.

"I will tell you," Marcus mused, "I've envied you your assistant."

"Really." Noah studied him and felt a now familiar curl of annoyance tighten inside him. When he'd seen Marcus and Tessa together, Noah hadn't been able to miss just how much Marcus admired her. Now he was forced to listen to the admiration?

"Oh, yes. When we ran into each other yesterday, she was a delight." Shaking his head, he smiled to himself. "She had any number of facts at the ready, off the top of her head. She's a stoater no doubt."

"She's a *what*?" Was that an insult or a compliment? Who the hell could tell? Either way, Noah didn't like it.

"A stoater, man." Marcus laughed shortly and picked

up his tea again. "It's Glaswegian slang. Means she's fantastic is all. The woman's a wonder."

Noah already knew that, so he didn't need Marcus telling him so—or noticing, for that matter.

Marcus gave him a wink. "Don't say anything to her, but I'm thinking I'll talk her into having a bite with me tonight."

"Yeah, that's not going to work," Noah said with no regret at all. "We're working tonight."

"Get off, man," Marcus said. "It's a conference. There's drinking and eating and dancing to be done. You can't work all the while."

"I'll keep it in mind," Noah said tightly.

The morning bustle in the dining room ensured that there were too many people talking and laughing to allow anyone to overhear their conversation. Soft gray light slipped through windows displaying a wide view of the busy London street beyond. Big surprise, it was raining again.

Marcus gave him a long look. "Well, I'll ask her anyway. Take my chances."

"Up to you," Noah said, though it cost him. He didn't want Tessa spending time with Marcus but didn't know how he could stop it, either. Not like Tessa was fond enough of him at the moment to pay any attention at all to what he had to say.

"You're a jammy man, Noah," Marcus was saying and that caught Noah's attention.

"I'm *jammy*?"

Marcus laughed to himself. "Glaswegian slang again, sorry. Means, you're a lucky man, having a woman like Tessa working for you as she's bloody brilliant."

Shaking his head in admiration, he sighed a little. "She makes my own Margaret seem a dafty roaster."

Noah held up one hand. "I'm not even going to ask what that one means. Are you sure Glaswegians speak English at all?"

Marcus grinned. "No we don't. We're Scots, man. And from Glasgow. We speak Weegie."

The man's constant good humor was only slightly less maddening than the sprinkling of bizarre words into a normal conversation.

Noah's frown deepened. "Weegie. Of course you do."

Tapping his fingers against the table top, Marcus asked, "So, is she happy? Tessa. At her job, I mean?"

Noah narrowed his gaze on the other man, suspicion rising. "Why?"

Marcus idly turned his teacup on its saucer. "Well, now, I might be considering making an offer, to steal her out from under you if I can."

For the first time around Marcus, Noah relaxed. "Won't work. She's already resigned—"

"Is that the truth, then?" Marcus leaned back in his chair and allowed himself a satisfied smile. "That's grand news to get on a gray morning."

"Yeah," Noah shook his head. "She quit because she has her own business she wants to devote her time to."

"A stoater, I told you," Marcus mused.

"Yeah, stoater or not, she's not going to move to Scotland to do a job she basically just quit in America."

"What's her business then?"

"She has an Etsy shop," Noah muttered, remembering the times in her kitchen, tying those stupid bows. Pouring candles and splashing hot wax on himself.

"Brilliant," Marcus crowed with a grin. "God bless the

internet. She can work on her business from Glasgow as easily as she can from California."

"She'll say no," Noah said, then frowned. At least he hoped to hell she would. He understood that he couldn't have Tessa, but damned if he'd be able to stand knowing that she was living in Scotland with Marcus. But, again, it wasn't like he could prevent it.

"Won't know until I try, will I?" Marcus signaled for the check and while they waited for the waiter to appear, he said, "I'll get the check this time, as a toast to our future business together."

"Thanks…"

"And, because I'm going to try to steal your Tessa for my own, it's the least I can do." He grinned again.

Scowling, Noah muttered, "You said jammy means luck?"

"I did."

"Well, you're gonna need a lot of jam."

"I'm swimmin' in it, Noah," Marcus said, eyebrows wiggling, grin widening. "Swimmin' in it."

While Noah took his morning meeting, Tessa attended a panel on European distribution. Fascinating? Not in any way. But she was there to gather information for Noah, so she dutifully made notes on her tablet.

As the panelists took turns explaining the steps taken in distribution, Tessa paid more attention to the speakers. You could tell a lot about people by the way they spoke about their employees, their business. Pride? Disinterest? Either one was a good indicator of what it might be like dealing with them.

While three of the men spoke about themselves and how they'd single-handedly built the biggest, the best—the fourth man instead heaped praise on his truck drivers and warehouse workers, the office help and everyone else who worked for him. He spoke of himself and his employees as a team and said it had been essential in building his company.

Tessa noted his name and the name of his business. The final decision would be Noah's, or maybe Steph's, but if they didn't want her opinion, they shouldn't send her to these things.

Her phone was on vibrate and she jumped when her pocket buzzed. Glancing at the screen, she saw Stephanie's name and keeping her voice in a whisper, she said, "Hi, Steph. Everything okay?"

"It's great, are you kidding?"

The man seated in front of Tessa turned around, glared at her and huffed out, "Shh!"

Wincing, Tessa hushed out, "Hang on," then she slipped down the aisle and out the door into a lobby that was full and bustling.

Finding the nearest chair, Tessa plopped down and said, "Hi again. Okay now I can talk."

"What happened?"

"I was at a panel, couldn't talk without getting the hate stare."

"Sorry."

"Don't be," Tessa assured her. "You did me a favor. I got what I needed, anyway. I think you should check out Harry Miller of Two Brothers trucking, based in Liverpool. I really liked what he had to say and I think he'd work out well for us—well, you."

"Okay, got it, thanks. I'll have Research do a run on them and then talk to Noah."

Tessa would tell Noah when she saw him, but giving Steph a heads-up would get things moving quickly. Funny, Tessa thought, but she would miss this part of what she did, too. Being trusted to find the right people for the right job. It was a good feeling to find someone like Harry Miller, who, if he contracted with Graystone, would see a huge leap in business.

But she couldn't stay. Especially after yesterday. Things had gone so wrong so fast, Tessa still wasn't sure what had happened. He'd turned from Mr. Charm into Mr. Who-The-Heck-Is-This in a blink of time. And though he'd sort of apologized, Tessa wasn't completely mollified. How could she be?

He might not know why he'd said all those things, but she did. He was scared. Something Noah would never admit. But she could see it. As she'd told him, things had been way too good between them. They'd meshed together so well that it had been almost effortless, and for Noah, that was worrying.

Since the tea shop, things had been so tense between them, it felt as if they were just acquaintances, trapped in a luxury hotel suite without a clue how to act toward each other. Heck, Tessa hadn't even left him yet and she already missed him. Missed the closeness, the laughter… *The sex, Tessa. You also miss the sex.* Yes, she did. They'd slept in the same bed last night, but they might as well have been on different planets. There'd been no touching, cuddling, kissing.

That argument had been right there in between them, like a wall neither of them could breach. And now, they had two more full days together before they left England on Friday. That was the day that, like Cinderella running from the ball at midnight, Tessa had planned to make her escape from Noah's world.

Now she didn't know if she could make it until then if this was how it was going to be.

After taking a steadying breath, Tessa forced cheer into her voice to talk to Stephanie because she really didn't want to get into this with her friend—and Noah's sister.

"So what's going on at home?"

"You will not believe how great the walls in this place look. And the floor, once it's finished, is going to be gorgeous. They've already got half the office done."

Right. She'd forgotten about Stephanie's plan to redo the office while Noah was gone. "Wow, that was fast!"

"The word *bonus*, remember?" Stephanie laughed a little. "I even got them to come in on Sunday so we could get a jump on it all."

"I always said you were impressive."

"And you are exceptionally perceptive," Stephanie said. "Enough about the now gorgeous office. How's England? Oooh. Better yet, how's my brother?"

Tessa took the easy question first. "England is great. Of course, December weather is cold and wet…"

"Sounds lovely."

"Actually, it is." Standing, Tessa moved over to a coffee bar, waited behind two other people and managed to snag herself a cup. She smiled at the woman next to her, then went back to her surprisingly uncomfortable chair. "We went to Stonehenge on Sunday."

"I'm sorry. I don't think I heard that right. Stonehenge?" Clearly incredulous, Stephanie said, "Noah went to a tourist attraction?"

"Well, it's not an amusement park, Steph. It's historic."

"You got that right," she said. "Getting Noah to take a day off is historic."

Laughing wryly, Tessa sipped at her coffee. It had been staggering that Noah had voluntarily taken time off. And then more time yesterday...okay, don't go there.

"It was wonderful, really. Even in the rain." She took a breath and said, "Yesterday, we did the Tower, Westminster Abbey and Buckingham Palace."

"A shame it's so early here," Stephanie muttered. "I need a drink."

Smiling, Tessa said, "It was really nice."

"Uh-huh." Stephanie paused for a moment, then said, "I can hear the tone of your voice, Tessa. Something besides tourist heaven is going on. What did Noah do?"

"Why do you think it was Noah?"

"Please."

Tessa nodded and lifted one hand in a wave to a woman she knew. "Okay yes, it was Noah. Yesterday afternoon, he said some things that really made me furious and we had a big fight and now, I just don't think I'm going to make it here until Friday."

"God, he's an idiot." Stephanie's sigh was audible. "Honestly, I've found that most men are, but even in this, Noah is a standout."

"I don't know what set him off, either."

"I can guess," Stephanie said.

"So can I," Tessa agreed. "But it doesn't really matter in the grand scheme, does it? We both said some things we shouldn't have and I don't see a way back from it."

"There's always a way back if you want it badly enough."

She stared out through the windows, watching the rain falling and the people strolling along the sidewalk. A sea of umbrellas bobbed and moved with the crowd.

"I used to think that, too."

"Damn it, Tessa," Steph snapped. "You already knew Noah. You loved him anyway. So *now* you've decided you can't take it?"

That sounded too close to the truth to be comfortable. Tessa had known Noah. She knew his good side, his bad side and everything in between.

"But I quit my job, Steph," she reminded her friend. "And this 'break' with Noah was always going to be temporary."

"It doesn't have to be."

Tessa laughed darkly. Shaking her head, she looked around the lobby and the hundreds of people milling about, chatting, studying conference schedules, sitting at the open bar. The hotel staff was busy, but everything was running smoothly. Well, she thought, not everything. She and Noah had hit a brick wall.

Everyone here at the conference had a purpose.

So did she and Noah.

Once that purpose was fulfilled, what was left?

Dinner that night started out tense. Noah had spent most of the day wondering what the hell he was going to say to Tessa. And he hadn't come up with a damn thing. At the end of the week, she would be gone. Her job done. This temporary seduction over. And where was that going to leave him?

Exactly where he had been when all of this started, he assured himself. Except he wouldn't have Tessa to bounce ideas off. He wouldn't have her making sure his business and, hell, his *life* were organized. He wouldn't see her every morning or get to eat the cinnamon Christmas cake she made every year. He'd forgotten about that until just that moment and it was yet another bitter pill to swallow.

He wouldn't have Tessa. But he would still have his family's legacy to prove. His grandfather's brand to build. Until he succeeded at that, he couldn't allow himself to consider anything else in his life.

No, he wouldn't have Tessa. She wouldn't be in his bed anymore because he'd begun to feel things for her, and that he simply couldn't allow.

"You're quiet," Tessa said, voice low, but carrying over the murmured conversations filling the hotel restaurant.

It was a palatial room. Tiled floors, cream-colored walls with images of England dotting those walls. Tuxedoed waiters moved between the small round tables and more private booths. There was subtle music filling the air from a pianist in the center of the room. Lighting was muted, with candles flickering on every table and hidden lighting along the crown molding on the ceiling. It was a stunning place and the food was delicious, yet it might as well have been cardboard for all Noah had tasted it.

Losing Tessa from his bed *and* his office was too much, so Noah was going to take a chance. "I've been doing some thinking."

He turned in the booth to face her and his breath stopped. Tessa was beautiful every day. But in candlelight, she was stunning. Shadows danced on her skin and flames flickered in her eyes. Her hair was loose, across her shoulders bared by the narrow straps of a black dress that boasted a short skirt and a diving neckline that kept capturing his attention.

"So have I," she said. "I wonder if we're thinking the same thing."

"Let's find out." He took a sip of wine, set the glass down again and met Tessa's gaze. "I want you to stay on at your job."

Tessa laughed shortly, then took a sip of her own wine and shook her head. "Well, question answered. We're not thinking of the same thing."

He frowned and had to wonder what had been in her mind. But he only said, "That's not an answer."

"You already know the answer, Noah," she said, shaking her hair back from her face. "I can't stay."

"Yes, you can," he said and told her what he'd come up with during the long day they'd spent apart. Noah knew he'd have to be damn good at this since he'd insulted her earlier.

"We'll write up a contract. Have Legal draw it."

"For what?"

"To lay out your hours," he said, warming to his theme. "What's expected of you at the job. No more on call twenty-four/seven, Tessa."

"Noah…"

"Just hear me out." He rubbed one hand across the back of his neck and forced himself to say, "I'm sorry. About before. I don't even have an explanation for what I said so maybe you were right to a point. That I was sabotaging us, I mean."

"Thanks for the apology. Really. I know the word *sorry* doesn't really hop into your lexicon very often."

"Because I'm rarely wrong," he said and smiled, hoping to ease some of the tension simmering between them. "Tessa, this affair or whatever it is we're doing is coming to an end."

She stiffened. He saw it and didn't like it. "We both knew that going in," he added.

"We did."

"But you can keep your job," he insisted. "We're adults. We can handle working together and not sleeping together. You'll have shorter hours, weekends off. You can get that dog you want and you can still be a part of Graystone." He was talking faster now, because he could feel that he was losing her. "Damn it, Tessa, you're good at it. You know the company almost as well as I do.

"And look what you've accomplished here at the conference alone. You've lined up two distributors and already have Legal looking into them. You set up that meeting with Marcus for me. You're good at this. Beyond good. I need you at work, Tessa. Stay."

She was watching him and he wished to hell he could read what was in her mind. But at least he didn't have to wait long to find out.

"No."

He jerked his head back. Hell, he'd made a lot of accommodation in his offer. Short hours, weekends off. What more could he do? "Just no? That's it?"

"Yes." She took a sip of her wine and lifted her chin. "That's it. I'm not staying, Noah. I can't."

"Why the hell not?"

She looked at him and the candle flame flickering there danced and swayed. "Because I love you."

Noah jerked back in his seat. This he hadn't expected. At all. He'd prepared himself to counter whatever argument she would give him, but this one had never crossed his mind. "Love?"

"Wow," she said with a broken laugh. "Way to nail the deer-in-the-headlights-expression." Sighing a little, she added, "Relax, Noah. You don't owe me anything. You don't even have to say anything."

"I don't know what to say," he admitted. Hell, no one but his mother had ever said those words to him. But to be fair, he'd lived his life in a way to avoid any kind of entanglement that might end with that particular admission.

"You know what?" She took another sip of wine and set her glass down again. "We started all this because I wanted to kiss you at least once. Remember?"

"Yeah, I do." That first kiss was still seared into his memory.

"Well," she said, "I wanted to say *I love you* once, too. I don't need anything from you, Noah. I just wanted to tell you *why* I won't keep working for you. I love you and you'll never love me—" she shrugged "—so I can't stay. I can't keep working for you, knowing what we had for a week and will never have again."

"Tessa—" He had to say *something*. But everything that raced through his mind just wasn't right. Noah didn't want to hurt her, but he couldn't make her the kind of promises she wanted from him.

"Oh, stop it, Noah," she said on a huff.

Surprised again, he asked, "Stop what?"

"Scrambling for something to say that won't hurt poor little Tessa."

"I wasn't—" He broke off, unable to deny it. "Fine. I was."

"I know." Her mouth curved. "You're not the mystery you think you are, Noah."

He didn't know how to take that, either. All he knew for sure was that this dinner hadn't gone the way he'd wanted it to—and Tessa loved him.

"Look," she said and Noah stopped thinking and started listening. "You and I had a wonderful time this last week, and that's how I want to end this. We can part friends and just move on."

"So I just let you walk away."

"You can't stop me," she said and her smile dissolved as she shook her head. "And if you're honest with yourself, if not with me…that's exactly what you want to do."

Before Noah could answer, a man's voice cut into the conversation.

"Excuse me. I don't mean to interrupt."

Noah gritted his teeth and swiveled his head to look at Marcus Campbell. He hadn't heard the man approach and now he wondered how long he'd been standing there. "What is it, Marcus?"

The man grinned and looked from Noah to Tessa. "I just wanted to ask Tessa if she would join me for a drink. Say in about an hour? I've something I'd like to talk to you about."

"Uh," she said, glancing at Noah before saying, "sure, I guess. The hotel bar?"

"Grand," Marcus said. "See you then." He nodded. "Noah."

"Marcus," he ground out and watched the man walk away before turning to Tessa and blurting out, "He wants to offer you a job."

"Really?" Clearly amused, she smiled.

"I told him you wouldn't be interested," he admitted.

"Did you?" She tipped her head to one side and stared at him.

Astounded, he asked, "Was I wrong? You'll quit working for me, but you'll move to Glasgow and work for Campbell?" There was absolutely no way he'd be able to deal with that.

"I won't know that until I hear his offer, will I?"

"Seriously?" It was a challenge to keep his voice low enough that it wouldn't carry beyond their booth, because frustration had Noah by the throat and was currently squeezing. "I can't give you what you want and you leave the *country*?"

Tessa's eyebrows lifted high on her forehead. "Wow. Believe it or not, Noah, this isn't about *you*."

"Of course it is. We have an argument, I make an ass of myself and you go to work in *Glasgow*."

Abruptly, she held up both hands and said, "You know what? Let's not. One argument a day is really my limit."

"Tessa." He reached out, grabbed one of her hands and held on. "I am sorry. About earlier. About now. I wish it could be different."

She lifted one hand and cupped his cheek. "No you don't, Noah. Or you would *make* it different."

He looked into her eyes and knew it was over. Whatever they'd shared this last week and more was done. Maybe it was the stupid argument and everything he'd said when his insides were churning with too many unfamiliar emotions and thoughts. And maybe it was just time for it to end.

He felt a cold hand squeezing his heart and didn't want to think about why it was happening. Noah felt the warmth of her hand on his face and let the heat of her touch slide into him for what would probably be the last time.

What felt like a great black hole opened up inside him and Noah knew it would be with him for a long time.

Ten

"You could work for me in Glasgow," Marcus said later, giving Tessa a warm, tempting smile.

But she was immune to charm and temptation now. Tessa knew who she loved and she knew he didn't love her back. What did she care about a different man's charm?

She'd thrown herself and her heart into the affair with Noah on the theory that if she'd been with him, she could at last walk away with some sort of satisfaction. Instead, she was left feeling emptier and colder and more alone than ever. She'd lost. Her job. Her heart. Her time with Noah. And now, she just wanted to be home, working on her business, doing normal things until that normal finally spilled into her soul and began to heal her.

"I appreciate the offer, Marcus. Really." She shook her head slowly and added, "But I'm not looking for another job."

There were a lot of people in the bar for a late-night drink and the music streaming through the speakers added a layer of cheer that Tessa just wasn't feeling.

"If not a job, why not an adventure?" Marcus leaned toward her and his eyes were fixed on hers. "Move to Glasgow for a year. Work for me—you'll have time for the business Noah says is so important to you—"

"He did?" Well, at least he'd listened to something she'd said.

"We've the internet in Scotland, too, you know. You could be happy there, Tessa. And I'd best whatever salary you were making at Noah's company."

"It's not about the money, Marcus. Really." She stirred her martini with the swizzle stick and watched the liquid slide around the inside of the glass as if hypnotized.

"Ah," he said. "So it's like that, is it?"

"What?" She looked at him.

"You're in love with the man."

"Am I that obvious?"

"Maybe not to everyone." He slapped one hand to his heart and sighed heavily. "This is a great disappointment to me. It's shattered my plans completely."

Tessa had to smile. Marcus Campbell was a man who knew how attractive he was and played it up for whatever woman was handy. And right now, his undeniable charisma was directed solely at her, so she had to admit it was a formidable weapon. At any other point in her life, she would have been enjoying herself. Marcus was gorgeous, fun, and oh my, that accent. But as long as she was in love with Noah, no other man interested her.

"Sorry your plans took a hit," she said, smiling. "I do appreciate the offer, though."

He waved that off. "I'll recover." Then he stared into her eyes. "Will you?"

Tessa took a sip of her martini and it tasted like dust. "Eventually."

Sighing again, Marcus drained the last of his drink, set the glass down and said, "Earlier today I told Noah that he was a lucky man. Now I'm thinking a man so foolish as to let you go, doesn't deserve luck."

"Why didn't I fall in love with you, Marcus?" A sad smile curved her mouth.

He reached out and gave her hand a quick pat. "A mystery to me, as well."

Tessa laughed as he'd meant her to and she was grateful.

Wednesday night was the big award ceremony, but Tessa wasn't attending in the mood she'd thought she would be. She was there, with Noah, but they were so separate, it was heartbreaking. At least, it was to her.

Noah seemed unaffected, which was exactly what she'd expected from him. He was so determined to avoid any kind of entanglement, she was only surprised he hadn't put her on the private jet to fly her home the moment she'd confessed that she loved him. As it was, she'd moved her things into the second bedroom of their suite and even the much smaller bed felt the size of a football field without him lying next to her. She hadn't slept much, so she was on edge and trying not to show it.

Tessa had worked alongside Noah for a long time, and this award ceremony had always been the carrot at the end of the stick. If the varietal vodka won tonight, Noah would have reached his first goal for honoring his grandfather.

She wondered if that award would be enough for him. Would he relax a bit, enjoy the win and start to wake up to life around him? Or, more likely, it would only focus him further in the race to capture *every* vodka award. To make the name Graystone interchangeable with the word *vodka*.

She glanced at him, sitting beside her in the crowded ballroom. There was dessert and champagne being served by silent, efficient waiters. A formal affair, the men in the crowd wore tuxedos and the women were dressed spectacularly in long, gorgeous gowns, with their necks and arms draped in priceless jewels.

Tessa's own dress, a deep scarlet, was strapless, clinging to her upper body and then sliding down the rest of her body in a bell shape. Her necklace had been made by Lynn, with faux rubies and diamonds, and the matching earrings completed the set.

Noah hadn't been able to hide the admiration in his gaze when she'd joined him in the suite, but since arriving at the awards, he'd hardly looked at her. Pain poked at her, but she ignored it. *Get used to it, Tessa. The fun and games are over and now it's back to grim reality.*

Except, her reality wasn't grim at all. And now she'd have the time to enjoy her life. Grow her business. Visit with her friends. And, in every other waking moment, miss Noah so much she would ache with it.

She took a breath, blew it out and reached for her flute of champagne. After a quick swallow, she felt she could speak and used her chance to say quietly, "Good luck, Noah."

He looked at her, so sternly handsome, her heart twisted. For one brief moment, his eyes warmed and she wished that moment would last forever. But then it was gone and he said only, "Thank you, Tessa. And whatever happens tonight, thank you for all your hard work in the past."

She nodded, because what could she say to that? Tessa felt as if he'd just handed her a gold watch and waved her off into retirement. There was no connection between them at all anymore. He'd sealed it off and she had to wonder again how he was capable of doing it so cleanly.

She'd seen him shut out other women over the years, but she'd never realized just how painful it could be.

For the next hour, they applauded politely for the winners and drank from the constantly refilled champagne glasses. But finally, the varietal vodka awards were announced. Tessa sensed Noah's tension and she shared it. No matter what had happened between them, she hoped Graystone Vodka won because Noah had worked so hard and for so long to reach this goal. As the master of ceremonies read off the finalists, Tessa reached out and laid her hand over Noah's. He instantly turned his hand over and closed his fingers over hers.

"The varietal vodka award goes to... Graystone Vodka for their Blackberry and Lime infusion."

Noah squeezed her hand hard, then released her and stood up to move through the room, accepting congratulations along the way. When he reached the stage, Tessa applauded with the crowd and watched as he accepted the gold medallion that he'd devoted most of his life to claiming. When he left the stage, people rushed to congratulate him and Tessa watched from afar as he accepted accolades from his peers.

I'm happy for him. Really happy. Then Anna Morgan rushed up to Noah and threw her arms around his neck. Tessa waited for Noah to break away, but instead, he threw himself into the moment, wrapped his arms around Anna and swung her in a circle while she laughed and his friends erupted into more cheers.

Tessa couldn't watch anymore. She grabbed her purse and headed out of the crowded room. The noise was deafening and she felt as if she were drowning in it all. Despite the heat of the room, she felt cold right down to her bones. For one brief moment when Noah had squeezed her hand, she'd felt that they were still a team. That they were in this together. But then he was gone and so was the moment.

Tessa didn't belong there anymore.

When Noah finally made it back to their table, Tessa was gone. He looked for her, but came up empty. After an hour spent accepting congratulations and looking for Tessa in the crowd, he at last took the elevator to their suite. But she wasn't there, either. Her room was empty. Suitcase gone. She'd left. Without a word.

"Why the hell would she leave?" he muttered, looking around fruitlessly for some kind of note. But there was nothing. It was as if she'd never been there at all.

"Fine then," he said aloud to the room, "no goodbye it is."

Noah stood in the shadows, his tuxedo jacket tossed across the nearest chair. He held on to the medallion he'd worked so hard to win and felt the heavy, cold metal bite into his skin. He looked down at it and the glint of gold winked up at him. This was the culmination of years. The settling of a debt he owed to the grandfather he loved.

He should be happy, damn it.

"Congratulations, Noah," he muttered. "You won."

"For the love of God," Stephanie said, two weeks later, letting her head drop to her desk top. "Go see Tessa. Talk to her. Please stop talking to *me*."

Noah stopped pacing in his sister's office and glared at her, even though she couldn't see it. "Tessa has nothing to do with this," he grumbled. "It's my new assistant. She keeps crying when she talks to me."

"I know the feeling," Stephanie muttered and lifted her head. "She's new, Noah. It's going to take her some time to get the hang of the job."

"She shouldn't even be here. It should be Tessa at that desk."

Tessa should be in his bed. In his arms.

"Well, Tessa's not. She quit and you let her go."

"This is *my* fault?" he countered.

"Of course it is." Stephanie took a breath and sighed it out. "She loves you, you love her and you were too cowardly to do anything about it."

That stopped him dead as he fired his sister a look that should have terrified her. But didn't. "Cowardly?"

"What would you call it?" Stephanie stood up. "You have that award you've been talking about for years. You have a woman who loves you enough to put up with you, which is damn near heroic if ask me..." He opened his mouth, but she held up one hand to keep him quiet because clearly she wasn't finished. "And you let her go, rather than admit that some things are more important than a promise you made when you were fourteen years old."

That slapped at him. Noah had vowed to his grandfather that he would restore the Graystone name. And he'd finally gotten to the point where he could make good on that promise. So he was supposed to stop? "So I just forget about Papa and what I owe him? What we owe him?"

"Nobody's saying that. You can have both, you know," Stephanie said. "You can succeed in business *and* love someone."

He shook his head. He'd done nothing but think about this since he returned from England and his mind kept going in circles. He hated being in his own damn home now because it was gigantic and empty and the silence seemed to mock him every time he entered. All he could think about was that cottage in Laguna where Tessa was, with light and warmth and... Tessa. Angrily, he shoved both hands through his hair and said, "You don't get it, Steph."

"Of course I get it, you idiot," she said and affection colored her tone in spite of her words. "We were raised by the same people. In the same house. Who else *could* get it?"

"Fine. Then you understand. I can't have Tessa and keep the vow I made to Papa."

"Okay," she said patiently, "let's try a new tactic. Who built this business?"

"Papa, of course."

"And was he a bachelor?"

"Are you delirious? No." He didn't know where she was going with this, but if she was trying to calm him down, she was doing a poor job of it.

"Exactly." Stephanie came around her desk, then sat on the edge of it to talk to him. "He was married to Nana for fifty-eight years until she died."

"What's your point?"

"Seriously? My point is, he had a full life *and* he built this company," she snapped. "He managed to love his wife and his idiot son and all of his grandchildren and *still* build a successful company. You think Papa would love knowing that you're sacrificing everything to keep a vow you made as a hurting kid?"

Was she right? Was he being an ass about all of this, refusing to take a risk on love and using the vow to his grandfather as an excuse?

Tension was still coiled inside him like a snake, ready to strike at his heart. His soul. Yet, as he stared at his sister, Noah felt as though something else was opening up inside him. Not enough to push aside the anger, the frustration and the damn ache that losing Tessa had caused him.

But enough to toss a little light into the shadows within.

"You talked to Stephanie again, didn't you?"

Tessa stopped wrapping the jasmine soaps and looked up at Lynn. "How can you tell?"

"Because you're a tiny bit happy. You've got this little satisfied smile on your face," Lynn said. "Being a gifted detective, this tells me Noah's sister has been telling you that the man is still miserable."

Really, Tessa thought, she had to work on her poker face. She was far too easy to read. And Lynn was right. Tessa had talked to Stephanie a few times since she'd been back from England. Which was how she knew that Noah was crabby and arguing with everyone.

She shouldn't be happy about that, but she was. Did that make her petty? If so, she could live with that.

"But that's the thing," she said as if she'd said all of that aloud, "he should be happy. He won the award. That's been his goal for years."

"Maybe he figured out that it's not as important as he once thought it was," Lynn said.

Tessa thought about that for a moment, then shook her head. "No. That was always Noah's driving force."

"Well, maybe losing you and winning the award on the same night took some of the shine off it. Besides, things change." Lynn waved a hand at the table, the island they were standing next to and the kitchen counter. Labeled boxes were stacked everywhere but the island where the two of them were still packing. "Look at you. Two weeks of having the time to work on the business and it's already taking off."

"Well, the internet ads haven't hurt, either," Tessa said. "But okay, you're right. I can see that. And it's been great. Being home. Working with you." She took a deep breath and let it out again. "Look at us. A week before Christmas and we're sending out maybe three times the product we did last year."

Then she went quiet and let her mind fill, as it had so often lately, with images of Noah, and their time together. It should make her smile, but it didn't because it was all over. And that was crazy, too, because she should be happy. She was working for herself. Now that she had the time, her business was growing. And she wasn't on call for Noah every minute of the day, and that, she thought, was why she wasn't happy.

She missed him. Tessa sighed. She would always miss him.

"You're doing it again."

Tessa looked over at Lynn. "What am I doing?"

"Sighing." Shaking her head, her friend said, "You have that sad smile on your face and your eyes went all soft."

"Well, don't I sound gorgeous?" Tessa muttered and cut off another ten inches of ribbon, this time yellow, to go with the jasmine soaps.

"Always," Lynn said with a smile. "So where were you?"

"At Stonehenge." Tessa shrugged. "It was great that day. Pounding rain, icy wind—"

"Yeah, sounds wonderful," Lynn said with a short laugh.

"I guess you had to be there." That day was only one of the memories that played over and over in her mind. Tessa tied the bow and moved on to the next order. Stacking three bars of yellow-and-white hand-cut soaps, she slipped the ribbon beneath them and tied the stack together.

This was what Tessa had wanted. But it wasn't turning out as she had hoped. Oh, she was making more sales and that was good, but there wasn't the joy she used to feel when she was working at home. Probably because she couldn't stop thinking about Noah.

"Have you heard anything from him?" Lynn's voice was soft, almost tentative.

"It's okay," Tessa said, "you can say his name. And no, haven't heard a word from Noah. But then, I didn't expect to."

"Really?" Lynn set the wrapped jewelry box aside and leaned against the kitchen island. "But from everything you told us, it seems to me that he was having as good a time as you were."

"He did." Tessa smiled at her friend. "Which is exactly why he's not talking to me now."

"That makes zero sense."

"Welcome to the world of Noah." Tessa smiled ruefully. He wouldn't spend any time exploring memories as she was. For Noah, when something was over, he was finished with it. Sad as it was to admit, he probably hadn't given her a second thought since they'd been home.

Suddenly tired of her own thoughts, Tessa set the last of the wrapped soaps aside, and asked, "Coffee?"

"Sure."

Tessa always had a fresh pot of coffee going, so she poured two cups, handed one to Lynn, then said, "Let's sit for a minute. I have some cookies my wonderful neighbor made me."

Lynn laughed. "Ah, my chocolate chips. They're all gone at my house. Carol says it's all Evan, but she gets up in the middle of the night to snack and thinks I don't know."

Tessa laughed and set the cookies in the center of the table. "Well, then, I'm glad I saved some for you."

"Me, too." Lynn took a bite then waved her cookie. "So tell me about the weird world of Noah."

"Not really weird," she allowed. "It all makes perfect sense to him."

"Okay…"

Tessa told Lynn about Noah and his father and grandfather and how he'd been working for years to make his late grandfather proud. "That's been the one thing driving him for most of his life. And now that he's won the varietal vodka award, there'll be no stopping him. He'll want to win for each of the other vodkas, as well."

"Sounds like obsession rather than devotion to duty," Lynn mused.

"It's not, really. He's just über-focused," Tessa said, wondering why she was still defending the man. She remembered sitting next to him on award night, feeling the tension radiating from him. That prize had meant everything to him and when he'd won, he'd been so proud.

And then he'd hugged Anna Morgan and— She broke that memory off fast. "Anyway, for him, he can't bring himself to make promises to a woman if he feels he can't keep them because of what he owes to the company. And his grandfather."

"Wow. You're being really reasonable here, Tessa. Almost unbearably so."

"I'm trying." Wryly, she smiled and added, "It's taken me a long time to get to this place and I'm really trying to stay there. Lynn, it doesn't do me any good at all to stay angry at Noah.

"What would be the point? He's already gone from my life, so staying furious only hurts me, not him."

"Again. So mature." Lynn studied her. "If it were me, I'd be throwing things and putting a curse on Carol. Your stability is starting to feel a little creepy."

"Would it make you feel better if I told you I have a Noah doll that I stick pins in occasionally?"

"Sadly yes," she admitted. "It would."

"Fine," Tessa said on a laugh. "I'll get one."

"Sure. So, a new subject."

"Thank you," Tessa said. It was bad enough that her thoughts and dreams were filled with Noah. She didn't want to keep talking about him, too. It just hurt too much.

"Have you decided to adopt Hugo?"

"I did…" She sipped at her coffee, then reached for a cookie. "He was perfect. A black Lab mix, two years old and I loved that little face. You remember, I showed you Hugo's picture."

"He is cute."

"Anyway, I finally decided to adopt him and I called them this morning. But someone else had adopted him already."

"Really?" Lynn shook her head and took a drink of coffee. "I'm sorry about that. But the right dog will find you."

She laughed a little. "We'll see. I am going to spread out, though. Try a shelter in Long Beach next week."

"Uh-huh." Lynn took a bite of the cookie. "So you're just fine and happy and moving on with your life."

"Absolutely." Tessa lifted her chin, plastered a brave, bright smile on her face and nodded.

"And," Lynn said, "you're lying."

Her shoulders slumped, her smile faded and she muttered, "Absolutely."

She couldn't move on until she got over Noah, and that, Tessa told herself sadly, was just never going to happen.

Two days later, Tessa was alone in the house when pounding erupted at her front door. After she jolted and clutched at her chest, she peeked out the front window and saw Noah's car parked outside the house.

Heartbeat suddenly pounding louder than his demanding knock, Tessa hurried to the door and threw it open. She stared up into his dark blue eyes blazing with heat and asked, "What are you doing here, Noah?"

"I'm done, Tessa. That's it. I've had it."

"What're you talking about?" He looked as handsome as ever in a pair of black jeans, boots and a dark green long-sleeved shirt. His hair was tousled as if he'd been stabbing his fingers through it and his jaw was tight, muscles flexing as if he were gritting his teeth.

It threw her off for a moment because she was so used to seeing him calm, cool, in control and wearing one of the suits that looked so amazing on him.

"I'm talking about *you*," he said, then paced to the edge of the porch and back again. "It's been two weeks and I'm still pissed. We won that damn award in England and you didn't even stick around to celebrate."

"That's what this visit is about?" She frowned at the memory of him swinging Anna Morgan around in circles in front of everyone. "It looked as though you and Anna were doing a good job of it without me."

He gaped at her, clearly stunned. "*That's* why you left? Hell, I only held on to the woman for a damn minute because at first I thought she was *you*, rushing up to share in the prize."

"Me? Come on." She didn't believe that for a second.

"If you'd stuck around," he told her, "you'd have seen me drop her like a rock and go looking for you."

Tessa was staggered by that and for the first time ever, didn't know what to say. Had she read the situation all wrong? Had she been so wrapped up in her own pain that she'd missed seeing the truth? But she stopped thinking and started listening because Noah wasn't finished yet.

"Then I got up to our suite and you were gone. Just... poof." He scrubbed one hand against the back of his neck. "Not even a damn note, Tessa. I had to find out from the concierge that you'd left for the airport."

"I almost left one," she said, but she'd convinced herself there was nothing left to say. Now she felt terrible.

"Almost doesn't count. But that's not why I'm here anyway, damn it." He frowned at her and blew out another sigh of frustration.

"Why don't we go inside and you can tell me. We don't have to stand on the porch."

"I'm not going anywhere until I say what I came to say," he ground out. And he didn't look happy about it.

"Fine," she said, crossing her arms over her chest in a clearly defensive posture. "Say it."

"The thing is, I'm here because I have a crappy new assistant who can't do the job without crying."

"Why do I care about that?" Okay, she did care, but she didn't want him to know it.

"Because it's your fault." He threw both hands up in the air helplessly. "She cries if I look at her. Cries if she can't get the printer to work. I swear, the whole office is going to be under water if this keeps up."

Tessa swallowed her smile, but not fast enough.

"Sure," he said, nodding. "You can laugh. You're not dealing with the mess you left behind when you resigned."

"You can't be blaming me," she argued.

"No, I'm blaming *me*." He took a breath and said, "Nothing's been right since you left, Tessa."

She liked hearing that. It made her heart a little less achy to know he missed her, but still. "I don't want my old job back, Noah."

"I'm not offering you your old job," he said, and grabbed her elbows.

From somewhere down the street, Christmas carols played softly and the cold wind off the ocean slid down the narrow road, rattling naked tree limbs.

"What's this about?" she asked, looking up into his eyes.

"I want you to come back to work," he said. "And I want you to marry me."

"What?" She pulled out of his grasp and shook her head. She couldn't believe this. Thinking back to all of the bribes he'd tried to use to get her to stay with the company, she felt her temper soar. "Noah, this is ridiculous and maybe the worst thing you've ever done. You offered to remodel my house and buy me a car and give me a raise to stay and keep working for you. But offering *marriage* as a job perk is really going too far."

"What? No." He scrubbed both hands over his face. "This is coming out all wrong. That's your fault, too."

"How?"

"Because you seriously messed me up when you left. I can't even think anymore!" Scowling furiously, he continued, "Marrying me isn't a perk, Tessa. Hell, it's practically a *sentence*. I'm not an easy person."

"True."

His frown deepened at her instant agreement. "And marriage to me will probably be hard," he added, "but I don't care, and you shouldn't either since you already admitted that you love me."

"I did, but—"

"Yeah, well, what you don't know is that I love you, too."

Tessa's knees buckled a little. She couldn't believe she was standing on her front porch, hearing the man she loved tell her he felt the same way.

"That's right. I love you. I need you," he added, "and damn it, I will have you."

Tessa had to laugh. He looked so frustrated and so... good. "You're such a romantic. I had no idea."

"You want romance? I can do romance. I brought you flowers, but I left them in the damn car and now they're probably gone."

"What?"

"Never mind. Marry me, Tessa." He reached out for her again, dropping his hands on her shoulders until the heat of his touch seeped down and into her bones, chasing away the chill she'd been living with since she left England.

"Look, I like that you've got your own business," he said. "I'll help whenever I can, but I won't tie bows anymore because mine always look like crap—"

"Agreed," she said, laughing.

"I can do romance, Tessa." His voice dropped until it was a low rumble against her heart. "I love you. I want you back working with me. Living with me. Loving me."

Tessa hardly knew what to say. He was offering her everything and all she could do was stare into those eyes of his. He wasn't hiding anything from her now. She read what he was feeling on his face. He loved her. He really did. "What about your vow to your grandfather?"

His features tightened. "I'll still make that come true. But it finally dawned on me that it was you and I together who won that award. We're a team, Tessa. One too good to break up. Together, we'll make Graystone the only vodka worth drinking."

Her heart was melting. She could feel it going soft

and gooey in her chest and it was the best feeling ever. "Oh, Noah…"

"Just say yes. Damn it, Tessa, I love you! And you love me!"

Tessa smiled and said, "I'll still want to keep my own business…"

"Of course," he said, eager to please. "I'll help any way I can, like I said."

"I'll come back to the office, but only part-time."

"That works for me," he said. "I'll transfer Crying Girl to Stephanie's office."

"That's just mean."

"Tessa," he said, leaning down to rest his forehead against hers. "Marry me."

"You'll have to go to Wyoming with me to meet my family."

"Wouldn't miss it," he said and his mouth began to curve into that satisfied smile she loved so much.

"And I'll want kids."

"As many as you want," he agreed, lifting his head to nod as he looked at the house and yard before turning back to meet her gaze. "But not in my house. I think we should live here. In your castle."

"Really?" Her heart finished melting and sent rivers of warmth coursing through her bloodstream. She could marry Noah and stay in her castle and have children and love and everything she'd ever dreamed of. This was really the best day of her life. "You want to live here?"

"Yeah, I really like it, though we might have to add on at some point. And, he'll need a fenced yard—"

"What? He who?"

"In a minute." Noah dug into his pocket and came up

with a pale blue box. He opened it up and showed her a sapphire-and-diamond ring. "Will you marry me, Tessa?"

Tessa's breath caught in her chest and she lifted one hand to her trembling mouth. It was happening. Her dreams were falling at her feet and all she had to do was pick them up and hold them close. She had to trust that Noah loved her and meant the promise he was making and it was so easy to do.

"Yes, Noah. I will marry you."

He grinned and slid the ring onto her finger, then sealed it with a kiss. "I do love you," he said. "Maybe I always have."

"Just so long as you always will," she said, reaching up to cup his cheek.

"Always," he whispered and leaned in for a kiss.

That kiss ended a few seconds later, when loud, insistent barking erupted out of nowhere. Tessa looked toward his car. "What's going on?"

"Hold on—I'll be right back. He's probably eating the back seat."

Tessa watched him run to the car, open the back door and reach inside. When he stood up again, he was holding a bedraggled bouquet of flowers in one arm and a squirming black dog in the other.

"Oh, my..." Rushing off the porch, she reached Noah in seconds, then scooped the dog out of his arms. About twenty pounds of love wriggling against her. "I don't believe this. It's Hugo. The dog I wanted to adopt from the shelter."

The Lab licked her cheeks, her eyes and anywhere he could reach as he wiggled with joy. Tessa laughed in delight and looked up at Noah. "How do you have him? You're the one who adopted him?"

"Yeah." He looked at what had once been an expensive bouquet, then scowled at the dog. "I've been talking to Lynn a bit—"

"You have?" Oh, her neighbor was sneakier than Tessa would have believed.

"Yes. And she told me you wanted Hugo, so I went and got him as a surprise—and kind of a bonus for if you said yes. We'll have to watch him every second, though." He frowned at the dog. "He ate my couch at my place. Hell, he eats *everything*." He stared at the bouquet that was now mostly stems. "Including roses, apparently."

She laughed and snuggled the dog. "We'll train him. Noah, I can't believe you did all of this."

Tessa wrapped one arm around Noah's waist and held on to Hugo with the other. She tipped her head back to stare up at him and basked in the warmth of his smile. "I've loved you for so long. I can't believe this is really happening."

"Believe it."

"All because I wanted to kiss you at least once."

He grinned and kissed her again. "We wasted five years, Tessa. You should have seduced me sooner."

* * * * *

SO RIGHT…WITH
MR WRONG

ANNA DEPALO

For Antonella, Alessandra & Valentina
cugine di sangue e del cuore

One

When she finally spotted the guy she'd been looking for, Mia knew there was only one thing to do—especially when she had less than two weeks to find a date before the Ruby Ball, an all-important fashion industry event, and her would-be escort had just married someone else.

She stepped from the alcove where she'd been lurking. The rooms on the top floor of the Brooklyn brownstone were dimly lit and otherwise deserted—all the other costumed partygoers were downstairs or in other rooms, mingling and laughing with the Halloween-obsessed hostess whose birthday it was. It was a cool spring evening, but the air on this uppermost level felt warm.

The man turned toward her and pocketed the cell phone he was holding.

Though a dark mask covered the upper half of his face, the height and build were right.

Sam. He'd given her only few hints about what he would be wearing.

"Look for me in a plain costume," he'd said with a quick grin. "I'm not one for lots of glitter."

She'd spotted him in the throng downstairs and had made her way across the crowded parlor floor when she'd seen him ascend the stairs. By the time she'd caught up with him on the sparsely furnished top floor, he'd had his back to her and had been speaking in a low voice into his cell phone—business call, no doubt. So she'd lurked beyond an open archway in an empty adjacent room, pretending as if she hadn't been stalking him. Waiting for him to come into sight again once he finished his call.

Mia pulled up the shoulder of her dress, which had a bad habit of slipping off. Unlike Sam's, her costume was anything but understated. The black-and-red concoction was all ruffles, with the skirt cut high in front—showing off her fishnet-clad legs—before dipping low in the back.

She and Sam had flirted at a couple of parties, and he'd brushed her lips with his when they'd last seen each other. It was all the encouragement that she'd required. She needed a new boyfriend *fast*—or at least someone who could pass as one.

The Ruby Ball wasn't only an *it* fashion event, it was also one where everyone came as a couple—the better to burnish their images and brands. Unfortunately, in a fit of bravado at the most recent Fashion Design Newcomers meeting, she'd let it be known that she *was* showing up with an escort—even if it wasn't her erstwhile boyfriend, since Carl was now very much married.

She had to pull this off. She *would* pull this off. As long as she had the guts. Time to accelerate her acquaintance with Sam...

He looked up in surprise as she stepped toward him. His dark eyes were shadowed in the low light cast by a table lamp.

With a sudden shot of nerve and adrenaline, she used gentle pressure to bring his head down and pressed her lips to his in greeting, taking up where they'd left off.

He stilled. But after a moment's pause, his hands settled on her waist, and he brought her more fully against him. His mouth moved over hers, caressing her lips and then settling deeper. His tongue touched hers, played with her.

She linked her arms around his neck, giving herself up to the encounter. This guy knew how to kiss—he put everything into it—and as she started to pull away, he followed, stroking her parted lips, coaxing a further response.

She made an involuntary sound in her throat and let him deepen the kiss.

His scent was deliciously warm and clean, and in counterpoint to the hard and lean body that now pressed against her, fitting to her curves and enveloping her.

Her heart thumped in time to the rhythm of the music reverberating through the house.

OMG. This was not what she'd been expecting. The last time they'd brushed lips, she'd gotten no clue about the smoldering heat that Sam could bring out in her. Maybe her plan wasn't so crazy after all…

When they finally broke apart, she sighed. *Wow.*

"Hi, Sam," she whispered.

"Who's Sam?"

She froze.

The voice was definitely *not* Sam.

Her eyes widened, his narrowed.

Then he lifted his mask, and Mia sucked in a breath.

Damian Musil.

She slammed the door on her inner wail and pushed away from him as if she'd been burned.

Why? Why did it have to be him of all people?

After years of sidestepping the enemy, she'd fallen into his arms—or thrown herself there. She winced inwardly.

There was no hint of surprise in his expression. "Do you always kiss masked men in dark rooms?"

"Don't be absurd," she snapped, covering her mortification. "Obviously it's a case of mistaken identity, and you know it."

"Who's Sam?" Damian asked again, his shadowed eyes betraying nothing.

"None of your business."

"I disagree, since minutes ago we were locking lips."

She took a deep breath, which served only to push her breasts up and draw his attention—*damn him*.

"Oh, right," she said sarcastically, "I forget that you like to warn away the guys I date."

"That's one way of looking at it," Damian responded.

Her temper sparked. Carl's small and quick wedding had had few guests, but since Damian had once been Carl's boss, he had been one of them. He'd supported her boyfriend's decision to break up with her for a kindergarten teacher he'd had a kismet moment with on a plane ride.

Sure, she and Carl hadn't been serious. After meeting at a party, they'd dated for three or four months. But his dumping her and immediately marrying someone else had still stung. Especially when she'd discovered through friends that Damian had encouraged the whole thing.

She wanted to stamp her foot and rail at the fates, which had left her not only boyfriend-less on the eve of one of her life's key moments, but now had her locking lips with the man responsible for her plight. How much humiliation could one woman take? And how could she ever have thought of Damian as attractive, even in passing, back in her teenage days?

He was several inches taller than her own five-foot-seven and built like a lightweight boxer. With a square jaw, dark hair and brown eyes blazing intelligence, she figured some women would say he packed a double or triple threat.

But she knew that he could be calculating and ruthless. Just like what she'd always been advised to expect from a Musil...

She raised her chin. "One way of looking at it? I suppose the other is that you were opening another front in the war between the Serenghettis and the Musils?"

He had the temerity to look amused. "Is that what you think?"

The Musils were her family's business nemesis, ever since her father, Serg Serenghetti, had suspected Damian's family of underhanded tactics to make it in the construction business and undercut competitors in western Massachusetts—namely, Serenghetti Construction. The bad blood had gone on for years.

Because Welsdale wasn't a big place, she knew Damian's real name was Demyan but that he went with the English instead of Ukrainian version. And once upon a time she'd even looked up its meaning: *tamer.* But she vowed that he wouldn't be taming anyone, especially a Serenghetti. Her family loyalties ran deep—even if she was known as the wild child.

In the years since high school, she'd moved to New York City to work in fashion and start her own label. And Damian had become a billionaire app developer with his startup company. She wondered darkly whether he'd succeeded in his chosen field only with the dodgy business tactics for which his family was known.

Musil. She remembered Damian correcting everyone back in high school. *It doesn't rhyme with mussel, it's Musil like Mew-seal.* Nowadays, there was no need to correct anyone's pronunciation. Everyone knew his name.

Mia straightened. It was time to end this meeting, instead of standing close together in the dark—as if this was some kind of clandestine romantic encounter.

"I need to go. I'm on my way to—"

"Look for an escort to the Ruby Ball. Right."

Mia's eyes widened. *He knew?* Things had suddenly gone from bad to worse.

Damian shrugged. "I overheard Nadia and Teresa talking earlier."

Mia muttered something under her breath.

"What are friends for, right?" He could still pick up her scent, feel the imprint of her curves, taste her on his lips…

"I'm not going to discuss this with you." She swung away. "In fact, this conversation is over."

"Which one?" he drawled. "The one about you kissing me? Or the fact that you're here to find someone other than Carl to accompany you to a career-making social event?"

She gave him the side-eye—looking for all intents like a woman who'd discovered a bug in her morning coffee.

"And they say the Musils are calculating."

She narrowed her eyes. "You are."

"Don't forget *dastardly* and *underhanded*."

"Those weren't the words I was thinking of," she remarked with a saccharine smile, "but thanks for supplying some nicer substitutes."

He cut off a laugh.

She swept him with a cool look. "Great costume. The masked villain is so appropriate."

"It's a Robin Hood costume." The character had been an easy and fast online pick.

"And considering that you're the reason why I need a substitute date," she went on, ignoring him, "I expect you to laugh diabolically at your victory."

He lifted the side of his mouth to get a rise out of her. "Or offer a lending hand because you're low on options. I'll check my calendar but a week from Saturday should be clear."

Mia parted her lips in a huff. "Not if you're—"

"—the last man on Earth. I know."

She threw up her hands. "Obviously you can't take a hint."

"Your signals have been more than a hint." He remembered her mouth under his. Soft, hot, sweet. She'd put real feeling into it—before she'd known who he was. And from what he'd been able to observe when they'd been around mutual friends and acquaintances over the years—first in Welsdale and now in New York City—Mia dove into everything with heart and soul.

Holy hell, after years of crossing paths with aloof and wary steps through a shared hometown and overlapping New York social circles, he'd finally settled any speculation about what it would be like to kiss Mia Serenghetti... and he hadn't let the opportunity pass him by. He hadn't even had time to think about why she'd suddenly come on to him. His jaw ticked at the thought of the unknown Sam, and he damned the other man to eternal oblivion.

Because right now Mia was a fantasy come to life dressed in a costume that a Las Vegas show girl might have worn. The outfit set off her shapely legs, long rich mahogany locks and almond-shaped moss-green eyes thickly fringed beneath sculpted brows.

His body tightened. The floor reverberated with music and laughter from below, but up here they were alone... If they were dating, he'd buy her the most outrageous sinful stockings. Lacy, black and sexy. And then he'd taste her full, cherry-painted mouth again while she wrapped her legs around him...

Wisely, though, he kept mum about all of it. "Listen, I had nothing to do with Carl marrying another woman."

"What?" She sucked in an outraged breath, which lifted her breasts. "I suppose supporting his breakup with me so he could hook up with someone else constitutes *nothing* in your book."

"It was what Carl wanted to do."

"But you gave him the encouragement he needed. You held the match to the powder keg."

Damian rubbed his chin. "That's a colorful analogy."

She raised her eyebrows. "It's accurate. You even offered him a private plane so he could get to Martha's Vineyard for his honeymoon."

He'd wondered what Mia had heard about his interactions with Carl—and what her reaction was. Now he knew. "You've got an outsized view of my influence."

"I'd say a plane qualifies as big," she snapped.

"Carl is happy."

"Because of you."

"Maybe," he admitted.

"And we'll never know whether he'd have gone for it without your help."

"I told him to follow his gut."

"Yes, and apparently that meant breaking up with me. Did it give you perverse satisfaction that a Serenghetti was going to take a hit in the process?"

"I've got nothing to do with JM Construction these days. That's my father and brother's gig."

She snorted. True, the family-owned construction company must be small fry to him these days, but she wasn't fooled for a minute. "Right, you're the tech founder with major bank…so I wonder why you'd care what a Serenghetti is doing or isn't."

"You're insisting this is about some ridiculous Serenghetti-Musil family feud."

"Isn't it?"

In his opinion, Mia and Carl hadn't been a good match. Mia was a take-charge type. A dynamo. Carl was a laid-back guy who strummed his guitar and was happy as a supporting player in one tech company after another. Hell, Damian had even employed the guy for a while and then had recommended him for an opportunity at another company.

But Carl had been in existential angst about switching girlfriends. So when the guy had asked his opinion over a couple of beers, Damian had given it.

"You're upset because the breakup with Carl happened right before a big event," he said calmly.

"No, I'm upset because your meddling caused the breakup with Carl to happen right before a big event."

"A situation I've offered to rectify for you."

She clenched her hands and then released them. "So you're the good guy? Un-believ-able."

He pointed to his costume. "Call it my hero complex."

Mia blew a breath, causing tendrils of hair to lift and resettle.

"If you're Robin Hood, what does that make me? Maid Marion?" she asked frostily.

Knowing it would provoke her, he scanned her ruffled costume, which revealed both leg and cleavage. "You don't look the part."

"Exactly."

"Too much fiery temper."

She frowned, annoyance stamping her face, before she smoothed her brow. "I agree, and that's why your offer would never work. I've got outfits in mind for the Ruby

Ball, and, let me tell you, nothing about them says they're right out of Sherwood Forest."

"Let me guess. Instead you're the femme fatale and your escort is—"

"Not you."

Under Damian's bemused gaze, she whirled away and stomped off.

But whether Mia liked it or not, their kiss couldn't so easily be left behind...

Two

He was the most infuriating man she'd ever met, and that was saying something considering she had three older brothers.

Mia pushed hair out of her face and looked around her cramped design studio, where her cousin Gia—who'd dropped by because she'd come to the city for a business meeting—was perched on a stool and responding to a text.

She'd tried to make a frank point to Damian about his help to Carl and their sparring families, and instead *he'd* reduced *her* to noting that Robin Hood didn't apply to their situation…

She caught herself touching her fingers to her lips *again*—the memory of their kiss was hard to erase—and yanked her hand back down. This whole situation was making her crazy…and desperate.

Gia tucked her phone away and regarded her levelly, picking up their conversation where they'd left off. "Are you out of your mind?"

Mia acknowledged there was no good answer, and that her chaotic surroundings hardly vouched for her sanity. Bolts of fabric were propped against the wall, a sewing machine was jammed into one corner, along with an ironing board, and there was hardly a place to sit. The buttons that she'd recently bought sat in a box nearby, and she knew she'd have to make another trip to Mood Fabrics. On the other hand, she was lucky. Many newbie designers worked right out of their apartments. At least she'd been able to rent a studio a couple of floors below her own one-bedroom walk-up in the Garment District.

"I know that asking Sam to reschedule his business trip to Singapore is a Hail Mary pass—"

"The Serenghettis play hockey, not football," Gia interjected, her hazel gaze doubtful.

Mia hadn't even confided in Nadia and Teresa at the party after her encounter with Damian. Now her fashion school friends were half a world away, having flown out for a cruise of the Mediterranean before they headed back to jobs at different clothing labels in Milan. And she was here, finally rehashing the experience with her cousin…

"I haven't misplaced my brain, if that's what you're thinking," Mia continued. "And for the record, it's my brothers who play hockey, not me. Jordan might still be in the NHL, but Cole stopped. And Rick never played. He was a wrestler in high school."

"Still, no football in the genes," her cousin said, shifting on her seat. "Face it, you haven't got the aim to complete a pass with low odds of success."

As if on cue, Mia's phone vibrated, and she snatched it off the table. She processed Sam's text, and her shoulders slumped. "Well, it was worth a shot."

With an *I told you so* expression, Gia folded her arms.

Mia sighed. Sam had eventually shown up at the brownstone party on Saturday, but before she could bring up the Ruby Ball, he'd announced that he'd be out of the country for two weeks. "Sam can't reschedule his business trip. Apparently, the timing is right for him to meet up with some of his former fraternity brothers in Japan."

"And you can't afford a guy who is into a boys' trip like *The Hangover*," Gia pointed out. "You already have a hangover."

"I don't have a hangover. I have a headache." One that was about to get much worse unless she came up with a date soon.

Her cousin nodded. "Yup. A sign you're a workaholic. You should be having fun to go along with the whole female empowerment message of your brand."

"Why do you think I need a date?" She tapped her finger against her mouth—glad that this time it wasn't because of the memory of a certain kiss lingering on her lips. "Maybe I can hire an escort…"

"Dear sweet heaven, girl, no. Why don't you find a male model to attend with? Isn't that an old PR ploy designed to get publicity?"

"First off, the Ruby Ball is a fashion industry event. Someone would probably recognize him from some photo shoot or other. Also, I don't merely require an escort. Preferably, I need an image boost with someone…impressive."

Sam had qualified, sort of, because he came from a well-connected family that had made its fortune in banking three generations back, even if Sam himself was a midlevel music exec.

Rats. She'd started her fashion label, MS Designs, for the modern woman ready to slay today—but thanks to Carl, she was looking like the furthest thing from her own target demographic.

"Isn't there a hockey player or somebody that one of your brothers can recruit?"

Mia rolled her eyes. "The last thing I'd do is ask one of my brothers to help me find a date." It would be a humbling experience, even apart from the teasing, especially given her long quest to stake her independence from her family. "Anyway, Jordan's team isn't in town on the night of the Ball, so it would definitely be an imposition."

"Well then, give Damian a chance," Gia said. "He fits the bill, and you said he's volunteered. Ask him. It's not like your family pays attention to the fashion press anyway."

Mia suddenly regretted sharing details of her run-in with Damian at the costume party, but she and Gia were as close as sisters. They were almost the same age and in artistic fields—Gia was a cartoonist with a widely circulating strip. And of course, they had rhyming names—which had led to no end of jokes over the years, particularly from Mia's brothers. "Maybe you should start the Damian Musil fan club."

Gia shrugged. "Alex likes him."

Gia's new husband was a millionaire in the tech field, so of course he'd crossed paths with Damian.

"Alex doesn't have the history with the Musils that the Serenghettis have," her cousin added, pushing back her newly straightened dark hair.

"Exactly. Anyway, I don't know how seriously to take Damian's offer to be my date. He might have just been needling me." Entirely possible given the Serenghetti-Musil feud. "And do you know how my family would react if they ever discovered I showed up as a couple with Damian?"

"When have you ever let that stop you?" Gia countered. "Isn't *rebel* your middle name?"

Right. The Serenghettis of Welsdale, Massachusetts

were all about construction—and hockey. And more lately, Hollywood, thanks to her middle brother, Rick, and his movie star wife, Chiara Feran. So naturally, Mia had gone to New York to study and work in fashion design…because her rebellious streak had started early and extended beyond triple-pierced ears.

Mia sighed again. She could have tried to attend with a friend, but she'd done a quick inventory, and she didn't have any guy friends that were completely unattached at the moment. But Damian…?

"You'll be seen by lots of people at the Ruby Ball, though." Gia worried her lower lip.

"I'd dump him the next day," Mia said jokingly. *ASAP.* Then she paused, her eyes widening in reflection.

"What are you thinking?" Gia asked suspiciously.

The idea of going out with Damian and then making it seem as if she'd dumped him quickly, if necessary, was gaining traction. Maybe a plan of attending the Ruby Ball with him wasn't so risky after all…

Mia bit her lip. "You know," she said thoughtfully, "the idea has some appeal."

Gia's eyes widened as understanding dawned.

"If anyone asks, our relationship had a quick and unfortunate end."

"Who's going to ask?"

"Oh, you know, if the question ever comes up." With any luck it wouldn't. But a few of the platitudes that celebrities relied on flashed across her mind like a Times Square news ticker. *We uncoupled, but I wish him nothing but the best. I've grown and learned so much from past relationships about what I really want and need in a partner.* The last was about subtly shifting the narrative, of course, without outright placing blame on the party who'd fallen short. She really needed to stop reading gossip sites…but then again, wasn't her brand about encouraging women to seize their power?

"Okay, how are you going to handle your family if they find out?" Gia rolled her eyes. "They'll be shocked."

Try horrified. "And relieved the dating was over in the blink of an eye. They'd be more worried if Damian was still in the picture."

Gia shook her head. "Okay, well, I'm glad you've realized Damian is maybe your best option for the Ruby Ball. As to everything else, there are ways this plan can go wrong."

"Now you're having cold feet?"

"Think of me as your living, breathing conscience making you think things through."

"Yeah—like when I suggested sneaking backstage at that concert," Mia muttered, the memory still fresh in her mind twenty years later.

"Hey, I told you it was a bad idea."

"Security was already chasing us in the arena's restricted access tunnel when you said that."

"Well, it was worth a shot at meeting the Backstreet Boys," Gia replied.

Yup. And her brother Jordan had done much more hell-raising back then—and she'd had a thing to prove about there being nothing her older siblings could do that she couldn't. "I guess you have a point there. Nothing ventured, nothing gained."

Still, Damian Musil?

There were upsides to being your own boss. Today was not one of them.

Damian rubbed the back of his neck and then leaned back in his office chair.

Absently, he nodded to one of his managers who walked

past beyond the glass wall of his office and saluted him with his takeaway coffee cup.

Victor broke his stride and poked his head in the door. "See you at the meeting at 11."

"I'll be there," Damian responded, noting the time at the bottom of his computer screen before the manager disappeared from view.

Frankly, Damian figured a meeting would be a welcome distraction right now.

He needed to hire a new exec to head his video streaming service, FanvaTV, and his messenger app—the core of CyberSilver, the company that he'd built—was running into software difficulties. He'd just read an email detailing the bugs that still needed to be worked out in the planned software update.

And *that* was only his work life. He wondered again if Mia had ever caught up with the mysterious Sam on Saturday night, and his jaw tightened.

He swiveled to face the window behind him, staring pensively over Madison Square Park below.

The trees were getting foliage, and the stray puffy white cloud was no match for the sun at midday. The occasional cherry tree added a dot of contrast to the deepening green canopy below. Everything was ripe for new beginnings—just like he'd felt once.

Ten years ago, when he'd taken his small inheritance from his mother and moved to New York City to start his business, he'd envisioned being here someday. Except things were supposed to be easier when he was flush with success. He'd spent years building, running, forgetting. To get as far away from his parents' hardscrabble existence as he could. And yet...

He still had problems, including his biggest one at the moment. With his growing new media company, Cyber-

Silver, some might wonder why he was interested in an aging local television company. But to him, buying the privately owned station in western Massachusetts would be the ultimate validation of his success. Yes, he'd left the family construction business to his father and brother, but buying back into the Massachusetts market in a big way would mean the Musil name would become associated with more than JM Construction.

The potential television station acquisition was personal on his part. A first…since he never let emotions influence his corporate decisions. But the satisfaction from owning WBEN-TV, along with the couple of other New England stations that came with it, wasn't something to be dismissed lightly… If only he could get the owner to sell to him.

Larry Bensen was suspicious of someone who had no background in television broadcasting, even if Damian owned a new media company and had roots in Massachusetts. Larry was ready to retire, but only if he could leave his company in good hands—since no one else in his family was interested in running it.

The truth, though, was the guy needed to sell to a bigger player. Larry had done everything in the past few years to keep his company competitive, including bringing in new management. But big conglomerates ruled media, old and new, these days. And Damian's biggest worry was that Larry would sell to someone else.

Especially since Larry's requirements included vetting a potential buyer's character—because he wanted a buyer who'd treat his company as if it were a family inheritance. Considering that Damian came from a fractured family and wasn't even close to starting one of his own—he wasn't even dating—that requirement put him at a distinct disadvantage. He was too tied to his job to have much of a social life, so at least he didn't have much in the way of negative publicity—no reality stars, baby mamas or lingerie models willing to tell all for the right price. But, on the other hand, he wasn't a poster boy for domesticity, either.

Damian idly reached for the computer mouse and re-opened the email from Larry that he'd gotten that morning.

I'll be in NYC next week for the Ruby Ball. Katie is covering it for *Brilliance* magazine, and Allison wants to go. Let's meet if you're in town.

Damian shook his head. Yup, Larry was all about family. He'd even named Alley Kat Media, his holding company, for his wife and daughter, Allison and Katie. And now Larry was coming to town because his daughter worked for a fashion magazine and his wife, a former model, was interested.

Damian turned again to stare thoughtfully out the window, and his lips quirked. This was the second time in a week that the Ruby Ball had cropped up as a topic of conversation in his life. Days ago he'd teased Mia about accompanying her to the celebrated event…

She'd turned him down, of course. Because she'd been bred to distrust and look down on a Musil.

But his body had hummed ever since their last encounter, when finally, finally, he'd been able to taste her lips. And the kiss had been hotter and better than he'd ever expected. She was a beautiful woman—growing into the potential that had been evident back when she still lived in Welsdale.

And lately, every time their paths had crossed, Damian had found her to be even more compelling and fascinating.

Damian steepled his fingers. He suddenly had a business interest in attending the Ruby Ball. He had not been able to get Mia off his mind, especially since Saturday's kiss, but now Larry would also be in town for the event...

No matter what Mia thought, however, the Musils weren't underhanded so much as ruthless. The business sense he'd learned from his family had served him well. He had more power and money than he'd ever dreamed of.

Damian contemplated his office view. Maybe it was time to cast doubt on everything that Mia heard about Musils over the years—as well as having her owe him one. In some ways, he couldn't have planned things better if he'd tried.

It looked as if he and Mia might be headed toward another rendezvous... He had only to beat the mysterious Sam to it...damn it.

Damian searched his mind for where he'd last crossed paths with Mia before the costume party. He knew a local trendy nightspot that was the usual haunt for some of their mutual acquaintances. He'd try there first on Friday night.

And with that thought, he straightened in his chair and leaned forward to reply to Larry's email.

Three

She was nursing dashed dreams but congratulating herself on her principles…so the last thing she needed was for temptation to walk through the door. But then, Mia had never felt especially lucky.

She watched with trepidation as Damian strode into the Twilight Club, as if he felt comfortable and welcome anywhere.

She'd temporarily separated herself from some acquaintances and gone to the bar for a drink. She'd seen Damian here in the past, but not so frequently that she'd been worried about him showing tonight…

Ask him. Gia's opinion sounded in her head.

Ugh. One week left till the Ruby Ball and of course enticement would walk in to test her resolve. She'd continued to waffle and had all but decided that Gia's suggestion of asking Damian was just too crazy—despite some of her brave words to her cousin—but now here he was…

Before Mia had a chance to make any decision, however, Damian strode right to her and parked himself at the bar, as if he too had been mulling a mission.

He nodded at the now-empty glass of Coke at her elbow. "Buy you a drink?" Then not waiting for an answer, he signaled the bartender. "Beer on tap. The darkest you have. And another round of soda for her."

"You like to take charge." She made the observation grudgingly.

"I'm a CEO."

"So am I." She, however, did not have the same pull. Already a couple of women had recognized him and were throwing sidelong looks in his direction.

Damian smiled at her. "How's it going with Sam? Have you run him to ground yet?"

Must he be so annoying? "Hardly. He's on a plane to Singapore."

"And the airline's departure gate closed before you got there?"

"Wouldn't you love it if I said I barely avoided arrest trying to stop him from boarding?"

He flashed a grin. "Somehow I doubt that's the kind of publicity you're looking for."

The waiter put her soda down on the counter, and she took a sip. "No publicity is bad publicity. Isn't that what they say?"

"I like a woman who goes after what she wants. So what's your backup plan?"

She eyed him. "What makes you think I have one?"

"Well, since I'm standing in front of you," he drawled, "I figured you'd be considering contingency options."

Damn him. "You?"

He nodded, leaving his beer untouched. "Me. As it happens, I now have a business reason to attend the Ruby Ball, and something tells me you have an extra ticket."

"I'll sell it to you."

Mia's mind buzzed with the pros and cons of Gia's idea all over again. She'd tried to convince herself that Damian had been merely joking at the costume party—but now he clearly wasn't. On the one hand, she was desperate, as much as it irked her that he knew it. And actually, did she have any other choice? On the other hand, Damian was a Musil. Her family would have a joint conniption if they found out. Even if Damian wasn't in charge of the family construction business, he had been and probably still was a beneficiary.

Then again, she'd never let family disapproval stop her, as Gia had pointed out. In fact, she'd often run into its open arms.

Like right now. Oh, Damian didn't literally have his arms open, but the man was…seductive. He seemed to know her weak spots.

She wavered. He waited.

Desperation won out, even if she was still suspicious. "Why would you be interested in an event that's all about high fashion?"

He quirked his lips, his expression rueful. "I'm not, but my client is. His wife was a model before they married. Now they're ready to retire, if they find the right buyer for their business. I aim to be Mr. Right."

Mia rolled her eyes. "So you're going to trot out your date, the fashion designer." *Me.*

He looked amused. "A bonus I wasn't looking for."

She figured it was a testament to her recent history with men that being referred to as an unexpected bonus didn't faze her. And Damian was a Musil, after all—she should keep her expectations low.

"And as it happens, a bonus for you, too. My client's daughter is covering the Ball because she's employed by *Brilliance* magazine."

Mia drew in a breath. He obviously knew she'd jump at the chance to make a connection at one of the foremost fashion magazines around. *Damn it.* Temptation had taken an irresistible turn.

Sure, she had some connections of her own—namely through her sister-in-law, actress Chiara Feran—but the whole point was being independent of her family. She wanted to make it on her own, not trade on her name, though she had done some cross-promotion with Chiara's former stylist, Emery, who'd started her own accessories line. And while her sister-in-law had friends in Hollywood who were walking billboards for designers, what Mia needed at this point wasn't simply to lend out her clothes for free publicity, but to expand her retail reach with department stores and boutiques. And for that she needed industry connections...fashion editors, store buyers, word-of-mouth in the trade. Anything that would get those orders coming in. Yes, she'd hired a publicist but her budget was no-frills, and fashion was a competitive business—she needed to work every angle.

Before she could let herself dwell on it any more, she blurted, "If anyone asks after the fact, I dumped you."

Paradoxically, mild amusement stamped Damian features, and then he quirked a brow. "Should we shake hands on it?"

He was playing her, using his bargaining skills. But she knew some of her own. "The can-can girl and the villain?"

He laughed, not missing her allusion to their recent encounter at the costume party. "Sounds like the name of—"

"—a low-budget movie." A disaster flick, hers. With the subtitle *Mia Runs Out of Options.*

The minute her palm came into contact with his, however, awareness shivered up her arm and spread outward.

Her lips parted, and she took a quick indrawn breath.

Damian held her gaze and the world fell away.

Why did she always have such a sensitized reaction to him? And what would it feel like to come into closer contact? Feel his lips on hers again and have him caress her with his hands while she moaned her pleasure… *OMG, no.*

It was bad enough that she was attracted to him even if she didn't totally trust him. Determinedly, she slipped her hand from his, and he let her go.

For now.

But there'd be a next time—the thought came unbidden.

Mia sipped her cocktail and regarded her youngest brother carefully.

Jordan was in town. *Rats.*

Sometimes one of her brothers visited New York. Usually not her oldest sibling, Cole, who now ran Serenghetti Construction. Occasionally it was her middle brother, Rick, who was a big-shot Hollywood movie producer—and still had plenty of contacts in New York City from his days as a Wall Street money man. Most often it was Jordan—her youngest brother and the older sibling closest to her age— since he played professionally with the New England Razors and traveled for his NHL away games.

Usually she was thrilled to see him, but the timing right now was awkward at best.

Since the Razors normally stayed at the Renaissance Hotel, which was a stone's throw away from her place in the Garment District, she didn't have a good excuse not to meet. And because the late afternoon was nice and sunny, they were meeting in one of the hotel's popular locations—the Versa restaurant, with its impressive indoor/ outdoor seating, retractable roof, potted greenery, and glass walls overlooking Midtown. She was glad at least that they weren't at the Renaissance's Thread Bar, since its fashion theme attracted a like-minded clientele—namely, people she was likely to know. Right now, there was only so much she could handle without someone in the industry mentioning the Ruby Ball in front of her brother. As it was, she'd had to swear Gia to secrecy...

"I thought Cole was coming to town this week. He mentioned he had one of those once-in-a-blue-moon business conferences."

Jordan's lips quirked. "He'd planned to, but the Musils are up to no good again."

Mia's stomach turned over, but she managed weakly, "Oh, really? I haven't heard a thing about the Musils in a long time."

Liar. Liar. But did Damian count if he wasn't in Welsdale anymore?

Jordan nodded. "They've been quiet, but now they're bidding to buy the same construction company, and for Cole it's personal."

Mia knew that Cole was looking to expand Serenghetti Construction in order to stay competitive. Construction was increasingly a business where the big players had an edge—and the little guys faced the threat of being left behind.

"Oh, please," she said lightly, "Cole's grow-or-die philosophy hardly means it's personal."

"For Cole, it's more than that. JM Construction has been a thorn in his side ever since they almost got the construction deal for that new gym."

Mia knew JM Construction was named for Damian's father, Jakob Musil. She'd learned that fun fact the way other kids learned their alphabet…because she was a Serenghetti. She shifted in her seat. "Oh, come on, Cole should be thanking the Musils. If JM Construction hadn't had the upper hand, Cole would never have volunteered to headline the fundraiser that Marisa was organizing for a new athletic facility at the school where she works. He would never have mended his relationship with Marisa, and they'd never have gotten married. There was a silver lining to the competition with the Musils."

Jordan's lips quirked. "In other words, the Musils did Cole a favor? I don't think he sees it that way."

Damn it. Why did the business rivalry with the Musils have to flare up right now? "Doesn't Cole have enough going on without worrying about the Musils? After all, with your plan to fund a new wing at the Children's Hospital, Serenghetti Construction will have more than enough business."

"Again, Cole doesn't see it that way. Besides, with existing projects, Serenghetti Construction is already stretched to the limit. If he wins the takeover battle, it'll ease some of the strain on resources."

Oops.

"Anyway, let's talk about you," Jordan said, seemingly oblivious.

Let's not.

"How are you doing?" He took a sip of his beer.

Mia waved her hand. "Oh, you know, business as usual."

Her brother quirked a brow. "You're leading the glamorous fashion designer life in the big city, and you don't have anything happening? Yeah, I believe that."

She had to get them off this topic fast. "You'll be surprised like everyone else when I make a splash."

Her brother laughed. "Okay, fair enough." Then he sobered. "It's nice to see you in a better mood, Mia. After Carl, we were all worried about you."

"Well, don't. Worry, that is. Carl is in the past." *And I've got bigger things to worry about these days.*

Jordan shook his head. "If I ever run into Carl—"

"You'll say hi and keep going. I can take care of myself." She'd escaped to New York, but sometimes it didn't seem far enough from her protective relatives. Sure Jordan was showing he cared, but she'd also been assigned a place in the family tree, and no one seemed interested in having her change her position.

"Maybe be choosier about who you date."

"Right." *Starting after Saturday.* "Says the guy who used to be a major player before he met his wife."

"Exactly. I speak from experience."

As a big NHL star, Jordan had gotten his share of headlines, including at least one woman trying to shake him down for his money and celebrity.

"I'm not a big enough designer to attract hangers-on."

"You will be."

"Thanks for the vote of confidence."

"In the meantime, better luck spotting the duds."

She shrugged. "It's New York City. There are literally thousands more single women than men in this town."

Jordan smiled. "Don't I know it. Or at least, I used to."

Mia wagged a finger at him in jest before they both sipped their drinks. The youngest of her brothers used to be in the running for hockey's most eligible bachelor. Tall, with dark hair and green eyes, he'd made women breathless with his underwear billboard ads.

Seriously, Jordan was in no position to judge…even if she did show up in public on the arm of a Musil.

And Damian might be many things, but he wasn't a

dud. The guy had major bank, industry respect and name recognition.

On top of it, she'd been working weeks toward the Ruby Ball. And plans were finally falling into place, sort of…

und, and her back and neck ached. Feeling woozy, Anya shut
her eyes again.

When she opened them, she was back in the waiting
hall, her name warm and steady on her shoulders, as—

Four

She'd gone bold for tonight, and her outfit was just the
start of it. The pink top was shaped like a suit jacket except the deep V in the front revealed what looked like the
top of a red bustier but was actually the cleverly accented
bodice of her dress. Below her waist, a pink satin skirt
was open at the front in a deep inverted V that revealed
long, shapely legs encased in red satin to match the bustier. The whole ensemble set off her dark mahogany hair
and tanned complexion.

If she wanted to invite attention, best to go all out, right?
She'd designed and made the gown herself, even though
MS Designs focused on ready-to-wear—at least till now—
and not haute couture. No use advertising someone else's
design chops instead of her own if she was dreaming big.
And if news filtered back to her family about the Ruby
Ball, maybe her daring gown would divert some attention
from her date. *Maybe.*

Still, Mia's bravado nearly deserted her when Damian closed the limo door behind her and she stepped forward on the pavement.

One intense look from him and her pulse kicked up. Her heart beat faster, and shivers of awareness danced over her skin.

Automatically, she touched the ruby resting above her cleavage, and his eyes became hooded. He'd invited her to make a loan appointment at a discreet Upper East Side shop and pick out matching jewels. He'd had access that she could only dream of, but despite some misgivings, she hadn't been able to resist.

Now that both she and Damian were dressed to thrill, however, she wasn't prepared for his effect on her senses. And the short limo ride from her apartment, where he'd picked her up, had done nothing to dull it—*drat*.

He looked hot, dark and intense in an impeccably tailored tux over a black satin shirt and tie. It was a modern, edgy look that complemented her dress. But though she'd given him some sartorial pointers when they'd communicated by text in the days leading up to the Ruby Ball, she wasn't prepared for the finished package. *What had she been thinking?*

He was big and tall, and he practically smoldered.

It was one thing when they crossed paths at a party or bar, it was another to handle Damian at a public event that she couldn't walk away from.

He led her forward with his hand at the small of her back—the imprint radiating out like warm, undulating waves carrying her off to...

Focus. Mia straightened and smiled as they approached the building entrance. The Vanderman Mansion was a New York landmark that often served as an event space and backdrop to some of the city's most lavish parties.

"Relax," Damian murmured. "You look stunning."

She cast him a side look. "Amazing how you can say that while smiling. Where did you learn ventriloquism?"

His smile broadened. "In the boardroom. You never know when you'll run into a lip reader when you're negotiating a business deal."

She let him guide her forward. "So that's the Musil trade secret?"

"There are others."

After running the gauntlet of reception, they stepped inside the event space, where sequined gowns and crystal chandeliers competed for dazzling allure.

Damian took two champagne flutes from a passing waiter and handed one to her.

"Cheers," he said, clinking his glass to hers. "You made it."

Mia took a deep breath and then a sip of her drink.

"Original design, by the way," Damian said, making the compliment sound both casual and incendiary.

How did he do it? Mia resisted the urge to blow a breath to cool her face. "I made it myself. MS Designs."

"Of course," he murmured. "Red suits you."

She cast him a sidelong look from under her lashes but was spared a reply as an older couple approached.

The gray-haired man clapped Damian on the shoulder. "Damian, good to see you. Not your crowd, I think, but glad you were able to make it."

"Of course," Damian replied smoothly. "How could I miss an opportunity to attend the Ruby Ball?"

Mia flushed because only she could know Damian's tongue-in-cheek meaning.

Damian turned toward her and made introductions to Larry Bensen and his wife, Allison. "Mia is a designer with her own label. MS Designs."

Allison leaned toward her, her chestnut hair gleaming. "It must be so exciting to have your own brand. I did some modeling when I was younger, but I was always fascinated by design. I never got beyond some fun sketches."

Mia smiled. "I hope you held on to those designs. What goes around comes around in fashion."

Allison laughed. "These days, our daughter Katie is the artistic one. She's why we're here tonight. She's covering this event for *Brilliance* magazine."

Larry cast an indulgent look at his wife. "No, we're here because you never lost your love of fashion. And I told you that your bolero jacket was the right choice for tonight."

Allison smiled at her husband, and then tugged at the lapel of the jade satin jacket that she wore over a beaded gown. "After more than thirty years of marriage, you've become an expert."

Larry chuckled. "Yes, but I also read *Brilliance* magazine because there are copies all over the house."

Damian looked around. "Speaking of which, where is Katie?"

"Working," Allison answered. "Or I should say, working the room and interviewing guests about their outfits for tonight."

Damian kept his smile in place and nodded toward Mia. "Then she should interview Mia."

Mia flushed again. "Now that's—"

"An excellent idea." Allison craned her neck as if looking for her daughter. "I'll try to wave Katie over."

"Allison likes her role as Katie's personal assistant," Larry joked before glancing from Mia to Damian. "So I guess you have a connection to the fashion world, too, Damian."

To Mia's surprise, Damian's arm circled her waist, and he pulled her closer. "Mia fills me in."

Larry looked thoughtful. "I like that you're getting out of the office." He cast a loving look at his wife. "Allison cured me of my workaholic tendencies a long time ago, and my doctor gives her credit for helping me avoid another heart attack."

"We stay active," Allison chimed in. "We play golf with another couple on weekends at a club between Welsdale to Springfield. Do you play Mia?"

"Er—yes." She wouldn't call her golf game anything but passable, though she'd learned to swing a club thanks to her brief stint on the high school golf team.

"You and Damian should join us one weekend," Larry put in. "Nothing like a little friendly competition, right?"

Mia blinked with a fixed smile. A golf date? She and Damian were ending their fake relationship after tonight.

"Mia comes from an athletic family," Damian said teasingly. "I wouldn't discount her skill on the golf course."

Just then a petite young woman came breezing up.

"Katie, there's someone I'd like to introduce you to," Allison began. "Damian is a business associate of your father's, and Mia is a fashion designer."

Katie gave her a sweeping look but her expression was friendly as they exchanged greetings.

"Are you based in New York, Mia?"

Mia cleared her throat. "Yes, and I have my own label. MS Designs."

She forced herself to stop and not blab. *You probably haven't heard of it.*

Katie tilted her head. "Mmm, I think I've heard of it."

Mia flushed. "I've done a few shows."

"More than a few," Damian put in.

Mia looked at him quizzically—was he trying to bolster her, or had he really been keeping tabs on her career? She found the latter hard to believe...

Katie tilted her head. "Great dress. Original, and the cut and tailoring are super. One of your own designs?"

"Yes, but right now, I market casual wear."

"Why don't you get in touch?" Katie said. "I know Editorial at *Brilliance* is always looking to shine a light on promising new names."

Mia smiled. "Fantastic."

She felt herself relax as Katie turned to her parents to chitchat.

Damian put his hand on the small of her back and leaned close. "Nice job. Your first contact of the evening."

For one wild moment, Mia thought he was referring to his touch at her back, but then she collected herself.

"Maybe my only contact," she responded lightly.

"Never underestimate."

Mia tingled, but there was no more time for private conversation.

Katie blended into the crowd again with a quick goodbye, and Larry addressed another question to Damian.

Mia glimpsed at Damian's smooth profile, which contrasted with the tux's darker hue.

His advice could just as easily apply to him. Because it wouldn't be wise for her to underestimate Damian Musil…

Hell, he should have anticipated Larry might complicate things. So here he was the next day, waiting for Mia to show up at the midtown café where she'd agreed to meet him at his request.

Damian shifted in his seat and then took a distracted swallow of his coffee.

When he'd gotten back to his place last night, his mind had buzzed with thoughts—fantasies—of Mia. Her dress had suited her—all red and pink and fiery just like her. And what had looked like a push-up bra peeking from beneath a satin jacket had played havoc with his concentration. He'd itched to unbutton her, spread those lapels, and let his mouth and hands roam those gorgeous breasts.

A snatch of conversation between them from the end of the evening replayed itself in his mind.

Are you sure you don't need help getting out of that dress?

I'm a fashion designer. I know all the tricks.

Too bad there's nothing I can teach you.

Just then, as if called forth by his thoughts, he looked up to see Mia walk in.

Today she was flushed and a little windswept, her lips rosy. The body-hugging jacket accentuated her curves, which were encased in leggings and knee-high boots. It was cooler and windier this afternoon than yesterday, and she'd obviously dressed accordingly.

As she sat down across from him at the small café table, he slid a cup toward her. "I ordered for you while I was waiting. It's lemon-scented chamomile tea, but if you prefer something else, I'll put in another request."

Her eyes widened fractionally.

"I noticed last night that's what you asked the waiter for at the end of the evening."

"Observant."

He wondered what she'd say if she knew he noticed everything about her. At the costume party, even in the dim light, he'd gotten close enough—finally—to notice that her eyes had a subtle mismatched green hue, and that her scent had been light but sexy and sultry. He'd never paid attention to a woman's scent before, or had it linger to haunt his thoughts.

Mia took a small sip of her tea, her eyelashes lowering, and then she sighed.

Damian shifted in his seat.

Setting her cup down, she looked up.

Their gazes clung for a moment, and she must have read something in his because her lips parted on an indrawn breath. Finally, she broke eye contact, and leaned down for the small brown shopping bag that she'd parked next to her when she'd sat. "Before I forget again—" she said, passing the bag to him "—thank you for arranging for the jewelry. I would have brought everything back today myself but the jeweler is closed on Sundays."

He was slightly amused by her haste to reassure him and cut ties. The ruby-and-diamond necklace, along with chandelier earrings, had suited her—emphasizing the vibrancy of her look. He couldn't have picked out something better himself. Mia had impeccable taste and a discerning eye.

Taking the bag and depositing it next to him, he said, "No worries."

She sat back with a glad-that's-taken-care-of look.

"But the jewelry isn't why I asked you to meet me."

Her eyes widened fractionally.

"How are we going to handle the invitation from the Bensens?" he asked, shifting gears to what he considered the real topic at hand.

She expelled a breath and brushed aside waves of dark brown hair that had fallen over her shoulder when she'd reached down. "Simple. One of us is going to fake illness."

"You've been thinking ahead," he remarked dryly.

"One of us has to."

"You know, it would be to both our benefits to go through with the golf date."

She blinked. "Near Springfield? That's like the back-yard for the Serenghetti-Musil family feud. Springfield is mere miles from Welsdale. Are we trying to widen the conflict?"

"That's up to you, but I'm thinking that Larry and Allison will want us to be on the same team. So they can, you know, beat us soundly."

"I'm not a regular golf player."

"You've got athletics in your genes. And anyway, we want to give them a run for the money but not embarrass them." He quirked his lips. "Bad for business."

"And here I was showing up today to publicly dump you," she replied tartly.

Somehow Damian wasn't surprised by her announcement. Still... "Why? Are you motivated by revenge or just distrust?"

Her eyes flared slightly. "You're blunt and direct."

"Comes with the business acumen." He curved his lips. "It's also where the instinct to look for additional mileage from our situation comes from."

"We agreed to attend the Ruby Ball together. That's all." She shrugged. "Before we get our families' hackles up."

"Ah."

"What? You don't care?"

He settled back in his chair and they bumped knees under the table. "I left Welsdale years ago. And so did you, come to think of it."

She leaned forward, a slight frown marring a face that could turn heads. "The Serenghettis and Musils are currently bidding to buy the same construction company, in case you didn't know."

He kept his expression neutral, even though it was bad timing for things to get stirred up between their families. "I don't know anything about it. I told you I'm not involved with JM Construction."

"But your family is."

"And you seem to worry a lot about what yours will think for someone who's struck out on her own in New York."

She seemed momentarily taken aback by his insight, but recovered quickly, her lips compressing.

Damian pressed his advantage. True, they'd agreed on showing up together only for the Ruby Ball, nothing more, but Larry had thrown a wrench in things. "We both stand to gain by accepting the Bensens' invitation. You get to curry favor with the parents of an important fashion editor, and I get to keep a potential business partner happy."

"I've already met Katie Bensen," she protested. "Last night. You're the one with more on the line here."

"A good businessperson isn't swayed by emotion…and that's what going our separate ways right now would be, especially when there's more to be gained by doing the opposite."

Mia jutted out her chin. "What about the satisfaction from tossing you aside?"

Over Mia's shoulder, Damian saw Carl walk in and cursed under his breath.

Mia followed his gaze, and her eyes widened. Then she swung back toward him. "Did you plan this?"

He quirked a brow. "No. The gods are laughing at me right now."

What the hell was Carl doing here? This was a trendy café, and both he and Carl—like Mia—lived in Midtown, but he must have run into Carl here only once before.

Before Damian could figure out what to do, Carl spotted them. Surprise, confusion and then shock flitted across the other man's face. After a momentary hitch in his pace, though, he started toward them.

Damian sighed. Carl had spotted them—of course, he had—and as awkward as it might be, there was no way to avoid the upcoming exchange of empty pleasantries.

Damian stood, smiling, and Mia got out of her seat, too. "Carl."

"Damian. Mia." Carl's tone was all fake jocularity. "This is a surprise."

"I was thinking the same thing." Damian slipped his arm around Mia's waist and felt her stiffen fractionally—but she didn't pull away.

Carl's gaze traveled between the two of them, and he shook his head bemusedly. "I got married, and you and Mia end up together. Go figure. Guess everyone winds up happy, huh? I mean now that I'm no longer standing in the way of everything getting sorted out."

Damian cursed underneath his breath as Mia gave a tight smile. *Carl needed to stop talking.*

As Mia opened her mouth, Damian cut in. "Mia and I were grabbing some tea."

It was the truth—though not all of it. As a non sequitur, it would work though.

Carl looked momentarily puzzled. "Well, I guess I'll be going. Just stopped in for some coffee. Two light roasts." His gaze passed from Damian to Mia and back. "Nice to see you."

When Carl moved away, Damian followed Mia's lead and sat back down. Neither of them said anything for a few minutes. Mia sipped her herbal tea, and Damian glanced out the window at the passing crowds.

It was only after Carl had gotten his order and departed that Mia raised her eyebrows and fixed him with a look. "Really?"

Damian didn't even pretend not to understand. "If your relationship had been serious, Carl might have had a different reaction right now."

"Or maybe he finally met the right person," Mia responded, something indecipherable flitting across her face.

"That, too," he acknowledged with a tip of the head.

"Either way, it would never have worked. Carl's too easy-going for you."

"Meaning I'm not good-natured?" Mia demanded.

No, you're hot, hot, hot. Just like his scalding cup of tea had been...until she'd walked in and everything else had faded in comparison.

Damian quirked his lips. "You were upset about the timing of the breakup, but the Ruby Ball went off without a hitch for you."

"Yes, except now there are other problems," she muttered. "Larry and Allison think we're a couple, and now Carl does, too."

"Don't tell me it doesn't give you some satisfaction to have him think you've moved on," he murmured, keeping his voice down as other patrons took a seat nearby.

Mia leaned forward. "Of course he thinks so. You put your arm around me."

"And you didn't move away."

A look of exasperation crossed her face.

"You're fiery. Carl is relaxed. And a little clueless."

She arched a brow. "Unlike you?"

"I'm willing to learn."

"On a golf course?"

He smiled. "If necessary."

She rolled her eyes. "You've got it all figured out, haven't you?"

Five

Mia ran the comb through her hair using the entry mirror in Damian's Welsdale condo while he took a business call in another room. It had been windy on the golf course earlier.

She felt as if she were still a teen in high school—and it wasn't a good feeling. The problem was that she was sneaking around, trying to make sure none of her family knew she was almost on their doorstep right now—with Damian Musil. Except for Gia, of course—but then, her cousin had always been her partner in crime.

And so far so good. No one in her immediate family had called or texted. The Ruby Ball was a longstanding event, but important only in fashion circles. She was counting on it being a distant memory if and when her family found out that she'd been there with Damian Musil. By then, of course, she could maintain that she and Damian had long since parted ways—for good.

Early this morning, she and Damian had driven up

to Massachusetts in his Lexus SUV. Fortunately it had been a beautiful sunny day—the weather had been perfect if a bit nippy—and the golf game had gone well. She and Damian had held their own even if they'd ultimately lost.

Afterward, they'd ended up here at the condo with the Bensons for drinks. At first she'd been taken aback—preferring to socialize at the course's clubhouse—but then Damian had clearly wanted to show off his local ties to Larry.

She'd also wondered idly if today's loss at golf had been an unusual event for Damian. He'd been so successful in his career, he probably hadn't experienced a true setback in years. Then she'd realized that he likely still thought of the day as a win. After all, before he'd left minutes ago, Larry Bensen had shaken hands on an agreement to a deal.

She deposited her comb in her handbag, which she'd placed on the console table below the mirror. As soon as Damian was done with his phone call, she was getting out of here—texting her mother that she was on her way over in a ride service, allegedly from the bus terminal.

As far as her relatives were concerned, she was coming up by bus sometime today for a short visit. She'd felt too guilty about not seeing them while she was in town, even if it made more sense to sneak back down to New York with no one the wiser. She'd fudged a little bit about when and how and why—the *other* why—she was coming up to town.

Still, as soon as she and Damian had driven into Welsdale after golf more than two hours ago, the back of her neck had pricked with the uncomfortable awareness that she might run into someone she knew…and would have to do some quick explaining—or covering up.

And right now, she didn't need any more curveballs.
Her early morning drive up to Massachusetts with Damian
had been eventful enough—and another silver lining to
dropping in on her parents was that she'd avoid a similar
ride back to New York. She'd been acutely aware of being
confined in a small space with him, unable to ignore his
strong and capable hands flexing on the steering wheel...
the clean, masculine scent that she'd come to identify as
his...and worst of all, his big frame folded into the seat
next to hers. And then thoughts of their kiss had intruded
again...

"Do we need to put on a show of affection for the
Bensens?" she'd blurted.

He'd glanced at her from the corner of his eyes. "Just
be yourself—"

She'd relaxed her shoulders.

"—unless, of course, you'd like to touch me."

She'd looked at him sharply and realized he was teasing.

She stared at herself in the mirror again. *Ugh.* This was
getting so complicated, and Damian was getting under her
skin. The condo seemed too small to avoid temptation.

Time to leave.

She wondered when Damian would be done talking
to whomever he was talking to. She supposed she could
sneak out of here—but that would be rude, wouldn't it?
And really, did she want Damian to think she was skulking
away? No, she was a Serenghetti. Resolute and resilient.

She glanced around the luxury condo. She remembered
when this complex had gone up in Welsdale while she'd
been in high school. Of course, Damian would pick one of
the ritziest addresses in town. The decor was understated,
but her designer's eye had picked up on the telling details
of luxury—the slate floor in the kitchen, the white mar-
ble in the bath... Naturally, though, Damian, had chosen

a building that hadn't been built by the Serenghettis—or JM Construction, come to think of it.

"Great job on the golf course," Damian announced, startling her.

She turned to watch him approach while still tucking his phone away. He loomed large and impossibly magnetic.

"You did most of the work." She could be magnanimous—and she'd bet he wasn't expecting that from a Serenghetti. At the same time, though, she fished out her own cell phone from her handbag. Time to text her mother that she'd be at her parents' door soon—they'd agreed she'd show up before dinnertime—and then summon a ride.

"I guess I'll have to give you lessons."

She didn't let herself think about what else he could teach her…and accidentally dropped her cell phone.

Flustered by her clumsiness, she bent to retrieve it.

Damian mirrored her move, and they bumped into each other.

After making a grab for the phone, she straightened and mumbled, "Sorry."

Could things get any more awkward?

"Are you all right?" His voice was low, soothing, concerned.

He gently rubbed her temple where they'd hit, and her breath caught.

She looked up and searched his gaze. "Yes."

"Mia."

Suddenly, it was as if all the pent-up sexual tension of the day—the car ride, making nice in front of the Bensens, breathing the same air alone in a quiet condo—snapped free of its taut hold.

Awareness sizzled between them. Desire and unmistakable need stamped his features, and Mia feared her own expression mirrored his.

His gaze dropped to her mouth.

"Are we about to bump lips, too?" she blurted.

He smiled slightly. "We can claim it was another accident."

As his head lowered, she said, "Or a victory celebration... except we didn't win the golf game."

"We gave them a run for the money, that's what counts," he murmured. "It would have been bad form to beat a potential business partner."

"If you say so."

"Mia, can we stop talking?"

And then he gently angled her head and covered her mouth.

She sighed against his mouth, and then snaked her hands around his shoulders, anchoring them both.

His lips moved over hers, searching, seeking, testing. The kiss quickly turned hotter, needier and more desperate.

Pressing against him, she felt the unmistakable sign of his arousal. Her breasts crushed against his chest, fueling their need.

He backed her against the foyer wall, and she rested her arms on his shoulders, tangling her free hand in his hair.

If this kept up, they'd soon end up naked right here inside his front door. The thought flashed through her mind, bringing her back to sanity, and she broke the kiss.

Gulping in a breath, she forced herself to say the obvious. "We can't do this."

A muscle ticked in his jaw, and his eyes glittered. "I want you."

It was a bald-faced statement that rocked her, and dear heaven, aroused her.

She closed her eyes briefly. "It would complicate things. This was supposed to have ended days ago."

"Nothing says it couldn't be more." He quirked his lips. "You want me…but you don't trust me, is that it?"

Wow, he was blunt. "Has anyone told you that subtlety isn't your strong suit?"

"You're the artist. I'm just a businessman."

"Please." He was *just* another entrepreneur in the same way that New York Fashion Week was just another garment industry event.

He bent to kiss her again, and she pushed against his chest.

She remembered Jordan's words—the Musils and Serenghettis were going head-to-head in business again. If only her brother knew that she was in Damian Musil's arms right now and fighting the urge to lose control with him. Right here. Right now.

Her cell phone vibrated, and she pushed away.

She punched at her screen while Damian continued to stand there, the personification of sex…

When she read her message, however, she groaned.

You're dating Damian Musil. What the hell.

Cole's text was like a dousing with icy water. She seemed to be on a bad luck streak these days, and the timing of her brother's message couldn't be worse. She was in Damian's apartment, in Welsdale, and her family had no idea she was in town.

Guilt ate at her.

Damian clasped her upper arms. "Mia—"

"I have to go." Then she added, "The cat's out of the bag with my family."

"Wha—"

"Cole thinks we're dating. Apparently my brothers have suddenly started reading *Women's Wear Daily* or some other fashion industry press." A brittle laugh almost bubbled up.

She swung toward the door, not bothering to deposit her phone back in her handbag, and with her other hand, grabbed the overnight bag that she'd brought in with her earlier. Anything to give the impression of the happy couple for the Bensens' sake, right? *Liar, liar.*

Mia winced inwardly. If she'd been able to forget for a moment who she was and who Damian was—while she'd been losing herself in his arms—reality had come crashing back.

And it looked as if she was overdue for an interesting family reunion...

When Mia arrived at her parents' Mediterranean-style home outside Welsdale, she immediately recognized her brother Cole's pickup on the circular driveway that wrapped around a central fountain. It was joined by Jordan's expensive SUV.

The sky overhead had darkened with rain clouds, as if foretelling the turn that today would take from her sunny outing this morning with the Bensens.

Damn it. She'd been hoping she could speak to her parents first before tackling Cole. But she should have realized that her brothers might be here. It was a weekend, after all, and both Cole and Jordan were local.

Cole lived close by—in a house he'd built for Marisa and their preschool-age daughter, Dahlia. He'd only taken over Serenghetti Construction after their father's stroke a few years ago.

These days, her father instead appeared on local television with *Wine Breaks with Serg!*—short slots devoted to wine recommendations and connected to his wife's cooking show. Mia was proud her mother had started a second career with *Flavors of Italy with Camilla Serenghetti*. Everyone, it seemed, was finding their niche except for her. But she was trying.

After depositing her overnight bag by the front door, she braced herself and entered the spacious living room. Cole turned to face her, while Jordan continued to lounge with deceptive calm in an armchair.

Her brothers shared the same dark hair and tall build, but Jordan's eyes were green while Cole's were hazel. And Cole had always been bigger, bulkier and rougher around the edges—his nose having been broken once.

At least her parents weren't in sight—yet.

"Are you nuts?" Cole asked, standing in the middle of the room.

"And hello to you, too, Cole," Mia replied dryly. "Thanks for not wasting time with pleasantries."

"Why bother when you've lost your mind? Showing up at a public event arm in arm with Damian Musil?"

"At least you've saved me the effort of filling you in." Mia eyed her brother but kept her tone light. "How did you find out?"

Cole raked his hand through his hair. "One of my employees mentioned that she'd read some coverage online about the Ruby Ball." Cole scowled. "She congratulated me on burying the hatchet with the Musils."

"Nobody was carrying a hatchet at the Ruby Ball, and no one was burying one either."

Cole fixed her with a look she recognized—a lecture from her oldest sibling was coming. "Do I need to remind you about the Musils' reputation?" Not waiting for an answer, he continued, "They've lured away more than one of our employees, tried to use personal connections to try to steal a potential business deal, and basically snuck around until they grew big enough to challenge Serenghetti Construction."

Mia glanced at Jordan—who merely raised his eyebrows—before focusing on Cole again. "Some people would call those tactics good business."

"They were cited for multiple violations on a commercial building job."

She sucked in a breath and then let it out slowly. "Well, that's their problem. What does that have to do with Serenghetti Construction?"

"The Musils targeted us with underhanded tactics. They aimed to succeed by pulling down Serenghetti Construction."

Mia raised her chin. "How do you know?" she challenged. Only because she wanted the truth, and not to defend Damian, she told herself.

"Listen, Mia, it's a fine line between ethics and corruption, especially in this business," Cole replied. "JM Construction was the winner when the VP of Kenable Management in Springfield was gathering bids for a job. Except now the strip mall exec also has a nice new guest house on his estate that he didn't pay for."

"A kickback or bribe?"

"What do you think?" Cole countered.

Mia threw up her hands.

Jordan cleared his throat. "Face it, Mia. You're not going to convince Cole or the rest of us that the Musils aren't bad news."

Mia rolled her eyes. "Thanks for the verdict."

"Oh, yeah, and you didn't mention Damian the last time I saw you in New York."

"For obvious reasons—"

Jordan nodded.

"—it wasn't any of your business."

Her sister-in-law Marisa walked in, breaking up the battle of words. She held a couple of breadsticks aloft. "Less queasiness this time," she announced, "but I'll be glad when this stage is over."

Cole smiled. "Dahlia is disappointed it's a boy this time."

As Mia widened her eyes, Marisa perched on the arm of an upholstered chair. "We didn't want a big gender reveal party."

Mia's lips twitched. "I'm sure Dahlia will come around."

"She has," her sister-in-law responded, sitting and moving aside a long brown curl that had fallen in front of her amber eyes. "I told her she'll be my helper with the baby while I'm on maternity leave next year."

Mia knew Marisa loved her job as assistant principal at the private school where she'd first met Cole. More importantly, she was glad to have the conversation diverted momentarily from her outing with Damian Musil. "Vincent will be thrilled."

She loved being an aunt to Dahlia, and to Rick and Chiara's son, Vincent. She even dabbled in making clothes for them. She supposed, though, she should thank her lucky stars that Rick, at least, was based in Hollywood and was not around to join the family pile-on today.

A wayward thought popped into her head about what her child and Damian's might look like, and she quickly squelched it. *What was wrong with her?*

Cole raked his hand through his hair again. "Let's get back to the topic at hand."

"Yeah. Damian Musil," Jordan added dryly.

Mia glowered at her youngest brother. "And if I'd mentioned him in New York, what would you have done? Ratted me out to the rest of the family?"

Jordan rubbed his chin. "Tough call."

Sera, Jordan's wife, walked into the room. She was taller than her cousin Marisa and, in contrast, a dark blonde—but the resemblance was there in the amber eyes. She waved a hand as she sat down on a sofa. "I couldn't help overhearing. And no, Jordan, you would have done no such thing. Not if I had anything to say about it."

Mia shot her a look of gratitude. Now that she had three sisters-in-law, she could count on some allies in family squabbles.

"After all," Sera continued as Mia's parents, Camilla and Serg, entered the room, "Mia didn't say a word to anyone when she caught us together in the cloakroom at Oliver's wedding."

All eyes turned to Jordan, who managed to look both sheepish and unapologetic. "Hey, no use upsetting everyone at cousin Oliver's reception with news about my big play."

"Oh, Giordano," Camilla cut in, her words tinged with an Italian accent, "I thought I raised you with better manners."

Jordan gave a lopsided smile. "Sorry, Mom."

Mia kissed her mother in greeting. Although Camilla had learned English at a young age, she still sprinkled her English with Italian. She'd only met her husband when he'd been vacationing in Tuscany and she'd been a twenty-one-year-old hotel front desk employee.

The doorbell rang, and Sera sprang up. "I'll get it."

"You should tell me, *cara*," her mother protested as she sat. "We could pick you up from the bus."

Mia started guiltily. "It wasn't necessary. Really."

"She's got your independent streak, Camilla," Serg grumbled as he also accepted Mia's quick peck on the cheek.

As her father took a seat in an armchair near his wife, Mia was glad to see that he seemed in good spirits. Evidently, Cole had not shared the news about Damian Musil with their parents…yet. And her parents' cheer at having family drop by might make the news go over…not catastrophically. At least she hoped so.

Instinctively Mia crossed her fingers behind her back.

She was happy, at least, to see that her father was looking healthy and vigorous—an older version of Cole with steel gray hair mixed with white at the sideburns. After his stroke a few years ago—when he'd stepped back from Serenghetti Construction and handed over the reins to Cole, Serg had fallen into a funk. But these days he was looking more chipper—as if his televised wine spots had injected a new vitality and purpose into his life.

Right when Mia looked away from her parents, however, Sera returned—followed by a familiar face…

Six

"Damian." Mia sucked in a breath. "What are you doing here?"

She drank in the sight of Damian. And then… *Oh, great. Oh, damn.*

Everyone's gaze swung to the entry.

Sera shrugged semi-apologetically. "He said you left something behind."

Cole muttered under his breath. "Musil."

Camilla looked shocked and dismayed, while Serg was patently suspicious.

"Who's going to take the first swing?" Jordan asked no one in particular, his lips twisted into a semblance of the killer smile that had won him underwear billboard ads.

"I'm confused," Serg grumbled.

Confused… Mia thought she could work with merely *confused*.

"And angry. Someone tell me what the hell is going on."

It was all a nightmare. Mia wished the floor would open and swallow her up.

Camilla placed a staying hand on her husband's arm. "Now, Serg."

Her father fixed Mia with a *care to explain* expression. "I may have had a stroke, but I'm understanding this…situation just as much or as little as everyone else."

Before Mia could react, her father turned to Damian. "You've got guts coming here, Musil."

"Compliment accepted, sir," Damian responded easily.

"What are you doing here?" Mia repeated, diverting his attention to her.

She thrummed with awareness. A short time ago, they'd been locked in an embrace. The world had fallen away, and now it was crashing back down on her.

Still, he was so big and calm as he strode over to her, despite the undercurrent of menace in the room. "I wasn't going to let you face your family alone."

"I can fight my own battles," she responded in a low voice.

"Now you don't have to."

"You're complicating things."

"Good."

Cole curled his hands. "Outside, Musil. Now."

"Oh, no, you don't." Mia moved to stand in front of Damian. Even if no punches were thrown, Cole and Jordan together were formidable. In fact, her brothers were all cut from the same cloth—tall, dark…and in excellent physical shape. "We're all staying right here."

"This is a…shock," Camilla remarked faintly.

"Nice to see you, Mrs. Serenghetti," Damian responded. "You're as lovely as your daughter."

Camilla looked flustered and then smiled. "Thank you."

Mia relaxed momentarily. Her mother at least seemed like she was going to maintain at least a semblance of politeness.

"Damn it, Musil," Cole growled, breaking the lull in hostilities. "Save the pretty compliments for the business deals over at JM Construction."

"I don't have anything to do with the construction company these days," Damian said calmly. "My father and brother run it."

"Well, that settles it," Jordan quipped. "In that case, someone invite him to stay for dinner."

Cole snorted. "You're still a Musil—unless you've been disowned?"

"I'm in touch with my family but I run my own business these days."

The understatement of the decade. Mia felt the full impact of what was left unstated. No one in the room needed any primer on how Damian Musil had launched Cyber-Silver and entered the ranks of the fabulously wealthy.

The tense moment was broken when Dahlia trotted in carrying a toy dump truck.

Spotting Damian, she stopped. "Who are you?"

"Damian Musil."

"I'm Dahlia."

He smiled. "I used to own a truck like that when I was little."

"Figures," Jordan muttered. "Construction is in the blood."

Cole's eyes narrowed. "Dahlia, go play in the rec room again."

The preschooler turned matching hazel eyes on her father. "Daddy, I'm talking to my new person."

Damian crouched and gave the truck a little flick so that it dumped its alphabet block load on the floor.

Dahlia squealed. "Do you want to come play? Daddy does sometimes."

Oh, my heart. Mia felt hers squeeze.

Cole gave an aggrieved sigh. "Dahlia."

Marisa rose and scooped up her daughter with an apologetic look at Damian. "Snack time."

After Marisa had left the room with her daughter, Jordan folded his arms. "You can charm the women in this family, Musil, but we see right through you."

Mia had had enough. "Damian hasn't pulled one over on me."

She'd been back in Welsdale for less than a day and already she seemed to have fallen back into a bad family dynamic—one where everyone thought they knew what was best for her.

On the other hand, she'd be damned if she'd admit to her family that her relationship with Damian was all a ruse—for the benefit of his business and hers. She was too riled up and annoyed.

"Mia," her father said warningly. "Someone explain to me how you've gotten to know—" he scanned Damian, sizing him up "—this guy."

"He grew up in Welsdale," she said in exasperation, throwing up her hands.

"And somehow, they ended up arm in arm at the Ruby Ball in New York," Cole put in menacingly, locking gazes with Damian.

Camilla's eyes widened while Serg muttered something under his breath—an echo of his eldest son.

"I'd explain," Mia huffed, "but I can see it'd be futile."

Then everyone seemed to be talking at once. Just like the mess of alphabet blocks on the floor, it was chaos... thanks to one deceptively placid-looking tech tycoon.

Mia raised her voice. "Damian and I are leaving. Obviously, no one here is in the mood for a civilized discussion."

As Damian pulled the car away from the Serenghettis' drive, Mia sat next to him in stony silence.

He chanced a glance at her out of the corner of his eye, but she gazed forward unwaveringly.

His arrival at the Serenghettis' had been met with exactly the reaction he'd expected. He'd be damned, though, if he'd let himself be tossed aside because Mia's family looked down on the Musils—especially after what he and Mia had started in his condo.

He hadn't liked the idea of her showing up and being outnumbered by the rest of her family in an argument. Besides, their underlying beef was with him.

Frankly, he now felt like a knight in shining armor riding off with the damsel in distress—except Mia would eviscerate him for that analogy. He had a car and not a horse, she was a woman who'd proven she could take care of herself, and his armor had a few chinks in it—not least because of his last name, at least as far as the Serenghettis were concerned.

"I can't believe you barged into Serenghetti Central like that," she announced finally, and then turned toward him.

"I didn't barge in," he corrected. "Your sister-in-law opened the door."

"After you misled her with some cooked-up explanation about my leaving something behind."

"You did. Me."

She rolled her eyes. "Yes, thanks for letting everyone know that I had been with you. What were you thinking?"

His hands tightened on the wheel. "I wasn't going to let you face the consequences alone."

"My brothers blowing off steam?" she huffed. "Please, I've dealt with it my whole life."

He bet she had. He and Jordan Serenghetti had crossed paths briefly at Welsdale High School when he'd been a junior and Jordan had nearly been out the door as a senior who was captain of the hockey team. Mia's two older brothers he knew less well. He'd occasionally crossed paths with them in Welsdale, and those interactions could most charitably have been described as an uneasy detente.

A detente that seemed to have ended minutes ago. "I think the correct response is *thank you.*"

He knew he'd irritate her, but hey, as long as they were having this out, he was going to defend himself.

"For what?" she huffed. "You gave everyone the impression that something is going on between us. First Carl, now my family."

He took his eyes off the road to glance at her, quirking a brow. "And you didn't contradict the idea."

"This is all business," she responded emphatically.

He didn't say anything but tightened his hands on the wheel again. Mia was deluding herself if she thought that this was only about business. It was about family feuds. It was about a tangled history of decisions overlaid by emotion and distrust. And most of all, it was about the two of them, and the undercurrent of desire running between them.

By the end of their golf outing with the Bensens, Larry had signaled that he would sign a letter of intent to sell his business to Damian, which meant they would be in good faith negotiations to the exclusion of other buyers. The lawyers were going to have to do due diligence, of course, while he and Larry hammered out details, so nothing was sewn up yet. Still, Damian knew he'd taken a major step toward buying Larry's company. Strangely, though, that felt like the least of his concerns right now.

"You act like you're always on a covert mission with your family," he said finally—because he knew better than to voice all his thoughts about the Serenghetti family dynamic he'd witnessed.

"Aren't you with yours? You're the outsider among the Musils, if you're to be believed."

"So we're both rebels with a cause."

She tossed hair away from her face. "Your oversharing was like throwing oil on the fire for Cole."

He allowed himself a small smile. "Putting a competitor off balance. Good for business."

"Nice try, but you said you're not directly involved with JM Construction—and what were you going to do when the punches started landing?"

"That wasn't going to happen. You jumped in front of me. Who'd have thought a Serenghetti would come to the defense of a Musil?"

"Between you and my brothers, you were the lesser evil."

He gave a short laugh. "Why so caustic when we make each other feel so good?"

She flushed. "Speak for yourself."

He'd been enjoying himself inside his condo until bad news had come barging in. If he could just get to kiss her again—third time was the charm, right? "You were magnificent. You held your own. No need for me to be the heavy, it turns out."

She opened and closed her mouth, seemingly flummoxed and unsure how to react to his words. "I forgot to sew myself a superhero cape."

He arched a brow at her. "You didn't need one. Anyway, aren't you the can-can girl? That costume I liked."

"Of course you did."

He flashed a grin. "For the record, I was on the wrestling team at Welsdale High School. Since then it's been martial arts." He didn't add that he had a black belt. All that focused energy had helped him deal with both his family and his career.

"Cole and Jordan box." It was her turn to raise her eyebrows. "For fun."

"Your brothers may have wanted to hustle me out of the house, but Cole has his business reputation to think about, and Jordan has a public image to maintain, not to mention plenty of endorsement deals. Besides, Dahlia was around. Adorable kid, by the way."

"Someone had to inject some cuteness into the situation."

"We're here," he said with false cheer, pulling into the parking lot beside the luxury condo complex.

A few stray raindrops hit the windshield. *Just in time.*

Mia sighed, and then opened the car door.

"When are we going back to New York?" she asked as she got out.

He followed suit, going around to the trunk for her bag. "Not until morning. Heavy rain and thunderstorms are coming, so we're staying put."

Seven

"What? You can't be serious!" Mia slammed the car door and then looked heavenward. "It doesn't look that bad to me."

Damian held out a hand, and a couple of large drops plopped onto his palm. "Famous last words before the skies open, and all hell breaks loose."

She watched, stupefaction rending her momentarily speechless, while he swung her bag out of the trunk and turned toward the condo complex.

Time to put her foot down, or her umbrella up—maybe both. Was there no end to today's man trouble?

She gesticulated with her hands as she struggled to keep up with him, rain hitting her face and hair with increasing rapidity. "It already poured. At my parents' house when you stormed in. That's why we should head back to New York."

She grabbed the strap of her overnight bag, forcing him

to stop. Raindrops had wet his hair. He blinked against a droplet that clung to his eyelashes, and she watched its trajectory as it made its way down to his sensual lips and chiseled jaw.

"There isn't another bus back to New York at this hour from Welsdale, and you know it."

"I'll rent a car then."

"You shouldn't drive back in this weather."

"Fine. I'll go to a hotel." They were toe to toe as they held on to her bag, getting wetter by the second.

"I've got a condo with a guest bedroom."

"Yes, and you come with it."

Damian's lips twitched, and then he leaned toward her so they were nose to nose, too. "What's the matter? Afraid you won't be able to resist me?"

She sucked in a breath, angry and embarrassed. "Oh, puh-leeze."

Still, his words irked her. She didn't like weakness—much less admitting to it. And wasn't Damian only voicing a variation of her brothers' suspicions—that she was in danger of losing her mind over him?

Damian straightened. "Good. Then there's no problem."

Sure, she'd thought back to their kiss at the costume party—their *accidental* kiss. Who wouldn't? It had been embarrassing. *And hot, seductive, pleasurable.* It had made all her dealings with him since then even more fraught.

The fact that the kiss had gone on repeat a short while earlier in his condo, *the one they were walking toward*—well, that was harder to explain away. But she had a long ride back to New York to mull it over—*alone*.

Damian stood like a rock, seemingly oblivious to the rain that continued to hit them. "For a moment there, I thought your opposition to the obvious solution meant—"

"Well, you were wrong."

"Glad that's settled."

She barely had time to process his words before the downpour began in earnest.

Damian cursed, grabbed her hand, and tugged her along.

Together they raced to the overhang sheltering a side entrance of the building.

When they were back inside his condo, they were cold and partly soaked.

Mia shivered and sent droplets flying.

Putting down her bag, Damian reached into a nearby closet and tossed her one of two towels. "Here. Use this."

"Thanks." She rubbed her face and hair, and then realized her white polo top was plastered to her front. Her lacy bra and erect nipples were outlined beneath.

And judging from the direction of Damian's stare, he'd noticed, too.

Her gaze traveled to his chest with its clearly defined muscles... She hugged the towel to her front.

He jerked his head toward the interior of the condo. "The guest bedroom is back there if you want to change."

"Thanks." She grabbed her bag and strode forward, intent on putting some distance between herself and Damian—and regrouping.

No way was she staying. Unfortunately for her, though, the torrential downpour continued unabated while she changed into drier clothes—sweats—and freshened up in the bathroom across the hall.

She was caught between a rock and a hard place. If she continued to insist on leaving, she'd seem mulish and put the lie to her denial that being alone with him...what? Made her aware of herself as a woman? She wouldn't give him the satisfaction. On the other hand, if she stayed, something *might* happen...

C'mon, Mia. You've dealt with more distracting situations than this one. She could trust herself...couldn't she?

When she wandered back to the front of the condo, she found Damian in the kitchen, contemplating the food arrayed on the counter before him.

She braced herself for some smugness or an I-told-you-so, but instead he gave her an apologetic look.

He gestured at the spread he'd laid out. "I don't stay here often, so it looks like our choice is mostly frozen pizza and hard seltzer."

She resolved to be gracious in her discomfiture. "Sounds exactly like what I was thinking."

While his hair was still damp, he'd changed into a T-shirt and jeans.

"Meaning you pegged me for the type to have an empty fridge with nothing but a container of leftover takeout?" he asked drolly.

Rather than answering, she moved closer to peer at the pizza box. "Feta, pineapple and pepperoni?"

"You've never tried it?" he said, feigning surprise.

"I'm more of a spinach and artichoke type. But I'm sure it's...delicious."

Damian lifted the side of his mouth. "Trust me."

Wasn't that the issue?

Her gaze skittered away from his, and she busied herself opening a can of wild cherry seltzer.

She focused on setting the table while he heated the pizza. Afterward, she made a pretense of scrolling through work emails on her phone while they waited for the food to be ready. Anything to distract herself from Damian moving around casually in the kitchen nearby.

When they finally sat down at the small dining table to eat, Mia took some bites of food and found herself unexpectedly relaxing. She'd been hungrier than she'd thought.

Damian eyed her plate. "Looks as if you like that pepperoni, pineapple and feta pizza after all."

She swallowed and dabbed at her mouth with a napkin. "Surprisingly good."

"See, try something new and—"

"The correct response is *thank you*?" she parried, echoing his words earlier.

He gave her a lopsided smile. "Sorry I couldn't deliver anything close to the home-cooked meal that you'd have gotten at your parents' house."

Struck by his unexpected apology, she found herself wanting to reassure him. "Yes, but then I would have had to deal with my relatives, and as you could tell, families can be difficult sometimes. It's like you're slotted into a role and typecast. At least that's how I feel."

Damian quirked his lips. "That's what happens with people who've known you for a long time."

She took a sip of her drink. "Please don't claim to be a rebel again. I think I've got that role locked up. Anyway, from all appearances, you're the American dream personified. The son of immigrants who climbed to the gazillionaire ranks."

"Yeah, but when you're an immigrant, family loyalty usually counts for more. In Jakob Musil's eyes, I should have stayed in Welsdale to raise JM Construction to new heights."

She could tell him a thing or two about family loyalty, too.

He leaned back in his chair. "And after my mother died, the family got even tighter. It was just me, my brother and my dad."

"I'm sorry." She knew that Damian's mother had died suddenly when he was thirteen. She'd been ten at the time but she'd heard people in town mentioning it.

Damian shrugged. "It was a long time ago."

"But the scar is still there." She didn't know why she made the comment—only that something in his eyes had belied his casual words.

"The scar is what made me who I am today. Though I don't think Dad understood it."

She tilted her head inquiringly.

"I fast-tracked my life. Not just to get away from the sadness at home, but because I got a firsthand look at the cliché that life is short. After she died, I let ambition fuel me."

Ambition was *her* fuel, too, but what a terrible thing to have it lit by the death of a parent.

"So I powered through Carnegie Mellon in five years for a joint computer science and MBA degree."

"And the rest is history," she said half-jokingly.

He arched a brow. "Only if you read the business press."

"You're not doing too shabbily on the New York social scene, either."

"Obviously," he deadpanned. "I showed up at the Ruby Ball with Mia Serenghetti as my date."

She flushed.

Did she want these insights into Damian Musil? It was so much easier to treat him as a two-dimensional character— a villain with sex appeal.

Mia curled up in a corner of the overstuffed sofa—and nursed her cup of chamomile. Outside the driving rain pounded against the Juliet balcony even though the hour already neared midnight. She saw a flash of lightning, and moments later, it was accompanied by claps of thunder.

She hadn't been able to sleep, even though it had been a long day. The Bensens were lovely people, but she'd still been unable to relax completely during the golf game. Not when she was aware of Damian's every move. At one point, she'd caught Allison giving her a knowing look. Who'd have thought that a Serenghetti and a Musil would ever be on the same team?

And then, of course, Damian had shocked her by turning up at her parents' house. He truly believed he'd come to her defense, and she in turn had jumped in to defend him. Now everyone thought they really were a couple.

"I thought I heard noise."

Mia jerked with surprise, and then put her sloshing mug down on an end table.

Damian stood silhouetted in the doorway. He was bare chested, and sweats hung low on his hips. If she'd thought he'd emanated sex appeal in jeans and a T-shirt, she was in no way prepared for the sight of a seminude Damian, his hair tousled from bed.

In the dim lighting afforded by a small lamp, Mia traced the lines of sculpted muscle—hard biceps, flat abs, ripped pecs. He worked out—*obviously*. And his stint on the wrestling team and his martial arts training didn't hurt.

When Damian's lips twitched, she averted her gaze. *Don't touch.* As long as there was no contact, she'd be fine...

He sauntered forward and sat down next to her.

"Sorry if I woke you," she mumbled.

"I had a hard time sleeping, too."

She was curled up, but Damian sprawled—his arm resting on the back of the sofa.

Her resolution about touching was getting harder to keep by the second. *Damn it.* Was he testing her? But no—he looked like the personification of ease while she verged on painful awareness.

"The thunder could wake anybody," he commented.

You could wake anyone. While she'd struggled to sleep

in the guest bedroom, she'd been aware of Damian beyond the bedroom wall in the next room. Her thoughts had hopped and skipped around, but Damian had been like a low hum in the back of her mind.

"What have you been thinking?"

She flushed. "Just contemplating the rain."

"Did storms bother you when you were a kid?"

"Not really."

"I guess there's no chance of you jumping into my arms with fright?" he teased.

She straightened on the sofa, uncurling her legs and planting her feet on the floor. "In your dreams."

He tilted his head. "I can almost taste you there, you know."

She gave a strained laugh. "Those must be some vivid dreams."

"Very."

A shiver of awareness chased down her spine, and she tingled all over.

"Do you want details?" His voice was low, intimate.

"What flavor am I?" she asked, her voice hitching.

No touching, no touching, no touching. She hung on to that resolution like a lifeline.

He quirked his lips. "What part of you am I sampling?"

Wow. Erotic images flashed through her mind. "Are you trying to seduce me?"

He reached for her hand and kissed the back of it. "You have no problems resisting me, remember?"

She sucked in a breath. "Right."

She'd resolved not to make the first move, but she searched her muddled mind about what was supposed to happen if *he* did.

"On the other hand, I want you badly."

"Oh." She wanted to ask since when—

"Your brothers saw right through me. Your family doesn't like it."

She drew in an offended breath. "Who cares?"

She stared at his lips, the plains of his chest visible in the semidarkness and then thrown into relief by a flash of lightning. She lifted her gaze and met his.

It was like he was willing her to make a move—coaxing her to touch him. The tension radiated from him like heat from a bonfire. Too bad the rain was outside and couldn't douse the flames licking her right now.

She wet her lips, and he made a sound.

Honestly, it was hard to hold on to the idea of him as the bad guy. *It was hard to think at all.* He'd walked right into the firestorm at her parents' house—and, traitorously, she'd momentarily thrilled at the sight of him after the initial shock. The whole situation had tested her loyalties, confusing her with her impulse to guard him from her family.

He was a Musil, but she'd started thinking of him as just Damian. Friend or enemy—or something else?

"I have no trouble resisting you." The words rang hollow even to her own ears.

"Ah. Yeah. But we didn't say anything about my resisting you."

If he'd touched her first, did that mean her own resolution about touching no longer applied? Plus, he'd found the weak chink in her armor by mentioning her family. She had a long insubordinate streak.

Slipping her hand over his shoulder, she exerted gentle pressure and brought his head forward.

"One last act of rebellion by getting it on with a Musil?" he muttered.

"Why not?" she whispered against his lips. "Everyone thinks I already have."

He groaned.

And then their lips touched, in a kiss that was hot and full of promise.

Damian angled her head and leisurely explored her mouth. She met him caress for caress as the kiss deepened. When he sought more, she tipped back and he leaned forward. And then he was bringing her legs onto his lap and following her down until her head rested on the arm of the sofa.

Still holding the kiss, he pushed back the gaping top of her pajama shirt.

Mia arched her back, her nipples brushing his chest and hardening. She shifted, seeking his touch, her body humming. Her pulse thrummed through her, hot and heavy with excitement…anticipation.

Damian fisted his hand in her shirt and pulled it down to expose her shoulder and the top of her breast. Then he trailed his lips along her jaw and down the side of her neck, pausing to nip her shoulder before stroking featherlight kisses on her breast.

"Do you always wander around the house without your shirt on?" she managed on a sigh.

He gave a low chuckle. "Hey, at least I put on my sweats before coming out here. I didn't want to scandalize you."

"We've been building to a scandal for weeks."

"Why stop now?" he murmured.

It was hard to come up with an answer.

And then his mouth was on her breast, and Mia forgot to think at all. Instead, she threaded her fingers through his hair and gave herself up to the sensation of Damian lavishing attention on the soft mound.

Sensation shot through her and pooled between her legs.

He moved to her other breast, and she whimpered.

"Mia," he said hoarsely when he lifted his head moments later. "You're even more spectacular than I imagined."

She breathed in deep. "What do I taste like?"

His eyes glittered in a flash of lightning. "Like heaven."

She pulled his head down for a lingering kiss until they were a tangle of limbs. His erection brushed against her, evidence that he was aroused.

When the kiss finally ended, he leveraged himself up and stood. Before she could react, he lifted her into his arms and she squeaked.

Instinctively, she linked her arms around his neck to anchor herself, and Damian strode across the room. Thunder rumbled outside and the rain came down with renewed fury.

"Is this to demonstrate how strong you are?" she teased weakly, adjusting to the unaccustomed sensation of being carried—literally swept off her feet. "I believed you about the martial arts and the rest, you know."

Damian kicked open his bedroom door. "This has nothing to do with showing off. I'm desperate, and I have protection in my room. Or at least I hope to hell I do."

Peripherally, Mia took note of the masculine bedroom done in muted neutrals that she'd glimpsed earlier through the partially open door. And then she found herself deposited on the rumpled king-size bed.

With a couple of fluid moves, Damian opened a small zippered travel pouch on the night table and placed a foil packet on the polished wood.

She raised herself on her elbows and glanced around at the tangle of sheets. "Looks like you were having a rough night."

"You have no idea." He began stripping off his sweats. *Dear sweet fashion gods.* "You don't need clothes."

"Afraid I'll put you out of business?" he teased.

She flushed.

"Yeah, I don't need clothes, I need you. Now."

Yes.

He clamped a hand on her ankle and pulled her toward him while she gave a small exclamation. When he stripped the sweatpants from her, he paused appreciatively. "Red panties."

She heated. "I was in a hurry and tossed them when I was changing."

He started unbuttoning her flannel shirt the rest of the way—and then fumbled.

His impatience—she'd never call Damian nervous—excited her further.

"Here let me."

While she worked at the buttons, he slid his hands up her legs and under her butt, and then trailed his lips up her inner thigh.

"Let's get these silky red panties off you."

She squirmed, and then his mouth found her hot core and she gasped.

With relief, she slid her arms out of her shirt sleeves and tugged him toward her.

"What do you want, Mia?" he breathed against her mouth.

"You. I want you."

They couldn't move fast enough then. He tossed the last pieces of clothing from the bed, and they were a tangle of limbs when thunder rumbled again. He touched her everywhere, arousing her with his mouth and hands.

Somehow they ended up switching positions, and she was on top, astride him. She caressed his length, aching to touch him, and watched him from under lowered lashes.

He closed his eyes on a hiss.

"Yes?"

"Mia."

She tasted him with her mouth, and his hand tangled in her hair.

Damian groaned but held still. "Sweet."

He jerked beneath her attentions, and his free hand fisted in the sheets.

When she sensed that he was on the brink, she straightened, brushed her hair aside, and rolled protection onto his length. She leaned down to kiss him again, and he surprised her by flipping her onto her back one more time.

Testing first, he then entered her in one fluid motion, and they both moaned.

Damian muttered something unintelligible against her neck. Moments later, he started moving, setting a tempo that she met with a counterpoint.

With the storm raging outside, Damian's arms seemed both the safer and more dangerous place to be. He adjusted her hips and suddenly he was hitting her in the exact right spot.

"Oh." Her breath came in gasps.

"Let it happen, Mia," he groaned into her ear. "Come for me."

It was the last encouragement she needed. She spasmed, her hips undulating against him and setting off his own orgasm.

They clung together, waves of sensation lifting them higher until they finally ebbed away, leaving them panting.

Moments later, Damian rolled off her and covered his eyes with his arm. "I went to heaven."

She giggled. "Better than your fantasies?"

Damian turned toward her and propped himself on an elbow. "Yup, and there were plenty of those."

He traced a finger down her chest between her breasts. "I used to wonder what the girl with the flashing eyes was thinking."

"Please, you hardly noticed me."

"I did," he insisted.

"I was a lowly freshman when you were a senior at Welsdale High."

"Remember Jacinda's pool party? I could barely take my eyes off you."

She recalled surreptitiously checking him out, too. "I remember shopping around for the perfect retro swimsuit."

"One that accented your curves."

He circled a finger around her breast, and her eyelids fluttered.

"One that flattered my coloring."

"If you say so."

"Mmm." She sighed languorously, and then turned her head when a glint of gold on the night table caught her attention. "You wear jewelry?"

She didn't recall Damian ever sporting any—not even a watch.

"It's a keepsake that I sometimes travel with." He paused and scanned her gaze. "A chain necklace that my mother bought when I was born."

"Ah. She's still part of who you are."

"Yes."

She was startled by the insight. Another sign that she was failing badly at keeping her distance from Damian. He'd even melted her heart by his interaction with Dahlia, in the midst of a charged conversation with the rest of her family.

She and Damian had kept their distance from each other over the years. Their families' rivalry had been like an insurmountable wall even in the face of any stirrings of attraction. But now that wall was crumbling. Her heart pounded. They'd dated, they'd kissed, they'd gotten to know each other better and realize how much they had in common... *They'd just had sex.* Wow, she was in deep...

Eight

The next morning, Damian woke to find Mia already gone from his bed. Then he realized the water was running in the guest bath. He was semi-aroused and disappointment that she wasn't still in bed with him washed away the remnants of sleep.

Turning his head, he saw the bedside clock said it wasn't even half past seven. He hadn't slept in—she'd gotten up early. With a mental shrug, he figured that maybe Mia was one of those women who didn't want to be seen first thing in the morning. She didn't strike him as the type, but then again, she was in the fashion business, where appearances were everything.

Settling back against the pillow, he stretched and folded his arms behind his head. It had been damn good between them last night. And if she'd still been tucked around him this morning, he'd have picked up where they'd left off.

He and Mia had slept together. His life had been one rapid climb, and yesterday he'd reached new heights.

He'd also faced the Serenghettis without getting ruffled... if you didn't count falling in lust with the firebrand of the family. Oh, yeah, he'd known he'd had a weakness. But he hadn't realized that getting closer to her would *increase* the pull of attraction instead of satisfying it once and for all. His past relationships had all been short-term. He'd been far more focused on the demands of his start-up business.

Instead, yesterday, he hadn't been so concerned about the satisfaction of having the Serenghettis face a Musil who'd legitimately grown more successful than they were as he'd been ready to defend Mia.

Crap, things couldn't get any more complicated. He was known for his cool unflappability in the boardroom—he'd counted on it carrying him through a mutually beneficial arrangement with Mia Serenghetti. Instead, he'd gotten more than he bargained for. More than a taste...more than a fleeting flirtation...more everything.

And he wanted more.

With a grunt of sexual frustration, he lowered his arms and threw back the sheets. He showered, dressed, and headed to the kitchen to make breakfast and answer some work emails.

When Mia appeared, she was wearing a yellow jumpsuit that wasn't revealing but nonetheless hugged her curves. She was like the sun emerging after a storm.

He felt a kick of lust and reined in his desire. He nodded apologetically at the food arrayed in front of him. "From frozen."

"I'm sure it's delicious," she responded brightly.

He'd rather feast on her. He eyed the overnight bag that she'd brought out with her. "In a hurry?"

"I wanted to be packed and ready to go," she said, flushing but setting down the bag. "I wasn't just taking my time to primp...in case you were wondering."

"Now why would I think that," he drawled, "when you're a fashion superstar?"

"Aspiring."

"You have to dream it before you live it."

She came closer and picked up an empty mug. "That's your mantra, huh?"

He poured some coffee while she breathed in the aroma and smiled appreciatively. "It worked out okay."

They stood at the kitchen counter and bit into the egg sandwiches he'd made. Sunlight shafted through the windows and onto the sofa in the nearby living room.

He watched the rays of light add to her luminescence. "The rain stopped, but it's still wet out."

"Mmm," she replied absently, and then swallowed.

Damian reached up and swiped the corner of her mouth with his thumb. "Crumb."

She stilled, and he brushed her lips with his.

"There, all better."

"Don't assume this means more than it does," she said after an awkward silence.

"What?" he joked. "Removing a speck of food from your lips?"

"You know what I mean."

"Isn't that usually the guy's line? No strings?"

She rolled her eyes. "It happened."

He smiled wolfishly. "It was good."

"I'm not into casual hookups—"

"Neither am I."

"I'm too busy with my career."

"Of course."

"But I'm a mature adult, so I know these things happen. We scratched that itch."

"What about if we want to do it again?"

"I don't respond to booty calls."

"Actually I prefer to text," he teased.

She sighed impatiently.

"Okay, what about a date?"

She widened her eyes. "Us? No, forget it."

"Why not?"

"You know why not, and it starts with our last names."

He thought fast. "The Bensens think we're a couple, so we need to play this one out."

"Until you get your business deal—"

"And you have a firm contact in Katie."

She looked momentarily disappointed. "Right."

"C'mon, you wouldn't want Carl to think that I was only a quick rebound relationship," he said half-jokingly. "Right now, he thinks you've moved on with his former boss. You're golden."

For some reason, the thought didn't seem to cheer her up.

"And let's not forget why we fell into bed." He lifted the side of his mouth.

"The storm—"

"Your rebellious streak. Face it, I'm your biggest rebellion yet."

"I'm more clearheaded this morning."

"Still gorgeous, though."

"My designs are meant to bring out the best in a woman."

Taking a sip of his coffee, he said, "Yeah, I figured the sexy jumpsuit was one of your own creations."

She wet her lips, but then took a step back, as if she didn't trust herself—them—not to speed back up the wrong ramp right now.

He sobered. "I've got a quick stop to make before we hit the road to New York."

She tilted her head.

"JM Construction. My father asked me to drop by, and—" he shrugged "—his office is on the road back to New York."

Her eyes widened, and then she shrugged. "We already had our moment with the Serenghettis, so I guess that's fair."

"A Serenghetti arguing to be fair to the Musils?" he murmured. "Never say never."

She raised her eyebrows at him before taking another sip of coffee.

Twenty minutes later, they made their way across the parking lot to his car.

Damian watched Mia sidestep a puddle. Then he opened the trunk and placed their bags inside. "It might be an extended conversation so you may want to come inside with me."

She adjusted the sunglasses perched on her head. "I guess you'll be protecting me from *your* big bad family this time."

Damian bit back a laugh. But damn it—why did the Serenghetti-Musil competition have to rear its head again right now? He didn't see the competition to buy the same construction company ending well. "You won't need protecting."

"Because I'm a badass?" she asked.

He snapped the trunk shut. "Yeah, and they'll be too busy gunning for me."

Her eyes widened. "You're the outlaw in a renegade clan?"

"Do two negatives cancel each other out?" he parried, searching her gaze. "Would that make me a paragon?"

"We'll see," she responded, giving him an oblique look.

"Anyway, with a Serenghetti on the premises, won't they be worried about, you know, corporate espionage…?"

He smiled slightly. "Come on. You can judge for yourself."

JM Construction was located in a nondescript commercial strip on one of the main roads leading out of Welsdale. Mia had driven by it plenty of times as a teen without giving it too much attention—except to occasionally wonder whether Damian was there.

He'd sometimes worked a summer job for the family business like her brothers did for Serenghetti Construction. One episode in particular was imprinted on her memory. She'd been heading to a frozen yogurt store to meet up with a couple of high school girlfriends. Damian had been hauling equipment out of the back of a pickup. Their gazes had collided—he'd given her a quick sweeping look, a slight nod of the head, and then an almost imperceptible smile. She'd swept her hair off her shoulder and walked on, pretending she hadn't noticed. Inside she'd sizzled. *With annoyance.* Or so she'd told herself.

He should have known that if he so much as looked in her direction, her brothers would pounce. And yet, years later, it hadn't stopped him…

They'd spent the whole night together. She'd woken twice in the middle of the night—once to find Damian's arm draped over her, and later, to find herself snuggled against him. When the sun had come up, she'd woken first and tiptoed back to the guest bedroom for a shower and to get ready—and to collect her thoughts.

Musils and Serenghettis did not date. Or have sex. She and Damian had simply entered a mutually advantageous agreement that had gotten complicated. But there was still time to get on the right track.

This was business. She kicked a pebble as they walked to the front door of JM Construction.

Moments later, Mia surveyed her surroundings. The office manager was busy on the phone, an employee in work boots was exiting via a side door and voices could be heard in the back office.

It was all rather mundane. Rather like Serenghetti Construction, actually—or rather what she remembered her family business being while she was growing up. The Musils' company, on the other hand, clearly remained small and scrappy—an opponent nipping at the heels.

Mia wasn't sure what she should have been expecting. Maybe something more ominous and forbidding. Darth Vader's theme song playing in the background, perhaps.

Damian gestured for her to follow him and they turned a corner to the back offices.

She recognized Jakob Musil instantly. An older version of Damian, he was standing in the hall talking to a younger man. His companion turned, and Mia recognized Valentin, Damian's younger brother. He'd still been in middle school when she'd crossed paths with Damian at Welsdale High.

"Damian, you're finally here." Jakob's voice was gruff but his perusal was a tad quizzical.

"Dad, this is Mia Serenghetti," Damian said, seeming to shrug off any implicit criticism in his father's greeting.

Mia steeled herself, but if they were shocked or surprised, neither Jakob nor Valentin showed it.

Instead, Jakob looked at her shrewdly for a couple of moments. "Ah, Mia Serenghetti. I remember when you were—"

He gestured with his hand to indicate a height under five feet.

Mia drew herself up. She might not match her brothers'

or Damian's six-foot frames, but at five-seven, she thought she held her own these days. "Nice to see you, Mr. Musil."

Jakob nodded his head. "Perhaps you've come as the family emissary ready to negotiate about the competition to buy Tevil Construction?"

"I know nothing about it, Mr. Musil," Mia responded. "The family construction company is my brother Cole's business to run these days."

Thanks to Jordan, she knew that Tevil Construction was the latest flashpoint between the Musils and Serenghettis. Well, except for the matter of her and Damian and their little arrangement...

"But you are still a Serenghetti, yes? And Serg's daughter."

"Yes, but—"

"Dad, Mia is here because we were invited to play a game of golf yesterday with another couple."

"Interesting," Valentin commented, finally speaking up.

"We were asked to make up a pair for golf," Mia added quickly, and then shrugged. "You know, so much business happens on the golf course..."

Not a couple, not a couple. Not in a real sense.

Damian shot her an amused look, and she pursed her lips.

What was wrong with him? The false advertising about their fake relationship was gaining a wider audience, day by day. At this rate, he should go ahead and take out a billboard in Times Square.

Perplexed, Jakob looked at her. "So you and my son are on the same team?"

"Not exactly."

Valentin quirked a brow. "Yeah, because who'd believe a Musil—"

Damian shot his brother a quelling look.

"It was a business outing," Mia offered lamely.

Valentin shrugged. "Right. Because we know Damian isn't in your league."

Mia heated and bit the inside of her cheek. Was Valentin suggesting that Damian wasn't good enough for her—or vice versa?

"Damian isn't in *our* league anymore, either," Jakob observed.

Well, that certainly cleared things up for her.

Damian's expression grew tense. "Dad—"

"Why else do you come back so little? That condo of yours is gathering dust."

Not last night.

Still, Mia felt a jolt and an inexplicable urge to defend Damian. After all, she could relate—to being overscheduled with a career and not wanting to fall back into a discouraging family dynamic, and for so many other reasons. But she clamped her mouth shut.

"I've been busy," Damian said without inflection.

"Yes, with the new Musil empire." Jakob looked around. "What was wrong with building on what's here?"

"We could use your fancy business degree," Valentin added dryly.

Mia glanced around at her surroundings again. They were bare bones, especially in comparison to Cole's glossy headquarters in Welsdale these days. But JM Construction would always be the upstart nipping at Serenghetti Construction's heels.

"Dad, construction was never my thing even though I worked plenty of summers here."

"Construction too old-fashioned for you? Working with your hands and getting dirty?"

Mia shifted uncomfortably. This was fast becoming an argument. Sort of like a mirror of her family, except she had no trouble mouthing off when it was another Serenghetti.

Damian sighed, as if this was a conversation he'd had before. "It wasn't that."

"How many generations does it take to wash the dirty money, eh?" Jakob mused, almost to himself.

Damian said nothing but a muscle ticked in his jaw.

Mia wanted to disappear but she was also transfixed.

"Just remember—" Jakob nodded at his surroundings "—this business paid the bills for your education."

Damian raked his hand through his hair.

Jakob turned to her. "What do you think?"

What? "I—"

"Let's leave Mia out of this."

"Why? She's obviously important if you brought her here."

Was no one listening to her protestations about a meaningless golf game?

"And she's also a Serenghetti. I'm sure she has strong opinions," Jakob added.

"Seems like we're going to retrace old ground," Damian muttered. "All of it."

Mia splayed her hands. "To be truthful, I went off to work in New York, too. I'm...biased."

"But you get home to visit?" Jakob pressed.

Yup, like yesterday—much to her regret. "Well, I—"

Jakob chuckled. "And you don't hold any animosity toward us Musils. Because you're not involved with Serenghetti Construction—" he gestured toward Damian "—but you are with my son." Jakob looked slyly between Damian and Mia. "Golf game, yes?"

"Well, to be fair, I do know that you and my family have some history."

Jakob lowered his brows at her words. "What history?"

"The incident with the Kenable exec, Dad," Damian

said, breaking in. "Let's start there, since we're rehashing things."

"What about it?" Jakob shot back, lowering his brows at Damian.

Mia was familiar with that look. She'd seen it on... Serg Serenghetti. She wondered what her father would think about the similarity to his rival and erstwhile nemesis.

Valentin sighed and leaned his shoulder against the hallway wall. "Here we go."

"Dad, he got a free guest house," Damian said.

"Only after he was not employed by the shopping mall developer anymore."

"But you discussed it with him before you got the contract."

"It came up in conversation. But why does it matter?" Jakob said impatiently. "JM Construction was the best for the job."

"And he got a new guest residence for giving you the business."

Mia supposed an underdog had to do what an underdog had to do. Didn't she know that herself these days, trying to break into the big time in the fashion business?

Jakob shook his head. "No, he paid for the raw materials, and we supplied labor for the guest house. It was a small project, and now he's a friend. What's wrong with doing a favor for a friend?"

Damian sighed. "Dad, we've been at an impasse on this issue for years. Let's just agree to disagree."

Suddenly, Jakob's shoulders lowered. "You think it's easy struggling with a new business and a young family? Then I lost my wife. I did what I had to do to survive... Maybe I would not make the same decision again."

Mia flushed and her heart squeezed. "Mr. Musil, I understand."

All three men stilled and looked at her. She wasn't sure who was most surprised.

"You do, eh?" Jakob finally asked.

"Yes. Sometimes it's not the facts but how we choose to interpret them—and our options—at the time." Her brother's indictment of the Musils had seemed damning. Maybe JM Construction had made a few missteps, particularly in its earlier days, but companies changed. People could change.

She understood—she was trying to build her own brand. She'd always striven to be ethical, but competition was stiff, like in every other business. And temptation could be lurking right around the next corner.

Damian's father relaxed a bit. "It's Jakob. And explain that to your brother Cole."

"I can't. We're not exactly on great terms right now."

Jakob looked between her and his son, a perceptive twinkle in his eye. "I don't ask why."

Damian muttered something, but it seemed as if the tension had broken.

"It's a little late in the game, but why did you want me to stop by, Dad?" Damian asked, his tone holding a note of forbearance.

Jakob suddenly chuckled and lightened. "Yes, I have something to give you." His gaze drifted to Mia. "And looks like the timing may be good."

They all followed him into the nearest office, which was sparsely furnished with a metal desk, two chairs and file cabinets.

Jakob picked up a small red box and held it out to Damian. "Here. Your mother wanted you to have this. Some of her personal possessions that she wanted divided between you and your brother by the time that you were both thirty. You weren't in Welsdale for Valentin's last birthday, so I'm doing it while I know you are here. This one's yours."

Damian took the box slowly. "Thanks."

Jakob nodded. "You don't have to open it now."

Damian rubbed the back of his neck. "Yup, I think Mia has seen enough drama."

All weekend. Mia took a deep breath. First her family, then the Musils, and she wasn't even counting the little interlude with Damian in between.

Dear sweet heaven, she'd slept with the enemy—and now she was having trouble remembering that's what he was supposed to be.

Things happened quickly after that. Jakob invited them to stay for coffee, and she quickly learned that for all the awkwardness and roughness, the Musils were bound by loss and a deep history. Jakob and Valentin were soon called away by business, however, and Damian announced that he and Mia needed to get on the road.

That's when Mia was brought back to the realization that she still had a long drive back to New York in close quarters with Damian...

Nine

"**W**ell, that went well," Damian remarked dryly as soon as he and Mia were on the road again.

"Hmm."

He glanced at her out of the corner of his eye. "Hmm?"

"I've never been inside JM Construction before."

He laughed. "I didn't think so, even though you had a reputation for being rebellious back in high school."

She turned her head toward him. "Meaning I might have broken in?"

"I said rebel, not spy. That wouldn't have fit the role."

"And what tipped you off? The purple hair? The nose ring?"

His lips twitched. "Yeah, what happened to that ring?"

She folded her arms. "I got bored with the experiment, and the hole closed by itself."

He chanced another glance at her. "You mean you'd achieved your goal of shocking your family, and it was time to move on."

She swept him with a look of mock affront. "You think so, Mr. Straight-and-Narrow?"

"Hardly."

She gestured at him. "Look at you. So clean-cut, there's barely a swerve to you."

"Meaning I had no surprise moves last night?" he parried.

She sucked in a breath.

"I love it when you get all bothered over me," he teased, before adopting a thoughtful expression. "You know, it surprised me when you went into fashion."

"Because of what I was like in high school?"

He nodded.

"It's not that surprising," she sniffed. "I have two aunts on my mother's side who were talented seamstresses before they sold their shop and retired. I spent a couple of summers with them in Italy, sort of apprenticing."

"Ah, no wonder I didn't see you in a new bikini every season."

She tossed him a quelling look. "Lots of Serenghettis are creative types. Even construction is an art form if you think about it."

"So I suppose that explains why you came to my father's defense back there. One artist backing another."

She opened and closed her mouth. "I wasn't choosing sides, just trying to see both."

He quirked a brow at her.

She glanced out the window. "My family doesn't like that JM Construction hired away some of their employees, but there's nothing illegal about it. And every construction company has run afoul of complicated codes over the years. With any luck, they weren't serious violations, and they've learned from them. Every company also tries to attract new business. As far as Kenable, though, your father admitted he might not make the same business decision today."

"Says the entrepreneur."

She tossed her hair. "Whatever. But yes, I've got some insight now that I'm running my own company."

"Naturally."

"You know, that was the first time he said that he might have made a mistake. Maybe it was the occasion of passing along heirlooms. Or maybe...it was because you were there."

She flushed.

He liked that Mia had warmed to his family. He also liked that she didn't think of his father as just another wrongdoer. Damn it, he liked *her*.

She shifted in her seat, as if uncomfortable with her own admissions. "Do you mind if we play some music?"

"That depends," he teased.

"On what?"

"Your musical tastes."

"You're impossible," she said, leaning forward and fiddling with the car stereo.

When she glanced out the window again, he caught the faint sounds of classic rock. They settled into a companionable silence, and he took the curves of the open road that wound between rolling hills.

She seemed lost in a reverie but eventually started mouthing some lyrics. Soon, to his amusement, the mouthing turned into humming and then singing under her breath.

"Caterwauling?" he commented.

She turned toward him. "What?"

"Do you always sing in the car?"

"Are you saying you don't like my voice?"

"I like it." He'd *dreamed* about it.

She tossed him a quizzical look. "I get the singing from my mother. She loves musicals. In fact, she named Cole after Cole Porter."

Damian rubbed his jaw thoughtfully, thinking it had escaped without even a punch yesterday. "Your brother lived up to his eloquent namesake yesterday. His words were music to my ears."

Mia tried and failed to suppress a smile.

"I should have guessed you took after your mother. Even aside from being beautiful, you also like music."

Mia grew flustered and glanced out at the passing landscape.

They drove in silence except for the low music, and the next time Damian glanced over at her, he was surprised to find that her eyes had fluttered shut. She'd dozed off.

A feeling suspiciously like tenderness swept over him. This weekend had tired her out. When he reached Manhattan, though, he knew he needed to rouse her because they would soon be at her place.

He turned up the volume and started crooning along to "My Girl."

Within minutes, Mia blinked and opened her eyes. Stretching, she asked, "What's that caterwauling?"

Damian laughed. "That's my girl…"

She rolled her eyes.

"What, you don't like the song? You know, we are in May, and you are—"

"Not sunshine. Please." She looked pained at his reference to the lyrics.

He grinned.

"You know, your singing voice isn't half bad," she sniffed.

"You should hear me in the shower," he purred.

"Caterwauling at the break of dawn."

He chuckled. "I'm not familiar with that song."

"Of course not."

When he pulled up in front of her building, there wasn't a parking spot in sight. *Damn it.* If they'd been at his place, he could have tossed the car keys to a doorman. But she lived in a walkup above her studio, in what looked like a renovated tenement on a side street in the Garment District. That much he'd established when he'd picked her up for the Ruby Ball—what seemed like eons ago.

Before their world had shifted. Before they'd hooked up. Before he'd met her family and she'd met his. Before she'd had his back, and he'd had hers, and they'd had each other...

She turned to look at him. "Thanks for the ride."

He nodded, flexing his hands on the steering wheel. Because otherwise it would be too tempting to reignite the passion between them, even with the passing pedestrians offering no privacy.

"I'd better get out before you, you know, get a ticket."

Nodding, he got out along with her. He was pulled up alongside some parked cars, and traffic continued to plow by on his driver's side.

After opening the trunk, he passed the overnight bag to her.

When their hands brushed, she stilled, and he quirked a knowing brow.

Her phone buzzed, and shifting, she fished it out of her handbag with her free hand. She frowned down at the screen for a moment. "I'd better get this. Work calls."

Text me. Call me. Sleep with me. But he said none of those things.

Instead, he shoved his hands in his pockets and watched her walk into her building.

But not out of his life.

They needed to see their arrangement through as far as the Bensons and their daughter were concerned.

And hell if he'd let himself be ghosted.

"I'm worried about you, *cara*."

"Stop, Mom. I'm fine. Really." Mia paced inside her work studio. The late afternoon sun filtered weakly through the security bars on the back windows, little particles of dust floating in the beams of light.

"I don't know... You don't seem yourself."

Mia blew out a breath. In other words, *let's talk about the kerfuffle that happened in Welsdale this weekend with Damian Musil.*

"Should I come down to New York to see you?"

Ack. No. It was enough trouble when her brothers dropped into the city. Mia absently twisted the tie on her denim jumpsuit.

Next time, she thought absently, she'd add a hidden cinch waist. She was always searching for ways to make her next design better...

"We could get reservations at a nice restaurant. There's a new place—"

"Mom, everything is okay." She'd gone restaurant hopping with her mother in the past, but right now the last thing Mia needed was for her mother to come to New York.

"Are you sure?"

Mia sighed. "You're really calling about Damian, aren't you?"

She needed to say she'd consigned Damian to the scrap heap—or pretend that she had. Or least admit they weren't in a real relationship. It was all a mutually-beneficial temporary arrangement, and anything that had happened in the bedroom had been one big mistake... But somehow the words wouldn't come.

"Your father wanted to call, but I said no. 'Serg, *fermati*. Stop.'"

Who was her mother kidding? *Calling* sounded so innocuous. *Yelling*, now that was more like it when it came to her father.

Camilla cleared her throat. "I—how do you say?—reasoned with him. I said, '*I know you are upset*, but Mia will make her decisions and tell us when she's ready.'"

Mia blinked. "Thanks, Mom."

Her mother had always been the one to run interference between her husband and her children, even if she remained a protective parent herself. Over the years, though, Mia had pulled and tugged on familial ties until they had stretched...all the way to New York.

"Did I tell you how your father and I met?" Camilla asked suddenly.

Of course, Mia knew the basic facts, having heard them discussed dozens of times. Her father had been a tourist in Tuscany when he'd first encountered her mother manning the front desk of a hotel. Before he'd checked out, a flame had been lit.

"My family didn't approve of him."

"You're kidding." This was news to her after thirty years.

"Your father doesn't like to bring it up."

"Of course." Her father had a lot of pride.

"But I had my heart set on Serg."

"Why didn't they approve?"

"They didn't know him, and they were suspicious. Too many Casanovas checked in and out of the *albergo*."

Mia choked back a startled sound. She'd never thought anyone would compare her father to Casanova. Still, she couldn't help being curious. "How did you know that Dad was the one?"

"He was *persistente*." Camilla laughed, her voice full of reminiscence. "I started dating someone else, and your father arranged another stay for himself at the *albergo*."

Damian was nothing if not persistent…

"Anyway, this is about you. I know your father and brothers are worried. You know they don't like the Musils."

"I met them," Mia blurted.

There was silence on the line. "And—"

"Mom, they seemed like any other family in the construction business. Except, you know, it was really up by your bootstraps because Damian's father didn't start his company until he moved to Welsdale. Then he lost his wife and had two young kids to raise."

Mia finished what she was going to say all in one breath. She'd heard enough about Jakob Musil and JM Construction over the years to know that Damian's father had arrived in Welsdale as a young man—whereas her own father had been born and bred in the area. If any of her relatives could appreciate being a new arrival and settling down in unfamiliar territory, it was her mother.

"Hmm."

Mia could tell her mother was torn between conflicting impulses. Camilla had been thrilled to see her sons married off, and she'd never been shy with questions about whether Mia was dating anyone. But no doubt, she'd never imagined the boyfriend candidate might be Damian Musil.

Wait, there was no candidate. No contender. No contestant.

"I don't know, Mia. Be careful."

Mia could practically picture her mother shaking her head resignedly. "There's nothing to be careful about," she responded lightly. "Damian and I aren't really a couple. We just had…a couple of dates."

There. Vague but accurate.

Her mother sighed, and Mia wondered if that was relief she heard.

"On the other hand, your father and I are heading toward forty-five years—"

"Yup, I know."

"—if we're lucky."

Mia perked up. She was glad for the change of topic, but this sounded *not good*. "*If we're lucky?*"

Her mother sighed. "You know the expression, no? How do you say? Don't count the eggs before they hatch?"

"Chickens, Mom. Don't count your chickens before they hatch."

"*Sì*, okay. What does it matter? You understand me, no?"

Mia was used to her mother's mashups of Italian and English. "Well, Dad seems to have put his stroke behind him these days," she said carefully, "so there's nothing to worry about, right?"

"Except for his new television career," her mother muttered.

Mia laughed, relaxing. "What? Don't tell me his *Wine Breaks with Serg!* segment has gone to his head?"

"He's giving me advice about my own show."

There'd been a time when her father had seemed threatened by her mother's second act as a local television personality—at the same time that he'd had to step back from the construction company that he'd built. But it had appeared that lately things were going well.

"Next he'll think we're rivals."

"Dad likes to think big. That's how he became a successful business owner. You know, he's competitive."

"Ha! You don't need to tell me."

Honestly, didn't her father's competitive streak also help explain why he'd held tight to his dim view of JM Construction? But on television, her mother was the established player, and her father was the upstart. "Just remind him that he owes his whole show business career to you. Without *Flavors of Italy*, there'd never be a *Wine Breaks with Serg!*"

"You remind him, *cara*," her mother huffed.

"Nice move, Mom. Why don't you let me know when he's ready to talk calmly with me?"

And Mia doubted that her father would appreciate her pointing out that these days he and Jakob Musil had something in common—they were both upstarts.

But he'd welcome any news that she currently had no plans to see Damian again. Now why didn't that make her feel relieved?

Ten

Since the weekend, and especially after the call with her mother, Mia had thrown herself into work.

Still, scenes from the weekend had replayed themselves in her mind, like an auto rewind. They'd pretended to be a couple for the Bensens. And then they'd had a confrontation with her brothers before jumping into an episode of *Meet the Musils!*

Why couldn't she stop thinking about Damian?

Yes, they'd had sex. Yes, it had been good. Yes, it had been spectacular. But now that part was over and never to be repeated…no matter what Damian thought.

Of course, she hadn't heard from him either in over forty-eight hours. And that's exactly how she wanted it, she told herself, unless he was getting in touch about the Bensens and Katie.

She moved bolts of fabric in a corner of her cramped studio, looking for the one that she planned to use for an

asymmetrical skirt for her new line. She wanted to expand
the range of her business.

The natural light in this ground-level space had never
been great, and today was overcast and wet. Maybe she'd
walk up the three flights of stairs to her own apartment
and work there since she didn't have anyone to supervise
today. She was between interns because the school term
at the nearby fashion schools was ending.

Her phone buzzed, and she straightened, pushing hair
away from her face.

Looking around, she spotted her cell peeking out from
underneath a copy of *Brilliance* magazine, which sat atop
Vogue, *InStyle*, and back issues of some other titles.

Glancing at the screen, she was surprised to discover
that the text was from Katie. She sucked in a breath. Ali-
son had insisted on passing along her personal contact info.

The word *interview* jumped out.

Excitement bubbled up.

Then she typed a reply. Sure...

Hitting Send, she blew some lingering stray strands
away from her face.

Soon enough, a reply came from Katie.

I'd like to include some words from Damian in the interview. It helps to round it out. I can also reach out to
any fashion industry names who'd like to say nice things
about you.

Ugh. Mia lowered her shoulders. Damian wasn't really
her boyfriend? Instead, she found herself typing again.
Sure.

Then she bit her lip. She couldn't even call Gia to talk.
Her cousin was abroad—accompanying her husband,

Alex, on a brief business trip to Japan. And anyway, there was a good chance Gia would egg her on.

She was about to land a prime spotlight on her company. She was beyond thrilled. But...

Before her bravado failed her, she raised her phone and called.

Thanks to planning for the Ruby Ball, she had Damian's number.

"Hello." The timber of his voice was low, deep, not at all surprised. "Mia."

His voice stole through her like the hit of a shot.

"Katie Bensen wants to interview me," she blurted.

"And that's a bad thing?"

"Yes... No."

"And here I was thinking this was the booty call that I was waiting for."

"Wishful thinking."

"Never stop dreaming."

His irreverence fortified her, and strangely helped overcome her anxiety and misgivings. "I need you—"

"Finally."

"Will you cut it out?"

"Why, when it's so much fun?"

"I need you to be interviewed, too."

"My turn in the limelight," he quipped.

She pasted a tight smile on her face even though he couldn't see it. "*Brilliance* magazine wants to include some words from you because Katie thinks we're—"

"Ah."

"—together," she finished lamely. "Everyone believes you're—"

"A boyfriend," he finished for her.

This was so humiliating. "Thanks partly to you!"

She should have gone with the idea of hiring a model

or escort to accompany her to the Ruby Ball. Now Katie had recommended making Damian a part of the magazine piece…and she'd agreed, jumping at a chance that was too good to pass up.

And, really, what else could she have said? No doubt the readers of *Brilliance* would savor every word about Damian… *If only they knew.* Their coupledom was a stunt. But if she was lucky, maybe a few of those single readers would contact him. The thought left a sour taste.

"All right, I have a suggestion."

Mia stilled.

"You conduct the interview at my offices."

"That's it?" She dropped her shoulders. The truth was, she hadn't relished the possibility of an interview in her cramped studio—one where she and an intern often had to sidestep each other.

"If you're doing the interview here, it'll lend credibility to our—"

"Coupledom?"

"Connection."

"Like the One Republic song?"

"You're a fan?"

"I have wide musical tastes. I was the designated DJ at slumber parties." When she hadn't been sneaking backstage at rock concerts…

Damian's rich laugh felt like a warm embrace. Then he started humming "All I Ever Need Is You."

His voice spread through her…heating, warming, kindling her senses. He had her off-balance, and thinking back to their weekend together, though she would never admit it. "You're going to make this ask as hard as possible, aren't you?"

Damian's voice trailed off. "Drop me a text with the

details, and I'll arrange an empty office space to conduct the interview."

"Great." She paused a beat. "Thanks."

"No problem. And since we're exchanging favors—"

"Exchanging?" Why did that word sound foreboding?

"I've got a charity dinner to attend at the end of next week. A lot of the East Coast tech crowd will be there. The extra ticket is yours."

Wait—what? It sounded a lot like...a date. "We're not a couple. We agreed."

"Did we?"

"You know we did. Or I said it, and you didn't disagree. So it was a meeting of the minds."

She pulled her thoughts away from the other ways they'd made a connection last weekend...

"Maybe I'm clueless."

"Oh, puh-leeze."

He gave a low laugh. "You don't believe me? It was just me, Dad and Valentin over at the Musil shack."

She snapped her mouth shut—chagrined. *Of course.* He'd lost his mother, and hadn't she spotted his remembrance necklace this weekend? But he couldn't be that clueless about women...could he?

She'd grown up with three older brothers who were all smooth guys, able to charm their way through innumerable girlfriends. Of course, her brothers had all been in the public eye and magnets for the opposite gender. Cole and Jordan had played for the NHL, and Rick had spent time as a stuntman with name-brand actresses on the big screen.

"On the other hand, you were holed up in the Serenghetti castle."

"Hardly."

He cut off a laugh. "I'm supposed to say I agree, right?"

"See, you are a quick study."

"What if I claimed I've learned a lot from you?"

She shivered with awareness even as she felt flustered by the flattery. For a guy who hadn't grown up around women, he was doing just *fine*. So instead of answering him directly, she said, "Fine, if that's what it takes to make this interview happen, get back to me with the details about the dinner."

"Great."

Just what she thought he might say. Sweet heaven...

Mia sat across from Katie in one of the empty glass-walled conference rooms at CyberSilver Technologies. They were taking a break from the interview so Katie could review her notes. The room was spare, as befitted a cutting-edge tech company, but plenty of light filtered in from the pre-war building's generous windows overlooking Fifth Avenue from twenty-three stories above.

Damian's employees walked by outside. They were dressed casually and seemed very laid-back, like they weren't at work. She could see them through the glass walls, but they couldn't hear her.

Fortunately. If they wondered what she and *Katie* were doing in their offices, no one said anything.

They could read all about it in *Brilliance*. And then she'd have some quick footwork and explaining to do with her family. She'd left her mother with the impression there was nothing to be concerned about beyond a few dates that had fizzled...

She'd have to claim that she and Damian had delayed their conscious uncoupling. She almost winced at the increasing tangle that she had to extricate herself from...

Mia shifted on her stool. It was hard to relax when this interview was so fraught with potential pitfalls.

So far, she'd been able to toss out some good details

about her business in response to Katie's questions. Her brand was affordable, environmentally conscious, and easy to wear. She'd hit all the keywords, sprinkling her answers with the bold terms in her business plan. All her best designs were displayed on some mannequins in the room. A photographer and assistant from *Brilliance* were busy photographing them. She'd also already emailed some pictures to the magazine.

Katie flipped a page in her notepad and looked up. "Ready to resume the interview?"

"Sure!" Had she sounded peppy enough?

"So tell me how you and Damian met," Katie gushed.

Huh? The questioning had suddenly taken a dangerous turn, and Mia straightened. "We grew up in the same town in Massachusetts, so, uh, of course we knew of each other."

"But there wasn't a spark of attraction back then?"

"Well, no." *Liar, liar.*

"We don't see you two together often. He doesn't show up on your social media."

"We wanted to keep our relationship private until now." *Yeah, right.* They'd done a crummy job keeping their non-relationship under wraps. The people whom she wanted most of all to keep in the dark—her family—had found out anyway.

"Isn't social media how you got your start in fashion?" Katie asked, changing her tactics.

Mia nodded. *Phew.* At least they were off the topic of Damian. "I started out as an influencer back in high school and college. Then I kept building a following." She laughed. "I spent too much time on filming videos and not so much on chemistry."

Katie grinned. "Me, too. Well, not so much making my own stuff, but posting what I liked about other designs.

I guess my father was disappointed. I didn't show much interest in the family company."

Mia found herself warming to Katie Bensen even apart from their work-related connection. "Hey, it's okay." She shrugged. "I wasn't much into construction, which was my family's business. The way I see it, I liked to create stuff but with different materials."

"So how do you stay fresh? With designs, I mean?"

"I take inspiration where I find it. It could be the color of a sunset." Or the look and feel of a thunderstorm on a night when you were trying not to be aware of temptation sleeping a few feet away.

At the sound of the door opening, they both turned. Damian sauntered in, looking every inch the rich tech startup owner, dressed down in jeans and an open-collar shirt. Since the interview was being conducted at Cyber-Silver, everyone had agreed that Damian would stop by in person for some questions from Katie.

There was an air of authority about Damian here in his corporate headquarters that was downplayed when he was socializing outside work. With her fashion eye, though, Mia could tell his shoes were expensive and his shirt was impeccably tailored—which helped advertise the lithe, muscular physique that she was all too well acquainted with.

Her heartbeat ticked up a notch.

She'd dressed carefully for this interview—striving for professional but edgy to match her brand. She'd finally settled on a black-and-white jumpsuit. The black trousers were attached to a white bodice with a sweetheart neckline and short puff sleeves. The bottom was conservative, but the top looked as if it could have been cut off a bridal dress. The construction was clever; it looked like two pieces when it was actually one, since jumpsuits had started as her signature item and her market niche...

She'd thought she'd hit the right note sartorially. But she hadn't anticipated Damian's look of appreciation—as if he was drinking her in.

He quickly replaced it with a bland expression and came toward her with a slight smile.

She shifted again on her seat and wished that she'd thought of nudging the empty stool next to her farther away. So she could breathe, think, focus.

Damian stopped next to her and leaned down. She widened her eyes.

He brushed her lips with his. "Hi, babe."

She sucked in a breath, and he gave her a slightly crooked smile.

Babe...? And what was he up to with the public display of affection?

When he sat next to her, she crossed her legs.

"I'm so glad you could join us," Katie bubbled. "And thanks for the use of your office. Mia suggested we'd be more comfortable here."

Mia avoided Damian's laughing eyes.

"No problem," he responded easily. "Anything to help."

Katie looked between them. "How long have you two been dating, if I can ask? I couldn't find anything about you before the Ruby Ball."

Mia knew she had to jump in. "Not long—"

"But I've been watching Mia forever."

Katie perked up. "Waiting for your chance?"

Along with Katie, Mia turned to look at Damian.

"Well, Mia was dating my former employee. You may have heard of him, Carl Eshoo."

Katie leaned forward. "Ooh, a love triangle."

"Not quite," Mia said hurriedly.

What was this? A fashion profile or a gossip piece?

Katie looked down at the pad in her hand. "My research showed he and Mia were an item—" she glanced at Mia apologetically "—but Carl recently got married."

So Katie had done her homework.

"His loss, my gain."

Wow, Damian was laying it on thick.

"But wait," Katie persisted, glancing from Mia to Damian and back, "if you've known each other for a long time, why did things never, uh, happen between you?"

Crap. "We were like two ships passing in the night—"

"And our families didn't like each other."

Mia resisted the urge to kick him. If she swung her crossed leg, could she make it look like an accident if it connected with his shin?

Katie, though, leaned back with delight. "Oh, so romantic. Like Romeo and Juliet."

Mia moved her elbow in position to give Damian a poke. He was inches away…but she had no room for error with a stealth maneuver.

"And it's so cute the way you finish each other's sentences."

Mia gave the semblance of a smile. "Isn't it just?"

This was playing out to her advantage in at least one way, she belatedly realized. The story now wasn't that she'd been dumped by a guy who'd raced to the altar with someone else. Instead, she'd moved on with the boss— who'd had the hots for her all along. While her family would have a conniption, the *Brilliance* readers would love it.

But what was Damian up to? It was one thing to tease her in bed about how he'd always been attracted to her. It was another to lay it on thick for a reporter…

Katie leaned in. "So your families are what kept you apart."

"Well, I can't speak for Mia," Damian demurred, "but I was crushing on her."

Both Katie and Damian turned to look at her, and Mia wet her lips.

"I, uh, was oblivious?" She tacked on a small laugh.

Damian lifted the side of his mouth. "Babe, you know I'm usually subtle—"

As a sledgehammer.

"—but you definitely had the hots for me."

She blinked at him—hard.

Katie, though, seemed to be eating up every juicy, duplicitous morsel.

Mia smiled brightly at the younger woman. "Well, there you have it. Damian is subtle...and I'm not."

Katie laughed. "Sort of like the Mia Serenghetti brand?"

As Mia widened her eyes, Damian nodded and folded his arms. "Bold, brave and badass."

Eleven

"I've instructed my lawyers to get everything in order for the closing date that we agreed to," Larry Bensen said, sounding pleasant and relaxed over the phone.

Damian sank back against his office chair. "Great. I'm looking forward to it. How does it feel now that things are nearly settled?"

Larry chuckled. "Like a weight has almost lifted from my shoulders."

"The company will be in good hands, Larry."

"I'm counting on it."

"I'm from Welsdale. It's important to me to help preserve the town and to keep connected to it." This was as personal as he'd ever gotten in a business deal.

"I figured as much."

They talked some more about the closing, and when the call ended, Damian rubbed the back of his neck.

The business with Larry was as good as a done deal.

All they needed was for the lawyers to finish the drafting of purchase documents. Because Larry had been ready to sell and had been looking for a buyer, he'd already had his house in order. With any luck, now the deal would close on time and without a hitch.

Soon, very soon, Damian would be the new owner of a local Welsdale television station. The native son done good and come home. The name Musil would be associated with a whole new venture and industry. Short of sticking his name on a park, street or impressive downtown building—but that might come in time—he'd gone a long way toward bolstering the family name. On top of it, he'd be investing in his hometown, which had helped mold him into who he was.

Damian thought back to Mia, because that's where his mind often went these days.

The interview with Katie had gone great. Sure, he'd laid it on a little thick—he could see the sparks in Mia's eyes when he'd called her *babe*—but he hadn't lied, either.

Because this was no longer solely about a business deal with Larry Bensen—if it ever was. Somewhere along the way, Damian acknowledged, his motives had morphed.

This was about the Serenghettis and Musils, and the fact that he and Mia had been dancing around each other for years because they'd gotten tangled up in simmering family rivalries.

Damian steepled his fingers, and then turned his chair to look out the windows behind his office desk. And now, damn it, that rivalry had raised its head again, threatening to upend things. Because JM Construction and Serenghetti Construction were vying to purchase the same company.

No doubt Mia's family was unhappy about her seeing him. He knew Mia was a rebel who'd buck any heavy-handed demand they made, but then again, he hadn't gotten to the top of the corporate world by letting the chips fall where they may. He needed a counterbalance.

Swinging around again, he tightened his hands on the chair rests. *Alex McDonough.*

The thought had first occurred to him before the call with Larry.

Alex was the husband of Mia's cousin, Gia Serenghetti. He'd crossed paths with him at tech gatherings over the years and respected him. More importantly, he knew Mia was close to her cousin—he'd seen them with their heads together at more than one New York party over the years. And he'd bought a whole table at this charity dinner and still had seats to fill…

He clicked on his computer mouse and opened a window to start an email to Alex. He quickly typed a few lines and then clicked to send. Then he leaned back, satisfied. *Almost.*

When he got his father on the phone, they exchanged pleasantries. Now that Jakob Musil was older, he stuck closer to JM Construction's management offices and delegated, so it didn't completely surprise Damian that he was able to get his father on a call on the first attempt.

"So," he said after they'd been on the phone a few minutes, "how are things going with the purchase of Tevil Construction?"

"They're no longer for sale."

Damian let silence reign for a moment. "So they've decided to go with the Serenghettis' offer?"

"I didn't say that," Jakob responded gruffly. "They've taken themselves off the market. They're no longer for sale."

Damian blew out a breath. "Well, that takes care of that problem."

"Maybe for you, but not for me. JM Construction needs to grow."

Damian zeroed in on the first part of his father's statement. "Maybe for me? You're suggesting—"

"If I had won the bid for Tevil Construction, it would have made complications for you with Mia Serenghetti."

True, but lately, his concerns were more nuanced. "I guess there's a silver lining."

"And you're wise these days, too."

Damian ignored the note of sarcasm. "Dad, you're sixty-two. Maybe it's time to start taking it easy instead of trying to expand the business."

"What?"

"Serg Serenghetti is already retired."

"He's older than I am. And he had a stroke." Jakob made a grumbling sound. "Besides, Serg has a son to run the company now."

"You've got Valentin."

"He just came aboard. How do you say? Reluctantly."

Damian knew his brother had kicked around bars in Welsdale, Springfield and beyond, playing gigs with his band and generally doing a good impression of being a footloose rocker. Still. "Listen, Dad, maybe Tevil is a headache that you're better off without."

Damian could practically hear his father's eyebrows lower over the phone.

"You should be getting ready to enjoy your golden years." Winding things down. *Like Larry Bensen.*

"So you jump ship, but now you want to advise me on how to steer?"

"Anyway, are you sure buying this company wasn't just about the satisfaction of outflanking the Serenghettis?"

Jakob spluttered. "Who put that foolish idea in your mind? Mia?"

"No, I came up with the dumb thought all by myself."

His father guffawed.

"I've got some good news for you." This should buoy his father and take his mind off Tevil. "I'm buying the local television station."

"What? Which?"

"WBEN-TV."

"I don't watch much television. Too busy with work."

Precisely my point earlier. There was no doubt he'd gotten his work ethic from his father.

"So you'll be back in Welsdale now with this company."

Damian found himself nodding against the phone. "Maybe not in the way you expected, but I'll be local."

"I always knew you'd come back." There was a bark of laughter. "Ah."

Damian smiled.

"The Musils are going into the television business."

"I guess they are, Dad."

"Did you open the box that I gave you?" Jakob asked, switching gears.

"Yes." It was no longer so painful to think of his mother. In fact, the memories brought fondness as much as sadness these days.

"Your mother wanted you to have them when you got married—"

What?

"—or you and Valentin reached thirty. You know which happened first."

Yup. He'd been working nonstop for years—until recently. Sure, he and Mia had started as a pretend couple for business reasons, but she'd soon become his focus.

His mother would have liked Mia.

Damian sighed and then answered his father. "I'm not sad when I think of Mom now. Maybe that's why I'm coming back. And to make her proud."

"*I'm* proud of you."

"I couldn't have done it without you, Dad."

Damian realized this was as close as he and his father had come—since he'd moved away from Welsdale—to acknowledging how much they were still connected.

"I'm glad to hear it," Jakob said gruffly.

"You've got to save me," Mia announced.

Then she knocked back some wine that she'd brought with her before her gaze connected with Gia's in the powder room mirror.

"Mmm," her cousin commented as she reapplied lipstick.

Beyond the hushed and upholstered confines of the anteroom to the ladies' restroom, hundreds of people dined at tables whose price per plate would certainly make her head spin, Mia thought. Gotham Hall was one of the city's premier event spaces—a nine-thousand-square-foot ballroom under a stained-glass dome. Its imposing neoclassical facade was a Broadway landmark.

Not that she knew the precise price tag of being here tonight. Damian had arranged everything. In fact, she'd been surprised to discover, when she'd arrived, that Gia and Alex were here, too, and seated at the same table. *She'd* only agreed to show up in a deal with the devil.

Or so she tried to convince herself. The words rang hollow to her own ears. But the more she tried to extricate herself from her ties to Damian, the more entangled she seemed to become. He was seductive and enticing.

She touched the fine filigree diamond necklace at her throat—one that came with matching earrings. *Another loan from the jewelers,* Damian had said. They had shown up at her door by courier after Damian had texted her to ask what color she'd be wearing tonight. She'd assumed

he'd asked so that he could coordinate his own attire—
not for the sake of picking out precious gemstones for her.

Of course, since she'd gotten to know him better, she'd
come to respect and…appreciate him. He wasn't a bad guy
just because of his last name—if she'd ever believed that
to be the case. He'd defended her to her family, had her
back with Carl and even been a pretend boyfriend during
her interview with Katie.

But anything more was too fraught with pitfalls…
too everything, for that matter. They could remain acquainted—friends even. She stiffened at the thought of
Damian dating another woman, and then shrugged off
the feeling.

Gia deposited her makeup in her handbag. "I think
things are going well."

"Are you kidding?" Mia responded. "The evening has
just begun, and Damian and I are practically striking
sparks off each other."

Gia tossed her a sidelong look. "You know, I was surprised when Alex told me that Damian had offered us seats
at his table for this event, especially since I'm a Serenghetti cousin and know all about the animosity between
your family and his."

Mia turned wide eyes on her cousin. "He offered you
seats?"

Gia smirked. "You didn't think it was a coincidence
that Alex and I are here tonight, did you? No, we didn't
buy seats ourselves. But why didn't you mention that *you*
would be here?"

"Why didn't you?" Mia flushed. "Anyway, you were out
of the country traveling. You were hard to get a hold of."

"And yet Damian managed to get off an email invite to
Alex while we were in Japan."

Guilty. She'd been keeping mum about her relationship with Damian. It wasn't that she didn't trust Gia. It was that talking about it would lead to questions that she wasn't prepared to answer. She wasn't even sure if she had all the answers.

"Then I realized that Alex and I may have been invited precisely because I'm a Serenghetti, not despite it."

Mia blinked. "What do you mean?"

Her cousin gave her a disbelieving look. "Mia, the guy seems hooked on you. But he also knows your immediate family is suspicious of him. Obviously, Alex and I are here to help smooth things. It might make you more comfortable, and Damian could try to win over some of your other relatives."

Mia was floored. She'd just assumed earlier that since this was a big event for the tech industry, Alex had decided to show up and had brought Gia. Had Damian really gone to so much trouble for her...?

Her cousin tossed her another sidelong look. "I see you took my advice that Damian might be worth more than one date."

"Whose side are you on?"

"Yours of course."

"You could have fooled me," Mia muttered under her breath.

"I never really liked Carl."

"Now you tell me?" Mia peered at herself critically in the mirror. "Next to Damian, he's a domesticated kitten."

"Exactly. Carl was too tame for you."

"So he got hitched to someone else to get away from the wild cat?"

Gia smiled. "Is that what Damian thinks of you?"

Mia flushed. "Who? Damian the tamer?"

Gia laughed. "He's got an appropriate name. Not boring."

Like Carl. Mia heard her cousin's unspoken words.

"Maybe he's got the right temperament for the board-room," she huffed. "But he's got another think coming if he aims to tame a Serenghetti."

"From the way he was looking at you during dinner," Gia murmured, "that's not what he has in mind. Eat you up is more like it."

Mia turned to face Gia. "Right, and this has to stop."

"Why?"

"He's a Musil." *And so many other reasons.* He unsettled her. He got under her skin.

"So you're not supposed to trust him but you want to, um, make it with him?"

She'd already done the deed with him—and it had been spectacular. And from all appearances, he wanted to be invited back for more. "He's…unpredictable."

She adjusted the shoulder strap of her dress.

"I think," Gia said, gazing at Mia's gown, "in this case you were done in by your own sartorial skills. Damian's reaction is very predictable…"

Mia bunched the skirt of her dress in one hand. "What? This?" *This old thing?* "I designed it for my senior project at Parsons years ago."

She had *not* gone to any great lengths to please Damian tonight.

"How can I forget?" her cousin responded lightly. "But cleavage never goes out of style."

Okay, so the gown was daring—but that had been the point when she'd been trying to earn a top grade at Parsons. She'd been a twenty-two-year-old who'd been starry-eyed at the end of a four-year college stint in New York City.

The neckline of the gown plunged between her breasts in the front and even lower in the back. The bodice was a deep blue velvet and the skirt a waterfall of tulle in an ombre pattern that ended in the palest of aqua at her feet. She'd had to use fashion tape to keep everything in place because she'd gotten curvier in the years since she'd graduated.

"You look like a mermaid emerging from the waves."

"Thanks for remembering my thesis show," Mia remarked dryly. "But did you have to mention it to Damian, too?"

Gia gave an impish smile. "Just making conversation. He seemed to...admire the handiwork."

Mia rolled her eyes. "I'm supposed to be the one who makes waves."

Gia laughed. "What can I say? Marriage agrees with me. I've started living outside the boxes of the comic strip that I draw. In fact, you should try it."

Mia widened her eyes. "What? Marriage?"

Gia turned to leave. "No, sex with a guy who gets hot under the collar merely looking at you."

Mia clamped her mouth shut. If only her cousin knew. Damian didn't just get hot under the collar, he got her hot...all over. Where was water to douse the flames when she needed it?

When she and Gia eventually got back to their table, Damian threw her simmering look, and Mia took another gulp of her wine.

Her cousin tossed her an amused little smile from across the table, and Mia responded with a small frown.

Glancing around, Mia spotted Carl and his wife chatting with other guests a few tables away. She nearly groaned aloud. *Great.* As if this evening could get any more awkward.

Carl was part of the tech world, too, and he and Damian likely still moved in overlapping circles...

Pasting a smile on her face, she leaned toward Damian.

Obligingly, he tilted in her direction, giving her his ear. His closeness made her breasts tingle.

"I didn't know Carl was going to be here," she murmured.

Raising his gaze, he gave her quizzical look. "Neither did I. Problem?"

Of course not.

Damian glanced past her. "Here they come."

Next thing she knew, Damian was draping an arm along the back of her chair, his fingers grazing her exposed spine in a passing caress.

When Carl hailed them, Damian turned and stood, and Mia reluctantly followed, depositing her napkin beside her plate. Damian slipped his arm around her in a signal of… support…affection?

Catching the interested expression on Gia's face, Mia could tell her cousin was savoring the show.

Drat.

Damian and Carl shook hands.

For the first time, Mia got a good look at Carl's wife. The woman she'd built up to be a bit of a femme fatale was actually…a bespectacled and feminine version of Carl. Curly dark hair framed her face in a style that was too wild to be a true pixie cut, and big brown eyes peeked at her from behind large frames.

It seemed, Mia thought bemusedly, she'd been dumped for someone who seemed to be Carl's complete counterpart.

"Laura, this is Mia Serenghetti," Carl said, looking a bit sheepish. "Ah…"

Laura jumped into the gap, grasping Mia's outstretched hand in both of hers and leaning in with an earnest smile. "It's such a pleasure to meet you."

Mia couldn't detect any smugness, just sincere interest.

Laura hadn't gone with the tried-and-true *I've heard so much about you*, which would have been awkward under the circumstances.

"It's nice to meet you, too," Mia murmured.

"We were making the rounds of, ah, the tables," Carl put in, "and thought we'd, ah, say hello."

"I'm such a fan of your work," Laura said, still grasping her hand.

"You are?" Mia couldn't keep the shocked surprise from her voice.

Laura nodded, finally dropping her hand. "Yes. I was at your fashion show two years ago with friends. I own a jumpsuit from the collection that you showed."

"Oh!" Bemusement turned to feeling flattered. If the timeline was right, Laura had known of her even before she'd met Carl.

"When Carl mentioned that he'd once dated you, I couldn't believe it." Laura's eyes sparkled behind her glasses.

Judging from the way Carl blanched, it seemed he hadn't gone into too many details with Laura about the precise timeline of his breakup.

Mia knew she had to play along; forgiveness was the best policy. "You should come by my studio for another jumpsuit." She winked. "Consider it a wedding gift."

Carl looked relieved, while Damian tossed her an amused look.

"I couldn't," Laura protested. "I know a boutique in Midtown that carries your designs—"

Mia waved a hand. "I'll be sending out next season's styles soon. I'll give you a peek."

Laura nodded. "Oh, right. You mentioned it in *Brilliance* magazine."

Mia blinked. "You read it?"

The issue with her interview wasn't supposed to be out until—

"They posted a teaser on their website."

Mia stilled. She needed to get her cell phone.

Carl and Damian made some small talk for a few more minutes.

Then Carl touched Laura's arm. "Well, it was great to run into you guys. We're going to keep circulating."

Carl and Damian shook hands before the other couple moved off.

Mia caught Gia's expression as she sat back down. Her cousin looked as if she could barely contain her curiosity.

"I guess that's what they call *conscious uncoupling*?" Damian murmured, retaking his seat.

"Who, me and Carl…?" Ironically, that's what she'd vowed she and Damian would do—first after the Ruby Ball, and then after Katie's interview. Except here they were.

Mia pulled up *Brilliance*'s web site on her phone and, after a quick scan of links, found the mention of her interview.

"Who else?" Damian replied dryly. "Well done, by the way. A lot harder to hold a grudge when you meet the enemy like that, isn't it?"

"Yup." She held up her phone. "And speaking of enemies, thanks to Katie's interview, everyone thinks the Serenghettis and Musils are lovers, not fighters."

Twelve

"So this is how the rich live."

"No, this is how I live," Damian corrected.

Mia placed her evening bag on the entry table and swiveled to face Damian.

She shivered. His penthouse duplex was in a new luxury tower. The condo was cool, muted and dim. The lights of the city twinkled outside sprawling windows.

"Cold?"

Must his voice be so sexy? "No, I'm fine."

While Damian consulted the apps on his cell phone, Mia took a moment to gather herself.

All during their chauffeured car ride back from the charity event, she'd mulled what she wanted to say, examined her feelings and tried to think things through. It was why she'd suggested going to his place. If Damian had been surprised—pleased?—he hadn't questioned her decision. The truth was, at his place, she was in control of when to end things and leave.

Mia heard the air conditioner in the condo picking up. Then velvet curtains automatically drew closed in the living room adjacent to the entry foyer. He was certainly high tech—but then what else should she have expected?

She pivoted. "Does the fireplace magically turn on? And where's the faint music? The lights are already dim, though."

He raised an eyebrow at her, amused…and a touch sheepish? "Drink?"

"No, thank you."

He paused.

She cleared her throat. Because she knew what she was here to do. She'd already ignored one *how's it going?* text from Gia.

Tilting her head forward to expose her nape, she removed the diamond necklace and then the earrings. Then she held them out to him. *She'd loved them.* Just as she had with the pieces for the Ruby Ball. "Thank you for another loan."

His lips twitched in wry amusement, but he took the jewelry—their fingers brushing—and pocketed them as if they were no more than plastic prizes dispensed by a toy vending machine.

"I wanted to talk."

"Problem?" Damian asked levelly.

She drew in a deep breath. "Thanks for giving me a graceful but public way tonight to put Carl in the rearview mirror. I know news of our crossing paths with the Eshoos will eventually filter out to people who know us."

He gave an imperceptible nod.

"And thanks for helping me open doors with Katie, and…having my back with my family when we were up in Welsdale."

"That's three thank-yous in a row. So why do I think

a kiss-off is coming?" he teased, his voice nevertheless holding a note of gravity.

There wouldn't be any kissing. That was the point.

"Let me guess—you're troubled because you realized that you built up the breakup with Carl to more than it was."

She shook her head—more vehemently than she'd meant to, so locks of hair tumbled around her shoulders. "No, I realized that the reason it bothered me so much was that *you* were involved."

Damian stilled and then his eyes gleamed. "Ah."

"Ah? That's it?"

"I'm hesitating in case I say the wrong thing."

"When have you ever let that stop you?"

He cut off a laugh. "I'm learning." Then he sobered and came closer, so she could still feel the energy coming off him, but didn't touch her. "And now? Does it still bother you?"

Her shoulders sagged and she blew a breath. "Carl's not the enemy...and neither are you even though I lumped you in with your family for a long time." She shrugged. "So of course when you were advising and helping Carl, I was suspicious."

"If I'm not the enemy, then what am I?" he asked softly.

Friend...lover. She raised her hands as if to hold him off, even though he hadn't taken another step. "This has gotten complicated—"

"Complicated is good," he joked.

"How can you say that?"

He lightly clasped her wrist and drew her even closer.

"Bold, brave and badass, really?" she argued faintly.

Damian smiled. "Those were my words, yes."

"It's also the headline of Katie's story, which is already live or at least teased on the *Brilliance* web site."

"Great."

"You have a starring role."

He studied her mouth. "Consider me flattered."

The back of her neck tingled with an awareness that soon seeped into other parts of her...

"You laid it on thick with Katie."

"That's assuming I didn't mean what I said."

"And that endearment—"

Damian laced his fingers with hers. *"Babe."*

What was she going to do with a man who could disarm her so easily? "You're—"

"Irresistible, irrepressible...irreplaceable?"

"It's so cute the way that we finish each other's sentences..." She made a halfhearted attempt at scoffing about Katie's comment.

He drew her into his arms. "No...it's so great the way that we make each other feel."

"Feel...is that what we do?"

"And kiss," he muttered. "Don't forget that."

He searched her gaze, and reading her eyes, bent his head.

She swallowed hard, moments before his lips settled on hers, and then twisted her hands in his lapels.

Damian made a sound at the back of his throat, and she sighed. There was a desperate, feverish quality to their kiss, as if hours at a stuffy industry dinner, politely listening to speaker after speaker, had fueled their suppressed need.

When they finally broke apart, Damian nuzzled the hair at her temple. Even in heels, she was three or four inches shorter.

"I'll make you a deal," he said huskily.

"Another one?"

He smiled against her hair. "You can invent a name for me, too. What do you want to call me?"

Tamer. "Insufferable?"

"Try harder, it doesn't roll off the tongue."

She was dimly aware that his hands were roaming, caressing her bare back as if looking for a zipper. *Or a key to her heart.*

He feathered kisses along the side of her face and down her neck. "Well?"

"I'm still thinking." She tilted her neck to accommodate him, letting her hair fall back.

"Ah, Mia."

Finally, when his hands came to rest on her shoulders, she had mercy on him. "Everything is held in place with fashion tape."

He muttered an expletive. "Tape doesn't belong on skin."

"It's an industry trick to prevent wardrobe malfunctions."

He looked at her with hooded eyes. "Hey, I like clothing... with glitches."

A breathless laugh escaped her. "You were right. I came here to give you the kiss-off..."

He raised his brows above smoky eyes. "Well, there'll be kissing and some things are coming off."

Holding his gaze, she placed her hands over his on her shoulders, and together they pulled apart her bodice.

He groaned. "Babe, you're bold, brave and badass."

Then he bent and trailed his lips down her cleavage, and her head fell back.

When Damian pulled her bodice all the way off so that the shoulder straps landed on her wrists, he inhaled sharply. The pads of his thumbs grazed her nipples, and then he settled his mouth over one breast.

She rested her forearms on his shoulders, losing herself in a fog of need.

When he finally straightened, he gave her a hard kiss, letting her feel his hunger.

Her fingers began to work at the buttons on his white shirt, and he shrugged out of his tuxedo jacket, letting it fall to the floor.

"I don't want to ruin the work of art that you're wearing," he murmured. "Someone will want to display your senior project in an exhibition someday."

"I can't believe Gia told you."

Damian nodded. "She noticed how I couldn't take my eyes off you in that dress."

"And that you wanted to get me out of it," Mia added, and then gave him an openmouthed kiss.

He lifted her off her feet and strode deeper into the dark recesses of the penthouse.

Moments later, Mia lifted her head and realized they were in Damian's oversized bedroom. White upholstery and bedding contrasted with dark-paneled wood. The lights of the city twinkled behind pale window blinds.

Slowly he lowered her so that her feet touched the floor again, letting her feel every inch of him on the slow slide to the ground.

He wanted her. That much was obvious.

Holding his gaze, she lowered the tiny hidden zipper at the side of her waist, and the whole dress fell in a heap at her feet, leaving her standing in panties and high-heeled sandals.

She forced herself to hold still under his hot gaze and lifted her chin a notch.

"You're beautiful," he said hoarsely.

"Now that's a b-word that you didn't use," she teased. "How did you leave out *beautiful* during the interview?"

Damian groaned self-deprecatingly, and then ran his fingers up and down her arms, before slipping them under the fabric of her panties and following the hourglass figure created by her waist. "Believe me, by the time we're done, you're going to hear a lot more from me."

She stroked the length of his erection. "Because you're *bothered*?"

He pulled his shirt out of his waistband. "How can you tell?"

She wet her lips, her mouth suddenly dry, and swallowed.

He tossed his shirt aside. "Step out of those blue waves pooling at your feet…*beautiful*."

She did, kicking off one sandal and then the other, and then he swung her up and deposited her on the bed.

"You need to stop carrying me."

"See, that's where we disagree. I haven't done it enough."

When he started to strip, she sat up straighter and then stood. "Let me."

She undid his belt and then he shucked his pants and briefs, stepping out of his shoes and pulling off his socks with them.

"Let me do this," she said throatily, stroking his rigid length.

His eyes flared and then closed on a hiss. "Ah, Mia."

She bent and her mouth closed around him.

She worked his length, and Damian made some guttural sounds. She savored the experience of making *him* weak.

Finally, he hauled her up, but when he would have tossed her on the bed again, she instead pushed him to a sitting position on the edge and straddled him.

Their mouths tangled, and the momentum sent him back against the bed.

"I've got to be inside you," he said on a half laugh with an edge of desperation.

She'd never heard Damian desperate before. *Desperate for her.* He was always so cool and in control—or seemed to be.

"I'm on the pill," she whispered against his mouth. "And I have a clean bill of health."

"Yeah, clean bill, too," he said thickly.

She guided him inside her, and they both sighed. She moved then, and he directed her with his hands on her hips, setting a rhythm that they both enjoyed.

Distantly from the other room, her cell phone buzzed, and she ignored it. The last thing she needed was for reality to intrude. This was about her and Damian…and now. A time and place where they didn't have last names, histories, animosities…

"Ignore it," he gritted, having the same idea.

"Yes," she whispered against his mouth.

He moved again, rocking against her, setting off tiny spasms of sensation that grew in ferocity as they fanned out through every inch of her body.

She called his name with her release, and with a final thrust, Damian came inside her, losing himself. They held each other while waves of emotion and sensation washed over them.

In his mind, the past couple of weeks had been a vacation.

Still, freshly showered, Damian threw on some clothes at Mia's place because he knew he'd have to get to the office soon.

He and Mia had fallen into a pattern of getting together without any discussion of the heavy issues that might still hang between them—or more particularly, between their families. Instead they'd lived in the moment...casually eating out, going for a bike ride near the High Line, or most recently, a concert at Madison Square Garden, where they'd sat by themselves in the CyberSilver box. Usually they'd end up at his place or hers, where they hadn't been able to keep their hands off each other.

They'd talked business occasionally, and he'd given her advice—one entrepreneur to another. He'd also put her in touch with his contacts—someone to review company finances, another to consult on marketing.

He looked around the bedroom of the walkup apartment now and spotted his wallet where he'd tossed it on a dresser last night. With a small smile, he retrieved it from where it peeked out from under Mia's bra.

Her bedroom was a small space at the back of an already-small apartment. The bed was covered with fluffy white counterpane that pooled on the floor like an oversized wedding dress. It was offset by exposed gray brick walls, a polished gray wood floor, and some dark furniture. Exactly what he would have expected from Mia: feminine but edgy.

Except he'd now breached the inner sanctum—so the sheets were mussed, thanks to their night together. Afterward, she'd curled up against him, their hearts beating in counterpoint as they'd drifted off to sleep.

Mia bounced into the room, her face lit up with excitement. "Good news. I got an email from a department store buyer. She saw Katie's article and wants to place a big order." She gave him an endearingly tentative smile. "I'm starting out in a few of their locations, so we'll see how things go."

He slipped his arms around her. "Congratulations. The start of something big."

She placed her hands on his chest. "I've got to get in touch with the factory today. There's no time to lose."

He gave her a quick kiss. "You'll be great. I have total faith in you." Then he smiled wolfishly. "But speaking of good news and the start of something."

Playfully, she pulled out of his arms and wagged a finger at him. "We've both got work to do."

He sighed good-naturedly. "Tonight then. I'll pick you up."

Twenty minutes later, she walked him downstairs so he could hail a cab to work, and she could unlock the street entrance to her ground-floor studio and start her day.

At the sidewalk, she clung to him for another kiss and then turned away toward her workspace.

Damian stepped into the street to flag a cab, but within moments, he heard someone call Mia's name.

A male someone.

He turned around and caught Mia's surprised look from where she had swiveled away from her front door.

"Sam."

Crap. So there really was a Sam. And he was back home. *Great timing.*

Damian sized up the other man, who—grinning from ear to ear—made his way toward Mia. Damian dropped his arm and curled his hand by his side. No way in hell was he missing this action.

Mia gave Sam a tight smile. "You're back. From Japan."

Yeah, this was awkward. Damian would give her that. Unfortunately only two out of three of them knew it. Sam kept steaming forward toward Mia like a train that could not be derailed.

"Yup, here I am." He threw his arms out expansively.

Damian's gaze connected with Mia's. *Wow, you sure can pick them.*

She frowned at him, and then directed a pleasant if uncomfortable look at Sam. "This is—"

"Yeah, I know." Sam grinned. "Surprise." He gestured to the door behind Mia. "I took a detour from my regular route to the office and stopped in the coffee shop across the street for a quick bagel since you weren't at work yet." Sam jerked his head to indicate the general direction that he'd come from, completely missing Damian.

Damian was hit by a mixture of skepticism and jealousy. She was going to show up at the Ruby Ball with this guy? *He* was the competition? Damian could see the passing resemblance between him and Sam in height and build—and especially in dim lighting and with a mask on at a costume party—but he was hands-down the better man. Even in a blind taste test. If he did so say himself.

Sam stepped closer to Mia—clearly intent on a reunion—and Damian sprang into action.

The other guy grasped Mia's hands and lowered his head.

"Mia." Damian made sure his voice cut into the tableau like scissors slicing a photo in half.

Sam froze, and then straightened and turned.

Damian saw it all as if in slow motion. "Thanks for penthouse sitting for me, babe." He winked. "I'll make it up to you this weekend. Reservations at Per Se."

Sam looked between Damian and Mia, and expressions flitted across his face—confusion, dawning understanding and then sheepish embarrassment.

Mia jumped into the void. "Sam, you know—"

"Damian Musil." Damian held out his hand, and after a blink, Sam grasped it.

Damian gave the other guy's hand a firm shake, making eye contact. "Japan. Nice place. I've been to Tokyo myself a couple of times."

Sam's expression wavered between a grimace and a smile. "Yeah, I've been away awhile."

Damian nodded. "Business trips can be a damper that way. You're out of the loop."

"No joke."

Sam turned back toward Mia. "It was nice seeing you, Mia." He shrugged. "The coffee shop was okay, but I'll be sticking to the one on my regular route."

Damian nodded. "Good idea."

"Well, see you around."

After Sam walked off, Damian observed Mia. She watched as Sam mounted a scooter parked farther down the block and took off.

Turning back to him, Mia raised her eyebrows, her gaze clashing with his.

"Territorial?"

Possessive. Maybe a bit jealous. But seriously? Damian raised his eyebrows to mirror hers. "He was your backup plan for the Ruby Ball?"

She lifted her chin. "Nice with the I'm-the-captain-of-industry routine."

"Hey, my quick reflexes let him off easy. Think about how much more embarrassing it would have been if he'd kissed you and then realized the guy who'd just spent the night was right behind him."

"Uh-huh." She looked unconvinced.

There didn't seem to be any end to the obstacle course that led to Mia's door. Her brothers, his family, Carl and now Sam. "Clearly he wasn't watching from the coffee shop window when I kissed you goodbye."

Mia's lips gave a telltale twitch.

"Might have been nice to be able to compare and contrast," she mused.

"Oh, yeah?" he queried, stepping closer. "Maybe my goodbye was too fast."

Damian lowered his gaze to her soft, plump lips. So full of promise. *Just like last night.*

His mouth was a hair's breadth from hers when Mia suddenly sprang back.

"Mom!"

Thirteen

Mia watched with apprehension—horror?—as her mother, who'd emerged from a cab, was handed her bag by the driver.

Damian had turned as well, and she could tell that within seconds he too had processed what was happening at the curb.

She also realized the tableau that she and Damian presented… She'd sprung back from Damian's kiss, but not before her gaze had connected with her mother's over his shoulder.

Now the expressions that flitted across her mother's face had moved from delight and puzzlement to surprise and concern.

"It's only an hour on the shuttle." Her mother's tone was mildly reproachful as she came closer.

"What a…surprise." It was a feeling very similar to what she'd experienced minutes ago at Sam's sudden appearance. Mia resisted the urge to pinch herself and make sure she wasn't dreaming all this.

Her mother smiled brightly. Too brightly. As if Damian wasn't standing right *there*... She set down her overnight bag. "I wanted to come to New York to try some restaurants."

Damian smiled. "Of course. How about Per Se?" He nodded at Mia. "I just mentioned making a reservation."

Her mother blinked. "I've never been, but I want to try it."

Mia looked at Damian as if he was crazy, but he winked at her.

"I know reservations are hard to get, so leave that part to me."

Of course. The perks of having an upwards of nine figure bank account.

She and Damian were taking her mother out to dinner. *No way.*

Damian reached down for her mother's bag. "Since you're planning to stay with Mia, let me take your bag up for you."

Smooth, smooth. Her brother Jordan could take pointers from Damian—even though her sibling had a reputation of gliding instead of walking, on and off the ice.

Mia stopped an eye roll and reluctantly handed her keys to Damian.

As Damian stepped away with the bag, Mia caught the bemused expression on her mother's face.

"I was thinking Eataly for lunch..." Camilla's voice trailed off.

Mia ushered her mother into her work studio and flipped on the lights. The smell of coffee wafted through the air. Mia had loved her mother's gift of an automatic espresso maker on a timer. She'd come to associate the scent with the start of the workday.

Before Mia could do more than prepare two demitasse cups, however, the front door to the studio cracked open and Damian's arm appeared, dangling her keys.

Mia hurried over to collect them and then shut the door.

It was nice of Damian not to intrude this time on what promised to be an awkward family conversation. He was learning…and coming along nicely as, yes, boyfriend material.

She took a deep breath and turned back toward her mother.

Camilla raised her cup of espresso and took a sip. "At least he doesn't have the keys to your apartment."

Mia raised her hands as if to ward off the reproach. "Mom, I didn't lie to you about him. Things have recently…changed."

"Of course." Pause. "And the mothers are always the last to know."

Mia could practically see the thought bubble above her mother's head. *Et tu, Brute?*

In the longstanding sibling game of making sure their parents got only select, carefully filtered information, she'd been behind…until recently. First, Cole and Marisa had sprung a surprise wedding on the family that they'd billed as only an engagement party. Then Rick and Chiara had been expecting a baby…and her mother had gotten the news through the gossip columns. And finally Jordan and Sera had managed to keep their relationship under wraps from the rest of the Serenghettis—at least until Mia had chanced upon them locked in an embrace at cousin Oliver's wedding.

But speaking of relationships… If she was going to legitimize hers with Damian, her mother was the best place to start.

"I'm confused. The last time you said that you and Damian are not a *coppia*."

When her mother set down her espresso cup, Mia took her hands in her own. "You know how you said that Dad wanted to win you over so he arranged another stay for himself at the *albergo*?"

Camilla widened her eyes. "Yes, and I said he stayed at a hotel, not my apartment."

"Just an updated version of the same thing, Mom."

Camilla sighed and searched her face. "And you have your heart set on him, too? Some things with love don't change. Doesn't matter the generation."

"Yes." *I love him.* Mia tested out the words as she dropped her mother's hands. *She'd fallen in love with Damian Musil.* Somehow, she wasn't sure exactly when, he'd snuck into her heart. Once she'd given up the fight against their attraction after the charity dinner two weeks ago— and stopped trying to keep him at a distance—she'd found a kindred soul.

Entrepreneur. Maverick. Risk taker. He'd teased and tantalized until she'd engaged...the enemy. Except she'd discovered she much preferred him as her friend and lover.

Her mother tapped a finger against her lips. "I've waited to be mother of the bride. But this is tricky. *Una situazione delicata.*"

"Mom," Mia protested, "Damian hasn't proposed."

Camilla's eyes gleamed. "He will...or you could."

Yes, she could. She'd always prided herself on her forward thinking and independent nature, hadn't she? On always being able to do what her brothers did—though proposing wasn't something that had crossed her mind.

But then she was caught in an uncharacteristic attack of nerves. Because she'd just realized how she felt, but Damian had never indicated—

"I see the way he looks at you, Mia."

Mia cleared her throat. "Yes, well. We'll see how things go, right?" she said brightly. "In the meantime, how are things with you and Dad? How is the budding sommelier?"

Her mother suddenly scowled. "The television personality is fine. He wanted to come to New York with me—"

Ugh. At least it hadn't been *both* her parents chancing upon her and Damian outside her door in the early morning.

"—but then he understood when I suggested a girls' weekend."

Mia bit the inside of her cheek. Her mother had never been like a girlfriend to her—too strict. Still, ever since Mia had turned twenty-five or so, her mother had fancied herself young at heart. "How about we compromise for now and put you in the role of mother of the fashionista? I'll text Gia. She'd love to see you while you're in town."

Some days were harder than others; they just made you want to run out for a margarita. As she surveyed the scraps of fabric and broken thread littering the floor of her design studio, Mia was thankful that at least it was finally Friday.

Her mother had returned to Welsdale midweek with the unspoken agreement that Camilla would mention nothing about running into Damian—but would nevertheless try to soften her husband and sons' stance toward Mia's involvement with a Musil. It had been only her and her mother for dinner at Per Se since Damian had gotten tied up at the office. The two of them had caught up with Gia for lunch the next day.

But just now, thanks to Katie, Mia was in the midst of sending more samples of her best designs over to *Brilliance*. And everything was in chaos. She had a call shortly with one of her suppliers so that all her raw material would arrive at the manufacturer at the same time. She was also due to speak with a small West Coast boutique chain that stocked her designs. On top of it, she had a meeting with her accountant tomorrow, for which she hadn't yet had time to prepare.

She longed for the days when she could concentrate on sketching and designing—and staring out the window for inspiration. The flow of creative juices had sometimes been slow, but her early career had been very fulfilling. Now, she was juggling more tasks, many of which were business related and not creative.

She mentally shrugged as she zipped a dress into a garment bag. On the plus side, at least she didn't have time to dwell on what was happening up in Welsdale—had her mother had a chance to bring up Damian yet?

Regardless, tonight Mia knew she'd see him. A thrill of anticipation ran up her spine. He was everything she'd been looking for, except she hadn't known it. And she resolved, whatever happened with her family or his, she wouldn't let it interfere with their deepening relationship from here on out.

Sure, it would be great if both the Serenghettis and Musils were on board, but at the end of the day, it was just her and Damian. They had built their own lives in New York, and now they'd become intertwined.

Of course, Damian hadn't said he loved her... A touch of doubt crept into the corners of her mind, and she swept it away. They hadn't talked about commitment even though their relationship was progressing rapidly. Still, it seemed as if they'd known each other forever and a day.

When her cell phone buzzed, and she noticed it was her mother, she nearly groaned aloud. She'd really like to find out if Camilla had broached the subject of Damian now that she was back in Welsdale, but she had enough to deal with today without adding potentially bad news.

"Hi, Mom. What's up?"

"Mia, my show has been canceled," Camilla said without preamble, sounding distressed.

Mia blinked and stilled. "What? How is that possible?"

"The station has been bought and the new owner wants to take it in a different direction."

"Oh, Mom."

"The new owner is Damian."

"What?" Shock made her voice rise. "Damian?"

"Yes."

"Mom, you must be wrong." *He would have told me. I would have known.*

She hadn't seen him while her mother had been in town, or since then. He'd been traveling and then having late nights at work. But still, a bombshell like this should have merited at least a phone call.

"There is no mistake, Mia," her mother replied, her voice thickening with her Italian accent because she was upset. "Damian owns Alley Kat Media."

"But your station in Welsdale is WBEN-TV."

"It is owned by Alley Kat Media."

Mia groaned. She'd actively avoided asking too many questions about Damian's association with Larry Bensen, because their two families had been rivals for years and she didn't want to seem as if she was on a reconnaissance mission to gather information for the Serenghettis.

Mia closed her eyes on a sigh—hadn't Larry mentioned being in the television business? But she'd never had occasion to mention her last name to Larry—only to Katie—so he'd never had a chance to make the connection between her and her mother.

She felt like an idiot for not putting two and two together.

Mia frowned. It was one thing when Damian's family was going head-to-head in business with hers. It was another for him to cancel her mother's cooking show. *How could he?*

Mia knew that *Flavors of Italy* was her mother's baby. Just like her, Camilla had staked an independent career apart from the family construction business.

Damian should understand better than most people how important realizing a dream like that was—why didn't he? Mia had fought so hard to realize her own dreams—she couldn't bear the idea of Damian stomping on her mother's. And then...had he done it deliberately to get back at the Serenghettis?

Her heart squeezed.

"I have two more episodes to tape," Camilla said, "and then *finito*."

"You're not finished, Mom," Mia reassured her, though her mind was working feverishly. "This is simply the beginning of a new chapter."

"Mia, I am past sixty."

"Mom, you still have game."

"I have what?"

"This is a temporary setback. I'll speak to Damian. I'm sure this can all be worked out."

There had to be some rational explanation. Because the worst-case scenario was that she'd played into the hands of the Musils in their latest battle against the Serenghettis. She'd helped Damian woo the Bensens—so he could become the new owner of WBEN-TV.

"Your father is very upset. *Wine Breaks with Serg!* is canceled, too—"

"By a Musil." Mia winced inwardly.

So much for thinking her family would come around to liking Damian. She'd been naive to think the two of them could put their family histories behind them.

Fourteen

Mia strode into Damian's glass-enclosed offices on the twenty-third floor of the pre-war building facing Fifth Avenue. New York's Flatiron District had been nicknamed Silicon Alley years ago for all the tech companies with headquarters in the neighborhood, and Damian's company was situated at a marquee address.

After the call from her mother, she'd restrained herself until after the end of the business day. She'd been busy, of course, but she also didn't want a full audience of his employees to witness their confrontation. As it was, it was seven in the evening, and there were still several people milling about the cavernous space. It was a tech company, after all, and long hours were fairly standard. Plus, Mia figured they had plenty of contacts on the West Coast in Silicon Valley, where it was still only four in the afternoon. Still, she couldn't wait forever to get this conversation over with.

The CyberSilver offices were within walking distance of her studio in the Garment District. Since they lived and worked not too far from each other, she hoped the island of Manhattan was big enough for them not to cross paths after this. But given her recent experiences running into Carl and Sam, she had her doubts.

Since Damian's offices were typical for a tech-savvy startup—lots of glass, lots of open space, and lots of windows—it made him easy to spot.

She'd sent a brief text to say that she was on her way.

His response had come while she'd been crossing Sixth Avenue. See you soon, babe.

There hadn't been an inkling that he had a clue that her world had gone topsy-turvy since they'd seen each other at the beginning of the week. She, on the other hand, was bursting with emotion, wanting answers.

When she got to the door of his office, Damian looked up, grinned and rose.

Striding across the carpet, she planted her hands on his desk and leaned forward. "How could you?"

He glanced down at himself. "What? Wrong T-shirt? Fashion faux pas?"

When she continued to fix him with a look, he seemed to realize she wasn't joking.

"You canceled my mother's cooking show."

"What are you talking about?"

She straightened, partly mollified. As unbelievable as it seemed, he looked genuinely perplexed. "My mother has a cooking show on WBEN-TV and its sister stations. And because of her, my father also has a gig fronting related short spots called *Wine Breaks with Serg!* Or should I say *ad*. He's been informed that he's kaput, too."

Damian's gaze grew more alert. "You're not kidding."

She pursed her lips. She could see how Damian hadn't necessarily realized the connection to the Serenghettis from the name *Wine Breaks with Serg!* but her mother's show was a different story. "Your lawyers' due diligence didn't reveal that Alley Kat broadcasts *Flavors of Italy with Camilla Serenghetti*?"

"Some junior lawyer must have drilled down to individual shows, but I only get summaries. Of course, I knew there were cooking shows…and I may have seen a list of programming." He frowned. "Probably something called *Flavors of Italy*."

"*Flavors of Italy* is what my mother's show used to be called, and how it's still sometimes referred to. But the name got expanded a few years ago to include identifying the host." Damn it, she was proud of her mother. And it made her so mad that she might have her spatula taken away from her. Especially, Mia admitted, when she herself had inadvertently played a role in bringing the whole thing about.

Damian sighed and came around his desk. "Mia, I had no idea that your mother had a cooking show on WBEN."

She blew a breath—palpable relief coursing through her. "So you won't be canceling her—them?"

He hesitated, his face closing. "That's a business decision. The station is being revamped to focus more on movies and less on original programming."

Hold on. She folded her arms.

"Who produces your mother's show?"

"Signa Entertainment." That much she knew.

"Yeah, that's the company that produces a number of shows on WBEN and Alley Kat's other stations. They're closing shop due to profitability issues."

Mia dropped her arms and raised her chin. "My mother

can get another production company. She can even produce it herself. Don't sidestep the issue."

Heck, Mia thought, if she could start her own fashion
label, her mother could go the do-it-yourself route, too.

"This isn't personal."

He came around his desk and reached out for her, but
she moved away.

The urge to touch him and have him wrap her in his
arms—and pretend this whole burgeoning fiasco wasn't
happening—was strong. She fought against it.

"Damian," she said in frustration, "it's all personal.
Our families have been engaged in a business rivalry
for years."

Damian frowned. "So when you came over here, you
thought I might be deliberately taking down a Serenghetti?"

Mia shook her head. "It doesn't matter what I thought.
Only that you make it right."

He stood there, looking like the gorgeous man she'd
snuggled against after a night of spectacular sex, but now
acting like a stranger.

Finally, Damian nodded. "Because once a Musil, always a Musil, right?"

How had this conversation gotten off course? Sure she'd
had some suspicions, but that was beside the point. Damian
could rectify this whole situation with a few strokes of the
pen—or taps on the computer keyboard.

"You were prepared to think the worst of me."

Mia shook her head. "Only momentarily—"

"And as long as I make sure the Serenghettis come out
okay, all is forgiven? Because your family loyalty over-
shadows any trust you have in me, right?"

No...wait. What was he saying?

"And what if I decide not to do a favor for the Sereng-hettis, Mia?" he asked softly. "What would you say?"

She huffed. *Favor?* There was no favor. Her mother had a damn good show. She'd even helped her father find a second act after his stroke—one that Damian had now closed the curtain on.

Damian got a cold, shut-down look on his face. "I think I've got my answer."

And she'd gotten hers. He wasn't going to commit to not canceling. And she wasn't going to grovel. Everything he'd said indicated that he wasn't changing his mind. In fact, he'd made it seem as if *she'd* done something wrong.

Mia blinked. She was flabbergasted. Angry. Annoyed. He was asking her to choose between him and her mother? "I guess there is nothing more to say then, is there?"

They stared at each other a moment longer, and then she swung away and marched out.

Damian raked his hand through his hair and glanced around his empty New York condo.

He'd already been to the gym and for a jog in order to work off excess energy and restlessness. It hadn't helped.

In his penthouse, he was literally and figuratively at the top—at the pinnacle of his life and career—and *alone*. And lonely.

When Mia had left his office last night, he'd been tempted to go after her, but something told him nothing would be accomplished in their current frames of mind. They needed to cool off.

Mia couldn't see this wasn't personal. Yes, it was her mother's cooking show. But since Mia was an entrepreneur herself—one who was used to dealing with financials and the need to turn a profit—she should be able to see it all boiled down to the bottom line.

But he had only himself to blame. He was knee-deep in entanglements with, logically, the last woman he should ever be seriously involved with. If this were purely a business calculation, he should have stopped at *hello* where Mia was concerned.

Tossing aside his usual deliberation, though, he'd pursued his attraction to Mia. Sure, Larry showing up at the Ruby Ball had been an opportunity that had been too good to pass up. But he hadn't stopped to think about his long-term goals with Mia—which was so unlike him.

Still, he wasn't guilty of using her as a pawn to get back at her family, no matter what she thought. But had his attraction to Mia been partly rooted in showing that the Musils were on a par with the Serenghettis? That a Musil was worthy of dating a Serenghetti? Even he couldn't separate out all his motives.

Damn, what a tangle. He paced restlessly. He'd had hours to think and be mad, and it had gotten him nowhere. Now that his annoyance was finally receding, he could think more clearly.

Belatedly, he acknowledged he'd put Mia in an impossible situation of divided loyalty between him and the Serenghettis. No, not just the Serenghettis, but worse—her mother, Camilla Serenghetti, in particular. The one member of Mia's immediate family who seemed to be—maybe—not so dead set against him. Not to mention, he'd handed Mia's father another reason to dislike him. *Way to go, Musil.*

He'd been bothered that Mia had thought he might have masterminded some kind of revenge plan using her as bait. On the other hand, the fact that she'd seemed torn—felt some loyalty to him as well as the rest of the Serenghettis—said something. Their relationship had moved fast...and could get only stronger going forward if they could work through this somehow.

On impulse, Damian picked up his cell phone. He was going to do what he couldn't remember ever doing in his adult life. *Ask his father for advice.*

The irony was, his rapprochement with his father had been facilitated by the Serenghettis—because Mia had helped him court the Bensens. His ownership of WBEN-TV meant he was coming back to Welsdale, which pleased Jakob.

He'd accused Mia of exhibiting loyalty to her family, but he was guilty of the same, he acknowledged ruefully. Still, he needed to get Jakob on board with a plan that was starting to form in his mind.

Damian didn't waste too much time on pleasantries when Jakob picked up. "Dad, I just fired Camilla and Serg Serenghetti from their television jobs."

"What?" The word came out almost as a bark.

Backtracking, he tried to explain the situation as best as he could, finishing with, "What should I do, Dad?"

"Grovel."

"Huh?" It was the last word that he expected to hear from his father's lips.

Jakob grumbled. "Damian, I raised two teenagers as a single parent. Sometimes I worried if I did a good job. So I'll get to the point. Make up with Mia Serenghetti."

Shouldn't his father be...gloating? Expressing some form of satisfaction?

"It's clear that Mia means a lot to you. Your mother died young. Life is short. Hold on to love when you find it."

Huh? Damian cut off a disbelieving laugh. "I expected—"

"I never harbored ill will toward Camilla. In fact, when your mother was alive, they were volunteers together at the soup kitchen."

"Mom never mentioned that."

"You were young, but she did not tell me either. I was shopping with her one day when she said hello to Camilla. She had to tell me how they knew each other."

"I doubt Camilla mentioned it to Serg, either," Damian remarked dryly.

Jakob chuckled. "Serves him right."

That was more like it. "Uh, Dad, you may need to learn to be nice to the Serenghettis."

"I'm counting on being able to learn new tricks." He laughed—a hint of self-satisfaction peeking through.

Damian felt like a huge load had been lifted from his shoulders. "Yeah?"

"I didn't believe that garbage about you and Mia just playing golf together for business."

Damian smiled. "We didn't fool you?"

"Mia likes you or she wouldn't be mad."

Well, *that* made a strange amount of sense.

"One of us has been married. Trust me. And you wouldn't be calling me if you didn't like her."

Damian suddenly heard Valentin in the background and realized he'd caught his father at JM Construction even though it was a Saturday morning. "Why are you at work?"

"Paperwork. Worse every year," Jakob grumbled. "Damn it, Valentin. Did you find that folder?"

In the distance, Damian heard his brother reply, and then his father must have covered the receiver, because there was some indistinct back and forth.

When his father got back on the line, Damian asked, "What did Valentin say?"

"He said you'd better get your rear end back to Wels-ale with Mia before the two of us throttle each other at he office. I substituted nicer words for his."

Damian laughed. "I'm looking forward to getting up to Welsdale again soon."

"And I'm going to enjoy Serg learning to be nice to me."

Damian stifled another laugh. He had his marching orders.

Except this was going to be a long, uncertain road. Maybe Mia would be waiting at the end...

If he was lucky.

Fifteen

"He's an underhanded sneak," Mia announced, "and I should have listened to my family."

"Now those are words I never thought would pass your lips," Gia replied.

"What? *Underhanded sneak*?"

"No, *I should have listened to my family*."

"How could I have been so gullible? So stupid?"

"Stop beating yourself up, Mia. Obviously the two of you have a relationship that's complicated by your last names."

"We have no relationship." She closed her eyes and sucked in a breath. "I haven't spoken to Damian since I confronted him in his office…and he hasn't tried to be in touch."

Two whole days. A whole weekend after the Friday night massacre at WBEN-TV, when staff had been informed that they were being let go—and told that Damian

Musil was the new owner. That much she'd gleaned in follow-up conversations with her mother.

Only dinner with Gia at a local noodle shop was saving her from hiding under her bedcovers—and never, ever coming out. She'd washed the sheets—nothing like a little laundry and mindless housework for the doldrums—but Damian's essence lingered in her apartment. *Damn it.*

Mia swallowed against a stab of pain. Obviously, Damian had had the weekend to think, too, and hadn't reconsidered.

"Oh, come on..."

"No, Gia, really. We had a relationship that was mutually advantageous for business. Now, it isn't anymore."

"Uh-huh."

"Whose side are you on?" she asked sharply. "I thought you said mine."

"You two have a thing for each other. Anyone can see it."

"Thanks. It's nice knowing I'm so transparent. See-through clothing...maybe that's the market niche I've been missing."

Her cousin laughed.

Mia hunched her shoulders and stabbed into her noodle bowl with chopsticks. "Don't humanize him. He's a beast."

"In or out of bed?" Gia's eyes were wide, guileless, but her mouth held a hint of a smirk.

Mia flushed. "I've been the victim of the biggest con of my life."

"He didn't know that he was canceling your parents—"

"But even when he found out, he tried to argue it was all business." Is that what their...relationship had been to him—all business?

Mia's phone buzzed, and she picked it up from the tabletop and scanned the screen. Another text from her brothers—this time Cole. *Ignore.* She hit a button and dropped the cell into the handbag dangling from her chair.

Gia angled her head. "Don't you think your reaction is because you see this as a personal betrayal?"

"What?" she scoffed.

"If Damian cared for you, he'd abandon his plans for the television station."

"You don't pull any punches, Gia," she joked.

Mia's heart squeezed. Her cousin was right. She was in love with Damian. It had happened without her knowing. He'd sneaked in. And now she'd gotten evidence that he didn't give a damn.

On the other hand, a little voice in her head whispered, if she cared about him—*loved him*—wouldn't she support him in doing what was best for his business? Even at the expense of her family?

What a mess. She couldn't really accuse Damian of not valuing their relationship without looking a wee bit hypocritical. Except she did think her mother had a damn good show—if only Damian could see that himself.

The dizzying mix of emotions slammed into her, and she grasped for something solid to steady her.

"I need to help my mother," she said resolutely.

With sudden clarity, Mia realized her family needed her at this moment as much as they thought she needed them. If anything, she could make a last-ditch effort to save her mother's show by demonstrating it was worth saving.

"Well, I don't see what you can do about it, short of blackmailing Damian."

"I'm the only one of my siblings who hasn't made a recent appearance on my mother's show, and now it's over. What's the saying? Make time for the important things in life?"

"Doesn't she have any shows left to tape?"

"One or two."

"Then get yourself up to Welsdale and put your misplaced guilt to rest."

Mia worried her bottom lip, because Gia had given voice to an idea that had started germinating in her own head. "You're right. It might not change things but—"

"You have a beautiful memory to make with your mother."

Yup. On the other hand, all of her memories with Damian were likely in the past…even if her appearance on her mother's show convinced him to keep it on the air.

Fortunately, it hadn't been hard to run Rick Serenghetti to ground. With a few phone calls back and forth between assistants, Damian had been able to determine that Mia's brother was in New York for business.

He'd been prepared to fly out to Los Angeles if necessary. Luck, it seemed, was on his side—at least this time. It had gone AWOL for a while.

Now he was finally meeting the middle Serenghetti brother in the lounge of a swanky Midtown hotel.

Rick eyed him from across a small table. This corner of the ground floor lounge was empty at four in the afternoon.

"You know," Rick mused, "I debated whether to meet you."

"I appreciate your time."

Rick shrugged, his casualness belied by the indecipherable look on his face. "But then I figured I had the chance to get a jump start on my brothers in laying into you."

Damian grimaced. He couldn't blame the guy when he'd managed to lay off his parents and break up with his sister in the same week. If it had been Cole, a physical altercation might have been a more serious possibility, but Rick

emained cool as a cucumber. Damian chalked it up to
nerves of steel honed as a movie stunt man. "Hear me out."

"Chiara convinced me that I should. She seems to think
you may have some redeeming qualities."

"Good to know the Serenghetti in-laws aren't quite
as—"

"—hostile as Mia's brothers?" Rick lounged back and
rested his arm along the back of the cushioned bench seat.
"I heard Mia prevented you from being hustled out the
door in Welsdale by Cole and Jordan. Crashing family
get-togethers is your thing?"

Damian rubbed his jaw—which had emerged from that
meeting still in good shape. "Yeah, but the Musils and
Serenghettis are no longer competing to acquire the same
construction company since Tevil Construction took itself
off the market. So two steps forward for Serenghetti-Musil
relations right there."

"Two little steps…and one big one back, too, since
then."

"I'm rectifying it."

Rick raised his eyebrows, looking intrigued.

In preparation for today's meeting, Damian had watched
a marathon of old *Flavors of Italy* episodes. It seemed a
lot had been going on in Welsdale since he'd moved away,
and the show definitely had its appealing qualities. It was
also clearly a family affair, with Camilla bringing on as-
sorted relatives and even their spouses as guests—until
Damian had brought down the butcher knife and cut off
any more episodes.

Still, watching the show had proved to be a good way to
get to know the Serenghettis. He'd been entertained by Cole
obviously salivating over his future wife, Marisa. Jordan
had vied against his own hockey teammates on a cook-off
that Sera had judged. And even Rick had been teased on

screen when his then-girlfriend, Chiara, had been a guest
Of course, Damian had eaten up every crumb of Mia's appearance on a couple of the early episodes, when she'd
looked as edible as the Italian cream pastry that she was
helping to prepare…

Before Damian could lay out his plan for Rick, however, an attractive woman walked in holding the hand of
a boy who looked to be close to Dahlia's age.

Even dressed casually in a striped sundress, with a pair
of shades obscuring her eyes, Damian recognized the actress Chiara Feran. He'd seen the news when her romance
with Rick Serenghetti had become public a few years ago.

As Rick stood, Damian followed suit.

"Vincent wanted to go for a walk," Chiara announced
with a smile, "so we're heading to the park for a bit."

Rick's face softened, and he hunched down. "Hey, bud,
take it easy with the stunts on the playground equipment,
okay?"

Vincent looked gleeful. "Stunts, stunts."

Chiara sighed. "Like father, like son."

Damian glanced at her. "Looks like the next generation
of Serenghettis is all cute."

"You've met Dahlia then, I take it?" she answered with
a smile.

"Let's just say she was the most welcoming of the
Serenghettis on that occasion."

As Chiara laughed, he held out his hand. "I'm Damian
Musil."

"Chiara Feran," she supplied, shaking his hand. "I've
heard so much about you."

Rick hooked the tops of his hands into his pockets. "Is
this really about taking Vincent for a walk?"

Chiara shot her husband an amused look. "Just taking a
small detour to say goodbye to you before we're on our way."

"Musil is still in one piece, as you can see," Rick muttered.
Chiara's lips twitched.

Damian figured that Chiara had done more than a little
onvincing to persuade her husband that this meeting was
orthwhile. For some reason, Mia's sisters-in-law were
eady to throw him a lifeline. But then he assumed it took
omen as strong as Mia to handle the Serenghetti brothers.

Rick ruffled his son's hair.

"Well, we'll be going then," Chiara said lightly.

Rick brushed her lips in a light kiss. "You look great,
nd I'm glad you're dressed for the weather. It's hot out
ere."

"Happy you like the dress." Chiara threw a significant
lance at Damian. "It's a Mia Serenghetti design. Isn't it
ntastic?"

Smoothly done.

Chiara turned, leading Vincent away. "Enjoy...your
lk."

Rick said something under his breath as both he and
amian took their seats again.

"Looks like the Serenghettis may have another stunt
an in their midst."

"Not if Chiara can help it," Rick supplied shortly. "But
nce we're on the topic, what's the purpose of this stunt
ou're pulling? I mean, this meeting."

"I've got a proposition, and I need your help."

"And I've got a news flash for you," Rick responded
ryly. "Serenghettis and Musils don't help each other."

"They don't date each other, either."

Rick's gaze flickered for an instant. "A lapse in judg-
ent on my sister's part that I hear she's since rectified."

"Then why did you agree to meet me? Aside from Chi-
a's influence, that is."

Rick's gaze flickered again. "I'm not supposed to say this,

but Mia is torn up. She blames herself for my parents'. predicament."

Damian felt like a jerk. "I want to make things righ with Mia."

"I don't think that's possible."

Yeah. But Damian had dealt with long odds before.

"Once my sister has made up her mind, it's hard, if no impossible, to change it."

"I know."

"So you must be delusional or—"

"I care about her." *I can't stop thinking about her. want to be with her.*

Rick regarded him silently but eventually sighe "Okay, spill it."

"I want you to help your mother start her own produc tion company."

Rick said nothing for a few seconds. "Nice, but whe will the show be slotted?" he probed. "An online strean ing service?"

"I want to keep broadcasting *Flavors of Italy* but I'd li the show to get a fresher look. The goal is to grow the a dience but keep the name of the program." He'd gleane a few things from watching Camilla's show, not only as viewer, but also as a shrewd entrepreneur.

Rick played with an empty coaster on the table. "Y know, I was mulling the idea of having the Serenghett produce the show ourselves. I own a production compan but it's only dealt with feature films up to now. It'd be be ter if my mother was set up with her own shop."

Great. If Camilla had a new production company, t problem would be solved—or half solved. Damian cou deal with the rest from his end.

"But why would we need you?" Rick asked pointed] "My mother could get broadcast anywhere."

"I'm assuming your mother still attaches some value to being on her hometown station. On the channel where she started and viewers are used to seeing her."

"Right, the Welsdale station that you now own. A fact you didn't share with my sister."

"I didn't know about the Serenghetti connection." *Had Mia mentioned that part?* Then he shrugged. "I'm not much of a cooking show kind of guy."

"If you hang around my sister much longer, you will be." *That's what I'm counting on.*

"Well, we agree on one thing," Rick conceded. "My mother needs her own production company."

Mia's brother hadn't exactly agreed to cooperate, but he'd given Damian an opening.

One Damian was ready to make the most of. He needed Rick to persuade the other Serenghettis... *Time to seal the deal.*

Sixteen

For her last show, Camilla announced that she wanted to make a millefoglie Italian wedding cake.

Mia mentally shrugged. She thought the choice was a little odd, but maybe her mother was putting the best face on a bad situation with her trademark optimistic style.

"We will assemble the cake right here," her mother said, speaking to the camera, "and with the help of some special guests."

Guests? As far as Mia was aware, she was the only guest.

"*Mia figlia*, Mia Serenghetti...and the new owner of this television station, Damian Musil."

The audience clapped.

Stunned, Mia watched Damian stride onto the set.

What was he doing here? Still, her bewildered senses feasted on him. He was tall, commanding...and seemingly relaxed. He looked as good, if not better, than when she'd last seen him. Dark hair, bedroom eyes, chiseled features

nd muscled body in slacks and an open-collar shirt. Her
eart felt a pang. He'd have a new girlfriend in no time.

When they'd last parted, he'd been cool and distant.
Now he was all smiles and insouciance.

Fortunately, the TV camera wasn't trained on her at the
moment, so she had an instant to compose herself.

She soon narrowed her eyes fractionally at her mother.
What was she up to? Or had Damian demanded to be
ut on air—so it wouldn't seem like he was the bad guy
who'd ended the show? Someone had some explaining
o do…

Mia cut off the flow of thoughts racing through her
ead. Because there was no more time to think. Because
Damian was up on stage, standing beside her, joining her
nd her mother in the worst cooking show casting *ever*.

While the camera focused on Camilla, Mia leaned
lightly toward Damian. "What are you doing here?"

"Lending a hand," he muttered back, keeping his smile
n place.

"And your good name."

"Something for everyone," he replied easily. "Smile for
he camera, Mia."

"For a Musil, you sure go out of your way to associate
vith Serenghettis," Mia responded in a low voice, while
er mother continued her explanation of baking for the
enefit of the studio audience and the television cameras.

Damian glanced at her, his eyes gleaming. "Maybe
ou've changed my mind."

Mia felt heat stamp her face. *At least they weren't live.*
f necessary, she could muscle her way into the production
oom later, and beg and plead for some strategic editing.

But first, she had to survive this taping. She'd already
owngraded her expectations from helping to make this
pisode her mother's best ever to…surviving. *Wonderful.*

After a producer trotted on stage to outfit Damian with a microphone, she and Damian worked together under her mother's direction to mix the ingredients. *Why, oh why did it have to be a wedding cake?*

It was a running family joke that her brothers and their wives had appeared on Camilla's show and soon after had gotten married. *Well, she and Damian were about to break the mold.*

Mia wasn't sure how she was going to make it through today. It was like the heat of a thousand suns. The audience...her family...the wedding theme... *Damian*. If she was still standing at the end of this episode, she'd plunge headfirst into the cake...

"Now Damian, Mia has helped me in the kitchen before, so you are the *secondo assistente, sì*?"

Mia nearly rolled her eyes.

"*Millefoglie* means a thousand layers in *italiano*," Camilla said. "The millefoglie wedding cake is *molto popolare in Italia*."

Mia scanned the audience, and her gaze came to rest on her family, including her father and brothers, sitting in the back. Why was no one glowering at Damian? Or better yet, jumping on stage to start an argument, so the show could go off the air with a real bang? Maybe they were all here to support her mother no matter what?

"First we will mix the ingredients for the vanilla custard," Camilla continued. "Then we will assemble with layers of pastry and fresh berries."

"Sounds delicious," Damian chimed in.

"Now a little birdie told me that you like strawberries Damian, so we will make this cake with those in addition to blueberries and raspberries."

"Thank you."

"*Prego.*"

Mia nearly gagged.

"I am showing everyone how to make the cake today, ut," Camilla added, "I've never had a personal opportu- ity. You know, I've never been the mother of the bride."

Mia wondered with chagrin what the heck she'd been ninking by agreeing to appear on her mother's last epi- ode...

"Have you ever had millefoglie, Damian?" Camilla sked benignly.

"No, I haven't. I've never been married," he joked.

Camilla tittered and then winked. "Maybe Mia can help ou at the end."

They both turned to look at Mia.

The audience murmured, and Mia pasted a tight smile n her face. What had she been saying about ending with bang? Apparently, though, her mother had the drama ngle covered all by herself.

"Sure," she said brightly. "Why not let Damian have is cake and eat it, too?"

The audience gasped and chuckled while Damian had ie audacity to laugh at her with his eyes.

Seriously, what was her mother thinking?

When they were finished making the cake, Mia almost igged with relief.

"Mia, why don't you offer Damian a taste?" Camilla sked, looking into the camera.

In slow motion, Mia cut into an edge of the cake with large spoon. Then bracing herself, she offered Damian sample.

Damian obligingly opened his mouth—but the look in s eyes said he'd rather eat her up. *Gia had called that one.*

When Damian swallowed his bite, Camilla asked, "How > you like it?"

"It's delicious," he said with a smile, his gaze on Mia.

"With any luck, I'll have one at my own wedding some day."

Mia kept a smile stuck on her face, but she wondered whether the cameras could pick up on the fact that she was being consumed by heat. Just a couple more minutes, and her mother would give her signature signoff...

"And now, I have big news," Camilla said.

Mia's gaze swiveled to her mother. *Please, no.* She didn't think she could take any more surprises.

Surely her mother wasn't going to announce the cancellation of her show right now? Right next to Damian? Right when Mia was imagining herself melting under the hot lights like so much gelatinous custard sitting in the sun too long?

"I have started my own production company," Camilla said with a flourish. "Dolci Productions. Now *Flavors of Italy* will have a new look." Her mother scanned the audience. "Thanks *mille* to my son, Rick Serenghetti, who helped arrange this."

A television camera panned to Rick in the audience. Her brother gave a slight smile and nod, while Serg, Col and Jordan all looked over at him in acknowledgment.

So her mother hoped to keep the show going somehow with her own company? Was that why her family was content to sit in the audience? Mia's spirits lifted and she stopped herself from throwing an unbeaten look in Damian's direction.

Her mother glanced beyond her to Damian, as if to give him his cue, but her expression was happy instead of victorious.

"Even though this is the last episode of the current program, Camilla will be back on-air next season with a whole new look for *Flavors of Italy*."

Mia blinked at Damian. She'd heard what he'd said, but

t wasn't processing. Still, she was able to note her father ooking pleased in the audience.

"*Alla prossima volta,*" Camilla ended gaily. "Till next ime, *buon appetito.*"

Wait…*what?* On air…where?

As soon as the cameras went off, Mia worked on de-aching her mic.

"Fantastic chemistry during this episode," one of the producers announced loudly, striding toward them. "We should have these two guests on together again soon."

Never. She didn't think she could survive it.

As her mother and Damian were waylaid by the pro-ducer, Mia hurried from the stage. She had a million ques-ions, but right now she had to get away from Damian.

She didn't know whether to laugh or cry. Sure, her mother's show had been saved, but she and Damian were still canceled…

Hurrying along a backstage hallway, Mia heard foot-teps behind her and then glanced over her shoulder.

"Mia, stop," Damian insisted.

"Forget it."

"I need to talk to you," he said, catching up with her.

She stopped. "No."

He opened the nearest door as if he hadn't heard her. In here will do."

"Your new office? How does it feel to be the owner of he station?" She had to protect her vulnerable heart.

"Fantastic. I thought I'd add a fashion show to the weekly lineup. You know, up-and-comers competing gainst each other."

"I'm sure you'll be able to find plenty of gullible design-rs with a penchant for Robin Hood costumes."

He had the audacity to chuckle. "You think so? Maybe I'll need some help."

She was done with offering him assistance...

They were attracting looks from staffers passing them in the hallway, so Mia chose the lesser evil and marched past him into the room. "Wouldn't a show along the lines of *Shark Bait* be more your speed? Every week people can tune in to see which competitor survives with their dreams intact."

He smiled and closed the door.

She stabbed a finger in his direction. "Did you enjoy your star turn on my mother's show?"

He opened his mouth, but she wasn't finished. "I sure hope so. Because she's poured her heart and soul into it."

"The cake was delicious—"

"I'm glad you agree." She placed her hands on her hips and cocked her head. "I was imagining you wearing it."

"I'm not sure berry is my color."

"Oh, it is. Take it from me." She pinned him with a look. "I've studied fashion, and what's trending right now is shades of red." *She was on fire.*

Damian quirked his lips. "I thought my acting skills were fairly good, even if it was just a cooking show."

"*Just* a cooking show?" She took a deep breath to brace herself. "This may not mean much to you, but my mother spent years being the behind-the-scenes supporter of a husband and four kids. Finally, she had time to pursue her dream, her second act, and what do you do? You—"

"Keep her on WBEN-TV as well as its sister stations and invest in her new production company?"

She stared at him blankly for a moment and then blinked.

"She's staying in her time slot with a revamped look for the show. Same name though."

"What?" She dropped her hands from her hips. So her mother wasn't only staying on-air with her own production company, she was going to continue to be broadcast on her regular station—where she already had an audience.

"I offered her a deal before today's show." He smiled. "Before I had my acting skills tested. Fortunately, I could mostly be myself since it was a reality-based show."

"You've been in negotiations with—" what had her mother called it? "—Dolci Productions."

"Not only that. I contacted Rick to talk about setting up the new company. With any luck, both of us can work out an even better syndication deal for her. She'll reach a wider market."

"How did I not know this?"

"I wanted to work behind the scenes." His lips quirked up again. "I've found that's best where the Serenghettis are concerned."

She waved her arms inanely. "My whole family was in the audience."

"I asked them not to say anything. Though your father was bursting to mention something about *Wine Breaks with Serg!* becoming its own spin-off show."

Good—her father needed his own turf, for both his and her mother's sakes. "So you swore them to silence…for the grand gesture?"

He nodded, rubbing the back of his neck. "I thought they'd enjoy watching a Musil brought to his knees."

She swallowed, her throat suddenly dry. "Why?"

He sauntered closer. "Don't you know?"

"Know what?"

He lowered his eyes, concealing his gaze. "I did it for you."

Mia studied his mouth. He was so close, her world had narrowed to him and what he was saying.

"For us."

She shook her head mutely—vestiges of a fight still in her. "There is no us."

"There could be."

She gave a nervous laugh. "Until the next time you cancel my mother's show?"

There were so many obstacles…and if she tried very hard right now, she'd remember some of them.

"I want you."

"And what Damian Musil wants, Damian Musil gets, is that it?" she huffed—because she was afraid to hope.

"No. I can't make you want me."

Oh… Her gaze traveled up to lock with his. "Stop poking holes in my reasons—"

"Love me, Mia."

"You—"

He wrapped his arms around her and covered her mouth with his.

The kiss was needy, desperate… She sighed against his lips, opening herself, and then shifted restlessly against him in order to get closer.

When he started to get aroused, they finally and reluctantly broke apart.

"I love you."

He softly brushed his lips against hers. "You're my heart."

She sighed against his mouth. "When I heard that my mother's show was being canceled, I assumed you were waging war on the Serenghettis."

"Shh, it's okay," he soothed, rubbing her arms. "You were upset."

She searched his gaze. "I couldn't believe I didn't figure out the business between you and Larry involved WBEN-TV. I was embarrassed…humiliated…and hurt for my parents—my mother in particular. They'd warned me about you, and I didn't listen. It seemed as if they'd been right all along, and I'd lived up to the image of rebellious Mia who doesn't know better."

He caressed the pulse at the side of her neck, the motion soothing. "Corporate holdings can be complicated and convoluted, and you were distracted by the potential fashion angle with Katie. Besides, I didn't put two and two together, either, and make the connection between your family and WBEN."

She smiled. "Because you're not into cooking shows."

The side of his mouth lifted.

Mia's smile turned tentative. "There will be other times when our families may clash. After all, the Musils and Serenghettis continue to be business rivals."

"And now that I'm your mother's boss, it's even more complicated, but it will never be boring," he teased.

"You can joke about it?"

He rested his forehead against hers. "I've moved boulders already for us to be together, Mia."

She widened her eyes and pulled back to search his.

He shrugged, the nonchalant movement belying the intensity of his expression. "I've been attracted to you for a long time, and it was clear you weren't going to give me an opening. A guy can only be so patient."

She swatted him playfully. "What attraction?"

He raised a brow. "I even envied Carl when he was dating you. When he started exploring other jobs, it was a relief."

"And you helped him walk out the door."

He nodded. "Guilty. Let's just say I had no problem providing a letter of recommendation."

"The way you helped him find another girlfriend, too?" she asked archly.

Damian looked uncharacteristically and endearingly

abashed. "I know that your feelings were hurt. I'd never have helped if—"

She touched a finger to his lips. "You were right. Carl and I would never have lasted. But I was too busy being mad at you for your role at the time to want to acknowledge it."

He kissed her finger before she moved it away. "Why are we talking about Carl?"

"Because you had the hots for me."

"And you didn't feel any spark of attraction ever?" he joked.

She caressed his jaw, unable to keep herself from touching him. "With our families, it always seemed like a bad idea to do any exploration where you were concerned."

He gave her a peck on the lips. "We'll work it out. Your family were all in on the plan for today's cooking show, so things are looking good already."

"All of them?" she gasped.

"Well, your mother and Rick put the word out."

"I can't believe they all showed up today."

"They want to see you happy. I think that convinced them."

"You convinced them that you'd make me happy," she teased.

"Okay, guilty." His eyes crinkled. "I think they were impressed that I braved the Serenghetti lair for you the last time we were in Welsdale."

"Why didn't you tell me before the taping?"

"Plan A was to show up before the show to talk to you," he admitted. "But I got stalled in New York on business."

"Oh!" No wonder everyone had been able to keep Damian's appearance a secret. He'd only just arrived.

"The season finale was supposed to end with my declaration of undying love for you. But without hashing things out with you first, I wasn't sure how you'd react."

The hint of vulnerability was her undoing.

"Your brothers missed out on witnessing that part."

Her heart squeezed. "Well, for my part, I'm not sure I'm up to the job of taking on the Musils." At Damian's surprised look, she added lightly, "I've had a hard enough time dealing with my brothers, and the Musils have their share of testosterone floating around."

Damian gave a lopsided smile, and then he wrapped her arms around his waist. "You're up to the challenge, don't worry. You'll have them tamed in no time."

"Aren't you supposed to be the tamer, with your name?" she teased.

"You can teach me all you know."

"Starting right now."

And then when Damian flipped the lock on the door, Mia gave herself up to being the biggest Serenghetti rebel of all...by loving a Musil.

Epilogue

The big Serenghetti family wedding was finally happening. Cole and Marisa had surprised everyone by turning their engagement party into a wedding. Rick and Chiara had had quick nuptials because Chiara was pregnant. And even Jordan and Sera had done a hasty scaled-down affair to coincide with the hockey off-season and in order to avoid too much press coverage.

Mia surveyed the proceedings. It was a fashion and culinary showcase all in one. Her desires and her mother's tastes had dovetailed nicely. At last, Camilla had found an offspring who was into the same fantasy wedding that she was.

Thanks to Katie's connections, Mia's wedding was also the cover story for an upcoming issue of *Wedding Bells* magazine. And of course, there was a millefoglie wedding cake complete with strawberries as well as raspberries and blueberries—because everyone knew the groom liked it that way.

Mia's gown was an ivory Chantilly lace with an off-the-shoulder bodice. She'd surprised even herself by going traditional. But then she'd added spectacular aquamarine teardrop earrings that Damian had gifted her for something blue, as well as the headpiece that her mother had worn at her own wedding to hold her veil. She'd borrowed her sister-in-law Chiara's diamond hair clips to hold her hair back. She'd even done the traditional Italian candied almond wedding favors, thanks to her mother's input.

Her engagement ring was an understated diamond that had been among the items in the box that Jakob Musil had given his son months ago in JM Construction's office. It turned out that Damian's mother had passed along her engagement ring to her son in addition to letters and other mementos. Mia treasured it as a gift from the mother-in-law she'd never get to know but who lived on through Damian.

The ring had even surpassed Damian's other surprise—because his wedding gift to her had turned out to be all the jewelry that she'd gotten on loan, including the ruby pieces that she'd loved and worn for the Ruby Ball, and the diamonds that she'd put on for the charity dinner. He'd never gotten around to returning them, and had claimed with a wink that he'd decided to make an investment in jewelry instead.

As the band struck up, Damian claimed her hand.

The lights in the reception hall dimmed, and she and Damian walked onto the dance floor and swayed to "Wonderful Tonight."

"Special request to the band," Damian murmured.

She felt chills race down her spine—as she often did around him.

Damian looked over her shoulder and scanned the ballroom around them. "Looks as if everyone is behaving."

"The photographer and writer from *Wedding Bells* are here. Plus, my mother read my brothers the riot act. She's finally got her turn as the mother of the bride, and she's going to show highlights on *Flavors of Italy*."

"Naturally," Damian deadpanned.

Mia smiled fondly at the two babies asleep in strollers in a quiet corner of the ballroom. Even her new nephews were apparently cooperating in making sure that the wedding went off without a hitch. Sergio had Cole's dark hair and hazel eyes, while Marco was fairer, as if Sera's blond locks and Jordan's darker hue had been mixed together. And now Rick and Chiara were expecting again, too—this time a girl.

Mia spied her father sitting at a table and chatting with Jakob Musil. "It seems my mother didn't have to worry about our fathers, either. They're chummy these days."

Damian followed her gaze and then smiled. "All is forgiven when your construction companies have joined forces and your kids are getting married to each other."

Serenghetti Construction had partnered with JM Construction to bid for more and bigger projects than either could handle alone. Though neither had ended up buying Tevil Construction, they'd found a way to work together to achieve the same benefits the purchase would have imparted.

"Next thing we know, they'll be playing bocce ball together," Mia remarked lightly.

"I've got news for you. They already have."

Mia threw back her head and laughed.

"You're wonderful tonight and every night," Damian murmured as the singer crooned the song's romantic refrain and other couples joined them.

"Remember how you felt that way when we have our next argument," she teased.

He quirked an eyebrow. "I thought we put all that behind us."

"We haven't gone through your closet yet."

He laughed. "I forgot. I'm now a fashion designer's accessory."

"My best accessory," she said firmly. "And my husband, lover—"

He swept his lips across hers. "Don't forget life partner."

Yes. Yes to everything. Yes to finally finding each other.

* * * * *

COMING
SOON!

We really hope you enjoyed reading this book.
If you're looking for more romance, be sure to
head to the shops when new books are
available on

Thursday 29th
April

To see which titles are coming soon, please visit
millsandboon.co.uk/nextmonth

LET'S TALK
Romance

For exclusive extracts, competitions
and special offers, find us online:

f facebook.com/millsandboon

🐦 @MillsandBoon

📷 @MillsandBoonUK

Get in touch on 01413 063232

For all the latest titles coming soon, visit
millsandboon.co.uk/nextmonth

MILLS & BOON

THE HEART OF ROMANCE

A ROMANCE FOR EVERY READER

MODERN

Prepare to be swept off your feet by sophisticated, sexy and seductive heroes, in some of the world's most glamourous and roman locations, where power and passion collide.

HISTORICAL

Escape with historical heroes from time gone by. Whether your passio for wicked Regency Rakes, muscled Vikings or rugged Highlanders, a the romance of the past.

MEDICAL

Set your pulse racing with dedicated, delectable doctors in the high-p sure world of medicine, where emotions run high and passion, comfo love are the best medicine.

True Love

Celebrate true love with tender stories of heartfelt romance, from the rush of falling in love to the joy a new baby can bring, and a focus o emotional heart of a relationship.

Desire

Indulge in secrets and scandal, intense drama and plenty of sizzling action with powerful and passionate heroes who have it all: wealth, s good looks…everything but the right woman.

HEROES

Experience all the excitement of a gripping thriller, with an intense mance at its heart. Resourceful, true-to-life women and strong, fearl face danger and desire - a killer combination!

To see which titles are coming soon, please visit

millsandboon.co.uk/nextmonth

JOIN US ON SOCIAL MEDIA!

Stay up to date with our latest releases, author
news and gossip, special offers and discounts, and
all the behind-the-scenes action
from Mills & Boon...

 millsandboon

 millsandboonuk

 millsandboon

might just be true love...

GET YOUR ROMANCE FIX!

MILLS & BOON
— *blog* —

Get the latest romance news, exclusive author interviews, story extracts and much more!